best sports stories 1978

best sports stories 1978

**A PANORAMA OF THE 1977 SPORTS WORLD
INCLUDING THE 1977 CHAMPIONS OF ALL SPORTS
WITH THE YEAR'S TOP PHOTOGRAPHS**

Edited by Irving T. Marsh and Edward Ehre

E. P. DUTTON / NEW YORK

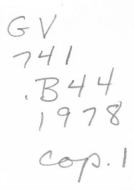
For information contact: E. P. Dutton, 2 Park Avenue,
New York, N.Y. 10016

Library of Congress Catalog Card Number: 45-35124
ISBN: 0-525-06624-1

Published simultaneously in Canada by Clarke, Irwin & Company
Limited, Toronto and Vancouver

10 9 8 7 6 5 4 3 2 1

First Edition

Dedicated to the late Wells Twombly
who saw sports and sports writing in
laughing perspective

Contents

Illustrations

THE PRIZE-WINNING PHOTOS

OTHER PHOTOS

Preface

Quick, now, when was the last time you read a sports piece by a university president—and a truly fine piece, at that? Well, you can find the answer to that question right here and now. *Best Sports Stories— 1978,* our thirty-fourth in the series that began in 1944, has the distinction of offering just that. We're pointing to the volume's prize-winning magazine story, "Tom Seaver's Farewell," by A. Bartlett Giamatti, newly named (last year) president of Yale University and quite obviously an ardent baseball fan. President Giamatti gained the accolade for this article with the Frank Merriwell sounding title (Frank was also a graduate of Yale) after publishing it originally in *Harper's Magazine.*

Dr. Giamatti appeared on the ballots of all three of our long-time judges: John Chamberlain, the syndicated newspaper columnist; John Hutchens, member of the selection panel of the Book-of-the-Month Club; and Jerry Nason, for many years sports editor of *The Boston Globe,* now retired, a previous winner of *Best Sports Stories* awards.

The winning story scored 6 points, 2 points more than the runner-up in the judging (see Box Score on following pages) on the basis of 3 points for a first-place vote, 3 for a second, and 1 for a third. Although according to his short biography at the end of this book, Dr. Giamatti has done a considerable amount of writing, "Tom Seaver's Farewell" is his first attempt at sports.

As to the other 1978 winners: In the news-coverage category Thomas Boswell has appeared in these anthologies three times before, but this one, his story on the winning game in the 1977 World Series ("The Sign Says 'Reg-gie, Reg-gie, Reg-gie'"), which appeared in *The Washington Post,* is his first victory. And for David Klein of the *Newark Star-Ledger* it was a second-time triumph with his deeply moving feature on Wells Twombly, that great sports writer and many-time contributor to *Best Sports Stories,* to whom the 1978 volume is dedicated. Second place in this category is a three-way tie among Sheila Moran, of the *Los Angeles Times* for her story on young tennis star Tracy Austin, Bob Rubin of the *Miami Herald* for that disgraceful Heisman Trophy presentation program on TV, and Joe Gergen of *Newsday* for his feature on Ted Turner, skipper of the America's Cup winning yacht, *Courageous.*

As has been the custom throughout this series, the stories were submitted to the judges blind, each identified only by a one-word "slug," newspaperese for such a label. Hence you will notice that each story was so called by the judges in the box score and in their comments, which follow:

THE BOX SCORE
(Winners in Caps)

News-Coverage Stories	Chamber-lain	Hutchens	Nason	Points * Total
SERIES [THE RIGHT-FIELD SIGN SAYS "REG-GIE, REG-GIE, REG-GIE" BY THOMAS BOSWELL]	2	2	3	7
Pele ["Love! Love! Love!" Cries Pele by Tony Kornheiser]	3	3	–	6
Randle [Randle's Big Explosion by Blackie Sherrod]	1	–	2	3
Fight [No Garden Party for Ali by John Schulian]	–	1	1	2

News-Feature Stories				
WELLS [WELLS TWOMBLY, 41; THE LAUGHTER STILL ECHOES BY DAVID KLEIN]	–	2	2	4
Tracy [A Wimbledon Story Waiting to Begin by Sheila Moran]	3	–	–	3
Heisman [What Some People Will Do for Money! by Bob Rubin]	–	3	–	3
Turner [Three Sheets to the Wind, and More by Joe Gergen]	–	–	3	3
Guthrie [A Mile of Style by Tracy Dodds]	2	–	–	2
Bull [The Bullring by D. L. Stewart]	1	–	–	1
Foul [Foul Play for Foul Balls by Jeff Meyers]	–	1	–	1
Pica [Who Are Those Guys Anyway? by Loel Schrader]	–	–	1	1

Magazine Stories

SEAVER [TOM SEAVER'S FAREWELL BY A. BARTLETT GIAMATTI]	3	1	2	6
Texas [If They Don't Win It's a Shame by Gene Lyons]	2	2	–	4
O'Grady [In This Corner: The Fighting O'Gradys! by David Wolf]	–	3	–	3
Lauda [Coming Back Blazing by Pete Bonventre]	–	–	3	3
Jerry [The Second Coming of Jerry West by Paul Hemphill]	1	–	–	1
Turkey [Far Afield, Far from Home by Monty Montgomery]	–	–	1	1

* Based on 3 points for a first-place vote, 2 for a second, 1 for a third.

JUDGES' COMMENTS

John Chamberlain

News-Coverage Stories

1. Pele ["Love! Love! Love!" Cries Pele by Tony Kornheiser]
2. Series [The Right-Field Sign Says "Reg-gie, Reg-gie, Reg-gie" by Thomas Boswell]
3. Randle [Randle's Big Explosion by Blackie Sherrod]

1. The story of Pele's presumably final retirement introduced me to a new world. It did it with force and emotion. And I liked the characterization of the world's preeminent soccer player. Since it was new and fresh to me, I may be confusing its newness with excellence. But it is genuinely exciting beyond the very good coverage of more orthodox American sports.

2. Reggie Jackson, like Pele, generates excitement. There is good dramatic quality in this spot-news story of three homes runs in three swings. Some of Jackson's own adrenaline gets into the prose.

3. This story of an incredible assault makes for horrifying reading, but it is handled with a clean directness and a sharp visual observation that make it truly outstanding. The irony of its conclusion (apparently manager Lucchesi was going to give Randle his chance to play after all) provides an extra wallop of its own.

News-Feature Stories

1. Tracy [A Wimbledon Story Waiting to Begin by Sheila Moran]
2. Guthrie [A Mile of Style by Tracy Dodds]
3. Bull [The Bullring by D. L. Stewart]

1. This is a very tender and perceptive account of the big-time debut of a teen-age star. What I like about it is that the author understands the teen-age mind as well as he [she—Ed.] understands tennis.

2. "She drove like a driver." Just as there is no nonsense about Janet Guthrie as a racer, so there is no nonsense about this story of the arrival of Women's Lib at the Indianapolis racetrack. If we had more Guthries and fewer Bella Abzugs, the Women's Lib movement would benefit. The author conveys this idea without uttering a word of preachment.

3. I've never been able to follow Ernest Hemingway on the glory of bullfights. I like this story of revulsion against needles torture for its candor in expressing an offbeat point of view.

John Hutchens

News-Coverage Stories

1. Pele ["Love! Love! Love!" Cries Pele by Tony Kornheiser]
2. Series [The Right-Field Sign Says "Reg-gie, Reg-gie, Reg-gie" by Thomas Boswell]
3. Fight [No Garden Party for Ali by John Schulian]

1. A fine, warmly felt and warmly written description of the exit of a great athlete. You may never have seen him play, and you may have no particular interest in soccer, but you can hardly read this without understanding the admiration of those who cherish the game and its most renowned performer.

2. Throughout a given season Reggie Jackson isn't everyone's baseball hero, but on this supreme day of his career to date, the last one in the 1977 World Series, he joined the company of the immortals. Just how he did it is made admirably clear in a first-rate piece of reporting.

3. Nor is Muhammad Ali everyone's favorite in the squared circle, but there was that final round that left even his detractors feeling that—as the ringside reporter of the title fight with challenger Shavers says—"annoying as Muhammad Ali is, you are going to miss him when he's gone." An excellent, vivid account.

News-Feature Stories

1. Heisman [What Some People Will Do for Money! by Bob Rubin]
2. Wells [Wells Twombly, 41; The Laughter Still Echoes by David Klein]
3. Foul [Foul Play for Foul Balls by Jeff Meyers]

1. A stirring shot at the sleazy, commercial demeaning of a major annual event in America sports, a severe and welcome contribution to the great tradition of indignation in sports writing as exemplified by, among others, Westbrook Pegler, Stanley Woodward, Red Smith.
2. A deeply moving tribute to a sports writer who had few peers in his time, one who was a figure of honor to journalism in general.
3. A lively, entertaining piece, which must certainly appeal to every fan who looks back on the days when as a youngster he carried a glove to a game in the fond hope that it would trap a ball hit by Cobb, Ruth, DiMaggio, Mays.

Magazine Stories

1. O'Grady [In This Corner: The Fighting O'Gradys! by David Wolf]
2. Texas [If They Don't Win It's a Shame by Gene Lyons]
3. Seaver [Tom Seaver's Farewell by A. Bartlett Giamatti]

1. A witty, sardonic, informative chronicle of an operator who must be unique in the prizefight business today, and of a teen-age boy's debut as a boxer.
2. An extraordinary picture of an outpost in minor-league baseball —what's left of it—that will fascinate, and quite possibly depress, old-timers who recall the role played in other years by even the lesser minors in shaping players for the big time.
3. A subtle and moving salute to a great pitcher that goes beyond his obvious brilliance on the mound to his character, the dignity and decency that place him in a rank with such immortals as Walter Johnson and Christy Mathewson.

Jerry Nason

News-Coverage Stories

1. Series [The Right-Field Sign Says "Reg-gie, Reg-gie, Reg-gie" by Thomas Boswell]
2. Randle [Randle's Big Explosion by Blackie Sherrod]
3. Fight [No Garden Party for Ali by John Schulian]

1. Proof of my aging contention that an outstanding sports performance is sure to generate at least one written report matching the event in quality, is the news piece on Reggie Jackson's three-homers epic in the concluding game of the World Series. Jackson's was a nocturnal thriller, and the writer had precious little time before edition deadline to tell his story fast, but good. This writer succeeded immensely, picking up where Reggie left off . . . smoothly, but explosively. A textbook example of how to perform at a typewriter "under the gun."

2. Only a super piece could charm me away from "Randle" as the No. 1 choice in the news category. The fact the writer of this unusual report was witness to the ball player's unprecedented physical assault on his manager gave him, the writer, the rare privilege of employing an "instant replay" writing technique. It is a remarkably vivid report on a nasty baseball incident.

3. M. Ali's narrow escape from the inspired fists of 'ol Ernie Shavers didn't make for a routine night for any boxing scribe. I saw the fight, and easily one of the most comprehensive, readable spot-news pieces of the year was this report of it.

News-Feature Stories

1. Turner [Three Sheets to the Wind, and More by Joe Gergen]
2. Wells [Wells Twombly, 41; The Laughter Still Echoes by David Klein]
3. Pica [Who Are Those Guys Anyway? by Loel Schrader]

1. The crop of submitted features or sports columns (as distinguished from news reports) was uniformly excellent and largely demanded that judgment be made in the area of subject material. In this respect, the piece on America's Cup skipper and celebrant Ted Turner was not only singular in this company, but possibly the most provocative piece to be found anywhere in this book. Turner's rocking of the fusty Cup decorum at Newport, in the manner of a parched cowhand at The Last Chance Saloon, I frankly found to be a fascinating passage of 1977 sports. A rare scene, and written in pace with Ted's unfettered celebration of a great victory.

2. Where "Wells" was concerned, this judge admits to a smidgen of prejudice. The writing of sports lost one of its very best this past year, Wells Twombly. The column one of his closest press-box friends wrote of him and his death, at 41, was done not morbidly, but with Twombly's infectious laugh and positive personality offering background music for the piece. A tough piece to wring out of a type-

writer. Wells would have loved the style and "class" in which it was carried off.

3. Possibly a reader would have to have done at least a brief stint in a newspaper or magazine shop to get the full flavor of "Pica." Who would believe it possible to get so much good writing and so many laughs out of such an insignificant typographical item as a baseball box score? This was one of the briefest pieces submitted, and infinitely the most cleverly conceived by, obviously, a writer's writer.

Magazine Stories

1. Lauda [Coming Back Blazing by Pete Bonventre]
2. Seaver [Tom Seaver's Farewell by A. Bartlett Giamatti]
3. Turkey [Far Afield, Far from Home by Monty Montgomery]

1. Automotive racing is not my bag—indeed, this judge is, if anything, an anti—but the story about Niki Lauda, a plastic surgery returnee to the Grand Prix "super bowl," begged to be read a second, even a third time. It is an expertly tuned-up human-interest piece. More than that, the writer of it spun into his story a fascinating fabric of racing information that cleanly profiled an extraordinary man against the backdrop of the dangerous sport in which he competed. Against really rugged competition it captured my nod.

2. Whereas the personality has been written almost threadbare for nearly a decade, pin-up pitcher Tom Seaver's abrupt and disconcerting departure from under the halo he apparently wore for the New York Mets gave a professional writer one more go at it. Seaver, his uniqueness as a ball player, his appeal as a person, his deep entrenchment in the affections of Mets' fans, were never better summed up than in this piece.

3. Out of some unknown outdoorsy magazine comes a little writing gem, "Turkey" . . . an Oklahoma turkey hunt with a lot of chuckles, a great deal of insight, and more than a quick dab of doubt as to the Plymouth Pilgrims' REAL main course on THAT Thanksgiving Day. The most relaxing story in this edition of BSS, you suspect.

As for the photos, which this year were vying for an increased award of $250, the prize-winning action shot, "The Day the Seismographs Broke Down," by George Waldman of the *Detroit News,* and the top feature photo, "A Child Shall Come Forth; Only He Wanted to Be First," by Charles R. Pugh, Jr., of the *Atlanta Journal-Consti-*

tution, impressed the editors with their hard-hitting impact. Both of the photo winners have taken prizes in this series before.

So, coming up, here is *Best Sports Stories—1978.* As we have said thirty-three times in the past: we hope you have fun.

Irving T. Marsh
Edward Ehre

THE PRIZE WINNING STORIES

Best News-Coverage Story

WORLD SERIES

THE RIGHT-FIELD SIGN SAYS "REG-GIE, REG-GIE, REG-GIE"

By Thomas Boswell

From The Washington Post
Copyright, ©, 1977, The Washington Post

Some say there isn't enough mustard in the world to cover Reggie Jackson. Tonight, there wasn't enough glory as the New York Yankees defeated the Los Angeles Dodgers, 8–4, to win the World Series.

"Reg-gie, Reg-gie, Reg-gie," says the sign in right field in Yankee Stadium, once the home of the mighty Ruth and now the residence of the prodigious Jackson. Tonight the sign was right all three times.

Jackson, the man who has swung New York between delight and exasperation since the day he was bought at modern auction for $3 million, hit three home runs in the sixth and final game of the Seventy-fourth World Series.

This Yankee victory over the Dodgers will go down as one of many milestones in this ancient rivalry. But Jackson's evening may in time be regarded as the single most dramatic slugging performance in Series history. "Nothing can top this," said Jackson, who saw only three strikes in his four at-bats tonight and hit each farther than the last. "Who in hell's ever again going to hit three home runs in a deciding World Series game. I won't.

"Babe Ruth, Hank Aaron, Joe DiMaggio . . . at least I was with them for one night."

Jackson was wrong there. He was ahead of them. If numbers tell any fraction of the truth, Jackson wrapped up the greatest statistical Series in history tonight.

Jackson became the first man to hit five home runs in a Series. In fact, he hit them in his last nine at-bats.

Jackson hit four of the homers on his last four swings. He connected on his final swing Sunday. After a four-pitch walk in the second inning tonight, Jackson hit the first pitch in each of his last three appearances.

His final blow in the eighth inning—the shot that made his achievement unique—was a truly Ruthian, 500-foot swat halfway up into the black bleachers in dead center off a Charlie Hough knuckleball.

Jackson scored four runs and drove home five tonight. His dozen total bases in the game tied a record, while his 25 bases for the Series broke the record of 24. His 10 runs scored for this October feast passed the old standards of Ruth and Gehrig by one.

Babe Ruth twice hit three homers in a Series game, the last time in 1928. No other man had. Until tonight.

Needless to say, Jackson, with his .450 batting average and his 1.250 slugging mark, won his second World Series MVP award. His other was in 1973.

On Jackson's night, Mike Torrez and Chris Chambliss carried spears with dignity. Chambliss tied the game, 2–2, with a homer after Jackson's walk in the second. Torrez struggled through a nine-hitter, his second triumph of this title affair.

Nevertheless, all the memorable theatrics tonight belonged to Jackson, the player above all others in baseball who longs for the spotlight and plays to it.

Jackson's first two homers were almost instant replays of each other—and both, though they traveled no more than 370 feet, were the sort that few other players have hit. In the fourth and fifth innings, each time with a man on first, Jackson crashed a low-inside fastball on a low, hooking line toward the right-field wall.

For other hitters the balls might have barely reached the warning track. In fact, right fielder Reggie Smith, who hit a solo homer of his own tonight, had his back to the plate preparing to field both balls when they banged off the wall. They never did.

Both plunged into the first row of seats perhaps 30 feet right of the 353 sign.

The first blast put the Yankees ahead, 4–3, and knocked out starter and loser Burt Hooton, whose curves were well-knuckled tonight. The second put the Yanks in front, 7–3, and knocked out reliever Elias Sosa, who in truth, was only so-so. Two Jackson swings, two pitchers sent to the showers.

If homers No. 1 and 2 decided this last Series game, giving the determined Torrez more cushion than he needed, it was the third homer that probably will live in legend longest.

In future years those who were here will say that Jackson's record-setter hit the Marlboro sign 650 feet away in center. Perhaps they will say it cleared everything and never came down.

In reality, if this game stayed within that boundary, Jackson's third blow looked like a gigantic pop-up. The crowd's cheer stuck in its throat for a second. Could a ball so high possibly reach the black bleachers, that no-man's-land attained by so few, behind the 417 sign?

But Jackson knew. He stood at the plate and watched. Why should he miss what other millions were admiring?

The fourth homer in four swings finally landed—pay attention, posterity—on the first row of backless seats above the exitway on the right side of the empty ebony bleachers. The first huge bounce hit the black wall beneath the Marlboro sign. Estimated distance: near 500 feet. With hop: close to 600.

Jackson leaped on second base with an enormous stride, pumped both fists between second and third, then clutched his chest with both hands, pulling his uniform away from his body to show how his heart was bursting, as he headed for home.

As Jackson took his home-run trot, one Dodger was awestruck. The L.A. first baseman, Steve Garvey, who had knocked home two first-inning runs with an opposite-field triple, said, "As he went around I was applauding into my glove.

"I have never seen anything like that in a championship game situation," the Dodgers first baseman said of Jackson's stunning performance.

"He beat us single-handedly. And actually that's exactly what he did. He knocked in five runs and we only scored four.

"I sure wish that I'd had a chance to talk to him at first base. But he didn't stay there long enough for conversation."

A saddened Dodger manager Lasorda called Jackson's performance the greatest he's ever seen in a World Series.

"We lived by the long ball all year and we got killed by the long ball tonight," said Lasorda.

The fans who had withheld their love so long poured it out in standing cheers that lasted and lasted.

When Torrez caught the final L.A. pop-up, Jackson ran for his life—faster by far than Ruth ever had, or ever needed to. Taking a great-circle route through center field, Jackson built a head of steam worthy of his 9.6 dashman's speed. He careened through bodies like a wild linebacker, then flew into the Yankee dugout bench so hard that he almost knocked himself senseless.

Jackson rose and staggered toward the waiting champagne, toward the tears of Yankee joy and relief. He staggered toward a place next to Ruth in the Yankee's World Series pantheon. He was New York's best-loved son at last.

Best News-Feature Story

GENERAL

WELLS TWOMBLY, 41;
THE LAUGHTER STILL ECHOES

By David Klein

From the Newark Star-Ledger
Copyright, ©, 1977, The Star-Ledger, Newark, N.J.

I was doing a piece on Frank Robinson yesterday when the guy walked back from the wire service machine.

"Hey, did you know this guy?"

"Which guy?"

"Wells Twombly. He died."

Yeah, I knew Wells Twombly. And in this business of road trips and airplanes and hotel rooms and gray cities and late nights in anonymous bars, he was my best friend.

And how do you start something like this and where does it go and what do you say and why make a private grief public and how the hell can Wells be dead anyway?

But the yellow machine paper makes it real, and the words spewed out letter by letter from the computer make it real. Funny. Yellow paper with printed words never screamed before. He was 41 years old and many people thought he was the best sports columnist in America and he's dead.

Snatches of memory flash, unbidden, unwanted, slides projected on a personal screen for an eternity of a second, scenes seen by no one else, times shared by no one else.

Summer in Montreal, three weeks of the Olympics, and it was Wells who kept it fun . . . Wells who made the dormitory bearable . . . Wells who got the journalist from East Germany so enraged when an argument turned into a screamer and he screamed about personal freedoms in his country and dared the East German to tell about his . . . Wells who wrote that the Canadian government was consigning an entire generation to massive debt in order to stage a three-week lawn party . . . Wells who did the piece on Esther Roth and the Israeli team that sang with emotion and tears.

And a week after the Olympics Wells and Peggy and the three boys and the baby drove down and turned another man's vacation into a ball and showed another man's family why this friendship was so deep and the house slept nine people and the laughter still echoes.

In the days after Joe Roth died, it was Wells who knew that the magnificent young quarterback's dream was to earn his college degree before cancer took him away . . . and it was Wells who fought and cajoled and finally convinced the regents of the California State University system to award that diploma posthumously.

It was Wells who resigned from the Houston *Chronicle* the day after Martin Luther King was assassinated, because he had written a column tinged with sadness that wasn't a sports column at all but a man's outrage at such madness and the editors chose not to run it because it might have offended Texans. And it was Wells who organized a family touch-football game every Thanksgiving in which there were no rules and no winners and no losers because he said that was the way sports should be.

And it was Wells, making Lenny Bruce proud, who named his dog Phineas T. Tirebiter and then had him ordained by mail as a priest in one of those whacko California religious cults for 10 bucks . . . Wells who covered the Democratic National Convention in New York City and wrote that "never has a teetotaler been launched to the presidency on such a sea of bourbon" and caused Jody Powell to phone him and admit that "the President does, on occasion, enjoy a glass of white wine."

Lord, did he laugh about that.

And a few weeks ago it was Wells who said on the telephone that he wasn't feeling well and might have to spend a few days in the hospital and that he was behind on another book he was writing.

And it was Wells who joked that his agent advised him a few years ago to change the title of a Bicentennial book he was writing to "Two Hundred and Two Years of Sports in America" so that it wouldn't be clearly late.

And all last week, when he was in the hospital in San Francisco, and things in New Jersey piled up, the last telephone call was never made. And now the phone is useless.

Let this be said about Wells Twombly: If there were 100 media members at a press conference, the loudest and most incisive question would come from Wells. And if there were 100 sports writers laboring at 100 typewriters in those gigantic press rooms, the finest piece of writing would come from Wells, too.

And after the machine spewed out its dreadful news, Wes Twombly, the oldest son, called. "He wanted you to know right away," Wes said.

Lord, how the press boxes of this country are going to echo.

Best Magazine Story

BASEBALL

TOM SEAVER'S FAREWELL

By A. Bartlett Giamatti

From Harper's Magazine
Copyright, ©, 1977, by Harper's Magazine

Shea Stadium is not Eden, and the picture of Tom and Nancy Seaver leaving its graceless precincts in tears did not immediately remind me of the *Expulsion of Adam and Eve* in the Brancacci Chapel. And yet, absorbing the feelings generated by Seaver's departure from New York led me to the kind of inflated cogitation that links Masaccio and the Mets, if only because the feelings were so outsized and anguished and intense. After all, Brad Parks had gone to Boston, and Namath to Los Angeles, and Julius Erving to, if you will, Philadelphia. Clearly evil had entered the world, and mortality had fixed us with its sting. If Seaver is different, and evidently he is, the reasons must be sought somewhere other than in the columns of the daily press. In fact, the reasons for Seaver's effect on us have to do with the nature of baseball, a sport that touches on what is most important in American life. Where Parks, Namath, and Erving are only superb at playing their sports, Seaver seems to embody his.

George Thomas Seaver almost did not become a Met. In February of 1966, the Atlanta Braves signed the University of Southern California undergraduate to a contract and assigned him to Richmond. At this point, Commissioner William Eckert stated that the signing violated the college rule. The contract was scrapped. USC, however, declared Seaver ineligible. The commissioner announced that any team, except Atlanta, matching the Richmond contract could enter a drawing for rights to negotiate. The Indians, the Phillies, and the Mets submitted to the wheel of fortune, the Mets were favored, and Seaver, signed in early April, went to Jacksonville of the International League. He was 21 and would spend one year in the minor leagues.

Seaver pitched .500 ball for Jacksonville, 12–12, with an earned-run average of 3.13. He would not have as weak a season again until 1974, when he would go 11–11, with an ERA of 3.20. Yet even at Jacksonville he struck out 188 batters, thus foreshadowing his extraordinary performance with the Mets, with whom, from 1968 to 1976, he would never strike out fewer than 200 batters a season— a major-league record. And from the beginning Seaver pitched as much with his head as with his legs and right arm, a remarkably compact, *concentrated* pitcher, brilliantly blending control and speed, those twin capacities for restraint and release that are the indispensable possessions of the great artist. There is no need to rehearse the achievements of Seaver with the Mets: three Cy Young awards; Rookie of the Year with a last-place ball club in 1967; the leading pitcher in the league at 25–7 (ERA 2.21) in 1969, the same year he took the Mets to their first World Series (and, in the process, re-elected John Lindsay as mayor of New York—a cause for the trade no one has yet explored). In 1970 and 1971, he led the league in strikeouts (283; 289—a league season record for right handers) and in ERA (2.81; 1.76—which is like having an IQ of 175, though the ERA is easier to document and vastly more useful). On one April day in 1970, Seaver struck out 10 Padres in a row, 19 in all—an auto-da-fé that has never been bettered. One could go on.

The late sixties and early seventies were celebrated or execrated for many things besides someone being able to throw a baseball consistently at 95 miles per hour. These were the days of the Movement, the Counterculture, and the Student Revolution; of civil-rights activism, antiwar battles, student "unrest." Yippies yipped, flower children blossomed and withered, America was being greened, by grass and by rock and by people who peddled them. This was a pastoral time, and it would, like all pastorals, turn sere, but for three or four years, while Seaver was gaining control over a block of space approximately 3 feet high, 18 inches wide, and 60 feet 6 inches long, many other of America's "young" were breaking loose. That great wave against structure and restraint—whatever its legitimacy—begun publicly by people like Mario Savio at Berkeley in 1964, was now rolling East, catching up in its powerful eddies and its froth everyone in the country. In 1964 Tom Seaver, Californian, was moving on from Fresno City College to USC, his move East to come two years later. Here are, I think, the origins of the Seaver mystique in New York, in the young Californian who brought control, in the "youth" who came East bearing—indeed, embodying—tradition.

Most Americans do not distinguish among Californians at all, and if they do, it is certainly not with the passionate self-absorption of the natives. Yet we should, for there are real differences among them, differences far more interesting than those implied by the contrast most favored by Californians themselves, the one between the self-conscious sophisticates of San Francisco and the self-conscious zanies of Los Angeles. There are, for instance, all those Californians, north and south, who are not self-conscious at all. Such is Seaver, who is from Fresno.

Fresno—the name means "ash tree," that is, something tangible, durable; not the name of a difficult saint, with all its implications about egotism and insecurity, nor a mass of heavenly spirits, with its notions of indistinct sprawl, but "ash tree"—Fresno is inland, about the middle of the state, the dominant city in San Joaquin Valley, that fertile scar that runs parallel to the ocean between the Coastal Ranges and the Sierra Nevada. Fresno is the kingdom sung by Saroyan—flat, green, hot, and fertile; the land of hardworking Armenians, Chicanos, Germans; the cradle of cotton, alfalfa, raisin grapes, melons, peaches, figs, wine. Fresno is not chic, but it is secure. You do not work that hard and reap so many of the earth's goods without knowing who you are and how you got that way. This is the California Seaver came from, and in many ways it accounts for his balance as a man as well as a pitcher, for his sense of self-worth and for his conviction that you work by the rules and that you are rewarded, therefore, according to the rule of merit.

All this Seaver brought East, along with his fastball and his luminous wife, Nancy. They were perceived as a couple long before this became a journalistic convenience or public-relations necessity. They were Golden West, but not Gilded, nor long-haired, nor "political," nor opinionated. They were attractive, articulate, photogenic. He was Tom Terrific, the nickname a tribute to his all-American quality, a recognition, ironic but affectionate, that only in comic strips and myth did characters like Seaver exist. I have no idea what opinions Seaver held then on race, politics, war, marijuana, and other ERA, but whatever they were or are, they are beside the point. The point is the way Seaver was perceived—as clean-cut, larger than life, a fastballer, "straight," all at a time when many young people, getting lots of newspaper coverage, were none of the above. And then there was something else, a quality he exuded.

I encountered this quality the only time I ever met Seaver. One evening in the winter of 1971 I spent several hours with the Seavers and their friends and neighbors the Schaaps (he is the NBC-TV broadcaster) in the apartment of Erich Segal, then at the height of his fame as the author of *Love Story*. The talk was light, easy, and bright, and was produced almost entirely by the Schaaps, Nancy Seaver, and Segal. Because I was about the only member of the gathering who was a household name only in my own household, I was content to listen, and to watch Seaver. He sat somewhat apart, not, I thought by design, not, surely, because he was aloof, but because it seemed natural to him. He was watchful, though in no sense wary, and had that attitude I have seen in the finest athletes and actors (similar breeds), of being relaxed but not in repose, the body being completely at ease but, because of thousands of hours of practice, always poised, ready at any instant to gather itself together and move. Candid in his gaze, there was a formality in his manner, a gravity, something autumnal in the man who played hard all summer. He sat as other men who work with their hands sit, the hands clasped chest high or folded in front of him, often in motion, omnipresent hands that, like favored children, are the objects of constant if unconscious attention and repositories of complete confidence.

Seaver had, to be brief, *dignitas*, all the more for never thinking for a moment that he had it at all. A dignity that manifested itself in an air of utter self-possession without any self-regard, it was a quality born of a radical equilibrium. Seaver could never be off balance because he knew what he was doing and why it was valuable. He contrasted completely with the part of the country he was known to come from and with the larger society that he was seen as surrounded by. With consummate effortlessness, his was the talent that summed up baseball tradition; his was the respect for the rules that embodied baseball's craving for law; his was the personality, intensely competitive, basically decent, with the artisan's dignity, that amid the brave but feckless Mets, in a boom time, of leisure soured by divisions and drugs, seemed to recall a cluster of virtues seemingly no longer valued.

And Seaver held up. His character proved as durable and strong as his arm. He was authentic; neither a goody two-shoes nor a flash in the pan, he matured into the best pitcher in baseball. Character and talent on this scale equaled a unique charisma. He was a national symbol, nowhere more honored than in New York, and in New York never more loved than by the guy who seemed in every other respect Seaver's antithesis, the guy who would never give a sucker an even break, who knew how corrupt they all were, who knew it was who you knew that counted, who knew how rotten it all really was—this guy loved Seaver because Seaver was a beautiful pitcher, a working guy who got rewarded; Seaver was someone who went by the rules and made it; Seaver carried the whole lousy team, God love 'em, on his back, and never shot his mouth off, and never gave in and did it right. The guy loved Seaver because Seaver did not have to be street-wise.

In bars in Queens, in clubs in the Bronx, in living rooms in front of Channel 9 in Suffolk and Nassau, out on Staten Island, everywhere, but particularly in the tattered reaches of Shea Stadium, they loved him for many things, but above all because he never thought he had to throw at anybody's head. From the Columbia riots to the brink of fiscal disaster, there was someone in New York who did not throw at anybody. They loved it in him, and in that act sought for it in themselves.

None of this reasoning, if such it is, would appeal to the dominant New York baseball writers, who have used the Seaver trade as a casus belli nor to M. (for, I think, Moralistic) Donald Grant, chairman of the board of the Mets, who would quickly tell us that Seaver wanted too much money, meaning by that something he would never say aloud but would certainly formulate within himself—that Tom wanted *too much.* Tom wanted, somehow, to cross the line between employee and equal, hired hand and golf partner, "boy" and man. What M. Donald Grant could not abide—after all, could he, Grant, ever become a Payson? Of course not. Everything is ordered. Doesn't anyone understand anything anymore?—Tom Seaver thought this was his due. He believed in the rules, in this game governed by law; if you were the best pitcher in baseball, you ought to get the best salary of any pitcher in baseball; and money—yes, money— ought to be spent so baseball's best pitcher would not have to work on baseball's worst-hitting team.

Of course Tom Seaver wanted money, and wanted money spent; he wanted it for itself, but he wanted it because, finally, Tom Seaver felt about the Mets the way the guy from Astoria felt about Seaver—he loved them for what they stood for and he wanted merit rewarded and quality improved. The irony is that Tom Seaver had in abundance precisely the quality that M. Donald Grant thinks he values most—institutional loyalty, the capacity to be faithful to an idea as well as to individuals. Grant ought to have seen that in Seaver; after all, the man worked for the Mets for eleven years. Grant ought to have had the wit to see a more spacious, generous version of what he prizes so highly in himself. Certainly the guy who had watched Seaver all those years knew it, knew Seaver was holding out for something, a principle that made sense in one who played baseball but that grew from somewhere within him untouched by baseball, from a conviction about what a man has earned and what is due him and what is right. The fan understood this and was devastated when his understanding, and Seaver's principle, were not honored. The anguish surrounding Seaver's departure stemmed from the realization that the chairman of the board and certain newspaper columnists thought money was more important than loyalty, and the fury stemmed from the realization that the chairman and certain writers thought everybody else agreed with them, or ought to agree with them.

On June 16, the day after Seaver was exiled to Cincinnati by way of Montreal, a sheet was hung from a railing at Shea bearing the following legend:

I WAS A
BELIEVER
BUT NOW WE'VE
LOST
SEAVER

I construe that text, and particularly its telling rhyme, to mean not that the author has lost faith in Seaver but that the author has lost faith in the Mets' ability to understand a simple, crucial fact: that among all the men who play baseball there is, very occasionally, a man of such qualities of heart and mind and body that he transcends even the great and glorious game, and that such a man is to be cherished, not sold.

Other Stories

SOCCER

"LOVE! LOVE! LOVE!" CRIES PELE

By Tony Kornheiser

From The New York Times
Copyright, ©, 1977, The New York Times Company
Reprinted by permission

It was his day, and everyone was properly respectful. When the diplomats and sporting celebrities were introduced, they waved to the crowd and remained silent in deference to his presence; even the unretiring Muhammad Ali stood mute.

When it came time for them to give him their gifts and praise, they did so as tersely as possible, and then they left the microphone to him, and the silence covered the stadium like a fog.

"Ladies and gentlemen," Pele said, putting his hands behind his head as if to support his quivering words. "I am very happy to be here with you in this greatest moment of my life. I want to thank you all, every single one of you. I want to take this opportunity to ask you to pay attention to the young of the world, the children, the kids. We need them too much. And I want to ask you because I think that, I believe that, love is the, the, the . . ."

Tears welled in his eyes, and he could no longer stem their flow. He tightened his grip on himself and continued, his words shaking, his voice cracking.

"Love is more important than what we can take in life. Everything pass. Please say with me, three times—love! love! love!"

As the message board flashed the word, Pele heard the crowd echo his message. Three times. Love! Love! Love! And it was all too much for him. He could say but one thing more before his voice was lost in his tears.

He said, "Thank you very much."

And then, as 75,646 persons watched, he covered his face with his hands and took comfort from his Cosmos teammate and countryman, Carlos Alberto. Then his wife and father came out to share the moment with him. Pele embraced them and they held him close and cried with him.

This was the day that Pele retired as a competitive professional soccer player. Warner Communications, which owns the Cosmos, set up this special exhibition game with Santos, the Brazilian team for which Pele had played most of his career. He played the first half with the Cosmos, the second with Santos.

The game ended with the Cosmos winning, 2–1. The big moment came with 2 minutes 34 seconds left in the first half. Pele, who had not attempted a shot for the Cosmos, was awarded a free kick from about 30 yards out. He drove the ball low and hard, a bullet keeping its line all the way to the left corner of the Santos goal, leaving the goalie sprawled out, watching as the shot went in. It was Pele's one thousand, two hundred and eighty-first goal of his career and it tied the game at 1–1.

In the second half he had five shots, two of which required saving. But try as they might, the Santos players could not set him up for the chippie the fans wanted to see him get. Still, the thrill of the day was not diminished in the slightest by Pele's having scored but one goal.

"I die a little bit today," Pele said after the game. "Now I am born again to another life. You see, I stop playing soccer because I want to stop, and that is important."

Warner spared no expense bringing the great and the almost great to be with Pele. Ali, Mick Jagger, Henry Kissinger, Claudette Colbert were there. So were the captains of the last five World Cup championship teams. So was Jeff Carter, the President's son, giving Pele a plaque and calling him, "Pay-Lay," with a Plains accent. Everyone but Bugs Bunny was there.

But the children touched the man the most. There were children from various soccer clubs in the metropolitan area. They did drills for Pele's approval, and some gave him flowers. And he bent to receive their gifts and kissed each youngster.

It was to be a love-in, and Pele, like the Pied Piper he is, led the way.

Although it began raining with six and a half minutes to play in the first half, this was not the kind of parade that could be rained out. At half time, Pele went to the center of the field for yet another ceremony. With his father at his side, he took off the No. 10 jersey he had worn as a Cosmos, a number that has now been officially retired by the team, waved it at the crowd, then embraced his father as he handed him the shirt.

As the rain continued, Pele put on the No. 10 jersey he used to wear with Santos. To the surprise of no one, it seemed to fit perfectly.

It had been thought that Pele would leave the field with two or three minutes left, but he played the entire game. When it ended, he embraced some players and stood in the center of the field, a familiar spot for him this day.

He gave his Santos shirt to his first coach and then, as the crowd shouted "Pele! Pele!" he took a victory lap around the field. The Cosmos' two goalkeepers, Shep Messing and Erol Yasin, then lifted him to their shoulders and carried him off the field. Bare-chested and dripping wet, he gave the fans his customary victory salute.

This was by no means Pele's final game. He has said he will play in exhibitions or charity games as he pleases. If you count all the times that he has previously "retired," today's game was his final, final, final, final one. Like Ali, whom Pele visited on the afternoon of his title defense against Earnie Shavers, Pele has waved good-bye so often that his arms must be weary.

In 1966, after the Brazilian national team had been eliminated from the World Cup competition in the quarter-final round, Pele went to the sidelines with tears in his eyes, saying, "Soccer is no longer fun." He told his close friends he was retiring, but the next season he was again playing for Santos.

In 1971 he said he was retiring from international competition, and 120,000 spectators cheered him so strongly that he wept. On October 2, 1974, he again retired after having played his last game for Santos. And in the book, *Pele's New World,* by Peter Bodo and David Hirshey, Pele spoke as follows about the feeling that came over him two days after that game:

"Finally came October 4 and I live the strangest moments of my life. It is difficult to say what I felt, because it was pure emotion, and not something I think. I look at public and players and say to myself, 'No more,' and it sound like the voice of another man."

Pele, obviously, is no stranger to retirement, nor is he a stranger to the emotional upheaval it causes. At a news conference two days ago, he called this latest retirement "the most important and most saddest moment in my life."

Taking a moment to compose himself and his thoughts, he continued: "This is life. You can't play one game all your life. Someday you have to stop. If I can't start all over my life again, I prefer to say good-bye."

This is not to suggest that Warner Communications and the Cosmos players did not do everything they could to get Pele to reconsider and play again. According to Shep Messing, the goalie, Warner put tremendous pressure on him to unretire, probably in the form of millions of dollars. The other players tried to talk him out of retiring throughout the North American Soccer League playoffs.

"We weren't really convinced that he would do it until after we won the championship," Messing said. "When he didn't change his mind then, we knew he was gone. He wanted to retire on top; he didn't want to be anything less than exceptional. And he wanted to spend more time with his family. So we bought him a gold plaque and inscribed it with our names. I mean, what can you buy Pele?"

Standing on a balcony, observing Pele's news conference, Messing admitted a deep feeling of sadness at watching Pele go out.

"I feel like quitting myself," he said.

Such is the effect of the man that all his teammates, and even all the other soccer players in the world, feel diminished by his leaving. His name has been synonymous with soccer the way Arnold Palmer's was with golf and Babe Ruth's with baseball. There is, rather was, but one Pele.

TENNIS

A WIMBLEDON STORY WAITING TO BEGIN

By Sheila Moran

From the Los Angeles Times
Copyright, ©, 1977, Los Angeles Times
Reprinted by permission

Her daily routine hasn't changed much, nine years after she described her life for a kindergarten assignment. But the world knows now that Tracy Austin plays tennis.

Having dominated the national junior ranks since she was nine, having knocked off a number of world-class players during her first foray on the pro tour this year, Tracy Austin is heading for another milestone later this month as the youngest to compete in the Wimbledon championships since 1887.

But at 14, Tracy is as much the adolescent off the court as her good friend Suzanne DeLangis, an eighth-grade classmate at the Dapplegray Intermediate School in Rolling Hills Estates. She wears her hair in pigtails and her smile reveals a mouthful of braces. She collects stuffed animals and stamps, attends to a growing gum-wrapper chain, tries not to miss *Blansky's Beauties* on television, and is concerned about her size.

Tracy is more apprehensive about starting high school in September than about her debut at Wimbledon and Forest Hills.

"When I think about high school, I think of big people," she said. "I think it should start in the tenth grade instead of the ninth. I'm too small."

Tracy is 5-feet-1, weighs 90 pounds, and the child-sized tennis dresses she wears with the sashes tied in back draw almost as much attention as her precocious volleys. But there are signs she might be ready to shoot up, like a dandelion after a rainstorm. She has large hands and a family precedent: Tracy's sister, Pam, 26, is 6 feet. Her brother, John, is 6-feet-4.

And, "I eat a lot and get tired a lot," she said.

Tracy spends most of her waking hours at the Jack Kramer Tennis Club near her home but had been grounded for several days with the chicken pox when she was visited recently by a reporter. She was curled up in jeans and a red parka-style sweat shirt on the living room couch in the family's three-bedroom house, working on an after-dinner dish of vanilla icre cream.

"I must have watched 40 hours of TV," she said wearily.

Tracy had tried sewing for the first time and displayed a red polka-dot apron she had just completed for her mother, a friendly, smiling woman who was seated in a chair nearby, still dressed in the tennis outfit she wore in the afternoon at the Kramer Club, where she works in the pro shop.

Tracy is poised among strangers in discussing tennis but seemed a trifle uncomfortable as she fielded questions about other things. While she takes her tennis achievements in stride, almost as if they were destined to happen, it appeared she does not yet understand that questions about other facets of her life also go with being a star.

Already, she admitted, she is "a little tired of it all." She receives "a lot of fan mail, about 200 letters since last year," and: "I don't usually read them all and it's too impossible to answer them all." Then, as if revealing a very important secret, she added: "Jimmy Connors only writes to people who send addressed envelopes."

So it was with some reluctance that Tracy allowed a reporter to visit her room. Her tiny sanctum includes a double-decker bed, the top bunk overflowing with stuffed animals and boxes of tennis shoes sent by doting manufacturers. Posters from tennis tournaments around the world—including one reading, "Feeling Groovy"—cover virtually every inch of wall, ceiling, and door space.

A pair of yellow anklets she borrowed from Chris Evert to wear in a tournament hang on a peg on the wall near the door. A child's typewriter sits by a wilting plant near her desk. Tacked on the door is that poster-paper essay from kindergarten, describing a regimen that is basically unchanged.

Tracy was born into a tennis family and was given her first racket when she was two. She started lessons at seven with her present coach, Bob Landsdorp, and "when I was nine, I started liking tennis a lot."

She is also adept at baseball, volleyball, and flag football, and at 10 broke both bones in her right leg ice-skating. She tried horseback riding, which is more popular in the bucolic Rolling Hills area than tennis.

"Horses. That's all my friends talk about," Tracy said. "You get on a horse and you feel like a midget. When I was seven, this friend, Annie Lou, would take me up in the hills and we'd ride all over the place."

Tracy's mother, Jeanne, and father, George, a nuclear physicist, took up tennis for fun when they moved to California in 1955 and produced five children, each of whom excels at the sport: Pam, who played five years on the women's pro circuit and now is a sales manager for the Los Angeles Strings; Jeff, 25, a circuit player ranked fifty-sixth in the United States; Doug, 23, No. 1 at Long Beach State; John, 19, a varsity player at UCLA; and, finally, Tracy.

Collectively, the Austins have won more than 400 trophies, which adorn a room off the kitchen that used to be filled with books. Mrs. Austin mentioned that there's no more space for trophies and added that perhaps the children might keep their winnings in their own apartments.

"No," Tracy said in a rare display of emotion. "Let it sit there. This is the house they grew up in. They won't take them away."

She speaks fondly of her brothers and sisters and of the family pets, four mongrels named Mama Dog, Little Bit, Joey, and Shortie. She describes the fun the family has playing tennis with the same importance she attaches to her own accomplishments.

"It's fun when my brothers and sisters come home," she said. "On Christmas, we all play doubles at the club."

How good is Tracy Austin?

Sports Illustrated put her on the cover when she was 13, with a caption proclaiming "A Star Is Born."

In slightly more than two months last winter, Tracy turned back more than $12,000 in prize money. Her startled victims included Dianne Fromholtz, No. 1 in Australia and No. 8 in the world, and Greer Stevens, No. 1 in South Africa. Tracy plans to continue competing in junior tournaments and selected tour events until she finishes high school. Then she wants to turn pro.

"She's a sweet girl," said Chris Evert, with whom Tracy is inevitably compared. "We'll know just how good she is by the time she is 17. By 17 or 18, if you haven't broken into the top three, you never will."

Tracy Austin's feelings about her future seem best expressed in a quotation by Ralph Waldo Emerson that hangs on her wall, in striking contrast to the childish artifacts in her room:

"The world makes way for the man who knows where he is going."

BASEBALL

IF THEY DON'T WIN IT'S A SHAME

By Gene Lyons

From Texas Monthly
Copyright, ©, 1977, by Texas Monthly
Reprinted by special permission of Texas Monthly Magazine

The wind blows in every night at the McAllen ball park at a steady 20 to 25 miles per hour from left field, carrying dust and occasional debris. On the bench it would be smarter to stay upwind of the snuff dippers and Redman chewers, but since everyone on the team has a mouthful of tobacco the best one can do is keep some distance and avoid the weak spitters. The McAllen team plays on a field rented from the city's high school. As there is no locker room, the visiting Corpus Christi Seagulls will have to shower in their motel rooms. The outfield grass is mostly brown from the midsummer sun, and not very smooth.

Though the players line up reverently before the game with their hats over their hearts while the scratchy press-box phonograph blares out a tinny version of the National Anthem, there is no flag on the premises to salute, or even a flagpole. During the first three or four innings the left fielders, shortstop, and third baseman stare directly into the setting sun. From left field it is impossible to follow a pitched ball at all, even with sunglasses; a player can only listen for the sound of ball hitting bat, wait for teammates to shout, and worry. The fielding statistics by which a ball player's future are in part determined will not record several innings of functional blindness. There will be no asterisk noting the dark spots on the field after the lights are turned on, or the odd bounces now and then. At third base the fear is more elemental: A line drive coming out of that sun could fracture a player's skull before he could raise his glove in self-defense.

By game time fewer than 130 paying customers have scattered themselves randomly on the rickety open bleachers on the McAllen

Dusters' side of the field. Behind the visitors' dugout there are exactly two: Bobby Flores's girl friend and Rick Buckner's date. Flores is a utility player—a baseball euphemism for a second-stringer—and Buckner the regular third baseman for the Seagulls. Considering last night's game it is a wonder anyone other than blood relatives of the players has come at all. The Dusters have the worst record in the league, having won 9 and lost 21. Corpus Christi has won 13 straight and is one win away from clinching the first-half pennant in their division. With 24 wins and 6 losses they have the best record in professional baseball.

The Seagulls' nearest league rivals, the Harlingen Suns, are 9 games behind with 10 to play and have only broken even in 30 games. Last night McAllen, arguably the worst professional baseball team in the United States, made 10 errors, including four in the second inning alone, gave up nine unearned runs and handed the game to Corpus Christi 11–0. Against Ken Palmer, a former University of Oklahoma pitcher who has yielded less than two earned runs a game, McAllen managed just four weak singles, no walks, and struck out 11 times.

By the late innings the Corpus Christi players were openly contemptuous of McAllen's lack of effort. For them there was neither joy nor honor in defeating a team that was not trying. McAllen has been a troubled, feuding club all season—primarily, the Corpus Christi players believe, because of second baseman Billy Gautreau, whose father owns the franchise and who they believe could not make the roster of any other team in the league, much less start. They are convinced the Gautreau controversy cost Mike Krizmanich, an outfielder who played for the Seagulls last year and won the league batting title with a .381 average, his job as McAllen's manager. By the end of the game the only thing that moved them to animation was the hope of knocking Gautreau down by sliding high and hard into second base. Like all ball players, they bitterly resent any trifling with the verities of their game. Such things are occasionally done in high school; it is not the way professional teams operate. Being professional is very important in the Lone Star League.

The Lone Star League is unique in professional baseball. It is the only independently franchised minor-league operation in the United States. With the exception of a couple of teams in the Pacific Northwest, every other professional baseball team in the country, and every player on each of those teams, is under contract to one of the 26 major-league organizations. But not the Lone Star League or its players. It is the last remnant of the way minor-league ball used to be, the boondocks of baseball.

Bobby Flores, who is from Robstown and played college ball at UT-Arlington, characterized his team as a "collection of oddballs, misfits, and old people, but a winner." What he means by oddballs and misfits is that, despite the Seagulls' gaudy record, no player was worthy of a current contract with one of the major-league teams (though a few Seagulls would qualify as oddballs by any definition); what he means by old people is that the Seagulls have two players who are actually 25, and a number of others over 22. Among the 18 Seagulls the 12 with previous pro experience have played for 33 other minor-league teams in 11 states. Manager Leo Mazzone was a left-handed pitcher for 10 years in the San Francisco Giants and Oakland A's farm systems, getting as high as Tucson in the AAA Pacific Coast League before being released, with stops along the way in Medford, Oregon; Decatur, Illinois; Amarillo; Monterrey, Mexico; and Birmingham, Alabama. Catcher Ron Lollis, 25, was drafted in the sixth round out of a Spokane high school in 1971 by the Oakland A's, turning down a baseball scholarship to Stanford. He played for teams in Oregon, Iowa, Alabama, and Florida (Key West) before making it two years ago to the top of the minor-league ladder, the Texas Rangers' AAA farm club back home in Spokane, but the word is that he had trouble hitting a slider. Fortunately for Lollis, not many in the Lone Star League can throw a good one, and he is murdering the ball again. But this time he is doing it on his own: He was released at the end of last season. The only one of the Seagull players who is married, L.O., as he is called, sold his house in Spokane to give it one more shot.

It is not hard to understand why, from Lollis's perspective, the sudden end to his career made no sense. There he was, moving up each year, still only 25—and then it's over. His experience sheds light on an aspect of baseball familiar to all players and virtually no fans: Professional baseball, often eulogized by intellectuals and traditionalists as a reminder of an older, more bucolic America, is in fact as bureaucratic as, and a good deal more relentlessly hierarchical than, such pursuits as banking, life insurance, and the teaching of comparative literature. Lollis was cut, not because he couldn't hit the slider, but because he was 25 and couldn't hit the slider. He was dropped to make room in the organization for the class of 1977, some of whom were 18 and 19 and had never *seen* a slider. Flores's characterization is apt: Most of the Seagulls are too old, even at 21 or 22, to be playing ball at this low level and retain much hope of making it to the big leagues, or even the high minors. For a very few it may be a beginning; for most it is the end. But they all have hope; without that, playing here for $400 a month would make no sense at all.

Minor-league baseball has not always been so cut-and-dried. Before television's drastic impact on virtually all public entertainment, from movies to sports, there were far more minor-league baseball franchises in medium- and smalled-sized cities all over the country. Until 1958, in fact, the only major-league team west of the Mississippi was the St. Louis Cardinals (the Browns moved to Baltimore in 1953), whose home park was a short walk from the river. In those days it was quite common for ball players to have long minor-league careers and to remain with one club for a considerable number of years; names like Eddie Knoblauch, Larry Miggins, and Jerry Witte are still familiar to postwar Texas League fans. Today a ball player seldom lingers for long in the minor leagues; Leo Mazzone's experience is unusual and, except for pitchers, almost unheard of.

In 1953, for example, there were 306 minor-league teams operating in 38 leagues around the United States and Canada, and an elaborate classification system that rated the quality of play from the AAA International and Pacific Coast leagues, through the AA Texas League and Southern Association, all the way down through Class A,B,C, and even D. There were leagues with colorful names and long traditions, like the Pony League (an acronym for Pennsylvania-Ohio-New York) and the Three-I League (Iowa-Illinois-Indiana). In Texas the current major-league cities, Houston and Dallas-Fort Worth (unhyphenated in those years), were in the AA Texas League, but 28 other Texas teams were in the Big State League, the West Texas-New Mexico League, the Arizona-Texas League, the Sooner State League, the Gulf Coast League, and the Longhorn League. Beaumont played in the same league with Houston, and Austin, Galveston, and San Angelo had franchises. Even towns as small as Gainesville, Paris, and Lemesa were respected. By 1976, though, there were just 16 minor leagues left, several of them for rookies only, and 100 or so teams. Besides the Lone Star League, the only minor-league teams left in Texas are in the four cities composing the Western Division of the Texas League: San Antonio, El Paso, Midland, and Amarillo. The majority of teams in the minors operate at little or no profit and are run by and for the major-league clubs that own them. Consequently, the minors are no longer so much a training ground for young players, a place to learn the subtleties of the game, but rather a testing ground: Put a player in the lineup, rate his ability to help the big club, and then move him up or move him out. Except for the Lone Star League, pro baseball is a closed shop.

The effect of this shrinkage upon the individual's career has been to speed things up considerably, as well as, from the player's point of view, to lend an air of capriciousness and mystery to the whole process. During his last season in AAA ball, Leo Mazzone was one of the few players able somehow to get a look at the scouting report written about him. He can give it to you word for word: "Big-league curveball, good change-up and slider, medium fastball. Short, very aggressive. Won't help anybody." In something over 1,000 innings, he says, he had a 62-58 record, mostly as a reliever, where won-lost percentages mean relatively little, along with 1,740 strikeouts—more than one an inning—and only 300 or so walks: very impressive statistics. One would think that anybody who could strike batters out at that rate and be around the plate so often would deserve a shot, at least, at some big-league club's bullpen. But the A's who released him evidently thought not. "What the hell does that mean?" Leo still wonders. "Short, very aggressive. Won't help anybody?" He can recite lists of short pitchers (he is 5-feet-9), commencing with Whitey Ford, who was 5-feet-10. As for aggressive, when he was with Amarillo, Leo once threw a ball clear out of the Memphis Blues stadium and into the Liberty Bowl when his manager came to take him out of a game. When Amarillo played at Little Rock he used to flash the Hook 'Em Horns sign at fans from the bullpen, although, being from Maryland, he doesn't really give a hang for them or the Hogs.

Leo's 10 years in the minors give him cause to sympathize with Mando Reyes, a right-handed pitcher for the Seagulls who as of this writing had given up just four earned runs in 30 innings and won three games against no losses with three saves. About the same height as Leo but with a slighter build, Reyes, who compiled an 18-2 won-lost record in two years at Pan American University, was ignored in the professional draft, probably because of his size. Anyone who follows major-league baseball must have noticed that young pitchers seem to be growing bigger each year: It appears that 6-feet-2 or so must be mandated minimum. Further affecting pitchers is the tyranny of velocity. Although there are any number of big-league pitchers who have done and continue to do well without blazing speed—it used to be said of San Francisco's Stu Miller that he couldn't throw a baseball through a wet tissue—anybody who can throw the ball 90 miles per hour or more and get it near the plate fairly often is virtually assured of a big bonus and every chance to make good. Baseball people—the ultimate realists—are aware, of course, that pitchers who rely on guile and deception can get batters out, but they are also aware that it takes a good deal of time and cunning for breaking ball pitchers to sharpen their skills sufficiently to fool big leaguers. But until they get to the top and learn the tricks of their trade, by which time a good deal of expertise and many dollars may have been expended on them, nobody can be sure they're worth the risk. So scouts put a radar gun to a pitcher's fastball, and if, like Ken Palmer's, it barely teases 85 miles per hour, even though he pitches lots of shutouts and hardly walks anybody, they write him off and he comes to the Lone Star League. Or if, like Dennis Olson, he has a bad day when the scouts show up, the same thing happens. Olson, who until early June pitched for the University of Missouri at St. Louis, thinks he has the velocity but had a terrible day in NCAA playoffs when the scouts came. It was so terrible, he says, "You could have timed my fastball with a sundial."

Other players encounter other problems. With millions going to free agents like Reggie Jackson, player development dollars must be carefully watched. The late bloomer or the very talented player who was drafted low or signed for little money has a built-in disadvantage against a rival in whom the organization has invested heavily. Put simply, Mazzone says, "A player they have put money into has to screw up badly; he has to play his way out of the lineup. The guy who got no bonus has to play his way in."

Politics plays a part too. For Marc Sinovich—whom you would recognize as a catcher even in black tie and tails, assuming anybody could get him to wear either—the problem was being labeled, he thinks unfairly, as a troublemaker. In the Oakland organization, Sinovich roomed during 1976 spring training with a player who for some reason set his alarm clock one time zone west of where they were, causing Sinovich to miss a bed check by a few minutes. He was fined $100. Called up to the big club the next day to catch batting practice, Sinovich made the mistake of complaining about the fine to Reggie Jackson, who was infuriated by the story and promised to pay the fine himself. Jackson called in pitcher Ken Holtzman, the A's player representative, who knew that fines were not to be levied in spring training against rookies with no big-league contracts. Holtzman called Charlie Finley, Oakland's owner, to complain; Finley reportedly called the minor-league manager responsible and gave him a dressing down, and 24 hours later Sinovich, who had had a good year in 1975 in AA ball at Birmingham and was hoping for an AAA contract, was given his release by the same manager. So last year he came to Corpus Christi, where he hit .317, had 11 home runs and 64 RBIs in 74 games for the Seagulls, performed excellently as a defensive catcher, Leo says, and hit two home runs in the final playoff game despite a broken finger. But he has been injured this year and in any case is getting long in the tooth. Like Lollis, he is 25.

Lloyd Thompson came out of the University of New Mexico in 1975 (as did right fielder Randy Rima and second baseman Mark Hiller) and signed with Montreal. Early on he hurt his shoulder sliding into second base to break up a double play. During corrective surgery in the off-season a large screw was improperly placed, so that to extend his left arm with the palm raised was impossible—rather inconvenient for a shortstop—and to follow through on his swing at the plate was agonizing. He played badly and was cut.

"There were too many young guys sitting on the bench for them to keep fooling with me," he says. When I remarked that 21, which he was then, seemed young enough to me, Thompson laughed. "We had two 16-year-old Puerto Ricans on that team." Last winter he had the faulty screw removed and on the advice of a scout came to Corpus Christi to try his luck as a pitcher, as he has what the players call "a good hose." But when Leo saw him in the field he went back to shortstop, where he is one of the players the manager thinks has a good shot at a second chance. He fields brilliantly and is hitting .300, so maybe he does.

Some players never know why they are cut. Unlike, say, the academic world, where someone dropped from the teaching roster can appeal to 17 committees and stick around for a full year after the decision is irrevocable, baseball teams do the deed with finality. Joe Kwasny, who was drafted in the tenth round and signed out of high school in Virginia Beach, Virginia, by the Yankees—"the same year and the same round as Mark 'The Bird' Fidrych; my dad always reminds me of that"—is a case in point. Kwasny, who had pitched, he thought pretty well, for three minor-league teams, came to his locker on the last day of spring training in 1976 to find it empty. "Usually they come to your room early in the morning, before anybody gets up," he says. "But they just cleaned me out, even my hat, which they usually let you keep. I got the point. I went to the manager and he said pack your stuff. They had me on a plane by noon. That night I was back home watching TV with my father. Then Leo called me up and asked me to come down, and here I am. I didn't know what I was going to do. I hate going to school, so that's out."

Kwasny starts the night of the second McAllen game, and I sit in the stands a couple of innings with Carl Sawatski, who caught for several major-league teams in the forties and fifties and is currently president of the AA Texas League. Sawatski is paying a series of honorary visits to the owners of the Lone Star League teams. I asked him what he would be looking for if he were scouting the teams tonight. In pitchers, he says, velocity. Do either Kwasny or Laconia Graham, the Dusters' pitcher, have it? In a word, he answers: "No." But Kwasny, I say, signed with the Yankees just three years ago at 18. Most athletes don't get their full strength until their middle or late twenties. What could have happened? "Either somebody made a mistake or he lost it." Which is likelier? "A mistake." But what about Stu Miller I go on; he got people out with no real fastball at all. "Not when he first came up," Sawatski says. "I knew Miller back in 1948 or 1949 when he first came into the minor leagues. He threw very hard then. He learned all that other stuff after he was up." Sawatski is a friendly and amiable man, but about baseball and particularly about pitchers, the former catcher's negative judgments are swift, confident, and severe. Kwasny's lack of a fastball to him is a fact, like the color of his hair.

Sawatski is able to stay only until the middle of the fourth inning and does not see Kwasny get really hammered, or the flaccid Seagulls do a passable imitation of McAllen's fielding display of the previous night. Before he is taken out with one out in the sixth, Joe has given up 11 hits and six runs, three of them earned. In the dugout for the rest of the game and all the way back to the motel he doesn't say a word. By the next morning he is joking about it. What else can he do? The loss is his second against five wins.

It is the maddening indeterminacy of baseball that makes it the cruelest game. If games offer any lessons for life, which I think they do, what this one teaches is humility. It is not simply that the Seagulls have been beaten 8–1 by a terrible team; it is that games like this happen all the time in baseball, every night at every level of the game: The worst teams beat the best ones. To be a successful baseball team you must win six out of 10 games; to achieve last place four of 10 will usually suffice. There are nights when Dad himself could play second base, or Mom for that matter, nights when a team could field a butterball turkey or no second baseman at all and still win. The indirectness and subtlety of baseball's competition is what makes it so productive of self-perpetuating illusions of greatness and finally so fascinating a game. At every level the bad news about one's prospects takes just a little longer to become apparent; often when it is most obvious to everyone else, it is least discernible to the individual player himself.

Consider batting, the most directly competitive and immediately quantifiable aspect of baseball. As of this writing the leading team for average in the major leagues is the Cincinnati Reds and the worst is the New York Mets. Virtually every hitter who comes to the plate for the Reds exudes an aura of menacing competence. Yet in round figures their team batting average translates to 29 hits in every 100 times at bat. The Mets, by contrast, seem as a group transfixed by feckless mediocrity. Their team percentage is roughly 24 hits per 100 tried— a difference of less than two hits a game. Coming a bit closer to home we find that the same point in the season the Corpus Christi Seagulls were batting .277 (or 27.7 hits per 100 at-bats) to the McAllen Dusters' .271 (or 27.1 hits per 100 at-bats). Yet Corpus Christi had scored 205 runs by that point to McAllen's 87, and no observer who had seen both teams play several times would mistake one for the other. It is this aspect of the game that makes a professional organization like the Lone Star League possible and provides its character.

Another thing easily lost in writing and reading about sports that are less than major league is that by any reasonable measure, these are extraordinary athletes. All of them have been stars everywhere they have played before now. Jim "Bear" Bratsen looks to have been made from the mold for God's own first baseman. When he was playing for Texas A&M he got some All-America mentions. Pitcher Fran Hirschy broke every record Long Island University ever had. When Mike Pagnotta and Jim Rainey, the left and center fields, come to the plate, they *look* like the good hitters they are. Everybody on the team can throw harder and more accurately than anybody I had ever played with—sandlot, high school, or anywhere else. If Joe Kwasny or Vern Snyder, or, for that matter, Leo Mazzone could today accept the collegiate athletic scholarships they could have had after high school, they would all be stars in the Southwest Conference. Yet here they are in the Lone Star League, which is as low as you can get in baseball and not be paid in beer instead of money. Even if they get the improbable break, the odds remain overwhelmingly against them. Making it to the big leagues is about as likely, statistically, as being elected to Congress. In all probability, there will be more turnover in Texas's top three political positions—two senators and a governor —in the next 10 years than in the Boston Red Sox outfield.

Traveling with a team of minor-league ball players is like spending a week with an athletic-minded college fraternity—except that physical conditions are more in keeping with the McAllen ball park than a plush frat house. The Seagulls started the season making round trips in a Dodge van, but one died before I got there and a second was lost on the way south when the hood flew up and smashed the windshield, so now they travel in private cars. The tone of most discussions, for anyone unfamiliar with such baseball literature as Jim Bouton's *Ball Four*, could not be described as elevated. The players talk about sports, but not in terms much more sophisticated than the average fan would use. Anyone eavesdropping in hopes of picking up the finer points of the game would remain unenlightened. The sole indication that these are athletes talking rather than fans is that they are more likely to challenge conventional wisdom. One such discussion raged over whether basketball superstar Julius Erving was overrated. But no one had any harsh words for any baseball major leaguers.

When they're not talking about sports, their competitiveness is expressed in continual ragging, teasing, and petty bickering, none of it serious on the Seagulls since they are winning. They talk about women, or more precisely, they talk about sex, even in the dugout.

"You call that a seven, man? I wouldn't give her a five."

"Well, Jesus, I didn't study her, I just looked. She's got a pair of big-league headlights on her."

"But look at the face. That's no seven."

"Well I didn't inspect her to see if she had tits or anything, I just looked quick. OK, a six."

"Six? Hey, c'mere and look at what he calls a six."

They talk about drinking, sometimes about fighting, about cards, and endlessly re-create, analyze, and laugh about things that have happened in games or on the road that illustrate foibles of their teammates or opponents.

"Did you see Medeiros act like he was trying to climb a 20-foot fence after that pop-up?"

"You gotta try to be as big an asshole as that. I bet he wears that helmet of his in the shower." (The player in question, the Harlingen catcher, wears an Oakland A's batting helmet he brought with him from an assignment there as bullpen catcher. It clashes obviously with his uniform.)

"Are you kidding, he wears it to *church.*" There is nothing secret about this ragging. But during games all the abuse is directed at the opposition. While I was with them, the Seagulls had a relief pitcher they had nicknamed "Psycho," on the grounds, I was told jokingly, that he was a potential mass murderer. As long as he was with the Seagulls his reputed hobbies of killing cats and stalking lizards at night with a baseball bat, crippling them, and blowing them to bits with firecrackers were tolerated uneasily. Now that he has been released, however, should he join an opposing club, he will hear about it from the dugout.

The daily routine of a ball club that plays seven night games a week is pretty predictable. In Corpus Christi, most of the Seagulls live four to a two-bedroom apartment in the same complex, making home indistinguishable from the McAllen Sheraton. If anything, things are better on the road, since they get $6 a day for food. After the game they drink beer, as often as possible in the company of the young women who flock to the ball parks to meet them. Even in the Lone Star League there are groupies (known as "Baseball Annies"):

In a crowd of 200, 50 or so will be women who are there to flirt with the players. Retiring anywhere between midnight and dawn, the players sleep until noon or later, then hang around their hotel rooms or apartments watching soap operas or whatever else happens to be on TV until it is time to dress for another game. Sometimes they go to the beach, although they are careful not to get too tired from the sun. What baseball players consider being in good physical condition is laughable compared to other professional athletes, or even serious amateurs, but a few jog or work with weights in the mornings. At $400 a month, a real spree is economically beyond reach, although I heard one starting pitcher brag all the way to the ball park about having been drunk and naked in a swimming pool at five that morning with a girl he had picked up in a bar. Privately, I suspect, most of the team thought him foolish and some may even have been irritated. The only public attitude permissible, though, was to wish that the girl had a friend. Mazzone says that if he were managing for a major-league organization or if the team were losing he would impose a curfew, but since each player's career here is his own affair, he dosen't see why he should. As in most such groups, there is a whole lot more talk than action.

From a conditioning point of view, the worst thing about the way the Seagulls live is the way they eat. Just before starting a long postgame drive from Harlingen back to Corpus Christi, the team actually *voted* to dine at a Seven-Eleven rather than stop at a restaurant. Even when you are near broke, you can do better than a six-pack and Doritos for supper.

The atmosphere of loose-jointed semiboredom and hilarity of men in such groups is communicable. Although I had anticipated a good deal of free time and brought along enough books to occupy me for a month, it took only a few hours to realize that reading anything at all that did not either list batting averages or show pictures of naked women would be unthinkable. What I really wanted, of course, was for Leo to look down the bench when Fran Hirschy had a couple of men on and a dangerous stick man coming to the plate and say something to me like: "If you can still throw that knuckle curve you had back in 1961, go loosen up your hose. We need a double-play ball here." I was not, if it matters here, a bad high school pitcher. But I was never privileged to pitch for a club where if you went in there and coaxed a sharply hit ball to the infield with a man on first, those boys would turn that double play over almost every time and you could go sit down.

Because that is finally what it is all about. What the Corpus Christi Seagulls are is a baseball team, nothing more or less, a thing that requires neither apology nor even explanation. They perform on summer evenings under uncertain lighting, with too much wind usually and too few fans, but when they do it well, which on this team is more often than not, it is a kind of artistry. Spending days and nights with them and watching them play every evening for a week I finally began to understand that the desire to warm up my hose and throw that sinker to get the double play is no more childish or shameful than my invariable wish when I read something that transports me: My God, I wish I'd written that. But I would rather spend two months on the road with the Corpus Christi Seagulls thank you, than two nights with a troupe of Shakespearean actors. I can remember telling a friend after hanging in suspense along with about half the nation through that incredible sixth game of the 1975 World Series between Boston and Cincinnati—the game that led Pete Rose to say in the locker room that even though his team lost he was proud and moved to have played in it—that watching it had been like reading a Dostoevski novel. The suspense and the hysteria were overshadowed in the end by pure aesthetics; the fact that who won was of no intrinsic importance in the "real world" was crucial to that feeling.

The last two games I saw the Seagulls play redeemed both messes in McAllen. The first of the two, in Harlingen against the Suns—after pregame nonsense including egg throws between teams of players, a home-run-hitting contest in which nobody hit a fair ball over the wall, and similar follies—was tight, crisp baseball, the kind of game that turns on points so minor that most casual fans would miss them. If Randy Rima had not held up at second a moment too long to see if a base hit was going to drop, if he had broken for the plate from third the instant an infielder committed himself to second base instead of waiting until the ball was almost there, if Pagnotta had not overslid second after having the base cleanly stolen, if Bratsen had let Rainey's perfect throw from center field go through to the plate and not cut it off at the mound and relayed it . . . if, if, if. And everybody understands these things so well that nothing has to be said. As Bratsen comes into the dugout after the inning all he has to do is catch Leo's eye to see if he knows it too. He does. The Seagulls lose the game 3–1. Harlingen has a pretty good club.

The next night in Corpus Christi, after the repast at the Seven-Eleven and the long ride back in the middle of the night, the Seagulls still need to win a game to wrap up the pennant. And Harlingen has driven up to play them head to head, arriving in a superannuated blue-and-white school bus with the motto "SHARE IN CHRIST'S LOVE" painted on the side. While we were gone it rained in Corpus

Christi and the dugout is flooded. The players take folding chairs from the "box seat" and sit in front; the mosquitoes that breed in there will be active tonight. Driving in uniform to the ball park in the van with cardboard taped over most of the broken windshield, an expired inspection sticker, and his Maryland driver's license in his pants back at the apartment, Leo gets stopped by a highway patrolman. The trooper says he could take him to jail, but as Leo is in his baseball suit and L.O. has his catcher's gear in his lap, he gets off with a warning. "You wanted to see the minor leagues," Leo says to me. "This is it."

The last time Mando Reyes pitched here in his hometown 2,000 fans showed up to see him and he shut out Harlingen on two hits. Tonight is *Corpus Christi Caller-Times* Night, and any kid who shows up in a shirt with an iron-on Seagulls patch that he clipped from the paper gets in free. Between 1,600 and 1,700 show up. Mando is not so effective as the last time, and the Seagulls' fielding is a bit shaky in the first three innings. The first batter reaches base each time. Each time he tries to steal second, and each time L.O. throws him out with a perfect strike. The crowd begins to get involved in the game. In the fourth Bear Bratsen hits a tremendous home run off the scoreboard in left center, and the way the game is going it feels as if that may be enough. But in the sixth Reyes gives up four base hits and two runs, getting out of the inning when Thompson makes a beautiful stop on a hard grounder and Hiller turns it over perfectly for a double play. The runs are the first Reyes has allowed in 25 innings. In the last of the sixth, Rainey walks and Bratsen hits one even farther than the last. Seagulls 3, Suns 2. On the bench I tell Thompson I am glad to see Bear tying into the ball, since after all I'd heard about his power I had been disappointed to see him limited to high fly balls and ground ball singles in the last week. Thompson reminds me that the difference between a 300-foot fly ball and a 380-foot home run is a matter of a fraction of an inch on the barrel of the bat meeting a moving object.

In the eighth Harlingen puts together a triple and a sacrifice fly to tie the score at 3. Soon Bratsen is at the plate again, with the bases loaded. This time he catches it a little farther out front and hits one, he says later, much harder than the other two, but the strong cross-wind that affects balls hit down the right-field line holds it in the ball park and it caroms off the wall for a three-run double. The score is now 6–3, and if Bratsen's future in professional baseball is an illusion, which Leo thinks it is not (although he hit poorly in his one year at San Jose in the Class A California League), he has with three wins fed that dream for at least another couple of months. But so what? For the rest of his life Bratsen will remember this as a perfect day. You don't get many of those.

Before the ninth inning starts, the press-box announcer reminds the crowd that the Seagulls are three outs from the pennant, which everyone on the bench regards as a portent of disaster. The Harlingen third-base coach tells Leo that leaving Reyes in will cost him the game. Leo responds with something brief and appropriate. Reyes gives up two doubles and a run, but third baseman Rick Buckner takes a one-hop line drive off the forehead and still gets the out at first base and the Seagulls win the pennant.

When I had spoken to him earlier in the week Bobby Flores had talked about his teammates who had no plans, no training, and perhaps no aptitude to do anything but play baseball. With a UT business degree, Flores plans to begin looking seriously for grown-ups work at the end of the season. Last year at Seguin, he says, he played better than he ever had in his life, but with the Seagulls he starts only intermittently (he is the only second stringer on the roster) and is hitting barely above .200. The others puzzle him. "I guess," he said, "most of them are too busy worrying about where their next piece of tail is coming from or how to find a nightclub to wonder, 'Where will I be tomorrow?' But it's weird to keep getting paid to play a kid's game, and unless I'm going someplace . . ." His voice trailed off and he shrugged.

Well, Flores is probably right, of course, from the mature point of view, but even after one week with the championship team in the lowest minor league there is, I can see what keeps them at it. I never made a conscious decision to quit playing baseball and cannot remember where or when I played my last game, but it has been more than 13 years. Even watching one of the Seagulls' star players alternating tobacco spits into the dirt with nervous pulls at a bottle of Maalox between innings was not enough to deter a powerful wave of nostalgia that hit me when I realized I had to leave the next morning. Before the last Harlingen game I played catch for a few minutes with Randy Rima to help him loosen up his arm. Returning to the bench I was struck for the first time with the realization that I was never going to play this game again. Suddenly I felt much older. I told Leo about it. "You try pitching 10 years of pro ball and have somebody tell you that," he said. Then he spit a stream of tobacco and walked down to see how Mando's warm-up was coming along.

BASEBALL .

RANDLE'S BIG EXPLOSION

By Blackie Sherrod

From the Dallas Times Herald
Copyright, ©, 1977, Dallas Times Herald

The sequence was all so incredibly swift, maybe four, five seconds at the most, and yet in afterthought, it hung there suspended in time, like slow motion or instant replay or the old newsreel films of the Hindenburg breaking apart reluctantly in dark Jersey skies.

There was the tableau of Frank Lucchesi and Lenny Randle talking, calmly it seemed to these witnessing eyeballs some 40 feet away —the Texas manager and his embittered player, once again debating Randle's past, present, and future with the Rangers. They stood maybe 18 inches apart, Lucchesi in his blue flowered shirt and gray slacks (he had not yet dressed for the game), Randle in his uniform, some 20 feet toward the Ranger dugout from the pregame batting cage.

There was no raising of voices, or even these jaded ears would have picked it up; no animation, no gestures, no jabbing of forefingers, no distending of neck veins. It seems to this memory that both men had their hands on hips, not belligerently but naturally as a couple guys on the street corner argue the respective talents of the Longhorns and Sooners. Three, four minutes the conversation continued while your eyewitness watched it idly, only vaguely curious at what appeared to be another review of Randle's discontent that he wasn't getting a full-scale chance at retaining his second base job from the challenge of rookie Bump Wills.

(The debate surfaced angrily last week when Lucchesi exploded that he was "sick and tired of some punks making $80,000 moaning and groaning about their jobs." The word *punk* was the fuse.)

Lucchesi had walked on the Minnesota spring diamond, said hello to a few fans, walked away for a private chat with Jim Russo, the Baltimore superscout. (Trade talk?)

The 48-year-old manager was en route back to the dugout tunnel to the locker room to get dressed when Randle approached. So the two men talked while Rangers took batting practice behind them, a cluster of players awaiting turns at the cage.

Suddenly with unbelievable quickness, Randle's right hand shot forth. No wild drawback nor windup, as a saloon brawler might use, but a straight strike from the body and here was Lucchesi falling slowly, turning to his right from the force, and there came a left with the same terrible rapidity. This was probably the blow that fractured Lucchesi's right cheekbone. Then another right and a left, all before the victim finally reached earth some 10 feet from where he was first struck. Your witness has seen the hand speed of Sugar Ray Robinson and the cobra strikes of Muhammad Ali, but the flurry of Randle's punches, all landing on the manager's face, must have broken all speed records.

After Lucchesi hit heavily on his right hip, his left arm curled above him in some helpless defense attempt, there were other Randle punches, maybe they landed, maybe not, before Bert Campaneris reacted from four strides away. He had frozen at first, probably as others stared in disbelief, but sprinted quickly to the scene, leaped astride the fallen Lucchesi and stretched his hands out, palms up, to fend off Randle. The furious player backed away, yelling, "Leave me alone!" while Jim Fregosi and others reached the dazed victim.

Then, while players carried Lucchesi to the dugout tunnel, his right eye already blue and puffing, blood trickling from his mouth, Randle preceded them to the dugout, pulled a bat from the rack and held it briefly, then dropped it and trotted to the outfield where he began to run wind sprints all alone. This was maybe the only positive move of the day, for who knows what player emotions might have followed. Ken Henderson, especially, had to be restrained when he saw Lucchesi, sitting propped against the tunnel wall while trainer Bill Zeigler tried to administer aid and judge the damage.

No witness could remember any similar baseball incident. Fights between players, surely, even spats between players and coaches, but never a player felling his manager. Eddie Robinson, the Ranger vice-president, arriving later, couldn't think of one. Sid Hudson, the veteran coach, shook his head. Burt Hawkins, the traveling secretary who watched Babe Ruth, also flunked.

So what prompted this unprecedented explosion? Randle, seemingly composed afterward, said Lucchesi had called him a "punk" again. Lucchesi, from his bed in Mercy Hospital, said this was a lie.

Was the Randle violent, savage action triggered by a remark in the apparent calm conversation? Was it a buildup of Randle emotions, of frustrations bred when he thought he was not being given enough chance to play?

A day earlier, Lenny had told Channel 4 interviewer Allan Stone, "I'm a volcano, getting ready to erupt."

"But," said Stone, "he was smiling when he said it."

If Randle's was a calculated action, would not a single punch have sufficed? What pushed him across the line into uncontrollable fury, an outburst that might end his baseball career forever? Probably no one will ever know.

In a corner of the dugout, by the bullpen telephone while Ranger players milled about in stunned airmlessness, a small white card glared from the wall. It was the lineup for Monday's game. The second line read: Randle, 2B.

GENERAL

WHAT SOME PEOPLE WILL DO FOR MONEY!

By Bob Rubin

From the Miami Herald
Copyright, ©, 1977, Miami Herald Publishing Co.

The network that brought you winner-take-all tennis matches in which the loser had a fat guarantee, the network that signed Olympic boxing gold medalist Howard Davis to a contract that allowed Davis to pick his opponents and pay them what he felt they were worth, used its magic touch on the Heisman Trophy presentation Thursday night.

CBS telecast an abortion called the Forty-third Heisman Award Show at 10 P.M. With the collaboration of the Downtown Athletic Club of New York, sponsor of the Heisman Trophy, and Trans World International, a firm that packages programs for the networks, CBS turned one of the important moments in sports into shlock show biz.

Shame on CBS. Shame on the DAC. Shame on TWI.

Before reviewing the gruesome details of the program, understand that there is one reason why the Heisman Award presentation was changed from a dignified postdinner affair to a tawdry hour of Elliott Gould, Leslie Uggams, Connie Stevens, Robert Klein, and 18 dancers and singers.

Money, of course.

CBS paid TWI $200,000 to do the show. TWI paid the DAC $164,000 and kept $36,000. CBS sold $900,000 worth of advertising. CBS has the option to do six more Heisman shows, raising its payment to the DAC $25,000 annually. If the show goes the full seven years, DAC stands to make $1,578,500; TWI $346,000, and CBS uncountable ad revenues.

Everyone wins—except the Heisman Trophy.

The show was a carbon copy of every award show you've ever seen

—the Oscars, Emmys, Tonys, Grammys, Whoopies, Zippies. (How about Heisies next year, CBS?)

It consisted of insipid, hastily thrown together song and dance numbers, celebrity presenters who continued the grand award-show tradition of inane chatter, a somber explanation of the rules down to the name of the accounting firm counting the votes, and occasional shots of big names in the audience—shame on you, Tom Harmon, Dick Kazmaier, Jay Berwanger, and other former Heisman winners for helping demean your own highest football achievement.

To pad out the hour, the show also introduced six new awards for top performers at different positions. It took the Heisman 43 years to achieve its status. Poof, in one night, CBS created instant tradition.

The show's lowlights:

Stevens and Uggams singing something called "Football Fever," accompanied by a group of, shall we say, delicate chorus boys dressed in skirts with Hs on them.

Klein doing an unfunny skit about bands.

Co-hosts Gould and O.J. Simpson singing together, surely one of the most terrible moments in show business history. Presenter Paul Hornung praised the effort, which makes one wonder whether Hornung took one shot too many with the Green Bay Packers.

The lone bright spots on this show were the ones that dealt with football, the dignity of the players in accepting their awards, and the film clips that preceded them.

The topper is producer Bob Wynn's aggressive defense of the show.

"This is primarily an entertainment show," he said. "By the sheer mention of the Heisman Trophy, we will attract football fans. We are loading it with entertainment to attract everyone else."

"If the 'old grads' don't like it, that's their problem. Times have changed. The caravan passes even though the coyotes howl."

BOXING

IN THIS CORNER: THE FIGHTING O'GRADYS!

By David Wolf

From Sport Magazine
Copyright, ©, 1977, M.V.P. Sports, Inc.

"I wanta promote the last bare-knuckle fight in the history of the world," says Pat O'Grady, tongue far from his cheek. "We'll use the old rules of the London prizefight: two known pros, toeing the mark, fighting in the dirt, till one guy can't get up anymore. Then we'll crown the last bare-knuckle champion of the world. Right here in Oklahoma City! The Chamber of Commerce will come out and tell me what a great guy I am."

"Are you sure they'll view it as positive publicity?" asks a visitor, envisioning the bloodbath.

"Why not? It'll draw international attention."

"So would a lynching."

"If that'll sell tickets," O'Grady replies, "we'll use it on the undercard."

Large, loud, and loquacious, 50-year-old Pat O'Grady is boxing's Barnum of the boondocks. Promoter, manager, matchmaker, trainer, cut-man, and publicist. O'Grady is a living relic, a slice of Americana cut from an era before television, when free-wheeling managers and promoters thrived in scores of small-town fight clubs from coast to coast.

Today those fight clubs are parking lots and supermarkets, and the independent promoter is extinct. Except for Pat O'Grady. On the first and third Tuesday of every month, O'Grady promotes a boxing card at the Ramada Inn Central in Oklahoma City.

Many of the bouts are of dubious artistry, a few even of dubious authenticity. Local heroes, with colorful nicknames (such as Tony "The K.O. King" Gardner), pile up glittering records that on close inspection reflect little more than O'Grady's skill as a matchmaker. But the cards are a spectator's delight. Most fights make up in action what they lack in finesse. Bloody brawls are frequent, knockouts are commonplace, and while the Marquis of Queensberry may be shadowboxing in his grave, the fans keep coming back for more.

O'Grady has no television contract, is not subsidized by a gambling casino or big city arena, and runs no wrestling shows to balance his books. Boxing is his sole occupation (the Pat O'Grady Sporting Goods advertised in his fight program is "just a closet full of boxing gear I'm trying to get rid of"). All of which probably makes Pat O'Grady the last truly independent boxing operator doing full-time business in the United States.

A child of the Depression, O'Grady was born in Ft. Worth, Texas, and raised by a stern grandfather. In 1942, at the age of 15, Pat used a forged birth certificate to enlist in the Marines. Badly wounded in the Pacific, he was awarded two Purple Hearts. He came home to seven months of hospitalization and a lifetime of wearing dentures and downing "antihostility pills (tranquilizers) that don't always work so good."

When he left the hospital, O'Grady began boxing "to strengthen myself," soon "fell in love with the sport," and—still a teen-ager—turned pro after just ten amateur bouts. Each summer he worked the "boxing booth" in a traveling carnival, fighting three times a day against all comers. His winters were spent on the Midwest club circuit, boxing "in every little dump town from Iowa to Montana."

"I fought as a lightweight, welter, middle, and light heavyweight," recalls O'Grady, who is now an overweight. "As a middleweight, I was no good. When I got to light heavy, I was lousy. The only thing I can boast about is that I had 80 knockouts in 123 recorded fights."

Why are only nine of those fights *recorded* in the *Ring Record Book*? "Because I fought under seven different names," Pat explains blithely. "For seven different managers."

The most noted manager, a venerable Iowan named Pinkie George, observed, "You count the house much better than you fight," and suggested that O'Grady increase his life expectancy by becoming a matchmaker.

In 1947, Pat put together his baptismal card, featuring two world-rated welterweights, for a promoter in Council Bluffs, Iowa. The day before the fight, O'Grady got his first taste of the perils of promotion. One of the main-event fighters demanded his entire $1,500 purse—in cash. Unimpressed by Pat's explanation that, it being Sunday, the banks were closed, the fighter left town. O'Grady could find only one substitute: himself. The "matchmaker" took a beating for seven rounds before the referee stopped the bout—whereupon, Pat went back to club fighting.

O'Grady believes it is the hard-knock lessons of those years that sustain him now. But survival is not to be confused with affluence. The glittering diamonds of Don King and the thick-carpeted boardrooms of Bob Arum have never been part of Pat O'Grady's world.

For almost 25 years, since he retired from the ring in 1953, Pat has prowled the hot, dusty tank towns of the Southwest, training and managing a succession of obscure—but often talented and always tough—fighters, openly matchmaking and promoting their bouts where it is legal to both manage and promote, and promoting through "front men" in states such as Texas, where it is not.

From Corpus Christi to Beaumont and Enid to Globe, he has scratched and scuffled, plowing his energies into the likes of Tony "The Bell-to-Bell Bomber" Longoria, Richard "Rocky" Medrano, Mel Barker, Anastacio "Tano" Serna, Claude "Humphrey" McBride, "Gentleman Jim" Brewer ("The dirtiest fighter you ever saw"), and Frank Duran, "who was known as 'Dummy' because he was deaf."

For 16 years, O'Grady's base was Austin, Texas, where he developed amateurs as director of the Montopolis Youth Center, and managed 33 pros at one time. He also represented the interests of an out-of-state sportsman, "who was really a pimp and a cardsharp." The man had a stable of fighters, which Pat booked in exchange for the manager's end of each purse. "All I had to do was send a letter, saying I'd paid him," recalls O'Grady. "That way he could account (to the IRS) for his income."

Meanwhile, Pat promoted behind the scenes, backing cards for his own fighters throughout Texas. Forty-two shows were in San Antonio, where he made some nice profits, but almost lost his hide when he was chased into the dressing room by a knife-wielding Mexican who was displeased by a decision favoring O'Grady's gringo welterweight.

Since moving to Oklahoma City in 1969, Pat has promoted an average of 25 shows a year. A disgruntled patron once punched him in the head, but no one has tried to knife him, and most of his promotions have turned a small profit.

Nevertheless, boxing has hardly made him rich.

The Oklahoma City office of Pat O'Grady Sports Promotions is an inauspicious one-story building that also houses Pat O'Grady, wife, and three children. Two signs in the porch window announce: "Boxing Tickets on Sale Here." The earsplitting clang of a ring bell accompanies each opening of the front door. The walls of the living room are covered from floor to ceiling with posters heralding Pat's

promotions. Somewhere underneath a tidal wave of clippings, programs, letters, and press releases are four file cabinets, three desks,
two telephones, and several chairs. The rest of the house is similarly
decorated.

With the O'Gradys, boxing is a family affair. Jeanie, who married
Pat in Austin when she was 19 in 1956, keeps the books ("I sent her
to H&R Block because the IRS scares the hell out of me"), writes
the program notes and press releases, oversees ticket sales and poster
distribution, takes excellent color films of every fight, and is—at
least nominally—the chief administrative officer of Starmaker, Inc.,
the corporation that manages most of the fighters who headline
O'Grady cards.

When she's at home, 20-year-old Coleen O'Grady, a dentistry
student at the University of Texas, runs the box office. Sweet Rosie
O'Grady, age 15, telephones potential ticket buyers, takes care of
the boxing equipment, and distributes programs on fight night.

Eighteen-year-old Sean O'Grady used to be listed in the program
as the "dressing room attendant." Now he is listed as the world's
second-ranked bantamweight by the World Boxing Association
(WBA) and is called, in all of Pat's publicity, "The Little Green
Machine." Someone else cleans the dressing rooms.

It is Sunday afternoon in mid-July and the temperature outside is
over 100 degrees. Sitting at his desk beneath a bumper sticker that
reads "The Green Machine Is Here," Pat O'Grady is even hotter.
In two days, Sean will fight for the first time since his most important
victory, a sizzling 10-round decision over veteran Davey Vasquez in
New York's Madison Square Garden. But only one of the three
local newspapers mentions the upcoming bout. "They don't give a
damn about boxing," Pat growls. "They've been waiting eight years
for me to fall on my face. We get no kinda coverage at all!"

O'Grady is not paranoid. The Oklahoma City press appears to
rate boxing as slightly less newsworthy than women's field hockey.
On Tuesday, one paper would not even cover the fight. Another
would send a stringer who—according to Pat—spent his time trying
to sign up a fighter under contract to the O'Gradys.

How does Pat make a living from boxing in a town where football
is discussed 12 months of the year and tourists are herded to the
Cowboy Hall of Fame? Through bulldog tenacity, much penny-
pinching, and a delightful affinity for the outrageous.

Among O'Grady's crowd-pulling accomplishments are the promotion of the first world championship bout in the state of Oklahoma,
the first Oriental kick-boxing card in the Southwest, the last scheduled 20-round fight in the world, and the first and last "Championship of the Super Heavyweight Division," which O'Grady invented

for the sole purpose of crowning a protégé named Claude "Humphrey" McBride.

In late 1970, the 340-pound, balding ex-divinity student had plodded into O'Grady's office with " a bible in one hand and a book of 10-year-old clippings in the other." After convincing himself that McBride had "incredible stamina for someone who was 34 years old and that overweight," Pat outfitted McBride in polka-dot shorts and cap, "like Humphrey Pennyworth in the Joe Palooka comic strip," and turned him into a drawing card.

In two years of thoughtful matchmaking McBride won 28 consecutive fights—against such titans as Chief Sonny Glass, Richard Schrum, and Baby Hughie—and became, according to an O'Grady press release, "the only white undefeated heavyweight in the world."

There was a momentary crisis when McBride became worried after a friend warned him that he might suffer brain damage in the ring. But Pat eased his fears, assuring McBride that his brain was "too small" to incur such an affliction, and even declared him heavyweight champion of Oklahoma. What remained but a world championship? Unfortunately, the heavyweight title holder, Joe Frazier, appeared a trifle advanced for Claude.

Undaunted, O'Grady proclaimed the birth of a new division, for "super heavyweights" over 240 pounds, and matched McBride—then down to a svelte 261—with the once-formidable Buster Mathis for the title.

"I really expected a win," Pat recalls. "Mathis was washed up and Humphrey really wasn't that bad. But at the prefight press conference, Mathis shook his left fist at Humphrey and said, 'This hand knocked out a horse!' Humphrey's eyes opened real wide and you could see the confidence drain out of him. I tried to tell him it was just a psych, but it was too late. The first left hand Mathis landed was a little tap. But Humphrey went down for the count. When it was over, I jumped in the ring. Humphrey could see I was furious, so he hopped up, like he'd never been hit, and moaned, 'That guy knocked out a horse.' I yelled back, 'Yeah, and now he's knocked out a dumb elephant!' So much for that championship!"

O'Grady can create champions and championships with impunity because Oklahoma has no state athletic commission or regulatory agency for boxing. "When I came here, I asked the governor and the legislature to appoint a commission," Pat declares. "But the members never did anything but ask for free tickets. So I went back to the legislature and had the commission abolished."

As a result, Oklahoma is boxing's version of the open range. The only law is O'Grady's. He selects the referee, judges, and physicians, conducts the infrequent weigh-ins, passes on the competitive fitness of fighters, and generally does whatever else he pleases. "One thing I don't do," he emphasizes, "is pay fighters more than the promotion can afford."

No one has accused him of unbridled generosity. "You don't need world champions on a club show," he says. "Just two guys with enough guts to hit each other in the head. What do I pay? Forty or 50 dollars for a four-rounder, and $75 for six rounds."

O'Grady is evasive about the size of Sean's purses ("Why should I pay him?" he jokes. "He owes me for making him a star!"). But without Sean, Pat's overhead for Tuesday night's typical card runs about $2,500. Since most of the 1,500 seats in the ballroom at the Ramada Inn are priced at $6 (there are four rows of $10 ringside), Pat needs about 400 customers to break even.

"We bypass the press in our promotions," he explains. "They don't cover us, so we go straight to our fans." A master of ballyhoo, O'Grady inundates the national media with releases and Xeroxed clippings on his stars. The same material is also sent to as many as 1,500 potential spectators. Then, in the days before each fight, Jeanie, Rosie, and a part-time employee telephone up to 2,000 fans. It's hard work, but it pays off. (For Sean's Tuesday night fight, despite direct competition from television of the major-league All-Star game, the paid attendance was to be an above-average 1,060.)

"If we draw," O'Grady says Sunday afternoon, "it'll be because of Sean. People come for two reasons: to see action and to root for the star. Right now, Sean is my star."

Over the years, O'Grady has coaxed such names as George Foreman, Ken Norton, Ron Lyle, and Jerry Quarry onto his Oklahoma City cards. But the bulk of his promotions have always been built around homegrown heroes. The man who must grow them is O'Grady.

A stern disciplinarian, Pat stresses exhaustive conditioning, but cares little for the nuances of boxing art. His fighters are taught to be aggressive, inflict pain, and work for knockouts. "I'm not Gil Clancy in New York, with 10 million people at his disposal and guys running at him with national champions to manage," Pat roars. "I'm not Angelo Dundee, who can sign up Muhammad Ali or Sugar Ray Leonard or King Kong. I'm in little towns and I've got to *make* fighters.

"I can't make runners, or hiders or fancy boxers," continues O'Grady, who once signed an aspiring junior welterweight on the advice of some awestruck Beaumont saloon patrons who had seen him bite off a man's ear and flush it down the toilet. "What my fans wanna see is a war. So I've got to make *warriors!*"

That he has done. But in his entire career, O'Grady has never had a world champion. "So what?" he snaps defensively. "I had two guys under contract that became champions, Curtis Cokes (welterweight) and Rudolfo Gonzales (lightweight), but I sold 'em for a couple of hundred dollars apiece. They were panhandlers, always asking me for money they hadn't earned. So I got rid of 'em. And I don't regret it!"

He begins a litany of names, painfully obscure: "I come from tank towns, but I brought fighters to Madison Square Garden that stood up! Mel Barker lost a split decision there to [Emile] Griffin [*sic*], 5-4-1. He lost 15 fights out of 76, and 11 were split decisions on the road. He coulda been champ. Frank Duran, too. A deaf-mute. I had to learn sign language. Duran *beat* the bantamweight champion, Jose Becerra, a nontitle fight in Nogales in 1959. But they gave Becerra a split decision and we couldn't get him to fight us again."

The anger and frustration spill out with the names. Finally O'Grady shakes his head and shrugs. "I know my methods win. Jeanie once figured out my won-lost percentage was 88. Eighty-eight percent! But back then, in Texas, I didn't know the politics. I didn't know how much you need the big promoters. To climb the ladder of success you first need the ladder. Now I understand."

In Oklahoma City, where potential talent is woefully thin, O'Grady has had no genuine contenders. Yet through hype and hustle, Pat has maneuvered two of his local stars—light heavyweight Brian Kelly and junior middleweight Tony Gardner—all the way to championship bouts. But confronted with a live opponent, both crumbled, lasting a total of five rounds.

Now, however, Pat O'Grady may finally have a future champion. His son.

He is a skinny teen-ager who likes to listen to The Eagles, eat chicken-fried steak, watch *The Gong Show*—and date girls. In T-shirt and jeans, his smooth unshaven features make him look even younger than his 18 years. If not for the swaybacked nose, there would be little to suggest that Sean O'Grady is a boxer, much less a three-year veteran, two days from his fiftieth professional fight.

But Sean has won 48 of 49 bouts, scored an incredible 43 knockouts, and by the end of the year can expect to challenge for either the World Boxing Association (WBA) or World Boxing Council (WBC) versions of the bantamweight (118 pounds) or featherweight (126 pounds) titles.

A September freshman at nearby Central State University, where he will major in premed and continue to live and train at home, the high school honor student is also deadly serious about becoming a doctor. "I've wanted that since I was four years old," he says glancing across the office at his father, who nods approval. "All my boxing money is being saved for medical school. Dad figures we'll need $50,000. With a title fight, we'll have it."

But boxing is more than a means-to-an-end for Sean. "It gives our family super togetherness," he says, "Mom cooks me high-protein breakfasts and some mornings she and Rosie even do a little roadwork. But I'm the lucky one. I'd be dumb if I didn't see how everyone is making sacrifices for me."

Sean also makes sacrifices. His training regime is brutal. Each morning he runs five miles. At midday he punches the heavy bag in the family garage. In the late afternoon, he spends between two and three hours in unusually grueling workouts in the gym. Sometimes he skips rope for 30 minutes without a break, then does 15 minutes of abdominal exercises. Since there are no local pros his size, the 5-foot-10, 118-pound youngster ends each day's training by sparring from five to 20 rounds against adults who outweigh him by as much as 75 pounds.

"I'm having a great experience," he says. "Partly it's the thrill of looking into the crowd and seeing people's mouths open with envy—the heroism, the big-city newsmen, all the fringe benefits. But the *boxing*, even training, is fun, too. Sometimes you get stale, but to me it's a way of life—and I love it."

Under his father's intense tutelage, Sean has become a title contender. Tall for a bantamweight, he has great handspeed, stamina, and punching power. Like all Pat O'Grady's fighters, Sean loves to rumble and is therefore easy to hit. Against a top boxer this could be his undoing. But he takes a good punch, and when his opponent is hurt, Sean is like a ravenous bird of prey.

"In a way, I'm two different guys," he says. "That's not the real Sean O'Grady in the ring, wanting to hurt people. That's The Green Machine. The Machine has no emotions. He wants to hurt people.

"I've been brought up to accept it," explains Sean, who has suffered five face cuts and a broken nose. "I get a thrill hitting someone and watching his legs buckle."

In winning 47 of his first 48 fights (all but six promoted by his father), Sean buckled many legs. He knocked out 20 opponents in the first round, eight in the second, and 10 in the third. But he was viewed with skepticism until last June when he fought in New York.

"The purse [$6,000] was rotten," says Pat, "but we took the Garden fight for exposure and credibility." They achieved both. Sean's 28-year-old opponent, 5-foot-2 Davey Vasquez, the New York State bantamweight champion and a former Olympian, was past his peak and never a puncher. But the cagey veteran turned back the clock, fighting with newfound determination. Crouched close to the canvas, he ducked most of Sean's haymakers and peppered his face with rapid combinations. Yet O'Grady dominated the fight.

Vasquez had never been knocked out, but Sean pressured him from the opening bell, giving the Garden fans—and the New York press— 10 rounds of nonstop action. O'Grady missed hundreds of punches, yet he never slowed the pace. Sean wobbled Vasquez with uppercuts, jarred him with overhand rights, and was awarded a unanimous decision.

If Sean's pre-Garden feats were viewed with skepticism, Pat has no one to blame but himself. O'Grady is unsurpassed as an architect of the prefabricated record. His first Oklahoma City hero, light heavyweight Brian Kelly, was an undistinguished journeyman until he came under Pat's wing. Suddenly Kelly became a star, rolling to 22 consecutive victories and even landing a title shot, which O'Grady promoted in 1971. But champion Bob Foster demolished Kelly in three rounds.

A close look at his 22 straight wins reveals that in the years immediately preceding their rendezvous with Kelly, the 19 opponents whose records could even be located had lost a total of 217 of 284 bouts and suffered 104 knockouts.

The suspicion is also widespread that some of O'Grady's imports are specifically instructed to lose—if they want to get paid. Pat vehemently denies this. "I won't tell a guy to lay down," he snaps.

"I never have and never will. Look, I don't have to. A good matchmaker can find the right opponent. If your kid's had five fights, you just get somebody with two fights, and let him knock 'em out!"

Sean scored first-round knockouts against eight of his first nine opponents, most of whom seemed poor bets to survive a round of shadowboxing. Typical was Muhammed Muffleh, a waiter at a local restaurant, who told Pat that he had "played box" in the Jordanian army, and would like to "play" with Sean. "Play" lasted about one minute.

"Sean was inexperienced, so I matched him with inexperienced guys," O'Grady tries to explain. "Sean was just 15 years old. We only turned him pro because he couldn't enter the novice division of the Wichita Golden Gloves. They said he was too experienced and he'd have to fight in the open division. That was bull! Sean only had 17 amateur fights. We weren't gonna put him in against 26-year-old men. So he got his amateur experience as a professional."

Fighting at least twice a month throughout 1975, Sean piled up 26 consecutive wins. Pat's posters described most opponents as "Mexican Contenders"—which was accurate to the extent that most were Mexicans. When the streak reached 29, Pat took a gamble—and a $10,000 purse from the Los Angeles Forum—matching Sean with Danny Lopez, a power-punching 23-year-old, who was to win the WBC featherweight title two bouts later.

Barely 17, Sean cracked under the pressure. "Dad told me to start slow," he recalls, "but I was so psyched up, I tore after Lopez and wore myself out." Though Sean won the first round, jarring the favorite several times, Lopez had taken control by the third. An occasional O'Grady punch stilled backed-up Lopez, but Sean was too hurt, tired, and inexperienced to pursue. When his son staggered to the corner after the fourth, Pat stopped the fight.

Sean returned to Oklahoma City—and victory. The opposition was more experienced, but not exactly frightening. Manuel Tarazon, who Sean stopped in three rounds, was billed as a "12-year veteran from Mexico." Actually, he was a 14-year veteran, who had not won a fight in eight years and had been knocked out in 13 of his previous 17 bouts.

Without consulting the North American Boxing Federation, which is supposed to administer such things, Pat announced that Sean's bout with Raul Carreon of Phoenix was for the "North American Super-Bantamweight Championship." Carreon, whom Sean knocked out in five rounds, was heralded as "Unbeaten in the Last Five Years." This was true. Of course, Carreon had not fought in the previous three years and 10 months.

Despite Pat's promotional shenanigans, there were signs that Sean was approaching legitimacy. He scored a first-round knockout over Victor Luna—who would later go the distance against three world-rated bantamweights—and stopped respected veteran Earl Large in the ninth round. After the win in New York, a title shot seemed assured.

Now on the afternoon of the July fight, the O'Gradys' home is a study in controlled chaos. While Sean tries to nap in his bedroom, the front doorbell clangs as fans troop in for tickets, one phone rings incessantly—"Boxing ticket office," Jeanie answers—and Pat blusters into the other.

"We got lots of title offers," he declares. "The Forum wants us to fight [Alfonso] Zamora [WBA bantamweight champion] and some guy wants us to fight him in Mexico. But we won't take a title fight for less than $25,000. Not when those Olympic kids are getting $50,000 to fight bums!

"I've offered Zamora $75,000 to fight Sean here. But he wants it tax free and that's too much. [Teddy] Brenner wants us back in the Garden against Rafael Ortega [WBA featherweight champion] for $15,000. I think he'll come around soon. But, till he does, we're open to any offers."

When Pat hangs up, he begins worrying about Sean's immediate opponent, one Ricardo (El Canguro) Flores, whose record, according to O'Grady's advertising, is "19 wins-3 losses." "That's what he *says* his record is," frets O'Grady. "A guy that speaks Spanish asked him. But he's one of Blackie Ramon's fighters, so you never know what to expect."

Ruben "Blackie" Ramon is the Southwest's leading distributor of practically dead bodies. Operating out of San Antonio, he has an inexhaustible supply of Mexican fighters, most of whom rarely win.

"I'm paying the fighter $250, plus plane fare from San Antonio, and I'm paying Blackie another $250, and I *still* don't know what I've got!" says O'Grady. "Blackie said the guy's had a lotta fights, that he's a puncher. But there isn't a mark on him. He showed up without a robe or trunks or hand straps. What kinda fighter is that? It'll look just great if he doesn't even know how to fight!"

O'Grady phones James Williamson, a local paperhanger, who will referee the bout, and tells him: "We might have trouble with this goose fighting Sean. Make sure the guy understands, no fight, no money. His nickname's The Kangaroo, so tell him to hop on it."

A few hours later, Pat is wishing he had kept his mouth shut. "El Canguro"—who spent most of the first round throwing occasional wild punches while staging an even wilder retreat from the stalking O'Grady—lands a sudden overhead right on Sean's temple early in the second round. As the crowd gasps, O'Grady freezes for an instant, then falls on his face.

Referee Williamson waves the startled Flores to a neutral corner, then looks toward the timekeeper to pick up the count. But the timekeeper, monitoring the rounds on his wristwatch, is even more stunned—and has forgotten to start counting. Later, there will be stories that Sean was on the canvas for as much as 20 seconds. Actually he has been down for five, possibly six seconds, and is starting to rise when Williamson—improvising accurately—yells "Five."

It is when Sean reaches his feet, still glassy-eyed, that Williamson offers some hometown assistance. He pushes the youngster against the ropes, places his hands on the fighter's chest, and pinches Sean's flesh—hard. Another five to 10 seconds pass before he signals the boxers to resume.

His son's first trip to the canvas does not shake Pat. Eyes fixed on Sean, he silently reaches for his medicine kit and removes a stick of smelling salts to apply between rounds.

The smelling salts are necessary, but not for Sean. Confused by his success, Flores approaches hesitantly. By the time "El Canguro" is once more throwing his wild punches, Sean's eyes are clearing. Though still groggy, he maneuvers Flores across the ring, then unleashes a rapid combination. At ringside, it appears he has landed two punches. Only with slow-motion film can it be seen that Sean has hit Flores five times. The final crunching left hook spins the Mexican down on his face.

A beaming Pat O'Grady screams "Yah-hoo!" and leaps from his seat, arms waving in truimph. Flores is unconscious. Williamson stops the count at 10, but could continue to 100.

"I was more embarrassed than hurt," Sean says the next day. "My first thought was 'What am I doing here?'" Rock music is playing softly on the stereo in his small bedroom. On his desk is a "Dr. Sean O'Grady" nameplate. On his eyelid, a patch covers an inch-long cut. "It was an experience I had to meet sometime," he adds. "My father says it's all part of becoming a champion."

Pat's politics are to the right of Genghis Khan ("I'm opposed to all rebellion against authority, and that goes double for South Africa!"), and his son is the somewhat-sheltered product of an upbringing in which adults command unwavering respect and obedience. Soft-spoken, shy, and polite till it comes out his oversized ears, Sean seems—on first impression—to be robotized by his father's presence.

But beneath the "yes sirs" and "no ma'ams" is an intelligent, introspective 18-year-old, capable of thinking for himself. "Dad's gonna make me a champion. I know that. But we're real different," Sean says, choosing his words carefully. "He had a tough life when he was young. I don't think he ever had a chance to be a kid. I've always been protected by my family—a Mamma's boy. Still Dad keeps thinking there's going to be trouble. He says 18 is the 'age of rebellion' and I'm 18 now.

"Dad didn't like it when I bought that stereo. He thinks hard rock is a sign of rebellion. I guess," Sean chuckles, "he thinks anything that's *fun*—anything away from boxing and schoolwork—is rebellion.

"He'd probably prefer I didn't *ever* date girls," the son adds. "He's right, as far as getting serious. While I'm boxing and working to become a doctor, I haven't got time. But, in my own mind, I feel that if I didn't go out with girls or have fun with the guys, I'd burn myself out. I don't think my father understands. But I think that's what happened to Tony Longoria."

Tony "Kid" Longoria, the "Bell-to-Bell Bomber," was Pat's most painful disappointment. "If I ever had a chance to be a millionaire, that was it," O'Grady says in his office that evening, as he watches a film of Longoria scoring a sensational first-round knockout. "Longoria could have been heavyweight champion of the world."

In 1962, when Longoria was 12 years old, O'Grady took him into his Austin home, became his legal guardian, and nurtured him through a brilliant amateur career. At age 16, Longoria turned pro and won his first 23 fights.

"Then came his eighteenth birthday, the age of rebellion, and everything went wrong," says Pat. "He'd always been *totally* dedicated, no distractions or dissipations. I was the dictator. He did whatever I said. Maybe I ruined him by pushing too hard. But all of a sudden, he didn't want to listen anymore. He wouldn't go to bed when I told him. He started to cut back on his training. Then he moved out of the house, got married, and just lost interest."

In his twenty-fourth professional fight, Longoria was knocked out in the second round by journeyman Memphis Al Jones. "I think he took a dive," O'Grady says bitterly. "I can't prove it, but I just feel he was looking for a way out of fighting—so he decided to lose. Longoria didn't throw a punch. I'd dedicated six years of my life to that kid. I was so mad I retired him, right then and there. And Longoria never fought again."

At that moment, a pair of large breasts enter the room—followed by the rest of Sean's current girl friend. Pat shakes his head and stares at his son. "There's another 18-year-old who I might have to retire," he grumps. "He's reached the age of rebellion, too."

When Sean and the girl have left, Pat launches into another harangue. "I'm not joking about retiring him," he says. "He can be champion, but the important thing is that he's gonna be a doctor. We're close enough to the money he'll need for medical school that I don't care if he fights anymore. If I retire him, I'll just make *another* fighter. I've been doing that all my life. I never wanted Sean to be a fighter, anyway."

Later, in the privacy of his room, Sean smiles knowingly when told of his father's threats. "In a way, it's true," he says gently. "Mom and Dad didn't want me to fight. They thought it was too rough. One night, before I turned pro, we talked it out. They asked me if I was really serious about fighting, and I told them I was. When they asked me why, I said I wanted trophies and then to make money. But that wasn't the whole thing."

Sean pauses and tilts his head toward the living room, where his father is shouting at someone over the phone. "Dad never pushed me to box," he finally continues, his voice a near whisper. "But I could see the pride in his eyes when I did well in the ring. He tries to hide it, but it's there even now. I wanted that more than anything. I still do. More than money, or a new car or being a doctor, the glory of my father's proudness is what I want most."

BOXING

NO GARDEN PARTY FOR ALI

By John Schulian

From the Chicago Daily News
Copyright, ©, 1977, Field Enterprises, Inc.

It had been a long time coming. Even Muhammad Ali, who is seemingly beyond blushing, must have been embarrassed by the delay. But at last there was a heavyweight championship fight that deserved the name.

The explanation for this startling development was so simple you would think someone would have thought of it before. What it boiled down to was that the other half of the human equation involving Ali was not Richard Dunn, a butterfly waiting for his wings to be picked off, nor was it Alfredo Evangelista, the walking Spanish omelet. It was Earnie Shavers, a brave man, a stubborn man, a tough man. And he was exactly what Ali needed to prove he can still deliver the quality on which he swears he has cornered the market—greatness. True to form, Ali waited as long as he could before doing it Thursday night. For 12 rounds, he stuck just enough stiff left hands in Shavers's face to turn it an ugly purple and pile up the points to be sure he would walk out of the Madison Square Garden ring wearing his crown. Then he woke up as Shavers tried desperately to knock him out.

The thuggish-looking challenger, 211 pounds of muscle packed under a shining dome, stormed out for the thirteenth and clouted Ali upside the head. "Hell, yeah, he hurt me," Ali said later. "He hurt me four or five times."

At least one more of those jolts came seconds after Shavers's first bomb. The rest came in the hailstorm that was the fourteenth.

Ali started the round by trying to show Shavers he hadn't been stunned. The ploy didn't work. Shavers went right back at him, tying him up against the ropes, banging away on Ali's kidneys and chucking him under the chin on the break. Then Shavers really got down to business.

He sent a looping right hand to Ali's head. And another. And another. Ali went stumbling backward into Shavers's corner looking dazed, ready to be finished. But Shavers didn't move in. He moved 10 feet away and stared at Ali as if it couldn't be true that Earnie Shavers, who just two years ago was fighting in dumpy gyms for 1,000 grubby dollars, could have done such a thing.

"I thought he was faking," Shavers said afterward in the gentle, almost fluty voice that seems foreign to the rest of him. "He's a pretty good faker."

The problem was, Ali wasn't faking. "I was out on my feet," he said.

It didn't matter. In his corner, Angelo Dundee, the brains of the outfit, kept telling Ali it didn't matter. Dundee had a man in the dressing room watching the round-by-round scores as they were flashed on television, and he knew that Ali had the fight won if he could stay upright.

That was all Ali had to do. You had to wonder if he was up to it when Shavers raced out and popped him with the nastiest left he had the strength to throw.

Ali struck back with a left of his own. Shavers was more startled than hurt. Ali pumped two more lefts into his face. Now Shavers was hurt. Ali didn't need anyone to shout the news to him from his corner. He unlimbered the right hand he used primarily for signing checks and rammed it upside Shavers's head. He was going for the kill. In a round that began with him in danger, in a round where he had to do nothing more than survive, he was putting on his greatest show since he and Joe Frazier gave us the Thrilla in Manila.

"He never hurt me bad," Shavers insisted. "I wasn't hurt."

If the round had lasted 30 seconds longer, Shavers would have known the truth. He would have been knocked out.

The brilliance of those final three minutes made a lot of things palatable afterward. You listened to Dundee say it was "the best fifteenth round I've seen in a long time," and you agreed with him.

"This is just Muhammad Ali," he said. "Muhammad always finds a way. He summons something up from out of nowhere and comes back. He's too much for all of us."

Even Ali, when he finally faced the press an hour and five minutes after he left the ring, had to be listened to seriously when he delivered his usual paean to himself. "I'm a courageous man," he said. "I have a whole lot of heart." Yes he does, and that is not all.

He had the ability to make us forget. Sad to say, there is much to be forgotten in this fight. There is the sleepwalking Ali did in the early rounds. There is the swing he took at Bundini Brown, his long-time good luck charm, after the fifth for telling him he should cut the comedy. There are the boos Ali heard when he tried to cover up some seventh-round soft-shoeing with a little showboating. And there are the boos Shavers's trainer, Frank Luca, is sure to hear for not being cagey enough to monitor the scoring on TV the way Dundee did.

It seems like an awful lot to be erased by just one round of boxing, just three minutes out of the lives of two men. But it happened, and when it was over, you realized something. Annoying as Muhammad Ali is, you are going to miss him when he's gone.

YACHTING

THREE SHEETS TO THE WIND, AND MORE

By Joe Gergen

From Newsday
Copyright, ©, 1977, Newsday, Inc.

Ted Turner was singing. He was weaving along the sidewalk of Memorial Boulevard, each arm supported by an officer of the Newport Police Department, and he was singing. He was a pie-eyed piper, leading a ragged band of 50 men, women, and children along one of his town's central thoroughfares, and he was singing.

". . . and crowned thy good with brotherhood," he was singing in his raspy southern drawl, "from sea to shining sea." And, in a very short time he was not singing alone.

They all joined in. They joined him in another chorus of "America the Beautiful," followed by "My Country, 'Tis of Thee," followed by a rousing rendition of "Rally Round the Flag." And all along the one-mile route from the waterfront to Salve Regina College, past the Canfield House and Jimmy's Saloon, people stopped their cars to stare at the sight. And then broke into applause. Ted Turner, defender of the America's Cup and offender of finer sensibilities, was at the center of the damnedest triumphal procession the sport of yachting has ever been a party to.

"We're doing pretty good for a bunch of drunks," said Turner, the skipper of the victorious *Courageous*, between songs. "I'm drunk. And I'm the first to admit it."

The admission was not entirely necessary. Only a few minutes earlier he had sat down behind a table in the press center at the National Guard Armory and quickly disappeared underneath. He emerged seconds later with a bump on his head and a bottle of Aquavit, which had been carried into the building by *Courageous* tactician Gary Jobson. Turner held it aloft, swallowed a slug, and slumped back in his seat.

What followed was the zaniest press conference in a competition that has been historically circumspect. The crew of the unsuccessful challenger, *Australia*, serenaded their conqueror thus: "Hooray for Ted, he's a horse's ass."

Turner blew cigar smoke in the face of the proper Bill Ficker, the 1970 defending skipper who was conducting the press conference in the manner of a funeral service. And two bottles were being passed around the podium simultaneously as winners and losers drank to each other's health, or what was left of it.

There were hundreds standing about the armory and the combination of the crowd, the television lights, and Turner's behavior brought beads of sweat to Ficker's bald head, which Turner occasionally rubbed playfully. Ficker, dressed in a New York Yacht Club blazer and tie, appeared mortified, cringing every time Turner leaned into a microphone. He had good cause.

No sooner had Turner expressed his love for the Aussies, for his crew, and for everyone in the room than he turned to Ficker. "And I like Bill Ficker, too," Turner said. "He's not a candy ass, and he's no fairy." It was about that time a few members of Turner's crew had the foresight to rush the podium, lift him to their shoulders, and carry him out like a sack of potatoes.

They attempted to dump the sack into the back of a pickup truck for the trip back to Conley Hall on the Salve Regina campus, where the *Courageous* crew had been headquartered all summer. Turner had other ideas. Regaining his equilibrium, he bolted across Thames Street and began jogging up the hill, much to the surprise of three policemen assigned to protect him.

After a short chase, right out of a Mack Sennett two-reeler, the police drew alongside. They suggested a nice safe ride in a car. Turner vetoed the suggestion. "We don't need anybody for anything," he said. "Are we doing super or are we doing super?" And he continued up Ann Street, past the cemetery, around the bend and onto Memorial Boulevard.

Dick Sadler, a grinder on the *Courageous* crew, soon pulled alongside in his MG. He stopped the car, opened the passenger door, and said, "Here, Ted, get in." Turner slammed shut the passenger door and kept walking. "I want an American car," he said. And once again broke into an American song.

It was on Annandale Road, the street leading from Memorial Boulevard to Salve Regina College, that Sadler and the puffing policemen finally were able to convince Turner to take a ride. That followed a 100-yard sprint down the road, setting another chase that left the neighborhood residents convulsed with laughter. The party, at last, was over.

It had been a ball to Turner, right from the start. He had come to Newport in June as a Rebel with cause, determined to prove himself and his crew worthy of defending the sacred cup. He had come as a distinct underdog, the third choice of many.

But *Courageous* had whipped *Independence,* the new 12-Meter from the same syndicate, and *Enterprise,* another new boat and allegedly the most advanced 12-Meter ever built. Turner and his crew proved eminently superior. They left no doubt, gave the NYYC no opportunity to name another boat, no matter what they personally thought about the loud, attention-seeking skipper from Atlanta. Terrible Ted. The Mouth of the South. Captain Outrageous. He was all of those, but he also was the best damned sailor in Newport.

And so Turner, his crew, and his three-year-old boat earned the right. And then they went out and blitzed perhaps the best foreign challenger of the last two decades, sweeping the series with four superbly sailed races. And along the way, Turner became a cult figure.

There were thousands of people waiting for him yesterday when *Courageous* was towed back to Newport Harbor. They stood on the rocks and the manicured lawns out by Castle Hill and they sat on their boats inside the harbor and they perched on the sloping rooftops of the boutiques and boatiques surrounding Bannister's Wharf.

One daring and resourceful fan even climbed to the top of the main mast of the Revolutionary War frigate *Rose,* 100 feet in the air, for a better view. They greeted him with bursts of cannon fire and blaring of horns and fireworks and applause, and he bowed to them all.

The party was just beginning. And neither Newport nor the America's Cup competition will be quite the same again.

AUTO RACING

COMING BACK BLAZING

By Pete Bonventre

From Newsweek
Copyright, ©, 1977, by Newsweek, Inc.

Niki Lauda's face is a testament to the dangers of his profession. A piece of his right ear is missing, and what flesh remains is grotesquely shriveled and discolored. A gruesome patch of wrinkled, light brown tissue covers his forehead and envelops his eyes and temples like a cheap Halloween mask. At first sight, he evokes horrified stares—but his boyish, buck-toothed grin and unself-pitying appraisal of his scarred visage immediately put people at east. "Anybody who has a little bit of brains doesn't take my looks into account," says the 28-year-old race-car driver. "When I talk, they know I'm not an idiot and that's what really matters. Anyway, a lot of people were born more ugly than I am now. At least I have the excuse of an accident."

Lauda was the reigning champion driver when the accident—a flaming crash at Germany's treacherous Nurburgring course—happened last August. That he survived was remarkable. That he is now pushing his blood-red 550 horsepower Ferrari 312T2 Formula 1 racer around the Grand Prix courses of the world at the peak of his form strains credulity. He has won two Grand Prix events so far this year, and last week he treated his fellow countrymen to a second-place finish in the Austrian Grand Prix at Zeltweg—extending his lead in the contest for the World Driving Championship to 16 points over his closest rival, Jody Scheckter of South Africa.

To call Lauda's return to racing a comeback is a gross understatement. Baseball pitchers make a comeback from sore shoulders, basketball players from knee surgery. Other Grand Prix drivers like Stirling Moss have also survived ghastly accidents and returned to the track.

But what Lauda did borders on the miraculous: He cheated death. His lungs had been seared when he sucked in flames, and the oxygen content in his blood was below the level theoretically necessary to support life. He had suffered burns on his head, face, and hands; a broken cheekbone; injuries to his left eye, and several broken ribs. On the night of the crash, a doctor told his wife he had no chance to live. Two nights later, he received the last rites. Not until the sixth day was he out of danger of dying—and a scant five weeks later he was back in the cockpit for the Italian Grand Prix at Monza.

"People thought I was crazy to go back to racing so quickly," he recalls. "They said that a man with a face like mine, not like a human being's but like a dead man's skull, should want to give up immediately. That is not my attitude toward life. I must work, and racing is my job. You aren't crazy when you go back to your job."

"Three things brought Lauda back," explains Enzo Ferrari, the crusty old patriarch of the fabled automotive empire. "The first is a pure thing—a love for cars. The second is pride, to prove after a bad accident that he could still practice his love. And the third is fame, and with it I include money."

Fame and fortune have always been two essential ingredients in the quest for high speed. For Lauda, however, they represent something more—a barometer to gauge how close he is to his goal of perfection. His dedication to racing is both singular and ruthless. "Niki is strong, and if you are not as strong, he puts you under his heel," says Ferrari team manager Roberto Nosetto. "He wants the best—always. He must be out of the pits first, and he wants his tires changed in the fastest time. When a car is not perfect, he wants it improved in the shortest time." Says Ferrari chief mechanic Ermanno Cuoghi, "He drives with his head, but not always with his heart."

Lauda represents a new breed of racing driver: serious and cynical, a technical whiz who lacks flamboyance and dash. He rarely drinks, never smokes, and has nothing but contempt for the silky Grand Prix groupies who hang around the tracks. He prefers instead to be on intimate terms with his car. He takes off one week a year for the Christmas holidays. Most drivers require more time to recover from the grind of a Grand Prix season—which extends across five continents, 10 months and 17 gut-wrenching races. But Lauda is almost fanatical about testing, making endless visits to the Ferrari test track in Maranello, Italy, where he will often keep driving long after the sun has gone down and push his crew to the brink of revolt by screaming, "One more time! I must go one more time!"

His ability to sort out his car's mechanical complexities is perhaps equal to his skill behind the wheel. It is also, many racing-car enthusiasts theorize, the secret to Lauda's success. Lauda himself prefers to credit other virtues, but he will not quibble with aficionados who place more importance on his technical expertise. "The best six or eight drivers in the world will do the same in the same car. The car has the same limit. Any of us go over that limit, we go off the road. What I must do is improve the limit of my car, make it higher than the others. So I must be clever. I must know every nut and bolt in my car, and I must be able to communicate what is wrong to my crew."

Gone are the days when a great driver could maneuver a second-rate car to victory. Gone, too, are the days when a gentleman could easily persuade wealthy friends to back him in a race car, spend his nights boozing and wenching—and then show up moments before a race, stick a cigarette in his mouth, and say to his crew, "OK, boys, let's see what this baby can do." Some critics blame Lauda for stripping a lot of romance away from Grand Prix racing with his scientific approach to the sport. But others insist that Lauda has merely adapted to the changing scene more shrewdly than anybody else.

For one thing, the enormous expense of supporting a racing team in this day and age has dimmed the eat-drink-and-be-merry aura. For another, the delicate, lethally quick Formula 1 cars of the 1970s demand sober and unswerving attention if a driver is to win a race—or survive it; they have also pompted a radical change in driving techniques. In the more romantic 1950s drivers would slide their heavy, front-engined cars around corners. The legendary Juan Manuel Fangio of Argentina, for example, had a cornering technique that one writer described as "a poem of mechanical artistry." He would hurtle down a straightaway under full power, then deliberately throw his car into a long controlled, high-speed slide that was breathtaking to watch. But if Fangio "overcooked" a corner in his Alfa 158, he could regain control of his car with a firm wrench of the steering wheel.

The modern Formula 1 car is unforgiving. It has immense cornering power because of its sophisticated rear-engine design, its emphasis on aerodynamics, and its wide, highly adhesive tires. Today's driver hardly ever slides around a corner and so looks less spectacular than the old-timers. Ironically, however, the margin of error is much narrower—and a slight slip in judgment could cause a driver to lose adhesion and fling his car against a barrier.

Most accidents in recent years have been the result of drivers misjudging a corner. "That's because they are too reckless," Lauda says almost disdainfully. "You have to drive with logic. You must use your head. It's not easy. Your instinct is to go faster, catch the other guy. But sometimes you have to settle for second or third place. Then you have to go back and test and hope you can get a higher limit next time."

When Lauda talks about auto racing, he likens himself to a physician, a lover, an art collector—people who thrive on passion and intelligence, patience and wit. He is not a man who seeks the fleeting, orgasmic thrill of high speed. Neither can he tolerate a driver who would tempt death to gain an advantage on a rival. Above all, he prizes thoroughness and ingenuity. "Sure, motor racing is dangerous," he says. "Sometimes you have to drive over the limit. But I don't take chances, I take calculated risks. A lap here, a lap there, when it's really worth it—and when the worst you can do is break your car, not kill yourself.

"Listen to me, I don't want to die," he goes on, his words rolling off his tongue in a lyrical accent. "I race for all the pleasure it gives me. Some people like oil paintings. I like the Ferrari. It's beautiful to look at. That's why I get pissed off when it doesn't handle well. I'm no engineering genius. I cannot design a car. But the car maker needs me if he wants his car to reach the limit of its potential. I am the diagnostician, not the surgeon. I tell my people the symptoms, what's wrong, and together we do the best with what we have.

"When the car responds to me, it's a fantastic feeling. After a crash you still want that feeling. That's why I returned to racing, not because I am brave but because I need that feeling. When a woman breaks your heart, do you stop pursuing her? No. Is that bravery? No. You do what you must do."

Lauda was born in Vienna in 1949, and grew up there, the son of a prosperous papermill owner. When he was 14, he had saved up enough money from odd jobs to purchase a 1949 Volkswagen. Along with the car came a construction manual, and young Niki promptly took the engine apart to see how it worked. He was hooked. Four years later, he quit school to race. When his father refused to finance his passion, Lauda talked his grandmother into sponsoring his first car by telling her he needed money to replace a friend's auto that he had wrecked.

Lauda began racing in hill climbs, then moved up the European ranks through Formulas 3 and 2. When he decided he was ready for Formula 1, he managed to get an Austrian bank to sponsor him, went to England and signed a contract with the March team. Upon returning to Austria, however, he discovered that his influential grandfather had gotten the bank to back down on the deal just before he died. "I have never forgiven him for that," Lauda says bitterly. "I never liked him. He was a pompous bastard, with all his houses and chauffeurs."

Lauda ended up going to another bank, which refused to sponsor him but allowed him to take a loan to buy his car. He borrowed $100,000 at 6 percent. He paid back the loan in two years—and then signed with Ferrari in 1974. That first year, Lauda won two Grand Prix races, finished fourth in the drivers' standings—and sparked Ferrari's return to the pinnacle of auto racing after almost a decade of decline. He also began polishing a style of driving that reminds the cognoscenti of several of the greatest racers of all time, including Fangio, the late Jim Clark, who died in a 1968 crash, and Jackie Stewart, who is now retired.

What makes a great race driver? What is more important, man or machine? The answer to the first question is highly subjective. The second question has ignited a debate as old as Grand Prix racing itself, and the answer is elusive. But there is no doubt that to win the championship, a driver must be at the wheel of a car that is at least as fast and handles as well as those of his rivals. His team's standards of preparation must be beyond reproach—and he needs more than his share of luck. "If he didn't have that Ferrari and that big testing ability," says Scheckter of Lauda, "he wouldn't be on top." But, almost in the same breath, Scheckter concedes, "Niki can be under all sorts of pressure, but he'll not do stupid things, like James Hunt. A lot of fast starters will sag in the middle of a race, but Niki establishes his limit and stays at it throughout the race."

"Niki seldom does something foolish," says Mario Andretti. "If he's had it, he won't fight. He rationalizes. Neck and neck and one inch away, you feel safe next to him."

In the cockpit, Lauda is smart, cool, and efficient, like a man filtering information through a computer rather than a mere brain. Many other drivers look hot and breathless, struggling fiercely with their wheel. Lauda is smooth and effortless, his eyes betraying little emotion. Like a jockey on his mount, he seems to become one with his car. "In theory," says Lauda, "another driver may have five seconds more talent than me—better eyes, reflexes, stamina, that sort of thing. But my ass is more sensitive than theirs. That's my secret, down there. I can feel a car sliding more quickly, for example, than the others, and correct it. If I didn't have that sensitivity, I wouldn't be so good."

Lauda almost always drives within the limits of his own ability and his car's—with consistency and precision and confidence. He knows the weaknesses of every driver on the circuit. His victories are usually the result of skill rather than bravado, practice rather than courage and patience rather than hard driving. He is less exciting to watch than other drivers—but he wins more often. "The easiest thing is to be in the lead," says Lauda. "Then you can create your own situations. You set the pace of the race, control the tempo, and don't do anything stupid. If I'm in the lead, the only thing I worry about is my own car. I say to myself, 'Car, please finish, don't break down.' You wish the race would be over on the next lap, so you have to hold your emotions in.

"If I'm behind, what I do depends on who's in front of me. If it's a good driver, I keep my car at the limit and hang on. If he's a nervous driver, if he gives up easy, I gauge how much I can use my car. I don't have to go all out to pass him. I pressure him into making a mistake. I may drive in a spot where he can't see me in the mirror. When he gets to the corner and he can't see me, he's saying to himself, 'Crap! Where is he?'—and he may miss his break point.

"Then," he continues, "there are some drivers who make stupid mistakes. They may take a corner too hard or break too early, so I wait. I'll stay third or fourth and wait for my chance. They'll have problems with fuel consumption or tire wear, and then I make my move."

Now, at the peak of his career, Lauda is displaying perhaps his greatest virtue. He has completely overcome the fear that his car might break—something even the most stoic drivers worry about. And after Nurburgring, that is an immense achievement.

Lauda had wanted no part of the Nurburgring course. Neither did most of the other drivers. It was the longest (14.2 miles per lap), most difficult (172 corners), and by far the most dangerous circuit in all of racing (nine Grand Prix drivers have died there). The drivers voted for a change of venue but pressure from the sponsors saved the race and all the drivers got was a promise of change for 1977.

Lauda was upset over the decision, but he raced anyway. To make matters worse, the weather was unpredictable. The day began in rain, then suddenly turned sunny. After the first lap, Lauda decided to switch from wet tires to dry slicks and make a pit stop. About 60 seconds later, while trying to negotiate a left and dipping bend on the second lap, Lauda flew straight off the road and crashed against a metal embankment at 140 miles per hour. The Ferrari bounced back onto the track—and was instantly smashed by two oncoming cars. Lauda's helmet was ripped from his head, and his 22-gallon fuel tanks burst into flames. "Niki was truly alight," recalls

Guy Edwards, one of three drivers who helped pull Lauda from the wreck. "There are fires where there is no chance. This once, there was a chance—a slim one."

At first, Lauda tried to work with his rescuers and free himself, but then he began passing out. Only his balaclava, a white fireproof head mask, prevented his head from incinerating. "The balaclava was turning black before our eyes," says Edwards. "Niki yelled, 'Get me out!' Then he lost consciousness."

Lauda was first taken to a hospital near the track. It was quickly decided to fly him by helicopter to Ludwigshafen Hospital, where there was a special burn unit. "The first thing I remember after the crash was the sound of the helicopter engine," Lauda recalls. "Then I remember thinking that I wasn't surprised it happened to me. I was prepared for the day when I might crash. That was good for me. I stayed calm and lost no time in recovery."

Luckily for Lauda, the chief doctor of Ludwigshafen was on duty, and he realized that the burns on Lauda's face were less a problem than his charred lungs. So Lauda was then dispatched to the intensive-care unit at Mannheim Clinic just across the Rhine, where he lay near death. "My brain was always functioning," he says, "but I felt my body giving up. There was a critical moment when I knew I was dying. It was when I realized to let go would be a joy, a release from pain. I got worried. My heart started beating faster, and I worked not to lose consciousness. I concentrated on the voices of the doctors and nurses around me. They were low and sounded far away, but I worked to hear them."

Two days later, doctors took X rays of his lungs, which seemed to be deteriorating. The oxygen content in his blood was perilously below normal. A priest was summoned to give him the last rites, and Lauda remembers him finishing his prayers by saying, "Goodbye, my friend." The words rattled Lauda's pysche. "The priest was wrong to say that," says Lauda. "I needed somebody to help me live, not pass on. My heart started beating faster again. I knew then if I had the slightest chance, I would survive. A fierce will to live? Not exactly. It's something in me, I respond to a challenge."

That response has made him a celebrity, but he has carefully organized his life to protect his privacy, first by limiting his endorsement contracts, then by charging an exorbitant fee of $3,000 for a public appearance to discourage requests. He earns about $800,000 a year, and he says that's more than enough. He lives no more ostentatiously than a successful doctor or lawyer, in a handsome chalet with a breathtaking view of the Austrian Alps and a four-car garage that contains a Volkswagen, a Fiat, a Jaguar, and a restored Bentley. Off the track, his passion is flying—he pilots an eight-seated jet provided free of charge from a nearby chartering service, and flies between races and testing sessions in Maranello.

Marlene, Lauda's wife, stayed with her husband at the hospital. She was there for the dozens of skin-graft operations, and later, at home, she was there for the long hours of physical therapy.

There were indeed some tense moments before Lauda himself knew he would be reborn as a driver. It was raining at Monza for the opening day of practice, and Lauda quit after just two laps, frustrated and distraught. "There is a corner there that I knew I could take flat out," he says. "But when I got there, I took my foot off the throttle. 'You idiot,' I said to myself. 'You idiot.' The next time around, I kept saying to myself, 'Take it flat out. There is no risk here, you can take it flat out.' But when I got there, my foot instinctively lifted again."

Lauda immediately pulled into the pits and complained about his car so he could buy time to think. That night in his hotel room, he kept asking himself, "What do you want? Do you want to race? Well, you must go out and find your capacity." The next day, Lauda went out and found the capacity to take that same corner flat out. But on race day, revving up his engine for the start, he didn't know if he could cope with traffic. "I eased my way through at the beginning," he says, "and kept telling myself. 'You want to race. You do, you do.' After one lap, my fear was over."

Before the crash, Lauda had won five of nine Grand Prix races and seemed well on his way to his second straight driver's championship. But his absence from the track and then trouble with his car enabled Britain's dashing James Hunt to catch up. Only three points separated them when the last race of the season in Japan rolled around. The weather was atrocious, and the drivers held two meetings to decide whether to race. The drizzle continued, fog had settled on the track, and twilight was descending when the drivers voted to race.

Hunt skidded through the first turn and took the lead. Lauda went once around the track in the blinding spray from Hunt's wheels and then retired. "Some things are more important than the world championship—like my life, for instance," says Lauda. "Was I a coward? Nonsense. I used my head. Listen. My accident taught me it is too easy to die. But when you add stupidity, it is even easier. Anyway, it took more guts for me to stop than to go on. I had the guts to take all the crap afterward. Some drivers only have to answer to one man. I lose, I must answer to Ferrari, the Fiat people who own Ferrari, their 6,000 workers, and the whole goddam fanatical Italian nation.

"The old man never said anything to me about quitting. If I were him, I guess I wouldn't be pleased, but if he wants an idiot for a driver, he should get an ape. I'm a human being with a brain."

Lauda has an intense love-hate relationship with the old man, 79-year-old Enzo Ferrari, and the people who work for him. Few drivers have survived for long the politics, emotions, and intrigues that swirl around the Maranello plant—and rumors abounded last week that Lauda may switch his allegiance to the Brabham-Alfa team. But Lauda has hung on so far because of his respect for the car and the man who is inextricably linked with Grand Prix racing in the mind of even the most casual fan. "If you go wrong with Ferrari, first it's the driver's fault," he says. "Then, it's the tires, and last of all it's the car. You don't get the support you do on a British team. There's no balance. But as soon as they know something's wrong with the car, they work like hell to get it right. They're superb at that. And when things really get crazy, I can always call Enzo to straighten them out."

One thing Lauda will never straighten out with Enzo is the cause of his accident at Nurburgring. Some say that Lauda hit a wet patch and his tires lost adhesion; others, including a vocal group of British racing writers, insist that a rear wheel fell off. Enzo staunchly defends his car—but still won't say anything critical about Lauda's driving. For his part, Lauda intimates that the car malfunctioned. "It was a left corner," he says, "and I went right. I wasn't asleep at the wheel. But why dwell on it? The accident is over."

Lauda was upset over the treatment he received from Ferrari after Japan. He is firmly convinced that Enzo and the crew thought he had lost his heart and would never be a great driver again. One indication was the releasing of Lauda's driving teammate, the veteran Clay Reggazzoni, and the hiring of brash Carlos Reutemann. It is no secret in racing circles that Reutemann and Lauda don't get along. Lauda won't comment directly on their relationship, but he says cagily, "We develop cars in different directions, which means there are many disagreements and more emotions."

When Reutemann captured the second Grand Prix race of the season in Brazil, he became the darling of the crew, and disputes over testing flared often. But then, Lauda won in South Africa and he regained his position as the top Ferrari driver. "When you win," says Lauda, "everybody loves you. When you lose, you're a nobody. It's a lot of crap."

Will Lauda know when to quit? "When I'm fed up," he says, "I'll leave. It's easy. When I have to think twice about driving, that's it. I may even quit sooner than that, if I find something that's more of a challenge. For instance, if someone offered me a jumbo jet and gave me a few years to pay it back, I'd do it. I'd fly cargo, people, anything. I'd fly day and night. I'd fly to all the dirty little corners of the world where nobody wants to go." Then, his eyes flash and he slams his fist on his dining-room table. "Better yet," he says, "give me 10 jumbo jets. I'll hire people like me, people who will work 36 hours a day. I'll put Austrian Airlines out of business. I'll be bigger than Pan Am. Now that's a challenge that would suit me."

FOOTBALL

THE TAMPA BAY BUCS WIN ONE AT LAST

By Hubert Mizell

From The St. Petersburg (Fla.) Times
Copyright, ©, 1977, The St. Petersburg Times

Hell can now freeze over. There can be a month of Sundays. The Good Lord was willing and this time the creek didn't rise.

They won one.

Jilted for 26 pro football Sundays, the Tampa Bay Buccaneers had an affair with victory on a December eleventh the New Orleans Saints fear will live in infamy.

America's foremost losers became winners. For the Buccaneers, butts of jokes and targets of pity, record 1 win, 26 losses had the taste of caviar.

Locker room heads, which had so regularly dropped, were held as high as a West Point cadet's. As always, there were tears. But this time it was like the crying at a wedding, instead of a funeral.

Hank Stram, coach of the victims, said his bedeviled Saints were "strangled by trauma." Instead of applause for Tampa Bay, Stram could only moan, "What a nightmare! It was the worst experience of my coaching career. We're ashamed for our people, our fans, our organization."

It was, perhaps, a similar line of thinking about the lowly Bucs that put the Saints in an inescapable hole before 40,124 mostly angry customers. Something Archie Manning had said privately to the NFL's best runner.

The New Orleans quarterback's thoughts were relayed to Buccaneer ears by the most distinguished of messengers, Chicago Bears yardage man Walter Payton.

After the Bears beat the Buccaneers 10–0 the previous week at Tampa Stadium, Payton mentioned a recent conversation with Manning. "Archie says New Orleans will be up for the game," Payton said, "because the Saints don't want to be the Bucs' first victims. He said it would be a disgrace."

The key word . . . *disgrace.*

Football coaches from the Pop Warner leagues to the pros turn such discouraging words into fire. Tampa Bay Coach John McKay reminded the Bucs before kickoff Sunday.

"When Coach McKay told us what he [Manning] had said, a powerful look came over our dressing room," said Tampa Bay's marvelous defensive end Lee Roy Selmon. Everybody seemed to burn inside, saying to themselves that it's time to end all this losing."

Rookie linebacker David Lewis, who oozes wih All-Pro potential, boiled even after the 33–14 miracle. He admitted going after the Saints' quarterback.

"Hey man, those are nasty words," Lewis said. "It's a case of respect. When a man says that, it's like . . . well, it's like somebody has been talking bad about your momma.

"When you don't give a man no respect, then you're messing with a man as a man, not just as a football player. I was after his ass."

McKay's hair already was gray when on Halloween 1975 he announced the jump to the pros, a five-year agreement with the Buccaneers for just under $1 million. As the 26 losing weeks passed, the gray seemed to whiten even more with each mounting disappointment.

"It's a relief for all of us," Johnny McKay, the coach's son and a Tampa Bay wide receiver, said of the win. "Best of all, we won one for our fans who have pulled so hard and sweated it out with us.

"It'll be a pleasure next week to run onto the field against St. Louis in Tampa Stadium a winner instead of a loser. It's good that we have another game, to try once more for our fans at home. Right now I wish we had 13 more games."

These 0–26 Buccaneers had not only been bad in weeks past, they had been as unlucky as a canary at a cat caucus. If the ball bounced, it bounced against them. But on Sunday, there was a 180-degree turning of the worm.

Victory was theirs.

AUTO RACING

A MILE OF STYLE

By Tracy Dodds

From the Milwaukee Journal
Copyright, ©, 1977, Milwaukee Journal

In company with the first lady ever to qualify for the Indianapolis
500 Mile Race, gentlemen, start your engines.
—Tony Hullman, Speedway Owner
The lady, Janet Guthrie, and the 32 gentlemen started their
engines and the annual Indianapolis 500 Mile Race was on.

The traditions of the Speedway did not suffer great injustice.

The hundreds of thousands of racing fans did not walk out in
indignant protest.

The gentlemen in the race did not have to make any special con-
cessions.

The woman driver did not cause mayhem on the track.

Quite the contrary.

The woman simply drove in the race. She drove like a driver.
She looked like a driver. She came into the pit and consulted with
her crew like a driver. She talked to reporters like a driver. She
endured the reality of mechanical failures like a driver. And she
looked toward next year like a driver.

She showed class.

"I must say that I have been very touched by the other drivers
who have congratulated me and offered support," Guthrie said.
"There is no running hostility. It is nice to see that develop over
the course of 1976."

What had happened to the hostility that she had faced when she
had attempted to qualify for the 1976 race? Simply, Guthrie had
proved herself with the kind of low-keyed, earnest professionalism
that she showed during the race Sunday.

On her first pit stop, just 16 laps into the race, her crew filled her tank with fuel and then continued to work on the car, trying to remedy a mystery problem that was plaguing the racer.

With the official temperature a humid 86 degrees, and with the sun beating down on the gleaming metal of the car, the fuel heated up and expanded, spilling out into the tub—into her lap, into her bucket seat. That's not gasoline. It's methanol fuel, alcohol.

"It's not very comfortable," Guthrie said. "It burns. It can cause blisters if it's on your skin long enough."

But her driving suit was soaked with it. She was sitting in a pool of it. Not only is it uncomfortable, but obviously dangerous. That fuel is highly flammable. What good is a fireproof suit when it is soaked with fuel?

Time to call it quits? No, time to flush out the tub with a water hose and pour water on the driving suit. It helped some.

She went back out on the track, but she was right back in the pits. Her crew members tried to explain that they were having trouble with the fuel injection, with the "brain" of the fuel control center. The car was just not running right.

This time she got out of the car, talked to reporters, sat on a stack of tires, cleaned her glasses, poured a container of water over the front of her soaked suit.

She went back out on the track for one lap, and came back in. The crew tried again. They replaced the ignition system. Again, she went back out for one lap and came back in.

She made six pit stops totaling more than 90 minutes. She was in the pit when the leaders, Gordon Johncock and A. J. Foyt, passed the 100-lap halfway mark, and in the pit again when the 150-lap mark was reached.

Finally, she and her failing car headed for Gasoline Alley.

She received a standing ovation from the fans in the grandstand, who had been cheering for her every time she gallantly tried again.

"We had a mystery on our hands," she said. "We tried everything. Each time we replaced an element, we thought we'd have it.

"Two or three times they told me that, at my option, we would quit. On the last one, then, I said, 'Let's try it, and if this doesn't do it, that's it.' "

No one would have blamed her for stopping sooner. Mechanical disorders are part of the game. After all, Johnny Rutherford had gone out after 12 laps because of his gearbox, and he was coolly watching the race from his pit while she sweltered in a fuel-soaked sweatbox.

"My mind was pretty well into the race," she said. "You have to do whatever is needed as long as there is still a chance to run."

But those were very trying waits in the pit while the race went flying by.

"One of the experienced drivers was telling me that, while you have to psych up for most races, for Indy you have to psych down," she said. "There is so much excitement and electricity with this race, that your problem is to keep your concentration.

"The chief characteristic of a good driver is concentration, clearing everything else from your mind."

She was concentrating on racing Sunday.

Not even the flammable fuel soaking could shake her from her concentrated cool.

Like when she realized that, under the circumstances, she had to take a shower, and there was only one shower. She didn't rant and rave. She had some of her mechanics help her build a makeshift shower stall with big sheets of metal, and she took a shower, letting all the joking reporters know that the problem was not just that it was a one-sex shower, but that one shower for all those people was hardly adequate.

And like when she answered the reporters who were asking her about rumors that her mechanics had taken a basically sound car and "fixed" it to the point that it wasn't running properly.

"I have two of the best mechanics in the business," she said, almost too defensively. "Both have been mechanics of the year here. Phil Casey and Chuck Loober. They did everything possible to get the bugs out."

And when that was pursued, when she was asked about her car being taken to George Bignotti's work area to be straightened out, she said, "Oh, I know where that started. We put it on George Bignotti's dynomometer to diagnose the problem. But any problems that we had, had been solved before the race."

And when she was asked about what she had proved by being the first woman in the race, she said, "I don't think I had to prove anything. I think it's a tremendous accomplishment for any driver to drive at Indianapolis."

BASKETBALL

THE SECOND COMING OF JERRY WEST

By Paul Hemphill

From New West Magazine
Copyright, ©, 1977, New West Magazine

For fourteen winters he had been one of the premier players in the National Basketball Association—a taut southern devil whose whole life had been basketball—but now his body was quitting on him. At the age of 36, all during the lonely summer of 1974, Jerry West was trying to get it going one more time. Every morning he would arise early and go through the ritual—exercise, golf, shooting basketballs alone in some vacant high school gymnasium, dieting, running against old age on the track at UCLA, trying to negate the groin injury that had cut his previous season in half—in hopes of playing that one last *good* year for the Los Angeles Lakers. The Lakers had been his life, the only professional team he had ever played for, and he wanted to end his career in grace; for them as well as for himself. Like Harry ("Rabbit") Angstrom, the hero of John Updike's novel *Rabbit Run*, West wanted to do what he knew he did best. Play basketball well. One more time.

Then, finally, shortly before the 1974–75 season, he realized that it wasn't going to work anymore. "I realized I didn't have anything else to give the Lakers," he says. "It was the most difficult time of my life. I knew I was going to have to give up something I had loved so much." He played in two exhibition games ("I was really bad"). He discovered he was so tired after working out that he could hardly walk. And so, after playing in an exhibition game against Portland at the Forum, but not well enough to satisfy himself, he went up to coach Bill Sharman and spoke the words. "The body won't do what I want it to do, Bill," he said. "I'm not going to embarrass myself." They tried to talk him out of retiring, but Jerry West had made up his mind.

Their first draft choice, in 1960 when the Minneapolis Lakers became the Los Angeles Lakers, was a wild-eyed gunner from West Virginia University named Jerry West. Quiet and intense and charming, West epitomized the Laker teams of the next decade and a half. For 14 consecutive years they made the National Basketball Association playoffs, and in 1972 everything came together; West and Elgin Baylor and Wilt Chamberlain and Gail Goodrich set an NBA record of 69 wins, won the division title by 18 games, blew out Chicago and Milwaukee in the playoffs and then took the New York Knicks in five games to become the best basketball team in the world.

It was a very good basketball team, for a very long time, and the soul of the team was Jerry West. They called him "Mister Clutch." He was 6-feet-3 and 180 pounds, with lazy eyes and sloped shoulders and a penchant for the stewardesses, and whenever the Lakers got into trouble, they gave the ball to Jerry and Jerry scored. During his 14 years as a player in the NBA he averaged 27 points and nearly seven assists per game, made the All-Star game 13 times, and to this day ranks first in NBA career playoff points. But then he quit, and the Lakers quit with him. For the first time in 14 seasons they failed to make the playoffs. During the two seasons following the retirement of Jerry West, they won 70 games and lost 94.

West, meanwhile, played golf and tickled the ladies and separated from his wife and sued the Lakers for money he felt was owed him from the 1974–75 preseason. Now and then he worked as a commentator on televised NBA games, but it was obvious the job didn't inspire him. What he really wanted to do was coach the Lakers, but that seemed out of the question because of the lawsuit. Next to being president of the United States there are few highs to match being a matinee idol, whether it is in sports or show business, and now it had abruptly ended for Jerry West. In place of 17,000 screaming fans there were a couple of double-knit golf partners. In place of sweaty palms and the tensions of going down to the last 35 seconds against the Knicks in Madison Square Garden there were lazy afternoons and mindless liaisons. He was going crazy—"It was such a shallow life," he says—and when Laker owner Jack Kent Cooke called last July and asked him to be head coach, West, of course, took the job. But he said, "I don't intend to make coaching my life's work." The people who saw the players he would be coaching agreed.

After floundering for two years, Jerry West could not now abide a failure, but the odds predicted one. He was a rookie coach, a retired superstar who had never had to *think* about how to play the game, much less articulate it to others. He had a personnel roster that was filled by the best player in the game, Kareem Abdul-Jabbar, and 11 basic trainees. "We're a bunch of misfits and rejects," said one of the assistant coaches, Stan Albeck. The roster that began with Abdul-Jabbar ended with an escapee from the American Basketball Association, a quiet gentleman of 26 named Marv Roberts, who had been on four teams in five years. As the Lakers' twelfth man, averaging little more than one minute per game, Marv would one day say that he didn't "know much about how it is to *play* for coach West, but I do enjoy *practicing* for him."

But. The word keeps coming up when you speak of the Los Angeles Lakers season of 1976–77. Here was a team not expected to make the playoffs. *But,* on a Thursday in February, nearly two-thirds through the schedule, the Lakers gathered for a road trip east leading the Pacific Division of the NBA and holding the second-best record in the entire league. Jerry West had turned them into winners. *But. How?*

West is pissed off. It is nine o'clock on Thursday morning and the Lakers are assembling at the TWA wing of Los Angeles International Airport for a flight to Boston, the first stop on their trip. The day before, a columnist wrote that West and Wilt Chamberlain never spoke to each other while they were teammates and the Lakers were winning championships. "You call that guy [the writer]," West tells Lynn Shackelford, the Lakers' traveling secretary and broadcaster, "and tell him he's a liar." West is in a lather. He is wiping his sweaty palms on his plaid wool slacks. "He's a lying son of a bitch. Tell him I said that. Tell him when I get back he can call me and I'll say it to his face. Christ. He oughta know when you're winning *everybody* talks to each other." Somebody changes the subject, saying the Lakers' best guard sits on the bench and wears a coat and tie. "Every time we get into overtime," says Stan Albeck, "I tell him, 'Suit up, Jerry. Just five minutes. Then you can retire again.'" West crosses his legs and blushes.

The team will play in Boston on Friday night, in Philadelphia on Sunday afternoon, at Madison Square Garden against the Knicks on Tuesday night, and in the snow up at Buffalo against the Braves on Wednesday. "The road being what it is," says Stan Albeck, "we should lose to the Celts and the Knicks and Philly. Buffalo we should win. If Portland messes up, we ought to be OK when we get back home." Portland is a close second in the Pacific Division.

We ought to be OK when we get back home. Indeed, basketball is a game too often influenced by outside factors—by referees whose objectivity is tilted by packs of screaming partisans; by wearisome travel. *Greyhound transfer airport/hotel/practice/hotel/game/hotel/ airport,* reads a typical day's schedule on the itinerary photocopied for the Lakers' traveling party. Up to this Thursday the home team has won 70.4 percent of all NBA games. The Lakers have won 20 straight at home.

Among the reasons for their success is the first decision West made upon accepting the job. Although most NBA teams have only one assistant coach, he got on the phone and hired two. West knew he needed help ("I tell you, I was scared about whether I could take care of 12 players all by myself") and he has got it from Stan Albeck and Jack McCloskey. The three have become inseparable, drinking together and going over game plans late into the night: West, the field commander, with a sense of the big picture; McCloskey, the master of defense out of Penn and Wake Forest; Albeck, the offensive genius who brought his "feed-the-big-man" attack from the Kentucky Colonels, where Artis Gilmore was the Kareem Abdul-Jabbar of the ABA.

Somewhere over the Rockies, in the rear of the first-class section, McCloskey, moustachioed and 50, scribbles notes with a felt-tipped pen. "Boston," McCloskey is saying. "We're going right back where it happened. Boston is where this club grew up. We went into Buffalo the first month and we were 4–4. We had a 20-point lead going into the fourth quarter. There was a fight, it ignited Buffalo and we lost in overtime. We went to Boston the next night. We battled and hustled, but we lost. That trip made us 4–6 and one of the writers said, 'Well that's it.' I told him he was wrong, that I knew then that we had a team. That was the night. Since that night we've gone 28–10. We grew up that night in Boston." It was not unlike what happens to a young boy when, in the symbolic story of growing up, he takes on the neighborhood bully and gets his nose bloodied and returns to his Charles Atlas course and then goes back and beats the living daylights out of the other guy. Manhood. The Lakers got embarrassed and then mad and, finally, mature on that first trip East.

When the plane lands, a bus carries the Lakers to Prudential Center. They have 20 minutes to check into the hotel, change to sweatsuits, and reboard the bus for a short workout at night in a dank little college gymnasium. After the hour-and-a-half workout, Albeck has a beer in the bar back at the hotel. Stan Albeck is an animated 45-year-old with a graying Brillo hairdo who is the cheerleader of the three coaches. His Lakers offense is so methodical that it resembles a troop movement. "We've got maybe two-dozen plays," he is saying, "but what it all boils down to is consistency. If the play isn't working and we're down to five seconds, we feed the ball to Kareem." He is talking over Muzak-fed Hawaiian music in a plastic bar called the Kon Tiki Ports. "You've got to figure the season is 100 games. There's no room for emotion. This game is decided by mistakes and injuries. When we go into the dressing room for half time we don't do any shouting. We go to the blackboard and show the guys what's working and what isn't working. That's the way Jerry played, and that's the way he coaches. We average 108 points a game, and we give up 103. That's the bottom line. When you do that, you win. Hell, we're a bunch of computers."

On Friday night, with 14,000 fierce Celtics fans looking on, Los Angeles blows a 10-point half time lead and loses by one. "Everybody wants to write about how great this team is, but we've been damned lucky so far," says West, flashing a white turtleneck and gray slacks and a royal-blue corduroy jacket outside the dressing room. "We didn't play smart at the end. Against a team like the Celtics, on the road, that's gonna get you beat." The writers traveling with the team are thinking that this is the kind of game Jerry West, "Mr. Clutch," would have won in the last second. "Hey," somebody asks on the glum bus ride back to the hotel, "how'd Portland come out tonight?" West is testy: "Screw Portland. I don't want to hear about Portland. How'd L.A. do? Son of a bitch."

They are grim when they check in at Logan Field on Saturday morning for the quick flight to Philadelphia and Sunday afternoon's nationally televised game against the Seventy-Sixers. The temperature is 25 degrees and snow is flurrying and West is annoyed because he has been told that, during half time the night before, Chick Hearn, broadcasting back to California, sang a love song to Jack Kent Cooke for "making this team what it is today" and never mentioned the coaches. "Shit," says West, "we've got the bodies of a YMCA pickup team when Cooke could've gone out and gotten Julius Erving and Paul Silas and guys like that. The only thing we've got going for us is, we have fun and we have Kareem. Look at Philly. They've got Erving and George McGinnis making a half-million each, and 10 other guys totaling $1.8 million a year, and our payroll is maybe $1.4 million. He promised me some help. Cooke promised. Then these players come up, and he doesn't move."

The makeup of this team is curious. There is Kareem Abdul-Jabbar, the dominant player in basketball today, and there is a motley supporting cast of 11. Normally, when you have such a superstar, jealousy will destroy. It has not been so with the Lakers and Kareem because he is a nice man and so obviously The Franchise. Philadelphia, for instance, has superstars competing against each other, but the very idea of another Laker presuming to compete with Kareem is ludicrous. "I just like to hang around and watch the man walk," is how one Laker puts it.

This is an extremely interesting man, Kareem Abdul-Jabbar, the former Lew Alcindor. He is in his eighth season with the pros and he is a cinch to become the NBA's Most Valuable Player for the fifth time. He is a gentle soul with a variety of interests—Oriental rugs, the Pyramids, books on sociology—and awesome physical gifts and very special problems. When you are 7-feet-3 and your face is forever on the cover of *Sports Illustrated*, it is impossible to walk unmolested through an airport. "About all I can do," he says, "is put the blinders on and look straight ahead. And walk fast." Nobody quite knows what his personal life is like. There was a marriage some five years ago, producing one child, and whenever the lady comes to L.A. from Washington, D.C., she stays with Kareem in his plush home. He recently wrote a brief essay about basketball for *The New York Times* and wants to someday write his autobiography without a ghost writer. This morning, on the flight to Philadelphia, he is lazing through a florid book on Oriental rugs put out by the Metropolitan Museum of Art. "I became interested in Oriental rugs my first year in basketball," he is saying. "I went to the museum once. I'd like to go while we're in New York, but there never is enough time. They have one rug there 1,600 years old. It was found in a tomb in what is now Russia. The tomb leaked water and the water froze. That's how the rug was preserved for so long." He has, he says, "quite a collection" of rugs himself.

Now, in his eighth year of pro basketball, it appears that Kareem is finally happy. The reason for this is Jerry West. That, in itself, is an upset because few superstars in any sport have gone on to excel as managers or coaches. A man becomes a great salesman or shortstop or writer, due, in most cases, to his inbred talent and instincts and hustle and ego. But to become a successful executive or major-league manager or editor means that one must sublimate one's ego; one must rely upon, and enjoy, the success of *other* men. Whether Jerry West —a born basketball player with the ability and the instincts and the body and the pride and the ego—could sit on a bench and summon up the patience to live with other men's successes and failures was the major concern of Lakers management and players and fans and West himself when he took the job. But he has used his old playing fame to his advantage ("Who's going to doubt one of the best basketball players of all time?" says Kareem). He has seen that his ego becomes infectious ("If everybody on this club hated to lose as much as Jerry does," says guard Johnny Neumann, "we'd be undefeated right now").

And the very bottom line on Jerry West as a successful coach may be his ability to communicate with other human beings—man-to-man, the way they learn it in West Virginia.

"Everything always came so easy for Jerry," play-by-play broadcaster Chick Hearn is saying Saturday night in the hotel bar. "I figured he'd blow his stack the first time a guard didn't do what *he* would have done. But he's got patience and the great instinct for knowing exactly when it's time to substitute. It's like baseball. The great manager is the one who knows—just plain *knows*—when to yank a pitcher. The poor manager leaves a pitcher in for one pitch too many and there goes a three-run homer and the ball game. You're born with that ability."

Lucius Allen, now 29 and in his eighth year as a pro, is reminiscent of those stoic black southern preachers who got their heads busted in civil-rights marches during the sixties. A quiet man who has played for four coaches and is charged with running the Lakers offense, Allen says, "Jerry is a people's person. He's honest with everybody, and you don't find that in pro basketball. I mean, if you're not playing you want to know why. Most coaches tell you everything but the truth. Like, 'Well, you can't shoot like the other guy' or 'He's a better dribbler.' Jerry says, 'You aren't playing because you aren't doing what I told you to do, and when you start doing what I want you to do, you'll start playing.' "

The Philadelphia Seventy-Sixers are a bunch of brutes who sometimes win out of sheer power and macho. Sinking under the basket and swarming all over Abdul-Jabbar, they muscle the Lakers and go to the dressing room at half time Sunday with a 51–37 lead. They win the game, 102–97.

Certain things on the road are relentless, among them the travel and the press. Here, after the Philly game, is a bearded young radio DJ with a tape recorder slung over his shoulder. He is shoving the microphone into West's face while they sit in a cavernous corridor beneath the stands. Steve Mix of the 'Sixers, who scored 37 points, is the subject.

"Did Mix hurt you today?"

"Anybody who scores 37 points hurts you," says West.

"How badly did Mix hurt you?"

"I'd say, offhand, about 37 points."

"If Mix hadn't played . . ."

West blinks. "Well, shit, if Mix hadn't played we would've won by 32 points. Hey, Jesus, we aren't getting anywhere with this." The radio guy and West smirk at each other for half a minute and finally the radio guy leaves.

The Lakers trudge through the snow to the bus that takes them to New York. "Hey, you know what?" Albeck says as the bus rocks north. "The guys were in there moping after the game. Christ, I told 'em they'd just lost two games on the road to two tough teams by a total of six points."

With the New York Knicks ahead of them, Tuesday night in Madison Square Garden, the Lakers are revising one of their early wishes. Up to now, upon hearing of a succession of games being canceled in Buffalo, they'd been hoping to be spared the snow there, too. Now, they are praying for a break in the weather so they can beat up on the Buffalo Braves Wednesday night. Otherwise, the road trip ends in New York. "The Knicks, in the Garden," says West. "We may not win a game on this trip."

In his room early Tuesday afternoon, West talks for nearly an hour about his life after he retired as a player. Soft sunlight filters through the sheer curtains. He is shirtless. When the phone rings three times he asks the operator to hold the calls. "I was looking forward to retirement," he says. "No more of the road and all of that." He digresses to emphasize that he "didn't quit; I retired with grace." He goes on: "I wanted to play golf and travel for a while, but I found out it wasn't a very good way to live. I won't go into detail, but that period played hell with my marriage.

"I guess I wanted to coach the Lakers one day. I mean, I *love* the Lakers. I always felt that loyalty was a tremendously important part in the life of an athlete. But I had this lawsuit going against Cooke and figured that would do it for me as coach of the Lakers. Then Cooke asked me if I wanted to coach the team. It was a tremendous adjustment. I guess I'd seen one Lakers game in two years. I called all of the players and told them I would be honest with them and that we were going to have fun. I went out and hired Stan and Jack because I hate organizational work and I needed a crutch to help me through that part. I'm still nervous. Sometimes I just don't know what to say to the players after a game. I'm still learning."

And the Lakers? "Look. This isn't a good team. We don't have any business being where we are. We need to upgrade ourselves in almost every area. I've got the best player in basketball, and two others I wouldn't trade: Earl Tatum and Kermit Washington. Both of those are young and hungry and have good bodies. They're winners. I'm not afraid to say that I think Cooke let me down when he didn't make a move to get me some quality players, like he said he would do, when they were available. It's disgraceful, the burden Kareem has to carry. Everywhere he goes he's double-teamed and triple-teamed. He's so easy to work with. Here, really, is a star. He's a class person. There's no animosity toward him or from him."

West is tired of talking. He has to put on his coat and tie for the game at the Garden. "Eighty percent of my personal problems," he says, "are due to those two years I spent away from basketball."

Working with the available material, West has set up a system in which every man is used whenever possible, which keeps the players happy and enables the coaches to exploit momentary hot hands. The philosophy is: Find our strengths and the opponents' weaknesses. Given West's fine instincts for substitutions at crucial moments, the Lakers excel at taking advantage of matchups. Nevertheless, they fall through the floor at the Garden. New York wins 125–107 and nobody bothers to mope this time because the loss is so definite. "They just beat the hell out of us," West says to the writers. "They put on a basketball clinic and we watched." Somebody asks if he ever has the urge, when down by 20 points, to put on a jersey and hit the floor. "No, never," West says. "Never."

Great God almighty, is it cold. The Big Snow came to Buffalo before Christmas and for two months not a day has passed when it has not been snowing or below freezing. Surely nobody lives in Buffalo on purpose. For the past two weeks there has been no mail service or garbage collection or Sunday church or public school or street movement or airport traffic or burials or, until yesterday, Buffalo Braves basketball games. One day at the Buffalo zoo snow piled so high that three reindeer escaped by simply walking over the fence.

If there is anything worse than the weather this winter in Buffalo, it's the Braves, who have the second worst record in the NBA. They did win last night, in their first home game in two weeks, but the Lakers are hot-eyed, ready to kill to come out of this road trip with at least one victory. Before the game, Kermit Washington is doing his stretch exercises next to the Laker bench when John Shumate of Buffalo happens by. Two months ago on the Lakers' pivotal initial trip to the East, Washington decked Shumate with two lightning rights to the jaw. "How's it going, man?" Shumate now asks Washington. Kermit, who is 6-feet-8 and 230 and can bench press 400 pounds, stares at Shumate, neither blinking nor speaking. An intimidated Shumate scores four points in 34 minutes and does not get close enough to Washington to draw a single personal foul.

Everything works for Los Angeles from the opening tipoff. It is 59–39 Lakers at the half. Buffalo can't do anything right; L.A. can't do anything wrong. The game ends, really, with five minutes to go, when Kareem, infuriated over missing an easy four-foot hook, takes the carom and rattles the glass backboard with a flying stuff that is absolutely terrifying. It is L.A. 105–90.

There is a flurry at the end. All night long a fat-bellied fan sitting directly behind the Lakers bench has been taking on Kareem Abdul-Jabbar. "Hey, Lew," he has yelled, using Kareem's pre-Muslim name. "You goddamn black-assed nigger, how's Mohammed doing?" The other Lakers have stared him down during the game, Kareem ignoring him, but the guy is still going when Kareem is ceremoniously taken from the game with 50 seconds to go. Trainer Del Tanner tosses Kareem a towel as he approaches the bench to applause. Kareem swipes at his forehead and then, before anybody can grasp what is happening, takes one giant step—*one giant step*—over a metal folding chair and is suddenly hovering over the fat kid and jabbing a finger in his face. "Did you want to take this up personally?" Kareem is saying in a rage. "Let's go outside in the snow." The kid flinches and giggles and pales. Six cops appear from nowhere. When Del Tanner bear hugs Kareem away he notes that Kareem's waist muscles are spasming out of control.

"Well," West says to the writers after the game. "I'd call it a great road trip. We left home in first place and now we're going back home in first place. If we beat Denver Friday night in L.A., we'll have the best record in basketball." With the questions running out, a writer asks West whom Kareem stepped over to go after the fan. "It looked to me," West says, "like he stepped over the world."

Not to be overlooked in West's hold over his players is his personal style. The kid from Cabin Creek has a loose insouciance—the grinning good old boy who has seen the mountaintop but still fondly recalls the night of the senior prom—that is not wasted on these rascally dudes with loose change in their pockets and a win immediately behind them and flashing looks in their eyes and lust in their hearts. Around midnight the leader of a Buffalo disco band is saying he is proud to recognize the famous Jerry West, coach of the Los Angeles Lakers, but West is too busy in the corner of the lounge to acknowledge the introduction. She is very pretty, about 21, red-haired and randy.

At nine o'clock the next morning Del Tanner stands at the front of the bus and takes a head count. There are snores, burps, yawns. "Hey," he says, "where the hell is Cazzie?"

"He got kidnapped," yelps Kareem.

"No shit. Anybody seen Cazzie?"

"I told you, man," says Kareem. "He got kidnapped. Idi Amin got him. Says he won't let him go until he teaches him the hook shot."

On Friday night, at home in the Forum, they brilliantly came down on the Denver Nuggets, but the postgame mood was somber. They understood to a man the irony. On the night they became the winningest team in basketball, the Lakers also, most likely, lost the championship. Midway through the third quarter Kermit Washington, the abrasive young forward who was beginning to symbolize the general meanness of these New Lakers, abruptly crashed to the floor while driving toward the basket and had to carried off the court. The Lakers had written every team in the NBA during preseason camp, trying to find a taker for Washington, but nobody had wanted him. Then, under West's needling and pushing, Washington had become an indefatigable rebounder with the endurance of a pack mule. He had become the only player on the team who could even presume to belly up to Kareem Abdul-Jabbar. And now they were going to operate on his knee and he would be out for the season. In a lounge, just off the floor of the Forum, Pat Washington tried to find somebody to look after one-year-old Dana so she could go and commiserate with her husband. Jerry West had a couple of beers and went home alone.

GOLF

WATSON IS THE MASTER

By Phil Taylor

From The Seattle Post-Intelligencer
Copyright, ©, 1977, The Seattle Post-Intelligencer

The kid who was supposed to choke made the entire Masters field—
including the greatest player in the world—gag on a mouthful of
birdies yesterday. He served them as appetizer, entrée, and dessert,
and he shoved them right down all those hungry gullets.

And Tom Watson, in earning the coveted green jacket, wiped away
the stigma, however undeserved, that has followed him from Sawgrass
and Hilton Head, where two big ones got away when they were easily
within his grasp.

Watson, 27, now sitting atop the golfing world, withstood all the
intense heat that could be generated from Jack Nicklaus and a cluster
of panting pursuers to post an eventual 12-under-par 276 and a two-
stroke victory in the forty-first rendition of this celebrated classic at
Augusta National.

In the final accounting, though few are likely to say it out loud, it
was Nicklaus, the man immune to mortal frailty, who faltered and
bogeyed himself right out of any fleeting hope of victory on the
seventy-second hole. He missed by two swings of the club and was
resigned to the unlikely runner-up spot at 278.

That left Tom Kite and Rick Massengale to share third at 280
figures, the only other guys who were in the hunt during another
delightfully warm Georgia day on a golf course begging to be taken.

This was Watson's day, really from the start, when he went out
co-holder of the lead at seven under par with unfortunate Ben Crenshaw, soon to hang himself on a noose of bogeys. Watson surrendered
the lead only once, then for perhaps half-a-hole, when Nicklaus went
11 under at the fifteenth, but he really thrust the dagger in for the
kill on the seventeenth, and the man most mortally wounded was
Nicklaus.

Both were 11 under par at the moment, Tom having birdied 15

right behind Jack. Watson, playing with Massengale, was on the seventeenth green as Nicklaus and Crenshaw teed off on 18.

By the time Nicklaus reached his well-placed drive, one of those special kind of Augusta eruptions from behind him tolled the shattering news: Watson has birdied the seventeenth.

Indeed he had. And he made it from 20 feet, a curling, right-to-left, downhill putt. It is not the kind of thing that comes from chokers, and Watson has reminded one and all he is not a choker.

Now Nicklaus could feel the tightening knot and, as he explained later, it changed his entire strategy.

"I had a good drive on 18," Nicklaus said, "and I was going to play to the middle of the green and make sure I got par. When I heard Tom making the birdie, it changed my strategy. I was going to hit a 6-iron hard past the pin, but I had a thin line. I tried to loft it and I hit it fat."

The "fat" 6-iron shot flew into the bunker and eventually led to a bogey, making the task of young Mr. Watson so very much easier.

Watson let Massengale, who started at six under, catch him on the second hole with a birdie, then began putting something together starting with the fifth hole.

In rapid succession, he birdied the difficult fifth from 10 feet, the short sixth from 15, the seventh from four, and the eighth from 12. Wham, bam, four birdies and an 11-under reading. Massengale, no hacker himself this crucial round, made three more birdies to be 10 under as the pair turned the corner for home. Massengale fell with a bogey on No. 11.

Nicklaus, meanwhile, found three birdies of his own going out to from a four-under start to seven under. And when he knocked in a five-footer at 10, a 12-footer at 13, and followed a drive and 3-iron with two putts from 40 feet on the par five thirteenth, he suddenly was 10 under.

Now Nicklaus surely would catch the kid. Didn't Watson squander a two-shot lead in the Tournament Players Championship and one of four strokes in the Heritage, each time with nine holes to play?

Not this time. Not this time. This one meant too much and Watson was too close to let it get away.

A lot of tournaments have been given away, but Watson's choker label is hardly justified. After all, he was the leading money winner coming into this event and now has a bankroll of $175,185 after yesterday's $40,000 check.

And, as he is quick to remind, "A lot of guys who have never choked, have never been in the position to do so."

He is the rightful champion of this tournament.

BULL FIGHTING

THE BULLRING

By D. L. Stewart

From The Dayton Journal Herald
Copyright, ©, 1977, The Journal Herald, Dayton, Ohio

On a midwinter Sunday afternoon, the place to be in Mexico City is at the bullring.

Being in Mexico in the winter and not going to a bullfiight is unthinkable. It is like being in downtown Dayton at night and not getting propositioned.

So at 3 o'clock on a warm Sunday afternoon, I am in a cab headed for the Plaza Mexico, the No. 1 bullring in the country.

The program does not begin until 4:30, but I have to get there early, because the ticket promised by my travel agency has failed to materialize.

As we weave through the heavy traffic on Calle San Antonio, I asked the cabbie how difficult it will be to get a ticket today.

He shrugs and blows his horn at a Renault he has just forced off the road.

"Normally, it would not be difficult," he says, swerving just in time to keep a bus from getting past us. "But this is the inauguration. The first fight of the season."

"Oh, wow, sort of like Opening Day in baseball." "Si," he says, giving a blast of his horn to a pedestrian crossing the street in front of us. While the cabbie leans on the horn and the pedestrian shakes his white cane at us, I sit back and consider the odds.

I have not had much experience with scalpers, especially in a foreign language. I don't even know how to say, "Psst, hey buddy," in Spanish.

In addition to which, I have no idea what a bullfight ticket looks like. I'm liable to shell out a couple of hundred pesos for a ticket entitling me to a free lube job with my next fill-up.

On the positive side, I have plenty of money in my pocket and the company's blessing to spend it. I think back to what they told me before I left the office.

"As long as you get a good bullfight story, we don't care what it costs," assignments editor Finster "Hi Roller" O'Shaughnessy declared. "Go as high as 10 bucks if you have to."

Then we are as near to the Plaza Mexico as the snarled traffic will permit. I hop out of the cab and pay the fare, which is 100 pesos. (The same ride back to my hotel after the fights will cost me 50 pesos. This is just one of the things that makes Mexico a land of mystery.)

Semi-confidently I joined the flow of one-way pedestrian traffic moving toward the stadium, until I am standing in the middle of Calle Augusto Rodin, the street that runs in front of Plaza Mexico.

The area is crammed with people. There are old people and young people, tall people and short people, fat people and skinny people. But they all have one thing in common: Not a one of them has an extra ticket.

For a while, I just stand around, waiting for a scalper to approach me. At 3:30 I still have hopes of buying a good seat in the *sombra*, the shady side of the ring. By 3:45, I am willing to take a seat in the sun. By 4 P.M., I am willing to sit next to the bull.

Perhaps I am being too subtle, I think. Maybe I should do something that will make it plain what I want. Like taping a $20 bill to my forehead.

At 4:10, a middle-aged man approaches me.

"Do you need a ticket?" he asks, in lightly accented English.

"Maybe. How much?"

"One hundred pesos."

I do some lightning quick mental math. It's 20 pesos to the dollar. Or is that 20 dollars to the peso? If it's 20 pesos to the dollar, that'll be $5. On the other hand, if it's 20 dollars to . . .

"I don't have all day, señor."

"Oh, sorry. OK, let me see the ticket."

He produces a pink and violet ticket with a picture of a man on a horse being chased by a bull. It's a bullfight ticket, all right. Either that or a ticket for a John Wayne movie. The price on the ticket is 45 pesos.

"OK," I say. I give the man his money.

"Follow me," he says.

Then I am inside the famed Plaza Mexico, the world's biggest bullring. As we walk to our seats, the man who sold me the ticket says that his name is Rodolfo Vasquez and he is an accountant who has traveled extensively in the United States.

Each year, he says, he buys two season tickets for himself and his wife. But his wife is sick this week and so Rodolfo Vasquez is doing what any red-blooded Mexican bullfight fan would do: He is going without her.

Our seats are in the *sombra*, high up in the lower deck. We reach them at precisely 4:30. Just as we sit down, there is a flourish of trumpets from somewhere in the stands above us.

It is the signal to begin the corrida, the running of the bulls.

At the opposite side of the ring a gate opens and the procession begins. That is what I have been waiting to see. The pageantry. The color. The spectacle.

The alguaciles, horsemen in sixteenth-century costumes, come first. They are followed by the picadors, the banderilleros, the matadors. Everyone is in the parade but the bulls. In bullfighting, only the home team gets introduced.

I snap a couple of pictures and look down to adjust my camera. When I look up, the ring is empty, again. I glance at my watch. It is 4:35. The pageantry, the color, the spectacle I have been hearing so much about takes just five minutes.

I have seen better ceremonies at the opening of a Burger Chef.

And then the first bull is in the ring, running, snorting, in search of an enemy. He finds many.

There are the picadors on their well-padded horses, who drive their lances into the large muscle at the back of the neck.

There are the banderilleros, agile men who plunge barbed staves into the wound to increase the flow of blood.

There are not one but three matadors, calling to him, taunting him, bewildering him, forcing him to run around the ring so that his heart will pump faster and the blood will flow more freely.

And then, when he is worn, weakened by the loss of blood, unable to hold up his head, unable to keep his tongue from dragging in the dust of the ring, one matador comes forth to challenge him.

Sometimes, it is said, a bull can win his life with an exceptional show of bravery. It does happen. About once every 50 years.

But the fight is almost always fixed. They wouldn't touch it in Vegas. Even a bull that defeats his final tormentor winds up being slaughtered, his meat given to the poor or sold right there at the bullring.

I sit through three fights, trying to understand what is happening down there, looking for the beauty that Hemingway found in the sight of men tormenting dumb animals.

But I am no Hemingway.

I see no beauty down there. I see only a depressing reminder of how little my species has progressed.

After the third killing, the one in which the matador slides his sword deep into the animal's back, puncturing a lung and causing gushers of blood to pump out of the bull's nose and mouth, I decide that I have had enough.

The program is only half over. The best fights are yet to come. The bravest bulls. The greatest macho.

Yet to come, too, is a tragic bit of foolishness when a young man vaults from the stands into the ring during the sixth fight and is badly gored. This, I learn, is becoming a tradition at bullfights. The flamboyant El Cordobes got his start that way, according to the legend.

But when the young man jumps into the ring at Plaza Mexico, I am no longer in my seat. I am wandering outside, sorting through the souvenirs, sampling the foods for sale at the booths that stand temporarily in the shadow of the stadium.

I doubt that I will ever return to Plaza Mexico. Or to any bullring.

It is not that I am bothered by the blood, although Lord knows there is plenty of that. Nor does the sight of a dead animal upset me. I enjoy steak as much as the next guy.

But, if you're going to kill an animal, get it over with. Shoot it. Hang it. Blow its head off with a bazooka.

But don't bleed it and torment it and wait until it is wild-eyed with fear and confusion while you do it. Don't spend 20 minutes torturing an animal and then tell me about your macho.

That's not macho. That's only another way of pulling the wings off of flies.

BOXING

DEATH OF THE DON KING TOURNAMENT

By Sam Toperoff

From Sport Magazine
Copyright, ©, 1977, M.V.P. Sports, Inc.

The steaming dressing room in the San Antonio Municipal Audi-
torium was crowded with well-wishers and newsmen one Friday
night last March. There was continual high-pitched chatter and an
occasional exultant shout in Spanish. The local favorite, Mexican-
American featherweight Mike Ayala, had won a big one.

The room quieted suddenly and the revelers parted. A small man
wearing a large stetson and a dark leather jacket stepped into the
room and made his way to the diminutive fighter sitting on the rub-
bing table. An old-timer standing next to me explained: "That's
Jesus Pimental, a great bantamweight in the sixties. He's a legend
down here." Pimental, who is now a small-time boxing promoter,
took the young fighter's face in his hands and said a few soft words.
He shook Ayala's hand and had some words of praise for the manager.
Then Pimental was gone.

Earlier tonight, Mike "Cyclone" Ayala had looked like the second
coming of Jesus Pimental, knocking out ex-world bantamweight
champion Romeo Anaya in six. It appeared that the 19-year-old Ayala
was aproaching world-class caliber, and at the lighter weights, very
few American fighters are recognized worldwide.

When the crowd finally left, I spoke with Mike and his father-
manager, Tony. They talked humbly about their hopes for the future,
a shot at world featherweight champion Danny Lopez. Then I said,
"Listen, I'm down here to cover Don King's U.S. Boxing Championships out at Randolph Air Force Base tomorrow. How'd you like to
be my guests?"

It was as though the Ayalas had been hit with the hardest punch
of the night. The son exhaled and slumped forward, lowering his

soft brown eyes. The father snapped, "Why'd we want to see a bunch of fixed fights!" But when they realized that my offer was not intended to offend, Mike said, "I wasn't even invited to fight in the tournament, and I'm ranked No. 2 in the United States in *Ring* magazine."

"It's an insult not even to be asked," said Tony. "And the money. They have second-rate fighters who will make three, four times what Mike made tonight fighting an ex-champ. It's a bad thing for boxing."

"Cause they control all the fighters and they know they couldn't control us," Tony said.

"But weren't they supposed to invite all the ranked fighters?" The Ayalas looked at me as though I were strange.

"The shame of it all," said Tony, "is the sacrifices we've made to get where we are. If you have any pride, it sticks in the throat. All the nights on the road sleeping in the car, living on soda and baloney sandwiches. Fighting all the toughest guys and not getting a fair shot at the big money. But you know who I feel most sorry for?"

"Who?"

"Jesus Pimental. You saw him in here? Well, he will have his picture in the paper with King, whom he is forced to do business with. And in his heart he knows it is rotten. He knows Mike could beat all of them in King's tournament, but he doesn't speak out about Mike's absence."

The moment had become too intense for words. I shook their hands and wished them luck. As I was leaving Mike Ayala asked, a trace of hope in his voice: "They can't get away with it, can they, mister?"

As far back as last January, when *Sport* assigned me to do a story on "The Resurgence of Boxing," I was in a unique position to see the possibilities of scandal in the Don King/ABC-TV U.S. Boxing Championships. As a college professor for 20 years, I was not well known on the boxing beat. But I had been attending most of the good matches at Madison Square Garden for the last 30 years. And I had married a woman whose father managed fighters in Miami in the mid-thirties.

His repertoire included having a variety of names and records for each of his fighters and of putting a couple of them in with each other to stage a "slugfest." He thus earned a nice piece of both fighters' purses. This ploy was at least partly due to the fact that whenever my father-in-law discovered a truly promising youngster, he always lost him to another manager who could get the kid better fights. I was to discover that Don King knew about this boxing "tradition."

A little background on King: Since 1972, when he came out of prison after serving four and one-half years for manslaughter, Don

King's rise in the boxing business has been mercurial. In his home-town of Cleveland, King signed up Richie Giachetti as his trainer and became manager of record of a few moderately prominent boxers, heavyweight Earnie Shavers being perhaps the best known. But King moved quickly from fight manager to fight promoter, and in 1974 he promoted the $10 million Muhammad Ali-George Foreman heavy-weight championship in Zaire and the next year, the $8 million Ali-Joe Frazier "Thrilla in Manila." King had apparently learned from such hugely successful earlier promoters as Tex Rickard, who charted the career of heavyweight champion Jack Dempsey, and Mike Jacobs, who controlled heavyweight champion Joe Louis: Through pro-motional control of key heavyweights, one can could dominate the sport. King achieved that dominant position when he promoted six Ali title fights. King then became the promoter of George Foreman, who, despite the loss to an aging Ali, seemed a good bet to regain his championship and reign for years. The Foreman-Jimmy Young fight in Puerto Rico last March is indicative of the kind of overall control of the heavyweight division King had attained—he had commitments on the future fights of *both* boxers.

Suddenly, boxing had become a major television attraction once again, and the man the networks had to see about acquiring rights to top fight promotions was, of course, Don King. Back in July 1976—even before the U.S. Olympic boxing team achieved excellent ratings in Montreal—ABC-TV had contracted to pay Don King Productions (DKP) $1.4 million in purse money and $40,000 per show for pro-duction costs to stage a U.S. Boxing Championships tournament. The ABC contract that King signed stated ". . . You acknowledge that the quality of the fighters participating in each weight category be the best possible, determined by rankings established by *Ring* maga-zine at the time the tournament starts." *Ring* was to be paid $70,000 for its services. James A. Farley, Jr., the chairman of the New York Athletic Commission (boxing and wrestling), agreed to act as unpaid overseer of the King tournament. King then set up a tournament supervisory committee, headed by Farley and including *Ring*'s editor-publisher, Nat Loubet, and associate editor, John Ort, plus two former members of the New York State Athletic Commission.

King supposedly invited all the *Ring*-rated fighters in eight weight classes to compete in the USBC. The purses were very attractive to up-and-coming fighters like Mike Ayala, who earned about $4,000 in beating Anaya. The USBC purses for boxers below middleweight started at $7,500 and progressed to $45,500 for title winners. Heavy-weights would receive $15,000 for each quarterfinal fight, $30,000 in the semifinals, and $135,000 to the winning finalist. Virtually all the fighters who accepted were required to sign contracts that gave King promotional control of the tournament champions for two years. Thus ABC, through its contract with King, would end up with an option to televise the bouts of some of the best young boxers for those two years.

In most stories I'd read about the former Cleveland numbers czar, King had been characterized as the second coming of Barnum, Mike Todd, and the Reverend Ike. When I spent a long, tiring day with him during that tournament in San Antonio last March 27, the image seemed appropriate. I asked how he maintained such a schedule, and he said, "I never gets tired because it ain't *my* energy that's being dispensed. It is *God* speaking through me."

God must have felt expansive this day because King's word cup overflowed, as he ran through quotes from Nietzsche, Freud, Thoreau, and Shakespeare. But even though he spoke openly, Don King seemed preoccupied. His tournament was already under fire.

On February 13 at the U.S. Naval Academy, Scott LeDoux, a journeyman heavyweight, lost a unanimous decision to Johnny Boudreaux and threw a tantrum in the ring. He said, "I was warned about this a month ago . . . I was told there was no way I could win in this tournament controlled by Don King, Paddy Flood, and Al Braverman." Flood and Braverman managed fighters in King's tournament and also served as "consultants" to King.

On March 24, Kenny Weldon, *Ring*'s tenth-ranked lightweight, who had been eliminated from the tournament, told a newsman that he had paid an international booking agent named George Kanter "a lot more [of his purse] than ten percent," the standard booking fee, to compete in the championships. But the fact that fighters had to pay for being booked into a tournament supposedly qualified for on merit was patently unethical. So, even though the tournament TV ratings were very promising—a 10.2 Nielsen, a 29 percent audience share—there had been some problems but nothing, King assured me, he couldn't handle.

"You see—your name's Sam, right?—you see, Sam, this ain't like no other business," King said. "Once you got a good idea, like I did with this tournament, everyone who doesn't have a piece of it will do whatever they can to bring you down. 'Specially if you're black folks. But I can assure you, it's strictly a case of sour grapes."

Whenever I asked a question that was even mildy critical of practices in his tournament, King either "sour graped" it, "stone walled" it ("These fighters have earned their way here on merit"), or invoked a higher authority: "Don't forget, my man, this entire tournament is sanctioned by the *Ring* magazine and fighter Ike

Fluellen, that named *Ring* as an integral part of the rating manipulations."

Fluellen, a Bellaire, Texas, policeman, swore that he had been contacted in September 1976 by manager Chris Cline, who was also the agent for Anthony House, Hilbert Stevenson, and his own son Biff Cline—all tournament fighters with falsified records. Fluellen said Cline promised him a national ranking in *Ring* and a place in the tournament if he, Fluellen, accepted Cline as his manager for the duration of the USBC. Since Fluellen had retired from boxing a year earlier and had never been ranked when he was active, the offer seemed absurd. But shortly thereafter, King invited Fluellen to enter the tournament, and the fighter agreed to accept Cline as his manager. Without having had a fight, Fluellen was listed as the tenth-ranked U.S. junior middleweight in the January 1977 *Ring*. Fluellen then called the magazine and spoke to Ort. "Mr. Ort asked me how many times I had fought in 1976, and I told him I hadn't fought . . . ." Fluellen said in his affidavit. "Not long after talking to Mr. Ort, Mr. Cline told me I would be ranked third the following month." He was.

Fuellen also said that "Mr. Cline informed me that the 1977 edition of the *Ring Record Book* would list two fights that took place in 1976 in Mexico. I did not fight in 1976." But the two fights were listed, as Cline promised, and in March, John Ort gave "Ike Fluellen" an honorable mention in *Ring*'s "Progress Award of the Year" feature.

But while Cline phoned Fluellen repeatedly to check on his condition, Cline was never able to give him a fighting date. Finally Fluellen called Jeff Ruhe, the assistant to ABC sports president Roone Arledge, and learned that he, Fluellen, was not in the tournament after all. Ruhe then convinced Fluellen to sign an affidavit on the Cline offer.

ABC disclosed that at least 11 fighters in the tournament were credited in the 1977 edition of *Ring Record Book* with fights that never took place. Among the more outrageous inaccuracies was a draw listed for March 26, 1976, between Hilbert Stevenson and Anthony House. Since Stevenson was a welterweight and House a lightweight, it is unlikely they would have been allowed in a ring together anywhere. And they had not been. Under Stevenson's name the *Ring Record Book* lists Wilkes-Barre, North Carolina, as the site of the fight, but under House's name the bout was in Winston-Salem, North Carolina.

Both House and Stevenson were handled by Chris Cline, who had long been accused of secretly giving John Ort a piece of his fighters in exchange for preferential treatment in the *Ring Record Book* and U.S. rankings, which Ort compiled. Ort heatedly denied the charges and offered to take a lie detector test.

I asked Ort if he could explain the overwhelming weight of evidence mounting against him. "It's not our fault if they sent us false records," said Ort, who then looked over at Loubet and asked, "is it?"

For support, Ort pointed to Michigan manager Hank Grooms, who claimed his secretary had mistakenly sent *Ring* erroneous records for all four of his fighters still in the tournament. Ort did not mention, however, that three other Grooms fighters had received credit in the *Record Book* for nonexistent victories, or that from September 1976 to March 1977 only one issue of *Ring* had not carried a feature story on a member of Grooms's stable.

I asked Ort how so many fighters who were unranked by *Ring* had qualified for the tournament. "I made up a supplementary list of five fighters in each weight class for ABC," he said, "and the fighters were picked from that."

"And ABC went along with those unranked selections of yours?"

"They did until today."

I asked Loubet if he was backing Ort. Loubet stood up as he said, "Maybe it's my Boy Scout training, but I don't believe in hitting a man when he's down. Especially when nothing's been proved. Yes, I do give John my unequivocal support—unless someone comes forward who can prove something against him."

Loubet—who for years had been warned by knowledgeable boxing people about Ort's questionable rating practices—walked me to the door and asked me in a tremulous voice: "What do you think will happen?"

"It'll be tough for a while, but I think you'll weather it," I lied.

"I hope so," he said.

I took a cab to King's town house to see what Braverman and Flood had to say about the tournament's suspension. But the "Boxing Department" sign had been peeled off the door and the secretary said coldly: "Mr. Braverman and Mr. Flood are no longer with us." King said he had fired them because "they were not acting in the best interest of the sport we all love."

Don King is the consummate salesman. He will sell you your own dreams on his terms. He had little trouble tapping James Aloysius Farley, Jr., as commissioner for his tournament, and he appeared on the face of it to be the perfect choice. Farley had a prominent name—his father was a former Democratic National chairman and Postmaster General—and the son himself was the former president of the Central State Bank and of Rheingold Breweries. Farley had style—ruggedly good-looking, easygoing backslapper—and he had the perfect credentials as chairman of the New York State Athletic Commission.

But professional opinion was divided on *why* Farley took the position. Some said he was just naïve and really didn't know a damned thing about boxing or the King setup. Others said he accepted the post because King—who continually claimed his influence reached all the way to the Carter White House—had convinced him that by establishing himself as the commissioner for the first national tournament, he would become the logical choice as the first federal boxing commissioner.

Every time I saw Farley on the scene as a boxing commissioner, I was struck by his blatant incompetence. He couldn't answer simple questions about tournament pairings. At the March weigh-in in San Antonio, when I asked him why Jesse Burnett, a light heavyweight who was scheduled to fight, wasn't present, Farley shrugged and said, "I don't know." Later, when Burnett still hadn't shown, I asked Farley if Burnett's opponent would advance into the semifinals. Farley said, "I'll find out." The commissioner didn't know the rules of his own tournament, which stated that a fighter whose opponent did not appear at the weigh-in automatically advanced to the next round. Actually, no rules had been distributed to either Farley or the so-called tournament rules committee. The only regulations for the tournament were in the DKP contracts with the fighters, which they signed, returned to King . . . and never saw again, according to the boxers I talked to.

When the tournament found itself publicly tainted after LeDoux and Weldon spoke out, Farley launched an "investigation." In San Antonio I overheard him and Loubet grilling fighters at the weigh-in. They asked each fighter three questions: "Who's your manager? How long has he been your manager? Any problems with your manager?" Some fighters faltered, but all of them passed the 20-second inquisition.

At an April 18 press conference, New York Governor Hugh Carey expressed outrage that Farley, acting as USBC overseer, had accepted airfare and lodgings for matches out of the state. It seemed as though New York had a moonlighting boxing commissioner. Farley's defense corroborated that suspicion: "I did it on weekends and I wasn't paid a cent for it. Sure I was paid for expenses." Farley was also concerned about allegations of wrongdoing: "Everybody is overreacting . . . I'm sure the tournament can go on. I don't think there's that much wrong with it."

Under fire in the press, Farley suspended himself as New York

State Athletic Commissioner on April 24. Since Farley's salary was being paid by the New York taxpayers, he deserved to be fired outright for simple negligence. While Farley was in Texas working for Don King on the evening of April 1, the New York State Athletic Commission approved a card at Sunnyside Gardens in Queens, New York, that included: a main-event fighter from Massachusetts with a 1–6 record who was billed as a boxer from Puerto Rico. A lightweight with 16 consecutive losses. A featherweight with 17 consecutive losses. Someone who fought under the name of Leo Randolph (who had been KO'd 21 times in compiling a 2–25 record)—even though he had been knocked out as "L. C. Mack" the night before in Bergen, New Jersey. The N.Y. State Commission's rules require that a fighter be suspended for 30 days after he has been knocked out.

Three days after it suspended the tournament, ABC announced the hiring of Michael Armstrong, former counsel for the Knapp Commission, which had exposed police corruption in New York City, to head its investigation.

I walked into the waiting room of Don King's town house on April 27 and heard from behind the former "Boxing Department" doors the promoter's angry, high-pitched voice. He used language that could not possibly have been sent by even a wrathful God: "Them freaking cock-roosters ain't got nothing on us. Only way they can get to us is by splitting us up, and I ain't gonna let that happen. All they got us on is that LeDoux decision." Al Braverman's voice announced, "We didn't fix no fights." Then I heard King, Braverman, and Paddy Flood agree they would all do better hanging together.

The next morning King announced that *his* "investigation" of his consultants had revealed nothing; the two were reinstated and the "Boxing Department" sign went back up on the door.

King vigorously defended himself throughout the spring and attempted to divert attention from his actions by arguing that he was being prejudged and villified in the press because he was black. The Reverend Jesse Jackson, national president of Operation PUSH, issued a very strong statement condemning "the endless vitriolic attacks . . . on brother King." Percy Sutton, a black mayoral candidate in New York City, embraced King warmly at a press conference. A group of respected black publishers issued a statement that found "the white press conspiring to discredit Don King in the boxing world, and therefore restore white promoters to the control of boxing." Muhammad Ali said, "They're out to get the coon, and I ain't gonna let it happen."

Now Don King was unleashing something a lot more destructive than a scandal-ridden boxing tournament. He was tapping a cultural history of racism that was still a distasteful reality in the lives of most Americans, black or white. A charge of racism from Don King was something I could not dismiss, when I recalled a long talk I had with a very sad, very bitter black man in Easton, Pennsylvania, named Earnee Butler.

Butler was the former manager of Larry Holmes, the Fourth-ranked American heavyweight and the favorite to win the USBC. You may have seen a half-page photograph of Holmes in a May 31, 1976, *Sports Illustrated* article on promising heavyweights. Holmes was in a victory pose after a fight, his trainer, Rich Giachetti, on one side, Don King, on the other. Their story did not mention that Butler had been eased out as Holmes's manager before the USBC was sold to ABC.

"I picked the kid off the street when he was 17, 18 years old. Taught him everything," Butler told me in early April. "Bringing him along slow, the right way. Then, just when he's ready to be something, Giachetti shows up and tells him Don King is interested in promoting his career. But he's got to sign with them. There's no way to keep a kid then. They tell me that I'll go along with them since I developed him. But when it came down to it, they didn't take me. Now he's making the big money in the phony tournament, and I'm still here in Easton teaching kids to fight."

On the day the tournament was suspended, the featured match was to have been the heavyweight semifinal between Holmes and Stan Ward. Ward's lawyer has since said that Ward, too, was under contract to King for a percentage of every purse. There was no way Don King could have lost the first USBC heavyweight finalist.

I had devoted almost four months to trying to discover the specific evils of the tournament, the "sins of commission," as my old ethics professor used to call them. But the bamboozle could not have gone as far as it had if the boxing press had covered their beat professionally. If some reporters had been curious about the selection of tournament fighters and checked records in back copies of *Ring.* Or, if they had spent a little more time in the gyms and investigated some of the leads provided by managers and fighters who had been excluded from this "open" tournament. The "sins of omission" had allowed the King operation to skip right along.

With the exception of Malcolm "Flash" Gordon, who publishes a boxing newsletter for insiders, *Tonight's Boxing Program*, there was nothing critical of the tournament in the New York press before LeDoux sounded off in mid-February. Even after *The Village Voice* on March 28 raised more serious questions about the tournament, there was little press criticism. It wasn't until after ABC suspended the tournament on April 16 that many of the New York reporters who had ignored the story attacked King and ABC.

Nowhere was moral indignation and self-rightousness greater than in the antiseptic hallways and executive offices at ABC. The press had castigated the network sports department for its association with the scandal, whereas ABC claimed to have been its chief victim.

One evening in early May over cocktails at New York's Hotel Dorset, Jim Spence briefed me on the network's position. Spence is ABC-TV's vice-president in charge of Sports Program Planning and the man who negotiated the tournament idea with King back in February 1976. "If you check," Spence said, "you'll discover that we took every possible precaution to keep the tournament clean. When problems did come up, it was ABC that brought them into the open. There's not a piece of evidence that hasn't been uncovered first by ABC." Roone Arledge, Spence's boss, had issued a similar statement.

"You know what gets me?" Spence said. "Putting Roone's picture in the paper between the likes of Braverman and King. Making all those comparisons with the movie *Network*. Hell, this is no *Network*. No one could have acted more responsibly than we have in this."

Nevertheless, soon after it suspended the tournament, ABC released the fact that, only hours before the first-round bouts on January 16, Roone Arledge had King, Ort, and Farley sign affidavits attesting that the USBC was legitimate and that the fighters' ratings were honest. So ABC itself had been suspicious of its show even before it opened.

I told Spence that, in light of those affidavits: "It looks funny now that you went ahead and did business with people you didn't fully trust."

"There was nothing we could prove at the time," Spence snapped. "Just rumors. Looking back is always easy. Monday morning quarterbacking."

I asked him about the general quality of the fighters ABC had got for the tournament, particularly the large number of fighters not ranked in the top ten. "Of course we wanted quality," Spence said, "but we just wanted to get the tournament off the ground this year. We were resigned to lesser fighters."

This seemed a very soft explanation. The purse money, especially for fighters below the heavyweight class, was so attractive that most good American boxers would certainly have given a truly "open" U.S. tournament a shot.

Finally I asked Spence: "If fighters qualified for the tournament on the basis of rankings, why then did they have to pay an agent's booking fee?"

"When we heard about the practice," Spence said, "we told King to stop it."

"When was that?"

"After LeDoux."

"Did you order King to return the fees that had been collected?"

"No, we didn't do that."

Before the results of any of the various investigations had been made public, ABC president Fred Pierce announced, "The role of ABC Sports in this situation under the leadership of Roone Arledge has been exemplary." And on May 1, Pierce named Arledge president of network Sports and News.

Every ABC executive I spoke to said Roone Arledge was most admired for his forthrightness. "He doesn't back away," said Irwin Brodsky, ABC Sports publicity man. "He takes personal responsibility for all sports decisions, the good and the bad."

Yet all of my efforts to interview Arledge were thwarted. Brodsky told me all I had to do to get an interview with Arledge was send him a letter stating my intentions and citing my writing credentials. I did. The letter did not work. Then I tried the phone. In the next two months, although several other sports writers talked with him, my 15 phone calls went unanswered and unreturned by Arledge.

There was, to my way of thinking, a murky quality in the moral stance at ABC. Its sports officials had bought something that may not have been wholly pure—why else the last-minute affidavits?—but that was doing very well in the ratings and had a promising future as a yearly national, and perhaps even international spectacle. Much of what had been done to "clean up the act" could also be interpreted as self-protection. "If it's at all possible," Spence said, "we'd like to do this thing next year. It's still too good a concept to lose."

The questionable activities of King and his colleagues have affected almost everyone connected with the sport. Of course, *Ring*'s reputation has been destroyed, and Commissioner Farley has resigned. More significantly, many small-time fighters and managers who are the fiber and lifeblood of the sport have been deprived of the bouts, purses, and TV exposure they deserve.

Not only has ABC cut back its boxing programming, but in late April CBS suspended its boxing shows in order to investigate and reappraise its handling of the sport. It cleared itself and was back on the air in three weeks. Another boxing tournament, the Don Elbaum-Hank Schwartz-produced "World Television Championships," which had been seen over many independent outlets, went off the air shortly after the USBC was suspended.

The King boxing empire appeared to be in serious trouble. Having jeopardized his relationship with ABC, King will no longer find it easy to attract and control the boxing flesh he's been peddling. ABC tried to withdraw from the King-promoted Ali-Evangelista fiasco on May 16. When King held the network to the contract, ABC televised a disclaimer before the fight showing the curious procedure the WBA and WBC used to rank Evangelista as high as tenth in the world. Earlier that week CBS dropped plans to televise a fight featuring WBC world lightweight champion Esteban DeJesus, whose contract King had assigned to Connie Harper—Don King's secretary. The CBS withdrawal resulted in the fight's "indefinite" postponement.

There were reports of defections among fighters important to King. Foreman had retired, and Ali had not been as vocal in his support of King.

Meanwhile, the investigations continue. The Baltimore Grand Jury, the FBI, the IRS, and the United States Justice Department were all searching for evidence of malfeasance, conspiracy, tax evasion, fraud, perjury, or extortion.

But such charges are never easy to prove. And if nothing *illegal* is established, King may still be very much in business.

Though more wary now, the networks still hunger for major fights and attractive fighters. If King can supply what they want, even his questionable ethics probably won't scare them away.

But the networks are unwilling and clearly unable to regulate the sport. With little sentiment in Congress for a federal commission, boxing's best hopes for the future reside with the courageous, fiercely independent managers and fighters like Tony and Mike Ayala. They let it be known that they could not accede to any control by the King organization, and Mike never got to fight in the USBC. Mike Ayala could easily have won the featherweight championship in the tournament, and in so doing would have earned $45,500 for three fights. Other fighters in the tournament sold their independence and gave up a chunk of their purse, but the Ayalas refused to.

Yet boxers who go the independent route travel a hard road. In order to get fights, they are often forced to take on anyone. On May 18 Mike Ayala went in against hard-hitting Rodolpho Martinez, the former world bantamweight champion. Ayala was TKO'd in the seventh. His purse came to less than $7,000.

Tony Ayala was philosophical about the defeat, saying, "Sometimes you learn more losing to very good fighters than by winning against pushovers."

I told Tony that since I'd last spoken to him, Braverman and Flood had said they had got in touch with him about Mike fighting in next year's USBC.

"They *never* talked to me," Tony said in disgust. "I never heard from them by phone, letter, or smoke signal—nothing. They're full of shit."

"Tony, if Don King does run a tournament next year, would you let Mike fight in it?" I asked.

"Let me put it this way," Tony Ayala said, pausing and choosing his words carefully. "Would you trust your little girl with a rapist?"

HORSE RACING

SEATTLE SLEW WANTED TO RUN

By Neil Milbert

From the Chicago Tribune
Copyright, ©, 1977, Chicago Tribune

Fulfilling his manifest destiny with power and glory, Seattle Slew was canonized as the first unbeaten Triple Crown winner in history this overcast Saturday afternoon.

He performed no miracles in winning the hundred and ninth running of the Belmont Stakes, but, as always, his conduct was flawless.

Seattle Slew simply refused to do anything wrong—and that has been the story of his racing life.

In the closing strides, jockey Jean Cruguet stood in the saddle and waved his arms in exultation. The Frenchman knew Seattle Slew's seven opponents didn't have a prayer.

At the wire, a distance of four lengths separated Seattle Slew from his nearest pursuer, Run Dusty Run, finishing in the money for the sixteenth time in his 17-racer career.

Racetrackers refer to Run Dusty Run as "an honest horse" because of that, and indeed he is. However, there is a vast difference between honesty and sanctity, one not measured in lengths or seconds.

It's a case of heart and soul.

Seattle Slew proved he had the heart to go the Belmont's grueling mile and a half. And something deep down told him that this day was his.

"We knew he was going to run," said Billy Turner, his 37-year-old trainer. "I could see that grim determination in his eyes this morning. I asked our exercise rider, Mike Kennedy, if we dared to gallop him and Mike said: 'I don't think so—he wants to run.'

"So, I decided we'd just jog him to the Belmont."

At 4:47, that pent-up potency unleashed itself before 70,229 on-lookers.

Breaking from the No. 5 post position, Seattle Slew shot to his left and seized the lead while remaining slightly off the rail.

Spirit Level, an inexperienced colt bearing the same blue and white Meadow Stable silks that adorned the last Triple Crown winner, Secretariat, in 1973, mounted the first challenge going into the first turn.

But this son of 1964 Belmont winner Quadrangle was making only a token gesture at upholding his stable and family traditions. That became obvious when Run Dusty Run, unhurried early, scurried between Seattle Slew and Spirit Level soon after entering the back-stretch.

The competition was keen, and Spirit Level couldn't cope.

Seattle Slew raced head and head with Run Dusty Run briefly. Then came another burst of speed, and Run Dusty Run was unable to match strides.

Shortly afterward Run Dusty Run was found wanting and the stretch-running Sanhedrin took his shot, blasting into second with a half-mile to go .

But Cruguet and Seattle Slew had spurned the temptation to do some speeding down the backstretch, and the horse had an abundance of energy in reserve.

Neither Sanhedrin's move nor the fact that Seattle Slew was being asked to run a quarter-mile farther than he had ever gone disquieted Cruguet's composure.

"Relaxation was the key," the jockey said. "I knew if I could make him relax, we'd have no trouble. The outside horse [Spirit Level] tried to run with me early so I had to go a little faster than I wanted to. But not too fast, I know I was all right.

"With about three-eighths of a mile to go I gave him his head and asked him to run a little more. He just pulled away. In the stretch I looked to make sure. He was going so beautifully, I knew nobody was going to catch him."

The Slew coasted under the wire in 2:29⅗. Though the time was nowhere near Secretariat's record 2:24, the threat of defeat was non-existent.

As was the case in his previous eight races, Seattle Slew didn't do everything. Winning—not time—is the only thing that puts him on a pedestal above the seven earlier Triple Crown winners.

The victory was the ninth in a row for the invincible one who is owned by Karen and Mickey Taylor and Dr. Jim and Sally Hill.

"All we wanted to do is keep Slew sound," said Mickey, acting as the spokesman for the quartet. "Billy Turner deserved all the credit for training him the way he has and Jean Cruguet for riding him the way he has. It's just a pleasure for us to be associated with people of their ability."

In addition to being the first undefeated Triple Crown winner, Seattle Slew is the first Triple Crown winner sold at auction. He was acquired at the Fasig-Tipton yearling sale in Lexington, Kentucky, for $17,500.

Sir Barton, the first Triple Crown winner in 1919, was sold privately. The other eight were bred by the stables that raced them.

Saturday's $109,080 share of the gross purse of $181,800 gives the son of Bold Reasoning-My Charmer by Poker a lifetime bankroll of $717,720. And his estimated worth—projected at $10 million going into the Belmont—probably has risen to $15 million.

For the $2 bettor, meanwhile, Seattle Slew's worth was translated into win, place, and show prices of $2.80, $2.60, and $2.20.

Run Dusty Run, who kept going after Sanhedrin faltered in the stretch, regained second and returned $3.20 and $2.40. Sanhedrin, two lengths behind the place horse, paid $2.60 to show bettors.

The track was labeled "muddy" for the Belmont following two days of rain.

"Yes, the track had me a little worried," said Turner. "I knew they were going to send early speed at us and I thought on a heavy track that could be a little bit of a problem.

"But when I saw them let him go a half mile in 48 seconds I knew it was over. I felt like a coach on the sideline and seeing a super athlete perform."

"He's the greatest horse that ever was," said Karen Taylor seconds after Seattle Slew carried her yellow and black colors to the winner's circle.

That statement is still open to conjecture. However, when Secretariat (1973), Citation (1948), Whirlaway (1941), War Admiral (1937), Omaha (1935), Gallant Fox (1930), and Sir Barton (1919) won the Triple Crown, they all had tasted the vinegar of defeat.

BASEBALL

FOUL PLAY FOR FOUL BALLS

By Jeff Meyers

From the St. Louis Post-Dispatch
Copyright, ©, 1977, St. Louis Post-Dispatch

Ever since I attended my first baseball game I have wanted to catch a foul ball. Not that I collected things—the ball probably would have wound up in the corner of a drawer beneath piles of old underwear. But a foul ball seemed to have some special meaning. It was a magical souvenir, a rare gift that somehow managed to reach your hand and nobody else's. I wanted one, but it never came my way.

A foul ball came John Santoro's way recently. He and his family were visiting Busch Stadium to watch the Cardinals play. Santoro, a burly machinist from Springfield, Illinois, was talking to one of his youngsters when the people around began to stir excitedly. A foul ball off the bat of Ken Reitz was heading toward Santoro like Haley's Comet. He stuck up his right hand just in time, caught the ball but couldn't hold on. It dropped into his lap. He wasn't spiritually prepared for what happened next.

"Before I knew what was going on," he said, "at least three or four guys behind me, and I think some women too, were grabbing at my crotch. It was awful. They weren't exactly being gentle. You can't imagine what it feels like to have five or six hands poking around down there."

Santoro kept the ball and his health, too, but not everybody is as lucky. When it comes to foul balls, a normal, peace-loving citizen can turn into a whacked-out maniac. He can be dangerous to himself and those around him. A foul ball in his (or her—women can be as equally nuts as men) vicinity can touch off a vicious display of scratching, stomping, clawing, and biting.

And vengeance. "A couple of years ago," said Busch Stadium chief usher Wayne Zeugin, "a guy reached over a lady and got a foul ball.

Well, she accused him of being fresh. They bantered back and forth for a few innings, and then he must have said something to really get her mad. She bought a couple of beers and threw them at him. But he ducked and she doused the guy behind him."

Despite the hazards involved, I decided to get serious about foul balls. Marty Hendin, the Redbirds' assistant public relations person, helped me determine the best locations in the stadium. We figured out that most fouls were hit down the right-field line behind the bullpen. So the other night, armed with my trusty Willie (Puddinhead) Jones antique glove, I ventured to Busch Stadium intent on making a leaping one-hand grab of a foul ball, although I would have gladly strong-armed one away from a small child.

My biggest mistake was lack of research. For future reference, I now know that pitchers are the biggest factors involved in selecting your seats in the stands. If a hard-throwing right hander is on the mound, most foul balls will wind up behind the visitors' dugout or bullpen —on the left-field side. The opposite applies when left handers pitch.

On the night I took my glove to the park, both pitchers were righties, the lineups were loaded with left handers, and the majority of foul balls flew into the left-field stands. While most fans were watching the action, I charted the foul balls: Eight were hit in the stands behind the plate, nine behind the visitors' dugout, seven into the left-field stands, and only five came anywhere close to me.

I wasn't the only person upset at the unfortunate turn of events. Mike Gibson came all the way from Sedalia to catch a foul ball. At 32 years of age, he seemed a bit too old to be sitting in the stands with a glove on. "I'm not wearing it to keep my hand warm," he assured me. "I've caught two foul balls—one hit by Stan Musial when I was a kid, the other by Pete Rose a couple of years ago. I love the excitement."

Indeed, foul balls can turn a dull game into a thriller. Kids are serious about taking home a baseball. Most of them wear their gloves, sit on the edge of their seats, and join the adults in screaming as a towering foul ball descends on them like a V-2 rocket. Landing among empty seats or rebounding crazily, it is pursued with reckless abandon by people who put a cowhide memento ahead of their safety or the safety of others.

Last year, an overweight man was sitting in the loge section at Busch Stadium. He reached over the railing in a desperate attempt to catch a foul ball, lost his balance, and plummeted 12 feet to the stands below. Fortunately, neither he nor anyone he splattered was injured.

"Last Saturday, a ball was hit into an area between two sections of stands," said Don Thompson, who guards the Cardinals' bullpen. "Some guy jumped over the side and his belt got caught on this hook. He was suspended in midair—his feet couldn't reach the ground and his hands couldn't reach the top of the stands. His friends finally had to unhook him."

Thompson and the other guards have seen many strange things that say a lot about human nature. There was a priest who jumped up to catch a foul ball and lost his pants. The old man who stands in the left-field corner waiting for foul balls. The guy who arrives early during batting practice and collects foul balls in a brown paper bag. Businessmen who gladly accept a shredded $200 suit in a successful fight for a foul ball.

"I even saw a father hold his kid over the rail by the seat of his pants so he could get a foul grounder," Thompson said.

Catcher Ted Simmons heard a story about a fan in Detroit. He was drinking a beer when a ball jumped off a player's bat and whistled right at his head. Flustered, the man juggled his beer, then finally decided to hold the cup in his mouth. He threw up his hand, caught the ball, and pitched over backward, nearly drowning as the beer poured down his throat.

It should be mentioned that a foul ball off the bat of the New York Mets' Steve Henderson nearly found me the other night. Henderson, a right-handed hitter, sliced a John Denny fastball about two rows behind me to my left. I had never been that close to a genuine foul ball. Unlike many of the people around me, I didn't freeze. I leaped to my feet and chose a course that would have brought my Willie (Puddinhead) Jones glove and the ball together at the same instant. But I stopped in my tracks.

"Ay, dat's my foot yer steppin' on, buster," grunted a guy who could have won a Conrad Dobler look-alike contest.

When I returned to my seat empty-handed, a 10-year-old kid sitting next to me said, "That's OK. You probably would have dropped it anyway."

OUTDOORS

FAR AFIELD, FAR FROM HOME

By Monty Montgomery

From Recreation (Boston Globe Sunday Magazine)
Copyright, ©, 1977, The Boston Globe
Courtesy of The Boston Globe

The nonresident hunter, heading north on 81, leaves the familiar behind on the outskirts of Oklahoma City. Oke City is ordinary America, airport, Kiwanis, Chamber of Commerce, suburbs, helicopter traffic reports, just one more of the cities of the Plains. He is driving to Enid, at the approximate geographical center of the United States of America to kill the American bird for the American holiday.

The American turkey is of three kinds: frozen, with a built-in red plastic meat thermometer that pops up when the bird is done; fresh-killed, which means that a bird of extremely dubious intelligence, given to such things as drowning in its water pan and smothering to death in a bizarre game of pile-on that turkeys are wont to play, has been hung, bled, scalded, plucked, beheaded, drawn, chilled, and delivered; and the wild turkey. The nonresident intends to eliminate the middleman, to deal directly with the turkey.

Highway 81: Qwik-Stop, Pumper-Up & Save, Food & Fuel, BarBQ & Beer, Self-Serv, See Indian City USA, EXXON-Diesel, Bunks & Showers, Stag Beer, Green River, Ordinance Enforced, Cimarron River, Two Storm Shelters (Is it Tornado Season? He scans the horizon for the funnel cloud). The road is lined with the bright green fields of winter wheat, just sprouted. On the skyline, oil well pumps rock up and down like automated dinosaurs. In the distance, in every direction, round concrete grain elevators poke up over the rolling hills. He wonders what he is doing amid so much alien grain.

The wild turkey can be hunted in 20-odd states, including Vermont. It cannot be hunted in Massachusetts, where some 350 years ago, to celebrate the first harvest, "the captain did allow four men to go fowling" in order to put out a little spread for assorted Pilgrims and Indians. It is extremely doubtful that John Alden, Squanto, Myles Standish, and so forth sat down that day to a fricassee of turkey. They've been digging through the garbage dumps of Plimoth Plantation for several years and they've found innumerable duck and goose bones, deer bones, but they've yet to find a genuine, certified, Wild Turkey Bone. Antique American hunting skills consisted mostly of loading up something resembling a small cannon with powder and scrap metal and sneaking up to the edge of a pond and hammering at whatever birds were sitting on the water. Ducks, which have the habit of waking up to a brand-new world every morning, lend themselves to Pilgrim hunting methods. Turkeys, if there were any, would have had the eyesight of an eagle and the temperament of a scalded cat. Turning four amateur woodsmen loose for one day to hunt turkeys makes about as much sense as putting Boy Scouts on the Vice Squad.

Of all the states where one is allowed to execute turkeys, the nonresident has chosen Oklahoma for the simplest of reasons. The best turkey hunter he has ever seen lives in Enid. He has never seen the turkey hunter actually kill a turkey, but he saw him hunt turkeys, once, in Vermont. The nonresident never saw Theodore S. Williams hit a home run, but he did, once, see him strike out three times in a row.

Mr. Williams, as many remember, was a more frightening hitter while striking out than most men are while hitting home runs. It was the awful intensity, the habit of taking a stance and holding it, disdaining to step out of the box, the attitude of the bat, the utter concentration of the man as he watched the pitcher, the long look after the third strike that said "I'll get you next time, you SOB."

The Oklahoman is that kind of a hunter. It is a personal quality unrelated to the success or failure of a day, and it can be seen in the moment of striking out.

The nonresident checks into the Mid-West Motel. The lady studies the reservation card. "You that fellow from Boston that's goin' huntin' with that Bland?" He says yes. "That Bland, he's the huntingest man. He's the best." The nonresident feels some of the glory rub off on him. The auspices are good.

It is necessary to eat, then to sleep. The turkey hunt will begin with a two-hour drive to Waynoka, west along the Cherokee Strip toward the Panhandle. He drives to Martin's Steak House and eats the small T-bone. The small T-bone is apparently the one that laps over the plate on only three sides. All through dinner, a woman plays dinner music on a small Hammond. She plays recognizable tunes, but with the tremolo and viola da gamba stops pulled out. The sound is exactly like that created in the better sort of funeral homes, excepting only the melodies. He retires early, in a combination of postprandial and funeral depression. He is beginning to have some doubts about whether he should be so far from home.

He rises in the morning and finds breakfast along Highway 81, Grits & Gravy, Sausage & Biscuits. He drives to 1125 North Oakwood Road. The sign says Dwain & Stella Bland. He begins to think he is in the land of the ampersand, the ornate printer's plus symbol. It is brutally cold, by Oklahoma standards, just below freezing with a breeze. They drive through the night from Enid through Carrie and Carmen. In much of the Plains, some very hard country is named for wives and daughters. If you drive further west toward the Panhandle, you get to Sharon, May, and Laverne. No Shirley.

Dwain is taking him to Max Olson's place on the edge of the Cimarron River Valley. There were always turkeys there. Just upstream is Sheridan's Roost, where General Philip Sheridan, noted genocide, took visiting dignitaries for a little recreational turkey hunting. Recreational turkey hunting in the nineteenth century consisted of sneaking up on the birds before dawn, as they slept unsuspecting in the cottonwood trees, and when you could see them silhouetted against the eastern sky, you poured the lead to them.

He is not going to do any roost-shooting at Max Olson's ranch. That is about as highly regarded as recreational drinking at a Women's Christian Temperance Union convention. They are going to go down in Max Olson's crick bottom, scatter the birds off the roost trees, and watch where they go.

There are three ways to hunt turkeys in the fall. If you can scatter the birds out into the knee-high sagebrush on the sandhills, they will freeze, and you can walk them up and they will flush like pheasants out of the sage and you can shoot them in the air. This is considered to be sporting by visiting hunters who are under the impression that it makes a difference in the scheme of things whether the bird is shot in the air. Shooting birds in the air is a game created by British gentlemen. It doesn't make any difference at all to the birds.

After the birds are scattered, you can try to call one in by pretending to be another lost turkey. Turkeys are wary, but gregarious. The third way is to ambush them. In both the latter cases, the hunter intends to shoot the bird on the ground. He will shoot it in the head, at close range. This is because he is more interested in eating an American bird on the American holiday than he is in pretending that he is a British gentleman. The large number of lead pellets that are found in birds shot while flying do nothing to improve the edibility of a turkey. But the nonresident does not really have a choice about how he will fresh-kill a turkey. That is up to the turkey.

He must, however, make a very important choice. It is legal, in Oklahoma, to shoot one turkey of either sex. Shooting hen turkeys is legal in somewhat the same way that messy divorces are legal. It is possible, but gentlemen, real Americans, and good old boys don't shoot hens. Hens are next year's crop. Even amateur turkey hunters can tell the difference between gobblers and hens, if the birds are on the ground walking toward you. Young hens and young gobblers (called "Jakes") are about the same size, and the red wattles of the spring gobbler in breeding season are barely noticeable. But the gobbler has a dark breast, almost black, and shiny, while the hen's breast is speckled gray and drab.

The nonresident wants to shoot his turkey on the ground, in the head, when he can see the dark breast. It is important to be more than legal, he wants to be right.

He follows Dwain Bland up a creek bottom. Chinaberry and cottonwood trees make leafless patterns against the dawn stars. Dark shapes in the trees are squirrel nests, loose oblong clusters of dried leaves. Down toward the Cimarron, the first coyote of the morning howls, and then the pack joins in, and the end of the night is filled with the hunting song of the pack.

The next tree with dark shapes on the bare branches is Max Olson's little ol' cottonwood roost tree. Against the false dawn the nonresident sees turkeys. There are at least 10 birds in the tree, high enough to show against the sky, and there are more obscured by the black background of the sides far side of the draw. He is looking at more turkeys than he has seen in six years of chasing them around Vermont and Pennsylvania. He thinks of Philip Sheridan a hundred years earlier, taking a foraging party up to the big roost on the Cimarron. It would be very easy to end an ordinary turkey hunt with a barrage into the cottonwood.

The turkeys hear the hunters, and a nervous *"put-put-put"* starts in the trees. In a moment, the air is filled with turkeys flying out of the big cottonwood and a dozen other trees. Thirty, maybe 40, turkeys, wings whistling in the still dawn air, fly out of the trees. He can hear them thump down on the ground, hear their great, hard three-toed feet pound along the sand bottom and through the sagebrush. The first step is accomplished. The turkeys are scattered.

It is 5:30 A.M. and the nonresident is about to spend the longest 11 hours of his life. For the first hour, he hunkers down in the chilled creek bottom, listening to turkeys, listening to Bland call turkeys. The call is the "flock call," the noise the birds make after they are scattered as they try to regroup. The *"put-put"* of alarm is the "Halt, who goes there?" The noise Bland is making, called a ki-ki-run, is the functional equivalent of the password, the reassuring "It's just us turkeys, y'all." It does not work. There are too many real turkeys down in the draw, and the scattered singles work themselves back into a flock, ignoring him. One of the three ways to fresh-kill your own turkey is a bust.

Around 7:30, they give up trying to call, and start working on the turkeys that are up in the sagebrush and sand burr-covered sandhills. The sagebrush is about two feet high, and the wild turkeys move through it head up, peering for miles across the rolling sandhills. Until 3:30 in the afternoon, the nonresident alternately walks, then runs, then crawls, up most of the sandhills on Max Olson's little ol' ranch. Anyone who thinks Oklahoma is flat is not a turkey hunter.

Four times during the day they catch the turkeys out in the open sagebrush. The turkeys freeze, invisible, and then explode underfoot, flushing like grouse against the blue sky. The nonresident has an arrangement with Bland. Bland will pick out the gobbler. Call the shot. Nonresident does not trust himself to avoid shooting a hen. Four times things go wrong. Only hens flush. One gobbler and four hens flush, but the gobbler is out of range. Two gobblers and two hens flush, and the nonresident is out of gun range. Then a single gobbler, 20 sandhills later, flushes. Bland tells him to shoot. He misses, wildly, from all possible excuses: short of breath, sweat in his eyes, surprise, disbelief in the flying speed of a turkey. Whatever. He is not disappointed, only embarrassed. He did not want to shoot a turkey in the air. He is intent on not spoiling the meat with a charge of shot.

The nonresident has few hunting skills, but excellent hearing. Most good hunters are slightly deaf from an excess of gunning. He is not that experienced. All day he has been the first to hear a turkey, and the last to see one. That is the difference between a natural gift and acquired skill.

The last hunt of the day begins. Bland, crawling through the sagebrush, has spotted part of the scattered flock of turkeys. They are picking their way through a baled hayfield, gleaning seed and small insects in the stubble.

The nonresident drops down on his belly, dragging his shotgun backward through the sand burrs, and crawls to the fence line at the edge of the field. The turkeys are grazing downhill toward the fence. There are turkey tracks everywhere in the dusty soil. They have found the birds, and they are lying along the edge of the route of march. It is a fair drove of turkeys in the hayfield. The field, viewed from belly-height, is a series of gentle rolls and drops. The turkeys graze toward the nonresident. Sometimes 20 birds are in view, sometimes none as they graze down into the low ground, then heads reappear, then bodies. The birds have come a quarter of a mile in 30 minutes.

Bland signals that he is going to leave. He will crawl away and move down one edge of the field. If the turkeys try to come out of the field before they get to the nonresident, Bland will make a small noise, perhaps show himself, to keep them headed south toward the ambush. He crawls over and whispers in the nonresident's ear: "Stay down. Pick out the biggest, blackest one. And remember, the first birds will be hens. They're always out in front."

He is alone now. The turkeys are within a hundred yards. Sand burrs are working their way through his camouflage jacket and pants, into his chest. The camouflage hat is pulled low, his face is blackened with streaks of camouflage paint. He remembers the paint, then, and wonders how much has sweated off. Bland had painted his face in the morning. It reminded him of grammar school plays, when he had turned his face up and had it painted by the teacher. The same helpless feeling as someone turned you into someone else with makeup. He wonders exactly who it is that is lying by the barbed-wire fence, waiting to kill a turkey. It is probably himself.

And the turkeys have disappeared. He raises his head for a better look, keeping it behind a small tumbleweed caught in the bottom strand of the fence. He had not noticed that there was another depression in the field right in front of the fence. He can hear the turkeys chattering, but they are out of sight, down in the swale. He realizes, for the first time, that if the turkeys walk directly toward him he will not see their heads until they are 20 feet, 25 at the most, away. If the hens are in front, they will be looking down at the hunter before the first gobbler walks up over the rise. He starts to shake a little.

Turkey heads appear in front of him. They are only 20 feet away. He looks up at them, through his dust-covered eyeglasses, just under his eyebrows, his face pressed in the sand. Four hens, gray headed, gray necked. They bend and peck and step toward him, grey-flecked breasts appear over the hay stubble. Another head, behind them, red flecks on the featherless jowls. A gobbler. He now realizes he is looking at the feet of the hens. If they are looking at him, they are looking down at him. The gobbler moves, and the black and glossy breast is visible. The nonresident pushes the safety on his shotgun from off to on. The movement of his right forefinger or the soft click alerts one of the hens, and she starts a wary "*put-put*." He is very glad to be alone. If there were two people, they would have to decide when to shoot, there would be a nudge, or a whisper. He looks one last time. He can see the four hens, the gobbler, and now several more turkey heads coming up over the rise. He aims the shotgun six inches over the head of the gobbler. At 20 feet, the normal spread of the shotgun pellets is no more than two inches, but always, in all shotguns, a few pellets spray outside the pattern, they are called fliers. It would be very easy to miss the turkey with the main pattern. He is counting on the fliers. The turkey is, in fact, too close.

Curiously, he did not hear the gun go off, or feel it. He remembers only that the air was filled with noise and flying turkeys, and somehow, without knowing how, he was on the other side of the high, four-stranded, barbed-wire fence. He does not think he climbed over it. He may have jumped over it, or just crawled through on his belly.

All of the turkeys but one are gone. The one turkey is lying breast down, wings spread, on the hay stubble. He turns it over, and the breast is very black. He stoops, and feels through the warm feathers. There is no red plastic built-in meat thermometer, just a short bunch of fibrous feathers hidden inside the glossy breast feathers. It is the beard of a male turkey.

The nonresident stood in the hayfield, quite alone. It was near sunset, and the first coyote of the evening began to howl, down toward the Cimarron. He looked up at the blue sky, and watched another flock of sandhill cranes drifting south on the wind. He could hear them, a loud rolling warble, calling to each other in the Oklahoma sky. There was no one there but him, himself and the fresh-killed turkey. It was time to go home.

TENNIS

BRITISH GLOW: WADE WINS WIMBLEDON

By Barry Lorge

From The Washington Post
Copyright, ©, 1977, The Washington Post

Virginia Wade, fulfilling a quest for what she resolutely refused to consider the impossible dream, today won the women's singles title in the Wimbledon tennis championships.

The first Englishwoman to win here since Ann Jones in 1969, Wade accepted the gold championship plate from Queen Elizabeth II amid an outpouring of patriotic sentiment at Center Court after beating Betty Stove, 4–6, 6–3, 6–1, in a match that, unfortunately, had little of the majesty of the occasion.

Wade, 31, who had never gone beyond the semifinals in 15 previous Wimbledons, won nine of the last 10 games in a contest that was more interesting for its emotion, psychology, and stately setting than for any memorable shotmaking.

The tennis was spotty at best, terrible at its worst. Ultimately, Wade was simply more purposeful and self-controlled than the 32-year-old Stove, who was in a big final for the first time.

At the end, when a Wade forehand return of serve forced the last low volleying error from the 6-foot-1, 160-pound Dutchwoman, the crowd of 15,000 erupted.

They gave what was by the standards of British reserve an unbridled display of affection for the new champion, who has always had a regal bearing but seemed destined by her own self-destructive temperament never to reign as queen of Wimbledon.

It took a couple of minutes after the final shot for the applause and cheering to die down enough for umpire Harry Collins to announce, "Ladies and gentlemen, the score was 4–6, 6–3, 6–1." The name of the victor he judged, correctly, to be superfluous.

As the queen made her way to the court where, on a round table draped with a Union Jack, the trophy lay for presentation, the duchess of Kent waved enthusiastically to Wade from the royal box.

Having put on an orchid cardigan to protect herself against the swirling breeze, Wade curtsied, chatted briefly with the queen, and then accepted the plate and a silver salver to commemorate the queen's jubilee. Then she held her prizes aloft for the gang of photographers who scrambled for position behind a restraining rope.

In the stands, delighted spectators waved flags and broke into a spontaneous, moving chorus of "For She's a Jolly Good Fellow." Hundreds of people had queued for two days outside the All England Lawn Tennis and Croquet Club to buy tickets, and they wanted "Our Ginny" to know that all her past failures were forgiven, if not forgotten.

"I don't think it was by any means the best match there has been this Wimbledon, but the atmosphere was just sensational," Wade said later, summing things up nicely.

"It was so friendly, and the duchess of Kent waving to me and saying, 'Well done,' and the singing. I mean, have you ever seen that before with an English crowd?"

Any words of wisdom the queen may have had got lost in the commotion, but that did not detract from Wade's jubilation.

"I was so excited, the whole thing was like a fairy-tale situation, with everybody cheering for the queen and cheering for me," she said. "It was so noisy that all I heard was, 'Well played. It must be very hard work.' Honestly, the rest of what she said got drowned. But I didn't mind. It was just great to see her lips moving and talking to me.

"I said, 'Yes, it was hard work.' I don't think I was quite at my most imaginative when I spoke to her."

Wade played a completely different and much more passive game than she did in defeating defending champ Chris Evert, whom she correctly labeled "the biggest obstacle to my winning the tournament," in the semifinals Wednesday.

But although she was not nearly as impressive in the backcourt, letting Stove force the play and make the mistakes, as she was in pressing Evert ferociously with bold approaches and flashing net play, Wade successfully guarded against an emotional letdown.

Wade knows that Stove has, as she proved again today, nerves that are even more suspect than her own. She gets rattled and will make errors if given the opportunity.

"I was wanting to be more keyed up than relaxed today, and I think it's inevitable that you're going to be a little tense against Betty because she hits a couple of incredible shots and then she misses some, so you feel a little insecure," Wade said.

Stove, the first Dutch player ever in a Wimbledon singles final, covers the court in long, slow strides and pulverizes the ball. She is an extremely bright woman, fluent in four languages, but she seldom plays points long enough to reveal much in the way of sophisticated tactics. Hers is hit-or-miss tennis, more blunt than artistic, or even craftsmanlike.

"Her style put me off a little bit in the first set because I felt I wasn't even really sweating," said Wade.

Wade never did much with her serve, spinning more of them in at three-quarters pace than going for big ones. She was afraid of playing serve-and-volley tennis with a slasher, and followed few serves to the net.

Initially, she didn't hit out often off her ground strokes either, but later she decided to answer pace with pace. In the final set Stove crumbled, and there were not many shots with pace coming in the court to answer.

Wade got into the match about the middle of the second set, after blowing a 3–0 lead.

"By the third set, I had hit enough balls and I found out I could generate the rest from myself," she said.

Wade lost her serve to 2–3 in the first set, broke right back at love as Stove served the second of nine double faults to 0–40, then was herself broken at love for 4–5.

Stove double-faulted to break point again the next game, but served out the set and exhaled a huge sigh of relief. It was short-lived. She immediately lost the next three games and, after breaking back to 3–3, won only one more. The longer it went, the more ragged she became, especially on her swinging forehand volley.

As Wade moved inexorably toward victory, she told herself to pay attention and not think ahead, lest her now very possible dream evaporate. "The hardest thing of all," she said, "is to stop letting all these stray dreams come in, to just be basic."

Wade earned $23,220, compared with Stove's $12,040, and will undoubtedly reap rich commercial spin-offs. But she said convincingly that thoughts of finance never entered her mind in all the months she prepared.

"The things I was dreaming when I beat Chris the other day were, 'Won't it be exciting playing the final with the queen there. . . . Imagine holding up the trophy,' things like that. Those were the things that excited me.

"The other thing was just to be able to say afterward that I did it. Those were my dreams, and I felt I had to control them because even those were dangerous."

This is indeed a new Virginia Wade.

"I think I'm much more secure as a person than I used to be. You can tell, just by general behavior, who is feeling at rest with themselves and who isn't. I felt this week that I was by far the strongest person in the tournament, that I had more guts than anybody else, and that would hold me through.

"I had more incentive than ever before. I really wanted to prove that I deserved to be out there among the champions."

GENERAL

WHO ARE THOSE GUYS ANYWAY?

By Loel Schrader

From the Long Beach (Cal.) Independent Press-Telegram
Copyright, ©, 1977, Twin Coast Newspapers, Inc.

While generations have searched for the Treasure of Sierra Madre, the Maltese Falcon, and Noah's Ark, I've been obsessed with trying to find the Lost Picas.

Picas are not an Indian tribe that has faded from existence. They are units of measurement in the printing trade.

When I had my first by-line over a sports story more than 36 years ago, newspapers had columns 13 picas in width.

But Cameron's immutable Iron Law of Picas decrees that a pica should be lost every decade. Now we're down to nine picas per column.

Cynics in the newspaper business have charged that the shrinkage in newspaper columns is a result of sharp increases in the price of newsprint, that publishers are giving less for more because they want to improve their profit and loss statements.

You know, instead of All the News That's Fit to Print, it's All the News That Fits We Print.

As a disciple of Cameron's Iron Law of Picas, I prefer to believe that newspaper columns have been reduced in size for aesthetic purposes.

But Cameron's Law has created some problems, especially with baseball box scores.

When I was a kid, I used to pore over baseball box scores and follow the hits and misses of Joe DiMaggio, Ted Williams, Dom Dallessandro, Swish Nicholson, Frenchy Bordagaray, Phil Cavaretta, Tony Cuccinello, and Frankie Baumholtz.

Newspapers used to carry full last names in box scores.

But Cameron's Law has made it virtually impossible to do that nowadays for names any longer than six characters.

The Associated Press, which transmits box scores on a high-speed computer wire, accommodates newspapers with nine-pica columns by employing some ingenious abbreviations.

For instance, the National League now has such players as Rtmnd (Rettenmund), RVtne (Robert Valentine), Stnntt (Stennett), Strgll (Stargell), Krrign (Kerrigan), Cncpcn (Concepcion), Stnhse (Stanhouse), Brrghs (Burroughs), Hrrlsn (Harrelson), and Bnnstr (Bannister).

Only the Dodgers are real people with Lopes, Cey, Garvey, Yeager, Smith, Monday, and Baker.

The American League has Cmpnrs (Campaneris), Ystmki (Yastrzemski), Wckfss (Wockemfuss), Sngllen (Sanguillen), Nrdbrk (Nordbrook), DeCncs (DeCinces), Chmbls (Chambliss), and Whlfrd (Wohlford).

These abbreviations obviously are unsettling to ballplayers, who spend many years trying to make it to the Big Top, only to be buried as RVtne or Bnnstr or Cmpnrs or Ystmki in baseball box scores.

Can't you picture all the people in Carl Yastrzemski's hometown, wondering what happened to the kid who used to hit the tar out of the ball? And all the time he's been in the big leagues as Ystmki.

Cameron's Iron Law of Picas has caused all sorts of language barriers, too.

I went to Anaheim Stadium the other night, looking for Wckfss. As a precaution, I took along an Associated Press box-score puncher as an interpreter.

I wandered around the clubhouse until I ran into a guy who looked like a Wckfss.

"Are you Wckfss? I asked.

"Wt're yu, sme knd of nt?" the guy replied.

"What did he say?" I asked the Associated Press interpreter.

"He wants to know if you're some kind of nut?"

I could see we were off to a bad beginning.

"No, no," I protested. "I'm really looking for a guy named Wckfss."

"Gt yr btt ot of the clbhse," the player growled.

I turned to the Associated Press interpreter. "Did you make that out?"

"Sure," he replied, "but I don't think you want the full interpretation. He's telling you to leave, only in different words."

I was indignant. "Who does he think he is?"

The AP man turned and conversed briefly with the player in nine-pica language.

"He says he's DiMggo Wllms, a rookie just called up from Shreveport."

I sneered. "Well, tell him he can go to Tkrs to Evrs to Chce." And I stormed out.

No gd dm rki cn tlk to me lke tht.

HORSE RACING

RACING'S BOY WONDER

By Pete Axthelm

From Newsweek
Copyright, ©, 1977, by Newsweek, Inc.
All rights reserved. Reprinted by permission

The bettors have already passed judgment on 16-year-old Steve
Cauthen. Day after chilly day, horseplayers huddle at New York's
Aqueduct racetrack and in the city's off-track betting parlors to
plunge recklessly on every horse Cauthen rides. When Steve is aboard
a desperate 10-to-1 shot, his worshipful followers are sure to bet him
down to about 4 to 1. Coming from hard-bitten, unsentimental
New York gamblers, this is a strange and touching affirmation of
blind faith. It is also being justified with astounding regularity; in
just over two months on racing's major-league circuit, the sensational apprentice Cauthen has won nearly 100 races and set or tied
almost every one-day and one-week victory record in the sport.

On several overnight shuttles to racing's other lucrative winter
center, California's Santa Anita, Cauthen has captured another
grandstand of admirers. Back in his home state of Kentucky, he has
left many fans searching beyond his statistics for new superlatives
to describe their beloved, baby-faced Kentucky Kid. "You're going
up to see Steve's family in Walton?" one farm owner joked last
week in fashionable Lexington. "Just turn right off the interstate
and look for the spot where racing's savior was born."

Cauthen has indeed emerged as a kind of savior for a troubled
sport—a glamorous child star infusing new drama into what too often
seems a shapeless numbers game. At the same time, he has become a
true hero for all seasons and all sports. One need not tear up any
perfecta tickets or lose any photo finishes to appreciate this engaging
prodigy who is whipping and driving to the very top of a fiercely
competitive adult game.

The star in Cauthen was born only in the sense that he grew up small enough to look like a jockey and gifted enough to ride like one. Beyond that Steve was made, by his own discipline and determination as well as the counsel of his remarkable, horse-oriented parents and their friends. He was raised around horses on a modest farm in Walton and introduced to racing at rugged nearby tracks of northern Kentucky and southern Ohio—where horses and riders alike tend to be ill-tempered and unforgiving. The hard land that produced Cauthen lies about 60 very long miles north of Lexington —and light-years from the bustling track where he is now flourishing. But that land remains perhaps the best place from which to view the Cauthen phenomenon.

"Sure, it's amazing," Steve says of his success. "But it's not lucky. I never stop to think of how lucky I am, because luck has nothing to do with it." That matter-of-fact statement from New York could easily be understood last week at the Latonia track in Florence, Kentucky, where the racing surface has been an unusable block of ice most of the winter and the only kind of luck for horsemen has been bad. For the raw-boned, leathery men who were drinking thick black coffee in the track kitchen and waiting for the weather to break, talk of the local kid who became a star was a bright diversion.

"I've seen some terrible horses around here," said trainer Lonnie Abshire. "Mean, speed-crazy horses that would run off with the strongest riders you could put on them. Then Steve came along and galloped them and he could handle them with a shoestring."

"The things the rest of us had to learn over the years," added a former rider, "came to Steve by the time he was 13."

"If I could raise a kid like Steve Cauthen," concluded trainer Jim Sayler, "I'd have a dozen of them. Even if he had never ridden a race in his life, he'd stand out as the kind of kid every man dreams of having for a son."

Across the small stained table, a quiet man in a fur hat puffed on a long cigarette and smiled at the remarks. "I must admit," Tex Cauthen said proudly, "that when people ask about Steve getting a big head or a smart-aleck attitude, I say that he's never given me much reason to worry."

As such conversations are traded and embellished, the skinny kid with the perfect poise on horseback emerges as a multifaceted hero —a 95-pound blend of the riding mastery of a Bill Shoemaker, the incredible precocity of a miniature Paul Bunyan, and the level-headed acceptance of sudden fame that distinguished America's last teen-age sports superstar, the 16-year-old Chris Evert. In fact, there are striking similarities between the modest, close-knit families of Evert and Cauthen. But if young Chris's debut at Forest Hills was the embodiment of a million suburban teen-age dreams, the tale of Steve Cauthen has a more "country" theme.

Steve was just a year old when his mother, Myra, propped him on a horse in Oklahoma to pose for a snapshot. By the time he was two, he was actually riding ponies. "Folks are making a lot of that now," says Tex, "but it wasn't all that unusual where I came from, in southwest Texas. That was bad farming country but good ranch country, and just about every kid got on a horse as soon as he or she could. I remember a cousin down there who could ride a pony bareback on the dead run when she was five."

As it turned out, so could Steve. He was five when his parents settled in Walton, and within a few years the word had spread through the Latonia stable area that Tex Cauthen's little kid "looked damn good on a horse."

Tex Cauthen, now 44, is a blacksmith by trade, earning $27 for each horse he shoes at Latonia or River Downs in Cincinnati. But he is also a keen student of the crooked bones and nagging infirmities found on racehorses at that level, and trainers commonly seek his advice. An all-round horseman, Tex enjoys breeding and keeping a few horses at a time on his farm—which happens to be an ideal setting for the legend of young Steve.

The neat, plain wooden farmhouse is tucked back behind a bridge over the railroad tracks in the south end of Walton, and Cauthen's patch of land stretches for 40 acres behind the house. Half a dozen horses in their shaggy winter coats roamed the snow-covered pastures last week. Doug Cauthen, 13, and Kerry, 8, were caring for them as Steve had done before them. But the most revealing sight on the farm was the fencing. The posts were railroad ties that most men couldn't even lift. Tex, a small man whose strength shows only in his blacksmith's forearms, once dragged every one of them into place by himself.

"Tex will fool you like that about a lot of things," says Lonnie Abshire. "Take that easy gentle attitude of his—it might make some guys try to take advantage. Years ago I saw him tried. We stopped to make a phone call in a rough bar in Collinsville, Illinois, and while Tex was on the phone a drunk started yelling at him and grabbing him. Before I could make a move, the drunk was landing against the wall on the other side of the joint. It was the only fight that Tex ever had, as far as I know. But he showed me he can go."

Steve showed Abshire the same kind of spirit as he tagged along with his father on his stable rounds. Once Steve watched in fascination as Abshire tended to his best horse, a stallion named Slade. The horse was as menacing as he was fast. "Hey, Steve," Abshire kidded, "you got your riding boots on? Want to ride this dude?"

"Yup."

"Put the tack on him, boys. You sure you can do it, Steve?"

"Yup."

For a moment Abshire hesitated to go through with the gag. Throwing this shy youngster up onto a fiery stallion might not have been very funny at all. But Steve insisted, and proceeded to mount Slade and walk him several times around the barn. "The first time they came around the corner I could hardly believe it," says Lonnie. "Old Slade was snorting, baring his teeth, throwing his head around something fierce. And Steve was laughing." Steve was seven years old.

Similar small adventures piled up over the next half-dozen years, and each one seemed to add to the rapid education of a race rider. In school, Steve was an all-round athlete, playing baseball, basketball, and football despite his size. But his enthusiasm always peaked when he was showing ponies at the 4-H Club, breaking yearlings on neighboring farms, or otherwise staying close to horses. "Even when I was very young," he says, "I knew I didn't want to grow up like the other guys. I didn't like riding around in cars or going to movies. I didn't enjoy dances or listening to records. All the guys did was run in a pack. I got bored with them and bored with school."

Cauthen now keeps up with a high school correspondence course out of a reluctant sense of duty; when he was still in the Walton-Verona school, even while his mind was off with Slade or some other horse, he managed a B average. But in his racing lessons, there were only straight A's.

If a university ever tried to teach a graduate course in the elusive art of riding and understanding horses, it could begin with the life of Steve Cauthen—as directed by Tex. First Steve learned the basics of grooming and galloping mounts; then he delved eagerly into specialized fine points. One summer, for example, he did little but hang around the starting gate, asking questions of the assistant starters and noticing "which riders helped their horses get out of there and which ones never quite seemed to be tied on when the gates opened." At another point he became a regular in the clockers' stand, watching thousands of workouts until he felt he could judge precisely how fast each horse was moving. Some riders go through entire careers wishing that they had been blessed with the "clock in the head" that marks the great ones. At 14, Steve Cauthen didn't wish. Through those tedious hours with the clockers, he virtually installed a clock in his own head.

Steve put almost as much time into developing his physical skills. His parents often found him alone in their barn, leaning forward on a bale of hay and slashing it rhythmically as he practiced handling and switching his whip. "I'm pretty strong for my age and size," he says, "but strength doesn't have much to do with getting the most out of a horse. It's usually a matter of technique. And technique is a matter of studying and hard work."

"Steve and I talked a lot about two topics that a lot of modern riders don't study—pace and wind resistance," says Tex. "I can't say he knows pace so well that he always knows how fast he's going —but I think he's right 95 percent of the time. And to cut wind resistance, he developed that good low seat he has on a horse."

On the track today, the Teletimer on the infield tote board usually verifies Cauthen's acute sense of pace. An appreciation of his "seat" and balance requires more subtle observation—but the result is just as striking. Almost any time Cauthen and other jockeys drive their horses to the wire in a tight finish, the other heads and backs can be seen bobbing at least slightly as the riders whip or hand-ride their mounts. Yet somehow, in a style reminiscent of Shoemaker and very few others, Cauthen controls his reins and whip as well as the others, while his back remains parallel to the ground and his head stays icily still. As one Aqueduct regular puts it, "You could serve drinks on the kid's back at the eighth pole and not spill a drop before the wire."

Only a technicality stopped Cauthen from showing off that form earlier: Kentuckians knew he was ready to ride at 15, but a jockey must be 16 to be licensed. So Steve waited, checking in at trainer Sayler's barn at 5:30 each morning to breeze horses, then getting the stable help to drive him to high school at 8. Last May 1, the day that Angel Cordero was winning the Kentucky Derby aboard Bold Forbes, Cauthen turned 16. On May 12 at Churchill Downs, he rode his first race in a chase that would eventually take him past Cordero in the New York jockey standings.

"I'll never forget the fear I felt that day," says Myra, Steve's attractive, athletic mother. "Watching him from the grandstand, I kept saying, 'Why did I ever let him do this?' Steve didn't look too confident himself." Steve's mount, a 136-1 shot, finished far back— but the experience was soothing all around. "When he came to the paddock for his next race that day," she recalls, "he already walked and looked better. And I started to feel better too. Now I'm pretty much over worrying about him getting hurt."

Five days later, Steve won his first race—and soon he was winning regularly, first at River Downs, then in Chicago and back in Kentucky. "At some places," he says, "riders aren't making much money and they're fighting to put food on the table. So maybe they'll think about dropping you. I was in one race where I thought a guy was trying to put me over the rail. I didn't let him, and he didn't win anyway."

"Steve's too modest about that," says a horseman who was there. "Those old riders at River Downs made him prove his guts again and again. In one sense, those races proved him as a good rider more than all his New York wins, because those old jocks kept putting him in tight spots—and he never once panicked or jerked his mount out of there. Of course, he knew Tex was watching every move with his binoculars, and he would have heard about that kind of mistake later." Steve didn't hear about too many mistakes at River Downs: He set a record with 94 winners in the 56-day meeting.

In the midst of their midwestern campaign, Tex and Steve spent one day at Saratoga last August—to check the possibility of a daring venture into New York. Steve rode two slow horses that afternoon and lost, but he and Tex also met agent Lenny Goodman. It was a winning day.

If Cauthen seems a model rider, Goodman is a model jockey's agent. In other words, he smokes good cigars, wears cashmere coats, talks out of the side of his mouth—and seems to know just a little bit more about everything than anyone else on the racetrack. Ordinarily Goodman, the molder of several champions' careers, wouldn't have considered taking on a mere apprentice. But Goodman's once magnificent client Braulio Baeza, 36, was suffering through a nightmare season of injuries and severe depression; his absences were forcing Lenny to look to his own future. And when Goodman's eye caught Cauthen on those Saratoga losers, he bid without hesitation: "Anytime you can arrange a place for Steve to stay in New York, Mr. Cauthen, just call me."

This winter the Cauthens arranged for Steve to live with a trainer in New York, and Tex called Lenny. Within days, the special chemistry of a hot rider and a shrewd agent was at work. "You know," growls Goodman, "in New York you've always got to prove yourself. But a lot of people believe in me, and when I told them I had something special, they listened. The first winner I rode was Illiterate. That trainer believed—and I've won two stakes with the horse since. Soon they all believed."

Soon Goodman was enjoying the luxury of choosing among several top horses in most races. He is smart enough to pick good ones, and

Cauthen has made them look even better. "A good ride can't make a bad horse win," says Goodman. "But sometimes he can squeeze a win out of the third or fourth best horse in a race. And he should never get beat with the best horse." Following that rough formula, Steve has grabbed victories in bunches. He is only the sixth rider in New York history to ride six winners in one day, and unless a superior record is concealed under a rock at some bush track, his total of 23 victories in a week is the best ever in American racing.

"Jockeys don't go into slumps," adds Goodman. "Agents do. As long as I keep finding fast horses, there'll be no bad slump." In his flat, unblinking manner that acknowledges success but stops well short of cockiness, Cauthen tends to agree: "I don't think I've rode a bad race here."

In a cynical business that takes nothing for granted, there have already been questions about Cauthen's future. Because he seems immune to the temptations of the wine-women-and-song variety, only three problems could eventually stop him. In ascending order of danger, they are the loss of the five-pound weight allowance enjoyed by an apprentice's mounts, injury—and growth.

Many riders have faded after losing the five-pound "bug," but Cauthen is too far advanced to become one of them after his apprenticeship ends in May. One proof is that he is already sought after to ride and win stakes races—in which the weight allowance does not apply. Serious accidents have also wrecked careers by damaging not only a jockey's bones but his nerve. Steve has not yet had a bad spill. "I'm not concerned about that," says Tex Cauthen. "If you've got true heart, there are ways to show it. And Steve's shown me."

Finally there is the specter of growth. Steve's large hands are an asset now, helping to give him his marvelous rapport with his mounts; but along with his size-6 boots, they also hint that he may be destined to get bigger—perhaps so big that he will be unable to make the riding weight. Since 116 pounds is near the upper limit for jockeys, the 5-foot-1 Cauthen clearly has about 20 pounds and at least several years to work with. As for what happens after that, Tex Cauthen is fatalistic. "I know he'll take care of himself and ride as long as he can," Tex says. "And if he has to stop after five years or so, well, it will have been a good five years."

The next four will have to be spectacular to top this first dizzying season. But Steve still has much to look forward to. The commercial potential of a teen-age WASP hero has not been lost on Goodman, and Cauthen's riding forays to Santa Anita have also been designed to gain media exposure. "Can you imagine what this kid could do pushing cereal or milk?" Goodman exults. Then there is the Derby. Although this year's leading contenders have booked riders, Steve is likely to pick up some mount for the race that he first attended when he was three—the same age as the horses.

"I may be too extreme," Jim Sayler said at Latonia, "but I think what we've got in Steve is a human Secretariat—a once-in-a-lifetime thing." Down the road in Walton, in front of the drugstore on the three-block Main Street, some citizens put the Kentucky Kid in another context. After giving directions to the Cauthen farm, one old man turned to his friends. "Another tourist," he grumbled. "The way that kid is goin', this town's gonna be as crowded as Plains."

FOOTBALL

THREE SECONDS TO GO

By Maury White

From the Des Moines Sunday Register
Copyright, ©, 1977, Des Moines Register & Tribune Co.

Uwe von Schamann gave one of the most audacious performances this side of the nearest bullfighting ring Saturday, directly under the gaze of one of the maestros in the art of taunting, and it brought a 29–28 victory.

There were three seconds left in a weird and exciting struggle of national football powers and the home team, Ohio State, was doing what little it could to cling to a 28–26 lead over Oklahoma.

That tiny bit that could be done wasn't much. The Big Eight team had had to take a time-out to stop the clock so that von Schamann, a native of Berlin who has lived in this country five years, could try for his third field goal.

A stiff wind was at his back, and that's important. That wind had helped bring a freakish game in which Oklahoma took a 20–0 lead, then went into an offensive hiatus until Elvis Peacock scored with 14 minutes remaining.

Buckeye linebacker Tom Blinco ruined a two-point try but then, to the deep groans of a frantic crowd of 88,119, third largest ever here, von Schamann delivered an on-side kick touched by Ohio State's Ricardo Volley and recovered by Sooner safety Mike Babb.

During the time-out by his forces, von Schamann kept his helmet on and knelt a dozen yards away from teammates, obviously concentrating. It was a 41-yard try, or a piece of cake for a man who has done 70 in practice.

When it was time to go to work, the Big Ten team lined up against the Big Eight power, Coach Woody Hayes used psychology, calling for another time-out to let von Schamann stew two minutes longer.

"I knew I was getting too tense," said von Schamann, now of Fort Worth, "so I ran up and shook hands with some teammates, then I decided to lead cheers for the crowd."

As the chant of "Block that kick!" started dominating the stadium, von Schamann raised each hand high and helped wave the cadence. And when it came time, he drilled the field goal far and true.

"I knew it was straight," he said in a humid dressing room. "I threw up my hands and 20 million players jumped on my back. I almost suffocated.

"As far as I'm concerned, this could be the last game of my career and I'd be satisfied. No! No! I'm only a junior and not thinking of quitting. But I like this feeling."

So did all followers of the Big Red of the Midlands, who won despite not having Thomas Lott at quarterback since shortly after getting the 20–0 lead. That hurt. The Buckeyes lost Ron Gerald late in the game. That hurt, too.

"We lost a great quarterback and a great linebacker [Tom Cousineau] by injury. Still we were doing all right until that fumble," said Hayes, the veteran who once removed his suit coat at Iowa City and pretended he was a matador fighting the crowd.

The fumble of which he spoke was by quarterback Greg Castignola late in the final period. Tackle Dave Hudgens made the hit and linebacker Reggie Kinlaw made the recovery to set up the winning drive at the end.

"Those ball games last 60 minutes, don't they?" sighed Oklahoma Coach Barry Switzer, after his team had stayed unbeaten at 3–0 as Ohio State fell to 2–1.

It was the first meeting ever of the perennial powers, who don't meet again until 1983. The Buckeyes, slight favorites, went into the game ranked No. 4 in the Associated Press poll with the Sooners No. 3.

In two previous interconference meetings this year, the Big Ten team had defeated the Big Eight. Oklahoma is now 5–2 against the Big Ten for life and Ohio State is 11–3 vs. the Big Eight, mainly Missouri.

This one had secondary billing as for the No Pass Collegiate championship of The World and at half time the Sooners hadn't tried one and the Buckeyes hadn't completed one. Later, a few fell in friendly hands.

The hitting was brisk, the tension was tremendous and the main thing decided was that two strong teams can play a whale of a game.

It threatened to rain the whole day and did a little in midafternoon. Ray Griffin did all his playing at tailback and W. W. Hayes has uncovered a new blaster in 222-pound freshman fullback Joel Payton.

"He'll be a good one," says Woody, so you can presume that Payton has found his place.

The pattern of the game was unreal. For starters, with all the fumbles bouncing right, Oklahoma scored the first four times it had the ball and led, 20–0, before Ohio State had a first down.

It wasn't surprising that Ohio State gave up a touchdown the first time it ever saw the wishbone run the way it should be, but the script was exciting.

Lott, intending to hand off the ball to Peacock, dropped it on the turf. It was clearly visible bouncing, then bodies got in the way, then Peacock suddenly had it and streaked 33 yards for a touchdown.

If Lott wasn't whistled for a double dribble, that was good for six. And he wasn't. Shortly thereafter, George Cumby recovered a fumble on the 16 and Billy Simms tore 15 for another touchdown.

Von Schamann, who kept drawing "oohs" for kicking the ball out of the end zone, came up with a pair of field goals. At this point, the Sooners looked like sprinters playing against kids wearing snowshoes.

That changed. Oh, how that changed! When Rod Gerald and Co. got the wind and some decent field position, they uncorked Ron Springson for a 31-yard scoring run, recovered a fumble, and sent Gerald 19 to score.

Things perked up a bit, then the home team got ahead early in the third quarter by recovering a fumble by sub-quarterback Jay Jimerson, a freshman, and driving in to send Payton over from a yard out.

Vlade Janakievski kicked the point for a 21–20 lead, which grew to 28–20 after Kevin Dansler intercepted a pass and, of all things, Castignola threw a 19-yard scoring pass to Jimmy Moore to make it 28–20.

The rest has mostly been told. The third quarter soon ended. By mid-fourth quarter, Oklahoma had quit coughing up the ball on about every possession.

"I was proud of the defense. I gave a game ball to everyone who played on defense—and gave a ball and a kiss to Uwe," said Switzer.

"We played the best we've played this year. One of the keys was late in our drive to the final touchdown, when they jumped offside and gave us a first down."

Hayes was philosophical about that.

"You can figure several other plays were costly. I'm not going to single out one boy for that play," said Woody. "We let it get away by not cashing scoring opportunities in the second half."

"Oh, the hell with exciting," snapped Hayes. "I'd rather be drab as hell and win. I thought we had won."

But Oklahoma won. You can look it up.

GENERAL

THE FLESH LOTTERY

By Wells Twombly

From the San Francisco Examiner
Copyright, ©, 1977, San Francisco Examiner

Through the graciousness and mercy of some judge who probably never had the decency to go out and pay to see some defensive tackle gnaw on a quarterback's leg, like a prehistoric beast discovering some raw roots, they actually managed to get the annual selection of collegiate flesh started yesterday. That certainly gladdened the hearts of saloonkeepers everywhere, because nothing stimulates the sale of beer like continuous arguments and nothing touches off more disputes than the annual professional football league draft, which was almost postponed forever because of various lawsuits and legal decisions. Thanks to judicial wisdom, halfback Tony Dorsett can either sign with (a) the Dallas Cowboys, or (b) the Toronto Argonauts, or (c) pump gas for a year and then pledge his sacred honor to whomever he pleases.

Now that may not be totally accurate, but the new agreement between athlete and clubowner in the National Football League is something only Melvin Belli could explain to you. It stands somewhere between the penal servitude of the past and the Bolshevik Revolution. It's a lot of fun trying to figure the whole thing out, especially if you started in the jock-writing swindle back in 1957 when everything seemed so simple.

There was nothing to it then. You dragged your portable typewriter, the one your mother gave you on the birthday just before you committed matrimony, and you asked damned difficult questions. A sample: "What was the turning point in the game, Bronko?" And if Bronko Jones had finished his postgame stalk of bananas, he would look at you through beady eyes and declare—for immortality—

"I guess when we ran the bleeping score up to 56–3 . . . arrgh." That's all you had to know.

Nobody in your newspaper's front office expected you to be an expert on labor law or social conditions. All you had to be was reasonably knowledgeable about the rules of two or three major sports, the ones the public wanted to read about anyway. If you are keeping score, and you certainly haven't been, it is now two decades to the very date since your beloved correspondent first earned a dishonest dollar writing about the games grown men have stolen from children. It isn't much, but it obviously beats working. There's something to be said for that.

"Yes, indeed," says Wells Twombly, Jr., somewhat cynically but with a measure of perception, "my father graduated from college 20 years ago and immediately retired." He had his point, but the period of time spent idling on the turf is nowhere near the record. Consider what the abnormally wry Prescott Sullivan, who never will be forgotten in San Francisco, said upon his retirement.

"It kind of got to me," he observed. "I was 71 years old and I had to walk up to some sweaty kid who could have been my great-grandson and ask, 'How are you going to do in the Big Game?' That was it. I decided it was time to take it easy, just as if I hadn't been taking it easy all these years. Somehow, 53 years at the ball park seemed like enough self-indulgence."

Everything was fine in this racket until they started educating some of these lads at the ball yard. The first time one of them earned a legitimate degree from a college or paid attention in high school, the simplicity of the subject was shot to bloody shreds. You can give a person $60,000 a year and explain that they are overpaid when the club owner is worth $200 million a year. Democracy has made a smashing change in things. Consider what a fine lovable creature John Montefusco was until somebody explained to him that he was sitting on a fortune. So this 14-game loser for the San Francisco Giants was able to shake down Bob Lurie, the gentle-hearted owner, for a massive amount of money because he managed to win two more games than he lost. Oh, wow!

Then, of course, he became a racetrack habitué, too good for the common herd and far too cosmopolitan to make those wonderfully fresh predictions that made him so pleasant in the first place. That's the way of all flesh and he can be easily forgiven for letting money muddle his mind, because he certainly isn't the first one. Still, it kind of irritates the nervous system and makes the spirit become unsettled when there are high school flunkouts asking for more money than any doctor could get if he was two months away from finding a cure for cancer. At least Montefusco went to college.

At a seminar for those who think journalism is a decent profession, somebody asked how long one newspaperman had been at the ball park and what did it take to find such a job. The young man was told that it took a fine gift of fantasy, plus a degree in seven technical skills, none of which the writer possessed, or ever thought was necessary. It seems that loyalty is lost completely, and that was the uplifting character of sports. If a man gets an urge to call his player a "punk," which is no admirable phrase, well, that player can turn around and shatter the manager's cheekbone. That is even worse than the silly, thoughtless remark.

A few days ago a little girl came up and asked her father if he was a celebrity. The standard line was that he wasn't. He was just a guy who wrote about celebrity-types, a regular bum in paradise. Now the thinking has changed and he certainly hasn't become somebody big. He's as small as he was when he left the University of Connecticut in 1955 and went to work as sports editor of the mighty Willimantic *Daily Chronicle* (circulation 12,562). Out he goes to the ball park and off he treads to the golf course, etc. There were heroes then on May 4, 1957. There aren't any left, just a bunch of guys who aren't any bigger than a guy who pounds a typewriter, only more wealthy and greedy for more.

SOCCER

THE COSMOS DANCE TO THE TITLE

By Bill Dixon

From The Coos Bay (Ore.) World
Copyright, ©, 1977, Southwestern Oregon Publishing Co., The World

That Giorgio Chinaglia dances like Quinn Buckner is nothing more than coincidence.

What makes it important is that both men have danced—well, boogied down—at great moments in their athletic careers. Buckner did it in front of 10,000 people in Montreal as the United States Olympic basketball team reclaimed the gold medal in 1976.

Chinaglia did his arm pumping, foot stomping number in front of 35,548 mostly young soccer fans in the second half of the 1977 North American Soccer League Championship game at Portland, Oregon, Sunday.

The New York Cosmos' forward had just slipped between two Seattle Sounder backs and driven a header into the Sounder goal for the winning score.

The shot culminated a Cosmos drive to the title that proved tougher than most experts said it would be. It put a championship finish on the 22-year competitive career of Pele, the Brazilian star who at one time was the world's highest paid athlete and the man who brought big-time crowds to the NASL.

Pele was supposed to be the difference in a game the Cosmos were supposed to win by two goals. But it took a field-spanning performance by forwards Steve Hunt and two near-misses by the Sounders to finally do the Pacific Conference champions in.

Hunt assisted on Chinaglia's goal with a perfect cross and made an incredible steal from Sounder goalie Tony Chursky to score the other.

During the interludes when he wasn't scoring, Hunt harassed the Sounders on offense and defense with his speed. He undoubtedly ran further than anyone else on the field, making steals on one end and getting down to the other end fast enough to give the Cosmos' attack the edge it needed.

For his efforts, Hunt earned an extra $1,500 as the game's most valuable player. That comes in addition to whatever share the Cosmos vote each other from the $37,500 the team earned in winning. (Seattle got $22,500 for losing.)

Hunt didn't exactly come out of nowhere to do it—he had already set a new playoff record for assists during the current six-game series —but he did come out of a crowd of bigger names.

The Cosmos also had Chinaglia, last year's leading scorer and a record-breaking scorer in the playoffs; Franz Breckendauer, this year's league MVP; and Pele, the richest Brazilian killer bee and the league's most prolific ticket machine.

When it counted most, however, the one who emerged was Hunt. He did it first with 19:05 elapsed in the game.

Chursky had just made a diving stop of a shot by Hunt and was looking for someone to pass to. He turned his back on the 5-foot-8, 160-pound Briton and started to dribble the ball with his left hand. On the second bounce, Hunt drilled his feet into the ball, tripping Chursky and knocking the ball toward the goal 10 yards away.

Both men got up quickly, but Hunt won the race and rolled in the score as players from both teams looked on in amazement.

Hunt said later he didn't expect a mistake like the one Chursky made. "I scored 100 or more goals, but I never scored one like that," he said. "It was just an opportunistic thing."

Chursky was disconsolate after the goal and after the game. He kept his head averted from reporters' eyes in the Sounder locker room and spoke in a new whisper.

"Mel Machin was hollering to me," Chursky said of the incident before Hunt struck. "But I have a deaf left ear, and I guess it must have been turned to him. I didn't see Hunt."

Chursky said he had never given up a goal in that way before. When he was asked if the Hunt goal was the one in his career that upset him most, he turned to the reporter and said between tight lips, "What do you think?"

The Sounders came back just four minutes after Hunt's goal with the tying goal. Midfielder Micky Cave drew the Cosmos' defense to him at the top of the penalty area, then flipped a pass to the charging forward Tommy Ord on the right. Cosmos' goalie Shep Messing went after Ord, but slipped on the rock-hard Civic Stadium rug as Ord faked.

Ord blasted the ball into the net just under Messing's outstretched fingers. That meant a tie, but the Sounders felt they should have had a 2–1 lead by then.

With only seven minutes gone in the game, they had converted Jocky Scott's steal from Pele into a goal on a header by Cave. Cave had played a rebound off a shot by Scott perfectly, but a referee disallowed the score because of an offside violation.

"Jocky shot the ball from 30 yards out, and I don't see how we could have had anybody offside," Sounder defender Mike England said after the game. England was as important to the Sounders as Hunt was to the Cosmos, breaking up at least five Cosmos charges on goal and making life miserable for Pele with his aggressive tackles.

But he also made a crucial mistake that allowed Chinaglia's winning goal with less than 13 minutes left to play in the game.

Hunt brought the ball down the left side of the field and crossed into what looked like an impossible situation: Chingalia was standing between England and another Sounder defender. However, neither checked him. The result was a header that the out-of-position Chursky was powerless to stop.

Then to the dance.

The Sounders missed five shots at the tying goal in the final 12 minutes.

The closest belonged to midfielder Steve Buttle. With 7:18 to go, he nearly broke the left goalpost with a shot out of a crowd. But the ball refused to go in and did the same with 6:12 left when the Sounders got a break and a four-on-four situation.

Scott was wide left on that one, Dave Gillett was the same with 4:36 to go, and Jimmy Robertson missed a limp shot from way out at 1:50 to wrap up all Sounder hopes.

HORSE RACING

DERBY WEEK: PARADES, PARTIES, PRESSURE

By Jenny Kellner

From The Record (Bergen County, N.J.)
Reprinted from the Record, Bergen County, N.J.

They do their utmost here to keep visitors from champing at the bit during Derby Week. There are, among other things, daily parades, nightly parties, a steamboat race, square-dancing contests, a mini-marathon, etc., etc., etc.

But the Derby is the main topic of everyone's conversation even if all they'll see of the race Saturday is a cloud of dust down the stretch.

The Derby is on the news morning and night, and trainers are interviewed on the radio, as are owners, grooms, hot walkers, jockeys, exercise riders, and anybody connected in any way with the biggest thing other than country music to ever hit this section of the country. Tons of newsprint are devoted to its coverage.

As trainer Bill Turner said, apropos of absolutely nothing: "And the plot thickens . . ."

Turner's charge, the undefeated Seattle Slew, and owners Karen and Mickey Taylor receive the most intense scrutiny of any of the 16 horses and owners pointed toward the race. So far the Taylors have been bearing up remarkably well, but then, as Mickey put it: "If you can't have fun here, you might as well have your heart taken out."

A great many people are rooting for Seattle Slew, who is the decided overdog on the early line at odds of 1 to 5. Hundreds of cars bear bumper stickers that say "Seattle Slew," people wear T-shirts with what passes for his face on it, and a replay of his victory in the Flamingo drew oohs and ahs from a group of breeders and owners Tuesday night.

But somehow, it's more than the desire for another Triple Crown champion. Horses are easy to like—they do not punch out managers, talk back, or ask for exorbitant salaries. And ones who run well are the easiest to like. And then there is the aura around the people who work with Seattle Slew.

Turner doesn't have the sullen genius of Leroy Jolley, or the flamboyant emotionalism of Laz Barrera, who trained Foolish Pleasure and Bold Forbes, the last two Derby winners. Instead, his unflagging graciousness is punctuated by mischievous, almost gleeful Irish wit.

Karen Taylor retains the same warm charm she must have displayed as an airline stewardess; while Mickey, a logger who favors boots and blue jeans, dispensed coffee from the camper parked in front of the barn before the crowds swelled to circus size.

Even John Polsten, the groom, and Mike Kennedy, the exercise rider, are as friendly and helpful as Boy Scouts. "If you don't get to know and respect the people around the horse, you don't really know the horse," said Karen Taylor.

The most important person around the horse, of course, is Turner.

There is a tremendous pressure on the 37-year-old trainer from the press and other trainers. He works Seattle Slew too slowly. Too fast. Too much. Not enough.

"I'm glad I read the papers because I wouldn't know what was going on otherwise," said Turner with a wry smile. "Every morning I pick up the paper and it tells me what I'm going to do that day."

But the strain is beginning to show a bit, or maybe he's just tired of answering the same questions every day. His nervous habit of scrubbing his hands together has increased in intensity so that it seems sparks will fly from them. Tuesday, while chatting with Polsten, a cry of "loose horse" went up and every ounce of color in Turner's face vaporized until he ascertained it wasn't Slew. That's pressure.

Jolley knows about pressure. He's come to Churchill Downs with three Derby favorites, and just Foolish Pleasure won. "I'm having more fun this year," said the trainer of For the Moment, who won the Blue Grass Stakes. "But I'd still like to have Seattle Slew."

Turner, however, is quite determined to hang onto Slew. He worked in relative obscurity before picking up the Bold Reasoning colt, although he did train 1970 Derby winner Dust Commander as a two-year-old. "I was fired," he said simply. "It was a bitter pill to swallow, though."

A son of Dust Commander, Run Dusty Run, is one of Seattle Slew's main rivals. And trainer Smiley Adams said Seattle Slew is "no cinch" to win the Derby. "He's a nice horse, but he's not unbeatable. I'm not running for second, you can count on that." Run

Dusty Run has been second in his last three starts, the Louisiana Derby, the Calumet Purse, and the Blue Grass Stakes.

"So far Seattle Slew has had things his own way," said Adams. "He may not be able to have them his own way in the Derby."

Other trainers think a lot more of the favorite. "Take Seattle Slew out of the race and every horse looks the same," said Barrera, who trains Affiliate.

And while no one will be even remotely surprised if Slew wins the Derby, there are those who are not particularly bitter about conceding the victory to the Taylor outfit. "Listen, they've done a great job with that horse," said John Fulton, who trains Steve's Friend. "There's no one who deserves it more than they do."

And so, the plot thickens.

GOLF

NICKLAUS!

By Nick Seitz

From 1977 PGA Tour Annual
Copyright, ©, 1977, Cardinal Publishing Company

Jack Nicklaus smokes as much as two packs of cigarettes a day—but
he never lights up on the golf course. A fellow smoker asked Nicklaus
how he can abstain from smoking for half a day and longer. Replied
Nicklaus, "I don't think about it." Nicklaus epitomizes mental discipline more dramatically than any other athlete in any sport. His
willpower is so intense it is visible to the naked eye. We may expect
him any day now to *stare* a putt into the hole from 20 feet. Golf is
above all the thinking man's game, and Nicklaus is the thinking
man's golfer. It is the mental dimension that sets him apart, that
already has enabled him to set records for major championships won
and for career money. He will tell you so, and so will his opponents,
who consider him no less than the greatest golfer of all time. Frank
Beard, the full-time golfer and sometime journalist, recently picked
a tour all-star team. He liked Al Geiberger with the driver, Ray
Floyd with the fairway woods, Tom Weiskopf with the long irons.
Beard worked his way through a half-dozen other categories, and
nowhere was Nicklaus mentioned. "That must mean there is more to
golf than striking the ball," Beard concluded. "There is—the mental
side. Nicklaus is the best in this department. His ability to organize
himself and maintain his discipline, concentration, and composure
is unparalleled. I've never seen Jack select the wrong club, hit a
stupid shot, or lose his cool. If you put together a composite best
golfer—the best driver, best putter, and so on—Nicklaus could give
him two a side." The implication should not be that Nicklaus leaves
a great deal to be desired physically. His physique, coordination, and
game all are near-bionic. He is blessed with massive legs, the gener-
ators of his awesome power. "His thighs are 29 inches around," says

Dave Hill, "which just happens to be the size of my waist." Nicklaus is perhaps 15 yards shorter off the tee than he was five years ago but still can move the ball as far as he has to. His is an entirely resourceful power.

He can hit his irons higher than anyone else on this particular planet, which means he can land a long iron more softly—"as softly as a butterfly with sore feet," it has been said on the tour.

Further, Nicklaus is the strongest player in golf out of the rough. He can bludgeon the ball into the green from 180 yards away with his forceful upright swing when others can only chop the ball out short.

Nicklaus's hand-eye coordination is fully as impressive as his power. Try this little test on a friend. Have him put his hands out in front of him, palms facing, six inches apart. Hold a dollar bill just above the gap between his hands, let the dollar go and see if he can catch it. Nicklaus can snare the dollar nine times out of 10, a facility that could keep him in pocket money if he needed it.

His coordination shows in a disciplined putting stroke that makes him the best fast-greens putter in the world and also the best pressure putter. Who else could take the putter away from the ball as deliberately as Nicklaus? If you had to choose a man to try one putt for everything you own—house, car, swizzle-stick collection—you would have to pick Nicklaus.

He is virtually impervious to pressure, which brings us back to the mental capacity that makes Nicklaus No. 1. "People don't appreciate that he thinks his way around a golf course better than anybody else," says Hale Irwin.

A dozen contemporary players hit the ball at least as purely as Nicklaus. There may be better putters day in and day out. But no one approaches Nicklaus in mental discipline, and ultimately it's a mental game.

"I define concentration," says Nicklaus, "as the ability to make my body do what my mind wants it to do. When I'm able to think clearly what I want to do and then make my body do it, that's when I'm concentrating."

Nicklaus suffers lapses in concentration, of course—if only about as often as you and I inherit a million dollars or jump over the moon—but almost never is he careless. As a youngster he developed the ability to focus on every shot as if it were his last.

From the time he took up golf at 10 Nicklaus has hit every single practice shot as if it counted. Consider what that means over the course of 26 years and literally hundreds of thousands of practice balls. Every shot becomes important.

In practice rounds before a tournament, most pros will casually drop and hit a second ball if a first shot doesn't come off. Not Nicklaus. He knows you get only one try when the tournament starts, and everything he does is geared to winning the tournament. Taking every shot seriously is a way of life with him.

As a result, Nicklaus is much less susceptible to final-round pressure than his rivals. Because he has treated every shot with total respect for so long, his anxiety level doesn't go up in the home stretch of a tournament. His mind is clear to deal with one shot at a time.

Dr. David Morley, a psychiatrist who knows Nicklaus, marvels at the clocklike workings of his mind. "He has this tremendous ability to concentrate in conditions where most of our minds would be going a hundred ways at once," says Morley. "It has to be his greatest single asset. A primary factor is the continual application of intellect, rather than emotion, to the job confronting him. He controls every move to a very specific end. There are no false starts, no blank spots, no slipping into neutral gear. The clutch of his mind responds quickly without pause or hitch."

If Nicklaus hits the odd bad shot, he summarily analyzes what went wrong, files the information away, and puts the shot out of his mind. He doesn't let the bad shot discourage him or affect his handling of the next shot.

Says a graying veteran of the tour, "Imagine that the mind is a quart jar. Nicklaus makes sure the jar is always full of positive thoughts—intentions of hitting good shots. The rest of us tend to fill the jar at least halfway with negative thoughts. We're thinking what can go wrong with a shot rather than what should go right. His mind is so permeated with the task at hand, there's no room for negatives."

Tom Weiskopf tells the story of being teamed with Nicklaus during the 1975 Ryder Cup Matches and joking as Nicklaus lined up a 15-foot putt, "You've never missed one of those in your life, have you, Jack?"

Nicklaus's icy blue eyes drilled his friend, and Nicklaus said, "Not in my mind, I haven't."

Many of his rivals cannot believe how little Nicklaus practices. He will warm up for 20 or 30 minutes before a round. After a round, when he believes practice is most productive, he will return to the range if he wants to work on something in particular. I have seen him hit five balls, find what he wanted and go home.

"I don't beat balls for the sake of beating balls like so many guys out here," he says. The truth is he doesn't have to. The years of thoughtful practice, respecting every shot, have matured his swing and concentration to the point they need only minor tune-ups, not major overhauls.

An imposing by-product of Nicklaus's physical and mental ability is his almost unassailable self-confidence. "He believes he has an absolute and inalienable right to win," says a PGA Tour executive. "He has never really experienced failure, and he has no fear of losing— or winning." That consummate confidence, stopping just short of arrogance, has characterized all the great golfers, from Vardon to Jones to Hogan to Palmer to Nicklaus. They felt—had to feel—they could figure a way to win under any circumstances.

"Nicklaus is the only man out here who can have two or three bad holes, then promptly turn his day around with two or three birdies," says another leading money winner.

Never was Nicklaus's capacity for righting a sinking ship more emphatically evident than in the last round of the 1976 World Series of Golf. Going to the third tee Sunday, Nicklaus was three strokes ahead of the field and looking as if he could beat the field's best ball the rest of the way.

But Nicklaus bogeyed the third hole and then played the fourth like a man wearing a straightjacket. He took four to get down from behind the fourth green, made a double-bogey six and tumbled back into a tie for the lead with Japan's Takashi Murakami.

Most golfers, their game plans slipping away from them under fourth-round pressure, become cautious or angry. In either case they are in no state of mind to start a comeback. They have lost their mental discipline.

Nicklaus didn't miss a beat. He parred the fifth hole, hit a towering 4-iron approach shot three feet from the cup to birdie the sixth, nearly birdied the 215-yard seventh, and birdied the long eighth with a second shot that deserves its own paragraph.

Nicklaus's drive on the eighth disappeared deep into the left rough. He now faced a 190-yard shot into the wind from a downhill lie in thick grass. He took a 7-iron (that is not a typographical error) and played an incredible low, British-type shot that ran onto the green and almost went in the hole. Birdie three. End of tournament.

There are assorted other instances of Nicklaus rescuing a round that looked to have gone down in flames. In the first Jackie Gleason-Inverrary tournament he was paired with "Cigar Joe" Campbell and began his opening round double bogey, bogey, double bogey.

Said Nicklaus to Campbell, "Isn't this a *bleep* of a way to start a tournament? I'll probably end up blowing it by a shot." Which is exactly what he did.

"How's that for confidence?" asks Steve Reid, a Tournament

Players Division official who was playing the tour at the time. "It never crossed his mind that he was out of it. I'd have been looking for a phone booth."

When you're talking about Nicklaus's mental assets, you cannot leave out his competitiveness. His friends talk about him as the most competitive animal they know, whether he's playing the tour or playing a neighborhood pickup softball game.

Nicklaus exudes the killer instinct peculiar to sports immortals. The breakfast of champions is not cereal, it's your opposition.

One of my favorite writers, William Price Fox, points out that Nicklaus needs a new nickname. Fox says "The Golden Bear" doesn't work because bears are not essentially killers. In Mexico, he says, Nicklaus would be known as "El Tigre"—the tiger—which would be fitting because tigers are ruthless stalkers that annihilate their prey.

"In one of Sugar Ray Robinson's fights," writes Fox, "his second-round victim let out the sad lament, 'I never knew the ring could be that small.' Against a killer the ring is always that small. That's the way it should be. You feel your strength draining as the suspicion hardens into the ice-cold fact that you're not going to be admired for being there, but simply and humiliatingly manhandled and disposed of. This is what Dempsey and Louis and Jones and Hogan did in style for years. And it is what Nicklaus is doing today."

Happily for golf, Nicklaus's killer instinct comes garbed in exemplary deportment. The game is fortunate to have him as its hero. He does not complain, he does not show temper conspicuously, he does not try to take advantage of the rules, which he knows practically down to the last footnote.

Perhaps the most remarkable feature of Nicklaus's entire career is the quiet grace with which he endured, as a mere teen-ager at first, overweight and underexposed, the obscene taunting of fans who resented his displacing of Arnold Palmer as king of the golfing hill. Not once did Nicklaus respond in kind, not in public at any rate.

In later years his graciousness once was put to a test during the Westchester Classic. The weather was a steam bath—temperature 102 degrees, humidity close behind. By now trim and popular with a resolute diet, Nicklaus was sought out on the clubhouse porch by an exuberant fan carrying two beers, one in each hand. The fan embraced Nicklaus—and spilled both beers on him.

Inquired Nicklaus with cool evenness, "Why don't you have another beer?"

It is speculated that Nicklaus is hurting his golf career by running a varied business empire. He spends considerable time designing golf courses, for example, such as his Murifield Village masterpiece in Ohio.

My own opinion—free of charge—is that Nicklaus's other interests benefit his golf and finally will prolong his career. His is the sort of active mind that must have diversity or else he quickly becomes bored. His mentality is such that he can focus 100 percent on one activity—and only one at a time—but can shift that searing focus to a wholly different subject as readily as you can switch on a light.

Let me give you an example. I wrote a film script about Nicklaus's new Memorial Tournament. He wanted several additional points made about the golf course. The first chance I had to discuss the film with him was at the World Series of Golf. Nicklaus noticed me during his Saturday round, as he was moving into the lead, and said he'd see me afterward in the press tent.

He came into the tent, reviewed his round in shot-by-shot detail for the assembled writers, and on his way from the tent to the locker room went over the film with me. He had seen the 30-minute film only once, but he remembered every key picture and line, and he made his suggestions—point by lucid point—in five minutes. Then he left and went to a business meeting on another, unrelated matter. Don't tell me it hurts his golf. He ran away with the tournament.

"Bobby Jones had that same kind of mind," said golf impresario Fred Corcoran. "He could practice law in the morning and win the U.S. Open in the afternoon."

Deane Beman, the PGA Tour Commissioner, says, "The first few years he was on the tour, Jack let Mark McCormack handle his business interests, and Jack had no distractions. When Jack took over his own business affairs, he was so well organized he was able to pursue other fields with the same intensity he brings to golf. But remember that his mental discipline started with his golf game."

At the summit, golf always has been a game of the mind, a contest not so much against outside forces as against oneself. It is his superiority in the mental aspects that makes Jack Nicklaus clearly preeminent. As one of his fellow pros puts it, he plays best that six-inch course between the ears.

BASEBALL

THE TEN-MINUTE COLLAPSE

By Bill Conlin

From the Philadelphia Daily News
Copyright, ©, 1977, Philadelphia Daily News

Dusty Baker hit a tough chopper to third and Mike Schmidt pounced on the wicked short hop like a jaguar running down a rabbit.

That was one out in the top of the ninth, seven straight ground balls thrown by Gene Garber. And 63,719 fans were on their feet, a shrieking chorus which all afternoon had roared with the bloodlust of a Roman Coliseum mob rooting for the lion.

Rick Monday bounced out to Teddy Sizemore. The Vet throng was chanting "DEEEFENCE." Eight straight ground balls by Geno. Game three was history. One more out, Geno, baby, and this was a 5–3 Phillies' victory. The Dodgers had coughed up two eighth-inning runs to go with three the crowd and plate umpire Harry Wendelstedt had bled from starter Burt Hooton in the second.

The Dodgers were down to their suspect bench. Ancient Vic Davalillo hauled his well-traveled bones to the plate, more wrinkles on his leathery face than there are base hits left in his bat.

On deck was Manny Mota, 39 years old, one final straw for Tommy Lasorda to clutch at should Davalillo reach first base.

Thus began the shortest, most devastating nightmare in the history of a town steeped in an athletic tradition of flood, fire, and famine, a town where some seasons, even down seemed like a long way up.

A funeral dirge would be appropriate at this point, Beethoven's *Eroica*, perhaps, or a few choruses from *Lohengrin.*

You thought the *Titanic* went down fast!

The 1964 Collapse took 10 games. This one took 10 minutes. It was like watching the shambles of 1964 compressed into an elapsed-time film sequence.

With two outs, the Phillies met the enemy and it was them.

Davalillo legged out a superb bunt to Sizemore, as if that is the normal play for a 39-year-old man with just 48 at-bats after the Dodgers picked him up for late-season insurance.

"If he had hollered, 'Hey, I'm gonna lay one down,' we still couldn't have stopped it," first baseman Richie Helmer said after the incredible 6–5 loss. "It was just a perfect bunt, a great play on Vic's part."

Mota came up swinging for a home run. He hit one in the final regular-season game last Sunday, hadn't hit one before that since the 1972 season.

He fouled a pitch back, then fell behind 0–2 with a swing so lusty it almost dislodged his batting helmet.

"Two strikes I am trying to just protect the plate," Mota said over the joyous babble of the winner's clubhouse. "I'm not a power hitter, I try to hit line drives. He threw me an inside slider."

Mota jumped on the pitch like a Santo Domingo street urchin putting the touch on a well-heeled gringo tourist. "Thank you, señor, may God bless you for this gift."

The fly ball carried driving Greg Luzinski back toward the bullpen fence in left. There was enough controversy in this schizophrenic game to keep a Warren Commission busy for weeks and this was one chapter.

Luzinski leaped at the fence. The ball lodged briefly in the webbing of his glove, then jarred loose, hit the fence, and nestled back into Bull's grasp. Wouldn't it have been a much easier play for fleet-footed Jerry Martin, often Luzinski's defensive caddy?

"He was the third batter up in the ninth," Danny Ozark said, wearing the dazed look of a train-wreck survivor. "I wanted him in the lineup in case the game was tied."

Davalillo was being held at third when Luzinski threw to second. The ball skidded through Sizemore's legs. Davalillo scored and Mota huffed to third on the second baseman's error.

The inning reached a 10 on the Richter Scale of natural disasters when Davey Lopes roped a one-hop shot off the heel of Schmidt's glove, off his knee, deflecting to Larry Bowa at shortstop. Bowa made a brilliant pickup and gunned a strike to Hebner. First base umpire Bruce Froemming, double-clutched, then spread his hands palm down. Hebner shrieked and stamped. Ozark erupted from the dugout. The veins in Bowa's neck bulged like telephone cables.

"If he had called the play right both me and Hebner would have been thrown out," Ozark seethed in his office after a calm performance in the mass interview room. "He didn't know what the bleep to call it, so he called it safe. He was stunned by Bowa's throw, as far as

I'm concerned. He just anticipated Bowa couldn't make the throw. He's got his hands stuffed in his pockets half the bleeping time."

For the second time in the tense war, the unwavering eye of the TV replay cameras would show Lopes out by a narrow margin, just as they proved from two angles that Steve Garvey never touched the plate on Bob Boone's superb block in the second.

Garber unfurled a pick-off move that skidded past Hebner and Lopes jetted to second. "It was a sinker that exploded," Hebner said. "I should have got more body in front of it."

The Phillies fiery Götterdämmerung was complete when Bill Russell bounced a single up the middle.

Mike Garman, sixth Los Angeles pitcher on an afternoon of baffling selection by Lasorda, retired Bowa and Schmidt, then drilled Luzinski with a high, tight fastball.

Hebner bounced Garman's first pitch to Steve Garvey and the crowd stood in a collective silence reserved for the demise of a great matador in a jammed Plaza de Toros.

Death had come to the executioners. The Phillies had met the enemy and it was them.

BASKETBALL

A LEGEND OF THE CITY GAME

By Robert Lipsyte

From the New York Post
Copyright, ©, 1977, New York Post Corporation
Reprinted by permission of the New York Post

The Goat is in jail again, living on dreams, jelly sandwiches, and the respect he always gets from fellow prisoners. "I'm in here with kidnappers and murders and kingpings of dope, and they say to me, 'Hey, man you shouldn't be here, you're a superstar. A legend.'"

The Goat shakes his head and smiles, a sweet, snaggle-toothed smile. His muddy brown eyes stare through a dusty window in the Bronx House of Detention. He can see Yankee Stadium a few blocks north. His smile fades. "I'm worried about my tournament," he says. "It's important to a lot of kids. On every corner there's a good basketball player getting the same treatment I got, don't have no books, more wiser in the street than in school, family messed up, no one to talk to.

"Most of the people on the street say, 'Why should I get you over, I didn't get over.' I talk to these kids. Last year I helped get 36 into school out of the city. There are people who can do more for others than for themselves, and I'm one of them."

The Goat is 32, and he has been famous on the black streets and playgrounds of New York for almost 20 years. His name is Earl Manigault and his claim—"If I could have got help I could have been as bad as Kareem"—is no idle boast; though barely 6-feet-1, he was once considered a player of incredible potential.

But he never had self-discipline, an ego, a sense of responsibility. His nickname, from the playground mispronunciation of Manigault, seems to fit him. The Goat is seen as a beautiful fool, a dreamer, victim, screwed-up. A loser.

He slipped through Benjamin Franklin HS in Harlem and Laurinburg Prep in South Carolina, but he never won the college basketball scholarship he had been groomed for. He drifted into the dope world. He became a petty thief and drug dealer to support his heroin habit.

Even as a junkie he was an asphalt king. He became a legend, a cult figure in the ghetto. But he is also a symbol of the system's failure; millions of black youngsters are diverted into basketball so they won't raid Sutton Place or storm the medical schools.

In 1970 Pete Axthelm's splendid book, *The City Game*, gave Manigault a measure of fame beyond the ghetto. He was in Green Haven State Prison at the time, on a drug-related crime, and when he got out he was given a tryout by the professional Utah Stars. It was a publicity stunt for the Stars. Manigault was 26 and out of shape and was cut from the team.

But it extended his reputation, and filled him with new purpose. He returned to Harlem and organized the Goat tournament, actually a summer basketball league for some 800 youngsters in a playground on Amsterdam Avenue near Ninety-eighth Street.

That first season was funded by drug dealers and pimps. It was a success. Since then, the tournament has got money from the International Ladies Garment Workers Union, through an old supporter, Bayard Rustin.

Through it all, Manigault never connected with a steady job or business, and the city never came through with a recreational plan that might have used his fame and skills.

Four weeks ago, six men were arrested outside a Bronx apartment house, and police allegedly found guns and dope. One of the six was Goat, wearing gym shorts, a tournament T-shirt, and hand-me-down sneakers from Bill Bradley.

Manigault's bail was set at $10,000. He expected the black community to ransom him quickly, yet again. But many of his longtime backers evidently felt that Earl had blown one chance too many and the reaction was slow. Then his case was forgotten in the wake of the blackout.

"What keeps you going?" I asked in a jailhouse interview room. "The roof." He begins to smile again. "One hour a day, five days a week they let us up on the roof. They've got two baskets up there, we play full court, but it's small enough so I can get a rebound, turn and shoot a jumper.

"Sometimes I throw one down, feel so good I stop and laugh and shout, 'Damn!' On the sidelines they say, 'Cut it out, Goat.' They're telling me I don't have to show them, they know who I am."

GENERAL

WHEN A FIGHT BREAKS OUT IT DOESN'T ALWAYS PLAY WELL ON TV

By William Barry Furlong

From TV Guide
Copyright, ©, 1977, by Triangle Publications, Inc., Radnor, Pennsylvania
Reprinted with permission from TV Guide Magazine

The richest irony in the media today is that the most intriguing and popular sports event on TV is the one that the networks try hardest to keep off the screen.

The event is the fight. Not the formal boxing matches that adorn (and sometimes disgrace) the TV schedule, but the hockey, baseball, basketball, and even boxing brawls that *aren't* scheduled. It's hard to get a rating on unscheduled events, but it's clear that the fight, not the game results, captures the headlines the next day; and it is the fight, not the score, that is certain to appear on local newscasts across the country.

For the fans know that the fights are not only the most dramatic moments of the game, but sometimes the most meaningful and the most costly as well. Ironically, the player who gets hit is often the least damaged. Early this season, Kareem Abdul-Jabbar of the Los Angeles Lakers clobbered basketball pro Kent Benson of the Milwaukee Bucks when Benson wasn't looking. Benson went down like a sack of sand. He was out cold, but recovered quickly. Jabbar, on the other hand, suffered a broken hand and a $5,000 fine. He missed more than a dozen games.

In a similar incident last summer, slugger Mike Schmidt of the Philadelphia Phillies, after being beaned by Bruce Kison of the Pittsburgh Pirates, threw a punch at Kison. Kison's pride was hurt, but Schmidt broke a finger and lost some of his knack for hitting home runs. Both fights were seen on local television. The networks don't always do so well. Sometimes when there's a fight, they show it. But, on other occasions, especially on ABC's *Monday Night Football,* they demurely avoid the fisticuffs. Why should the networks try to keep them off the screen if the fights are so popular? There are several reasons.

Reason one: The fights arouse questions that the networks would just as soon everybody ignored. Boxer Scott LeDoux, for example, was infuriated when he suspected he'd been robbed of a decision over Johnny Boudreaux on one of the ABC-televised fights. His anger resulted in some scuffling in which Howard Cosell's hairpiece was knocked awry.

Whatever LeDoux's protest lacked in elegance, it made up for in effectiveness. It not only attracted headlines but also the FBI and a federal grand jury, because LeDoux alleged that Boudreaux was secretly owned by somebody in the fight-promoting camp. All this was embarrassing for ABC. At first, the network denied everything. Then it investigated everything. Then it dropped everything—including the boxing series. And all because of one fight it *didn't* want.

Baseball sidestepped a similar problem after a massive melee in Cleveland's Municipal Stadium three years ago. The fracas started when a number of fans jumped onto the field late in the game and tried to liberate the cap of a Texas Ranger outfielder. The outfielder objected, and the rest of the Rangers (including those on the bench) grabbed bats and began chasing after the fans. They caught some, and one fan was sent to the hospital.

What ensued was a memorable brawl and TV spectacular, and tapes of the scene were run over and over again on stations all across the country. Both baseball and TV executives burst out with the usual derogatory statements about the fans. But there was no discussion, on TV or within baseball, of the real cause of the free-for-all: The home team had promoted the game as one where the fan could get a beer for 10 cents. It was, in effect, an open invitation to the fans to come to the ball park for a cheap drunk. Not surprisingly, some fans accepted the invitation. *That* was the real cause of the brawl, but the baseball establishment wouldn't face the facts.

Reason two: Spontaneous fights are very hard for TV to cover. George Finkel, a producer of sports shows for NBC, remembers the time when Pete Rose of the Cincinnati Reds slid hard into Bud Harrelson of the New York Mets and touched off a big brawl during a 1973 National League playoff game. NBC's cameras caught almost everything—the battle of the players, the hysteria of the fans, the garbage-and-bottle-throwing from people in the left-field bleachers when Rose ventured to his outfield position. They missed only one thing: the start of the fight. In fact, for a few crucial moments, they didn't know the fight had started.

When Harrelson tagged second base to retire Rose and then threw to first base for the double play, "We went to first base with the ball," says Finkel. "So, we've got John Milner [the Mets' first baseman] on the air with the putout and we're starting to go to the commercial when we realize that all hell has broken loose." Finkel quickly switched an on-the-air camera that recorded Rose's dash to second base. It had recorded everything that happened at second base, including Rose's hard, spike-slashing slide and the start of the fight. "On the 'isolate' we had everything, from the start of the leadoff into the start of the fight," says Finkel. It was great, but lucky, television and it did not do much to convince the front-office types that unscheduled bloodlettings are easy to cover.

Reason three: Unscheduled fights embarrass TV as much by one extreme as by another. When Dave Forbes of the Boston Bruins expressed dissatisfaction—via his stick—with Henry Boucha of the Minnesota North Stars several years ago, the whole civilized world began agonizing over the quantity of blood being spilled in sports events. Women and editorial writers were appalled, children were sent out of the room, and prosecutors were aroused because of the inclination of some to seek reason at the end of a bludgeon. Dave Forbes was ultimately released after a jury was unable to decide the issue in criminal court in Minnesota, but the public and media reaction to the fight was so fierce that TV and the sports executives felt they had to do something about the violence. They looked for a way to replace it with something else. Not with nonviolence, but with dull violence.

The difficulty is that even when hockey fights are genuinely brisk, the telecast can be hurt by dullness. George Finkel recalls working a game between the Philadelphia Flyers and the Montreal Canadiens before the National Hockey League put in the rule penalizing players for rushing off the bench to join a fight. The fight started just before an intermission and it was a hard, bitter brawl—"even though," says Finkel, "it lasted only a short time. Both benches emptied and all the players joined in. After the fight, it took 20 minutes to clean the ice."

Then the players resumed hockey for a few seconds and trooped off for a 20-minute intermission. So, with the exception of those few seconds of action, NBC had 40 minutes of dead time on its network—40 minutes in which it lost viewers, sponsors and, as it turned out, further interest in telecasting hockey.

Another aspect of getting caught by one extreme or another was demonstrated by CBS during the last NBA basketball seaason. At best, CBS has a good many difficulties trying to keep these telecasts from being overwhelmingly dull. There are those who feel that pro basketball isn't a game so much as an affliction, that the points go on the scoreboard so fast you'd think it had developed a stutter and that the best way to watch is in absentia—wait until the first 200 or 250 points have been scored, then tune in for the last 10 seconds to see who wins. The willingness of many fans to do this, combined with ABC's programming (Superstars, the American Sportsman, Wide World of Sports, and occasionally the U.S. Boxing Championships), put a lot of ratings pressure on CBS.

Thus when a string of fights broke out in NBC games, it appeared that it couldn't do anything but help the ratings. Fans would be tempted to stick with a CBS telecast all the way through in the hopes of seeing not basketball, but a really good fight. Instead, it seemed to hurt. Two conflicting views emerged over the fights. One was that any fight on the CBS telecast was a sham that *had* to be staged to arouse interest in a ho-hum piece of programming. The other was that the fights were so genuine and destructive that CBS and the NBA were guilty of offering *violence* to the American people. Either way, TV was in the wrong. Finally, NBA commissioner Larry O'Brien stepped in to set things right. ". . . As far as violence is concerned, I will not tolerate it," he thundered. It was a bravura performance, for in one statement he banished the notion that NBA games were becoming violent for violence's sake and yet he seemed—by that denial—to be insisting that the fights were genuine.

In the end, TV is caught by the contradiction of the fights—their popularity with the viewers and the difficulties they offer the networks. Today, TV knows it can't promote the fights. It can't end them, either, and it can't pretend they're not there. All it can do is sob a little in the night, learn to live with the richest irony in the business—and make the most of the money it attracts.

BASKETBALL

THE ENJOYABLE CHESS GAME

By Maynard Eilers

From The Florida Times-Union (Jacksonville, Fla.)
Copyright, ©, 1977, The Florida Times-Union

The two generals, Al McGuire and Dean Smith, barked orders from the sidelines in rapid succession. For one, it was to be his last war, his final battle, his culminating victory.

"We played a chess game," said McGuire, the victor. "It was most enjoyable."

And so it was that the forces of Marquette outmaneuvered the forces of North Carolina, 67–59, in the NCAA championship skirmish Monday night at the Omni.

McGuire, the general—no, dictator—received the only injury, a sprained toe, when he kicked the scorers' table. And he cried on the way to the dressing room, not because of the pain but because of the pleasure and because this was his last walk to the dressing room before his retirement from coaching.

"I'm not ashamed of crying, I just don't like to do it in front of people," McGuire said in front of five reporters in an otherwise empty dressing quarters. "It seems like destiny, but I don't like those words because they sound like they come from sandlots and TV announcers.

"I thank my family and I thank God, even though I'm a hypocrite. I personally think Dean deserved it . . . not to take anything away from my players."

McGuire the general notwithstanding, it was his players who fought the war and won the battle. It was especially Butch Lee, named the tournament's outstanding player after scoring 19 points, and the victory also belongs to Warriors Bo Ellis and Jerome White-head, named to the all-tournament team along with freshman

Mike O'Koren and Walter Davis of North Carolina and Cedric Maxwell of UNC-Charlotte.

It was North Carolina's fabled four-corner offense which eventually led to its downfall after 15 straight victories, the nation's longest winning streak. With the Tar Heels, now 28–5, coming off a 39–27 half-time deficit with 14 of 16 points to tie the score at 41, the four-corner proved to only be a time-waster.

North Carolina wasted three minutes of precious time before missing with 9:45 to play, and then it was Marquette which snubbed the Tar Heels by using its own slowdown tactics. The only difference was that Marquette's worked.

From that point on, Marquette scored an amazing 16 of 17 free throws—also a North Carolina tactic in games past—and blew open the game with 43 seconds left, enough time for the tears to well in McGuire's eyes and the Marquette followers to wave their yellow pom-poms until the stuffings fell out.

"We psyched them out, kinda," said guard Jim Boylan, who was snubbed by Carolina when he wanted to transfer there. "I don't know many teams who would try a stall against them, especially after they had just tried it against us.

"They couldn't handle our man-to-man. Nobody could cover anybody else one-on-one."

Smith said, "We went into the four-corner to get them out of the zone. That's a great zone with three 6-foot-9 players—Bo Ellis, Bernard Toone, and Jerome Whitehead—in there. [Bruce] Buckley went in for a lay-up and either Bo or Whitehead blocked it. Then they went into their delay game. They hit all their free throws down the stretch. Of course, that's what we did to get there."

The beginning of the first half was a stalemate, with the lead changing hands nine times until Toone's lay-up gave the Warriors a 14–11 lead. From there, Marquette's advantage went to 25–17, then to 29–18 and finally to 12 points before Carolina's spurt in the second half.

Lee's two free throws with 6:09 left gave Marquette the lead for good. Still, with 47 seconds left, Davis's free throw made the score 59–55, but Gary Rosenberger hit two free throws, Lee scored on a drive, and Boylan made two more free throws, which sealed Carolina's fate at 65–55 with 19 seconds to play.

Ellis and Boylan had 14 points apiece for Marquette, whose 25–7 record contained the most losses ever for an NCAA champion, while Davis scored 20 points and O'Koren had 14. O'Koren and senior guard John Kuester each fouled out in the final three minutes with

O'Koren being charged with four fouls in 43 seconds and Kuester three in less than two minutes.

"I've been through so much of this spotlight stuff," said McGuire before he received his championship trophy. "I wanted it for the guys. There was so much excitement that I felt like a ticket taker on a trolley car in St. Louis.

"I've tried before, but this time the numbers came up right." Exit General McGuire. Victorious.

In the consolation game, Nevada-Las Vegas overcame a 55–50 deficit at half time to outscore University of North Carolina-Charlotte by 56–39 in the second 20 minutes en route to a 106–94 victory.

It was a five-man show with two Vegas players—Eddie Owens with 34 points and Reggie Theus with 24—combining for 58 points and three of Charlotte's starters—Cedric "Cornbread" Maxwell and Chad Kinch with 30 apiece and Lew Massey with 22—hitting for all but 12 of the 49ers points.

"I still don't like consolation games," said Vegas Coach Jerry Tarkanian. "But I told the players that it would be a real test of their character and pride for them to come back and win and I was very proud of them.

"We were ranked in the top five and 10 all year and Charlotte wasn't, so I was a bit concerned that they would want the game more than we did. When you don't really feel like playing, it's harder to press and run."

Vegas got down by 14–11 but scored 16 points in a row in only 25 seconds to take a 27–14 lead, Charlotte then went on a 28–9 spurt to tie the score at 44 later in the half.

The Runnin' Rebels went ahead for good, 74–71, on a three-point play by Lewis Brown with 12:23 to play, and a 10-point streak ended Charlotte's chances at the 10:20 mark with an 86–73 Vegas lead.

BASEBALL

PAGING JOE DiMAGGIO!

By Peter Bodo

From New York Magazine
Copyright, ©, 1977, NYM Corporation

"There's a lot more noise here now, a lot more kidding around. Before, we were a reserved, quiet group. We have a different type of player now," said Roy White, the last of the quiet Yankees, a dignified, soft-spoken man who broke in with the baseball club in 1965, the year the most glamorous dynasty in American sports crumbled. He sat before a row of lockers bulging with platform shoes, blowdriers, exotic creams and lotions, S-E-X cologne, esoteric shampoos, albedo shirts advertising the charms of Art Deco women, bubble gum, tobacco, and Afro-Sheen.

"The big argument now is that we're entertainers; people are interested in our salaries, and in what we do off the field. I don't like that sort of attention. Entertainment is planned, but when we go on the field, it's spontaneous, the game happens. There's nothing planned about it, and we're still under the same pressures as ball players years ago. But I wouldn't say I'm uncomfortable. There have been a lot of changes over the last few years, particularly since Steinbrenner has taken over. It's been surprising, but it's been good."

The old Yankees dominated baseball from 1949 through 1964, an aloof and arrogant collection of talents who were whittled to perfect dimensions and pressed neatly into the proper cavities by club owner George Weiss. The club offered immortality, and the price was conformity. It was no choice at all for the fair-haired heroes and rubes who considered Yankeehood the highest state of athletic grace. At heart, the classic sports hero was an organization man, and the Yankees were first and foremost organization men.

Today, with a new season beginning Thursday, all that has

changed. Ball players have climbed out of the hayloft and won their freedom; they are no longer willing to die for the cause of the front office. "The little-boy fantasies have dissolved," says Ken Holtzman, a Yankee pitcher. "We are not robots anymore." The transition has been perhaps hardest on the Yankees—the conservative, image-conscious, blue-blooded Yankees.

The new Yankees, last season's American League champions, are no longer reluctant to allow a black player to wear their pinstripes. The old Yankees were notoriously slow to integrate their club, and did so only grudgingly. The only black player of any stature during the dynasty was Elston Howard, and it is impossible to say how much sooner he might have become a star if he had been white. Unlike the Mets, who are the laughingstock of black ball players because of their insistence upon retaining a virtually bleached club, the new Yankees will have one of the best outfields in baseball, consisting of three blacks: Roy White, Mickey Rivers, and Reggie Jackson. The team's silken second baseman, Willie Randolph, is also black and a typical New York hero who grew up playing ball on the cracked pavement and ravaged playgrounds of Canarsie. And it was the Yankees' black first baseman, Chris Chambliss, who hit the pennant-winning home run last year. "This isn't the old Yankees," laughs Dock Ellis, a vibrant, controversial pitcher who is fond of flattering his right ear with a gold earring. "Nobody's gonna mistake Mickey [Rivers] for Mickey Mantle, or Reggie Jackson for Babe Ruth. And I sure ain't no Don Larsen. We could never be the old Yankees. We got too many niggers on this club for that."

The black Yankees are extremely conscious of the changing complexion of the team without making it a matter of public debate, or allowing it to interfere with that often illusory, always fragile quality known as team unity. Since the beginning of spring training, press reports have speculated upon the likelihood of dissension on a club laden with major-league talents. The team has been formed with judicious training and heavy spending, but remains by and large a puzzle which has yet to be assembled. Nobody quite knows what personality will emerge from this team, but every player understands that the club will be resented, hunted, and subjected to the highest critical standards. "We will be the little foxes that everybody wants to outthink and kill" is how Ellis put it.

When I visited the Yankees at their Fort Lauderdale spring-training base, I expected to find them defensive and uncertain, squirming under the pressure that is already beginning to bake the back of their collective neck. Surprisingly, the Yankees were an open ball club, responsive and frank, despite the fact that it is a team slightly uneasy in its own company, resembling a wedding reception dominated by too many distant relations.

The Yankees' fortunes in 1977 may very well hinge upon the personalities of two men, provided that the rest of the team plays up to potential. They are Thurman Munson, the team captain and the American League's Most Valuable Player in 1976, and Reggie Jackson, the newly acquired free agent who is probably the most electrifying hitter in the game today. Each is a brilliant player, as well as a sensitive psyche disposed to demanding his pound of flesh, and fully prepared to carve it from the most tender portion of a detractor's anatomy. They are men of big egos, and a number of sports writers have predicted that those egos will clash. But without those egos, each of them might still be in Podunk, playing softball for the local tavern. What will be important about their egos is less a matter of size than flexibility, but this much has already been shown: The new Yankees will never be accused of camouflaging their personalities behind the corporate facade.

Thurman Munson crossed the clubhouse, wearing baggy cotton long johns cut off above the knee, and blue leggings fastened to high white sweat socks with three turns of adhesive tape. He selected a hard-boiled egg from the foil-lined tray, and examined it carefully, as if he expected a fabulous insect to erupt from the pale oval. Munson salted the egg heavily, broke it in two, and pushed a half in his mouth, olive-colored particles of the yolk clinging to a moustache that helps give his countenance the perpetually dour expression of a walrus.

"Hey, Thurm, you comin' to the party?" Rivers shouted across the room.

Munson chewed the dry egg.

"Thurm, I'm talkin' to you! You comin' Thurm?"

The Yankee catcher swallowed hard and answered, "Do I gotta bring a hostage?"

"You jus' bring yo'self, Thurm. . . ."

Munson laughed at his own joke. "Do I gotta bring a hostage? I thought you had to bring a hostage these days. . . ." He drifted back to his locker and flopped heavily on the hard wooden bench before it. Munson is completely at home in a locker room, comfortable with the racial and genital humor, satisfied with his role as the Yankee team leader and resident "red ass," a term commonly used to describe the kind of moody, cantankerous athlete whose day-to-day brilliance is often obscured by a pose suggesting that his very presence on a team is a matter over which he has little choice, and which causes him profound pain.

There is very little about Munson that suggests the qualities of an athlete—he is a stump of a man who in street clothes might very easily be mistaken for a paunchy, gruff fan. Munson is bottom-heavy, his hips flared wide to accommodate massive thighs that give him the low center of gravity so invaluable to a catcher. His shape suggests a bowling pin, and he moves with a waddle. Ellis calls him "the little nigger" because of his protuberant rump.

"I'm unconventional," Munson said. "I'm a bit awkward, so my mistakes show up more. I'm not flashy."

This deceptive ungainliness has caused Munson a great deal of anguish, and he spent his first six years in the major leagues fighting for the recognition he deserves. Since he is the kind of fellow whose idea of a good time is insulting a stranger and then reveling in his discomfort, Munson's efforts at self-promotion have often served to alienate rather than convince.

Gene Michael, a former teammate, put it best when he called Munson "the most selfish team ball player in the league." He is without doubt the Yankee dynamo, but still enough of a hayseed to function smoothly through the daily drudgeries of a life spent passing from the lobby of one Holiday Inn to another, showering with 25 other men, crouching day after scorching day in the dust behind home plate in the claustrophobic gear of his trade, the ball blistering and lacerating his fingers and the bat stinging his palms and jarring his elbows.

In his caustic persona, Munson also bears a deep desire to be admired and looked to for leadership.

"I like to be appreciated," Munson acknowledged, "but I like to be left alone too. I like to be recognized, but I don't want to be hounded. All players overrate themselves and think they're getting a raw deal. That was kind of my problem in the first six years. But in the last two seasons, it's changed some. Sure I have an ego, but for me that's a feeling, I guess, of self-gratification. I feel like I've fulfilled my potential in the last two seasons. I used to go into a shell because a lot of the time I don't understand the press. They write about what you say, not what you do. So everybody wrote that I was a crybaby, when I just wanted them to write about what I'd done on the field. It's different now; things are coming around. Hell, I'm not envious of anyone. Why should I be?"

Yet the spirit of the poor relation is still easily kindled in Munson, the son of a truck driver. His attitude toward money is reverential; he dresses badly and invests well, stuffing his money into things a little more productive than the mattress, a little less risky than movie production. While this has no bearing on his abilities in the

game, it is significant that the first clash between Munson and
Yankee management was over money, shortly after Jackson signed
his lucrative five-year contract. Munson claimed that Steinbrenner
had promised to renegotiate his contract if the Yankees won the
pennant in 1976, and personally guaranteed that Munson would be
the highest-paid Yankee besides Catfish Hunter.

Early in the year, Munson discovered that Jackson's total annual
salary of $332,000 still exceeded his own, due to a complicated
deferred-payment scheme. Outraged, he considered buying out his
contract, or demanding that he be traded, before the matter was
finally resolved. Overtly, the matter engendered no conflict between
Jackson and Munson, but it probably served to put the aggrieved
catcher on the defensive, and may have added credence to any
suspicion Munson entertained upon realizing that just when he had
finally filled out his pinstriped uniform and gained ascendancy as
the Yankee captain, the club secured the services of a man who may
be no greater as a player, but whose star certainly shines with a far
more brilliant light.

Reggie Jackson carefully squeezed a dollop of white cream from
a bottle of Musk hand-and-body lotion into his hand, and began to
massage it into his other arm with painstaking care. A porcine fellow
wearing the uniform of a Little League umpire sat on the bench
alongside Jackson, his round face crimson from exposure to a star,
his hand extending a tape recorder toward Jackson's face.

"Reggie, I understand ya collect cars. . . ."

Jackson nodded, and recited the names of a dozen vintage auto-
mobiles which he keeps garaged in his Tempe, Arizona, business
headquarters.

"I didn't hear you say a Mercedes, Reggie. I drive a Mercedes, a
real honey. I thought maybe ya had a Mercedes or two, ya know,
wonada classic models."

Jackson closed the cap on his lotion, wiped the top and placed it
carefully on the uppermost shelf of his locker. He took a container
of Johnson's baby powder down and began to dust his thighs and
midsection.

"A Mercedes," he said. "Yeah, I bought my attorney a Mercedes. . . ."

The man laughed nervously. "What didja get 'im, a 450?"

"450 SL."

"Yeah, ha-ha, that's what I got, 450 SL."

"I'd like to have a nice Cadillac Eldorado convertible," Jackson
said, pulling pale-green boxer shorts over his dark olive skin. "Not
that I like the car that much, but it's a good sound investment." He

sat down and looked his interviewer square in the eye. "The one I like best is my Corniche. It gives me a lot of freedom when I drive it." He paused, measuring his words. "You don't buy a car like that with a $500 down payment. You have to work for it. You have to strive to get to a certain position so you can afford it. . . . It's a comforting type of feeling, to be able to drive it. It's hard work, a certain kind of accomplishment. The car is a beautiful car in itself; it's a nice ride, it gives you a great feeling, but to be able to drive that kind of a car you have to make so many sacrifices, put in so much time. It shows that you have reached a certain standard, a certain level, in life-style and living. You've come from someplace."

The interviewer sat rapt; when Jackson finished speaking he asked the man if he knew what a Corniche was.

"No, I'm afraid not, Reggie, ha-ha, I'm afraid I don't. . . ."

"It's the top of the line Rolls-Royce. . . ."

Jackson is a star—a controversial, intense, deeply ambitious man who has mastered the art of celebrity. He is both perceptive and informal as a television commentator, but he can also translate the enormous power harnessed in his body into his words and gestures. When he senses gravity in a topic, or feels as if he is under pressure, he can make whomever he is speaking with break out in sweat. And Jackson is under great pressure these days.

He has been considered disruptive by a number of baseball people who do not like young men in uniform to speak their mind. Jackson is conscious of this and deeply embittered by it. "People always want to create some minuses for me," he said, after satisfying his first interviewer. "They don't like to say that I'm a great ball player. It's like wherever I go it's always what I can't do. What I won't do. How I will hurt, or disrupt. . . ."

That reputation developed in Oakland, where he helped the brilliant, enigmatic A's to three World Series titles, won an MVP award and the American League home-run title twice, and helped the flamboyant club become legendary for its dissension and clubhouse fistfights. The A's were larger than life, a condition which suited Jackson temperamentally. He was traded to Baltimore last year, refused to play for the offered wage for a part of the early season, and ultimately became a free agent, finally signing with the Yankees. He has his detractors, yet the fact remains that he plays with proud intensity, symbolized by his swing, a smooth but savage explosion.

Jackson knows that he has arrived at the reckoning point of his career and must now prove his contention that "if I played in New York, they would name a candy bar after me." Thus, while he has been characteristically gracious with the press, his quiescence has been disturbing, his concentration so intense that when he picks up a bat one half expects him to snap it in two.

"I know the great names of the old Yankees, what this club always meant in terms of power and overall excellence. I don't have illusions. I don't want to bring them down to my level, but to play up to theirs." Yet at the same time, Jackson is ambivalent about wearing the Yankee pinstripes, because he is far too much of an individualist, far too much the contemporary star. "What are you supposed to say when they ask you about putting on 'the old pinstripes,' or about Yankee pride or the stadium? There's only one answer you can really give to that, so the question doesn't mean anything. The Yankee image? Well, it isn't really all that appealing to me."

Jackson does not possess the ideal temperament for a team sport; his needs are those of a star, and while he believes the Yankees can only win if he is "a cog in the wheel," he will not sacrifice self-expression, or alter his own priorities for any team image.

"It would be nice to become the Yankees' first black superstar," Jackson reflected, leaning against the batting cage, squinting in the sun. "The old Yankees were an all-white team; the front office was racist and bigoted. They didn't want no black superstars. I'm not knocking the players; the players had nothing to do with it. The Yankees were what the Mets are today, lily-white. It isn't comfortable to say, but somebody has to say it."

Jackson has been deeply hurt by the insinuations and charges of black activists who have been openly critical of his dating white women, his traveling in primarily white circles. He has donated both time and money to poor youth, and racial critics fail to perceive that Jackson's ego resists limitations of color. He is a man who strives toward perfection, period.

"I told Reggie that he can bring the city out of debt," said Ellis. "I told him he can get his candy bar. It's all on him. I hope he can do it. I know he can do it." The biggest problems Jackson will have to face are those of adjustment and acceptance.

"The toughest thing for me will be to fit in socially. This club has a lot of leaders, guys like Munson and Hunter. My job is to fit my personality to theirs, not for them to fit in with me."

This is true for the whole club in a larger sense, the sense that they will have to find some base of communication despite the high turnover of players, the transitional nature of the franchise. It is disconcerting to scan the list of players who have not signed contracts. The party line maintains that once a player takes the field, squabbles with management are forgotten. This is patent nonsense in most cases. "You know what it takes to win," said Ellis. "It takes egos and money. We may not have the money part straight, but we sure got the egos."

Those egos are as diverse as they are large. Crucial to the Yankees' hopes this year will be the behavior of Mickey Rivers, the temperamental outfielder who has angered manager Billy Martin by his tendency to sulk, for reasons, refreshingly enough, which have nothing to do with his salary. Rivers feels that Martin has tried to alter his playing style, and has also let some unspecified problems unrelated to baseball affect his play. Less refreshing is the case of Graig Nettles, last year's American League home-run champion. The Yankee third baseman has been trying to renegotiate his three-year, $390,000 contract and feels that his placid character and manner have encouraged Steinbrenner to turn a deaf ear toward his problems. "It seems like the guys who make money on this club are the flamboyant, controversial guys. Maybe I should pull something controversial."

The pride of the new Yankees is as thorny as the pride of the old, only it is the pride of individuals, perhaps still lacking the kind of charitable pride that can knit a team together. That pride will have to develop in the crucible, while they are prey to all the giant-killing instincts of teams with lesser talent, or more experience in molding it. They are in a number of ways the ball club of the future, given the increasing freedom demanded by the players, their increasing preoccupation with money, the increasingly frantic shuffling of talent by owners who need to make a winner to make a budget. They are everything the old Yankees were not, the flagship of baseball's future. It will be a heavy burden for them to carry.

Munson and Jackson, initially cool to each other when training camp opened, later began circling each other, sniffing the air, trying to pick out signals of compatibility or antagonism. They were sitting in the dugout one morning, chatting with Tony Kubek, a former Yankee, while the batting cage was being wheeled into place.

"I got more hits in my first seven years in baseball than any catcher," Munson said to Kubek, swinging a bat idly, releasing a lazy gob of spit now and then.

"More than Berra?" asked Jackson.

"Yeah, more than *anybody*."

"Yeah, but if we were on the old Yankee club, we'd both be sittin' the pines," Jackson suggested. "The bench."

"How the f--k do you know?"

The cage was in place. The conversation ended with the anxious clatter of their spikes on the cement steps of the dugout. It was time to hit.

GOLF

WOMEN'S GOLF TOUR:
STAINED BY TEARS AND DRUDGERY

By James Tuite

From The New York Times
Copyright, ©, 1977, The New York Times Company
Reprinted by permission

Carol Mann is 6-feet-3, slim as a No. 2 iron, and has banked half a million dollars by whacking a golf ball across more courses than she can remember.

She cried into the pillow of a San Diego motel last week and she very well may weep again in Chagrin Falls or Wheeling or Omaha or a score of other cities on the women's golf tour. Half a million dollars cannot dam a woman's emotions.

"You wake up in the morning saying, 'Where am I? What city is this? What day? What month?'

"Soon life became nothing more than a mattress, a box spring, a bathroom, and four walls. You say to yourself, 'Is that all there is?' and you cry a lot."

Miss Mann is the third highest in career earnings in women's golf. She has won 38 tournaments in 16 years as a professional, including four first-place finishes in 1975. Yet she talks of the present as a "comeback," because in 1969 she was the top money winner.

If one of the stars of the tour can cry a lot, what do the newer, young players do, the "hungry" kids who would settle for even a slice of the purse?

"They cry, too. I know; I've been there. I went broke 20 times along the way. My father once figured out my hourly wage when I was new on the tour. I made 15 cents an hour.

"It's dreadful as hell for losers. I learned after 1969 that I had to expand my life to survive. Now I have a town house in Baltimore and grow tulips and forget about golf when I take a rest from the tour."

Carol Mann is also in love. That helps.

"When I started out," she said, "there was nothing to do but go back to your room and sit alone at night. Now it's easier to have male companionship. Attitudes have changed. You can go to a bar, if you want, not to drink because you can't drink and play golf, but you can dance or meet guys."

What about those women who, out of loneliness, turn to the other women for solace.

"We're damned if we do," said Miss Mann, "and we're damned if we don't."

But Carol Mann is 36 years old now, and while Louise Suggs (54) and Patty Berg (59) are still around, the younger players who are nudging them out see women's golf through a different kaleidoscope. Take Amy Alcott, for example. She's 21.

"The hardest thing," said Miss Alcott, a fierce competitor whose very stride bespeaks confidence, "was being young and coming onto the tour right out of high school and a very close home environment. I think the thing I miss most is my mother's homemade soup."

Chicken soup?

"Any kind of soup. The thing is, because I was young and success-ful, I would feel the jealousy of the other girls because they knew I was taking a big chunk of their money, and they didn't like it."

She was rookie of the year for 1975 with record earnings of $26,000.

"I just stayed away from the others. I made my own friends. I'm just out to win and I don't care what anybody thinks."

"Amy Alcott is a loner," Carol Mann observed.

Is there a great deal of jealousy among the women golfers?

"I don't think you can call it jealousy," said Joann Washam, a 27-year-old pixie-faced golfer who is said to be one of the best-liked players on the tour.

"Sure, I feel annoyed when I win tournaments and Laura Baugh makes all the money because she's prettier and gets the testimonials, but I think it's envy more than jealousy."

"There are cliques," said Miss Washam. "But why not. The top players have earned the right to sit together. Some other kids come along for the ride, eat at McDonald's, rent a Caddy, shoot a 90, and eventually disappear. Why shouldn't the top players have a right to stay to themselves."

Only the top players were here for the $305,000 Colgate-Dinah

Shore tournament, which began today. This was not a place for losers.

"I'm here to make money and have fun," said Miss Washam. "I don't cry myself to sleep for loneliness. I go back to my room, eat dinner, watch television, and that's all right for me.

"Some of the girls are chasing guys all the time. Others just stay in their room. They don't bother me, I don't bother them."

Carol Mann seems to agree.

"I've never seen any player do anything to hurt another player."

But then she sadly recalls some incidents:

"In 1968, in Michigan, I was having severe problems with my eye and with my back. I found a bottle of placebo tablets in my mailbox with a note: 'This is good for what ails you.' Then in Texas, I hurt my back when I was awakened suddenly but got it put in traction and went out on crutches and won the tournament. And they thought I was faking it! Can you imagine!"

"I used to run with a crowd that would always make snide remarks, but I got away from it," Miss Mann added.

Her effusive personality has reaped some strange rewards. There is one letter-writer, a white man in a primarily black Maryland prison, who kept writing her to "be my savior," and get him out.

"Then there was this one I call 'the Bike Man of Atlanta.' He would ride his bike to wherever I was playing, Cincinnati, New Orleans, anywhere. It became a big joke on the tour. But then he got arrested and wired me for $300 to bail him out. That ended that."

When the Dinah Shore ends Sunday, the elite join the tour again at Hilton Head, South Carolina, one of 30 cities and 30 tournaments.

"Oh well," said the ebullient Miss Mann, "another opening, another show!"

OUTDOORS

THE DAY OF THE ELK

By Jack Samson

From Field & Stream
Copyright, ©, 1977, CBS Publications, the Consumer Publishing Division
   of CBS, Inc.

We had been walking for almost three hours and the wind was gust-
ing intermittently at about 40 knots, carrying with it the fine powder
snow that tugged at an exposed cheek with all the delicacy of a wood
rasp.

The air, which had seemed to congeal at 22 below zero at 4 A.M.,
had soared up to somewhere near 5 below by midmorning as the
sun climbed into the incredible blue of the New Mexico sky. But
the northwest wind, whipped down from the arcticlike air at the
top of Costilla Peak and Ash Mountain, added a wind-chill factor
that was bone-penetrating. With me was Bob Dougherty, my red-
haired, red-moustached, red-bearded guide. He was lean and as
rugged as the twisted, wind-wrenched cedars that studded the rocky
ridge below where we had been breaking trail in the knee-deep
snow. More than 20 years younger than I, Bob did not notice the
lack of oxygen at almost 9,000 feet. Like most of the hands who
worked year-round on the half-million-acre Vermejo Park ranch,
his lungs had adjusted to the altitude. Mine, used to the sea level
of New York (and probably still tinged with carbon monoxide from
the deafeningly loud Madison Avenue buses, plus half a dozen other
toxic chemicals spread over Manhattan by Con Edison, taxis, and
the Jersey oil refineries), were struggling to keep me alive, let alone
moving.

We had hoped to find the elk in a big meadow just to the east
of a saddle between two small hills. Bob said they had been there
four days ago when he had ridden by, herding a recalcitrant Here-

ford bull that had evaded the other ranch hands who had driven the cattle down to winter range a month earlier.

We had reached the meadow an hour before—just at sunup. There had been no elk and no tracks. The weather had changed all the rules, and with several mountain ranges on the 750 square miles of ranch, it was anybody's guess where the elk were. After failing to locate them near the meadow, we had tried scouting ridges, hoping to cut sign of traveling elk moving down to the lower canyons and mesas that were spread out below us like an undulating sea of dark-green trees and gray rocks poking up through the glare of sunstruck snow. Still, there had been no tracks of elk. We had come across the pugmarks of one lion—fairly small by the prints—a couple of coyote trails, and some mule deer sign. Our glasses failed to pick out elk at the base of the peaks or any fresh tracks in or near heavy spruce timber.

"Hard to tell," Bob said, lowering his glasses. "The storm could have them all down in the heavy spruce at the bottom of the slopes, or then"—he rubbed a mitten across his moustache, white with frozen moisture from his breathing—"they could be all the way down to the scrub oak if they had really been hurried by the big freeze."

I doubted it and I knew Bob did too. Elk will move down to winter range when the big storms hit the high country, but they usually feed down—not rushing all at once. They might come off the peaks in a hurry if a huge blizzard struck, stumbling and poking their way down the steep trails almost head-to-tail in the swirling snow (as I had seen them do once in Wyoming), but only down to the heavy blowdown spruce timber for shelter. Once the storm abated they would emerge and paw through the new fall for grass in the high peaks and meadows, continuing their slow descent to the flats and foothills.

"Tell you what," I said, shifting a numb foot in the deep snow, "let's try behind the Wall. They might have come down behind it."

Bob thought a moment then nodded slowly. He stuffed his glasses inside his fur-lined parka.

"Might just work," he said. "It's going to be some walk in this snow." He stopped and grinned. "You up to it?"

"I'm up to it," I said. "Yesterday didn't kill me and I guess today won't. Besides, you're breaking trail."

It made a difference walking behind the one who had to plow through the wind-packed drifts. In most places it was about knee-deep, but there were areas where it was thigh-deep and it was necessary to thrash through these low spots. We could have hunted on horseback, but I don't like wearing a horse down in deep snow. A good mountain horse will go until it can barely walk in soft snow, but it can't speak to tell you how damn rough it really is. I *know* when I reach the edge of exhaustion and I can always stop, rest, and eat some raisins or sip hot, sweetened tea while resting in the lee of a big tree or boulder. Besides, I like to hunt afoot. I like to hunt any way I can, or for that matter, anywhere.

It does cause problems. Having one's body stationed in Manhattan, overlooking Madison Avenue—and one's heart in the Rockies, or Kenya, or on a caribou tundra near Ungava Bay or a Virginia marsh, can cause the mind to bend some.

"Why must you hunt?" asks another of the very bright ladies at yet another of the endless New York cocktail parties. "We have come a long way from having to hunt for food. You can buy anything you need to eat at this time in history. Is it a need to hunt for trophies? Do you kill for sport? Tell me, I have an open mind. Why must you hunt?"

That is the time of the mind bending.

No, dear lady, I do not *have* to hunt for food in 1977, nor did I in 1937 nor will I in 1987 or 1997, if I am granted life long enough to hunt then, but I *will* still hunt. I will not go into all the reasons why hunting is a legitimate wildlife management tool—as I have done for decades—because you will not accept my logic. In spite of what you say, you have already made up your mind. I am a hunter because I grew up one and I must be one until I am too old to hunt anymore. And few men love nature or its wild creatures more than I do.

Each year my freezer is filled with the delicious meat of white-tailed deer, elk, mule deer, antelope, caribou, upland game birds, waterfowl, and all the freshwater and saltwater fish I am able to catch.

You may keep your USDA-inspected beef, your butterball turkeys, your kosher corned beef, your plastic hamburgers and hot dogs; your Colonel whosit's chicken, and your Mrs. what's-her-name's breaded fish. You can have somebody else do your killing for you if you wish, and you may absorb all the chemicals for quick fattening and artificial coloring they pump into growing, living things today as long as you wish. I will get my antelope steaks after a long, careful stalk under the endless blue sky; my venison backstrap after a successful shot at a white-tailed buck; and my caribou roasts from the plump young bull climbing the slope above the river. I savor magnificent roast Canada goose I dropped from a flock climbing out of a cornfield; succulent quail from coveys that burst from a palmetto patch; pheasant from the magnificent cock bird that almost outflew a pattern of No. 6 shot last year; and roast ducks from the myriad of mallards, blacks, teal, widgeons, pintail, and other waterfowl that have brought me so much joy.

And if I am able to keep up with this strong young man breaking snow ahead of me, and if we are lucky enough to run across the elk moving down from the frozen peaks in the wake of the big blizzard, I am going to dine on elk steaks—the best-tasting meat I know of—all next year.

The blizzard, lashing and savage, roared across the Southwest in early December, piling snow spruce-tip high in the mountain passes, bringing cross-country driving to a halt on the drift-choked highways, and sending temperatures plummeting far below zero.

Three days earlier, near the border of Colorado and New Mexico, the temperature had dropped to 22 below zero. That was the night I landed at Albuquerque's airport on the jet from New York, and already the streets were several inches deep in blowing powder snow, whipping along on the surface of an inch thickness of glare ice. By morning, when I started the drive to Raton, New Mexico, at 7 A.M. in a rental car equipped with steel-belted radial tires (having forgotten to request snow tires), the local radio stations were already awash with fender-bender accidents on the news and storm and highway reports from the Continental Divide on the west to the Texas border on the east. The thermometer had registered an all-time record low in many of the towns and cities of New Mexico—with a bone-chilling 14 below for Albuquerque.

The trip, which would be a normal 3½- to 4-hour drive from Albuquerque, took almost 12 hours. From Santa Fe to Las Vegas, New Mexico, there were a dozen cars and several semi-trailers off the highway. Cars were forced to stay within icy ruts on the main highways and anything over 40 miles per hour was extremely dangerous. I had a sandwich and a beer in Las Vegas and had the gas tank filled. The young man operating the gas hose, seeing the gun case on the rear seat, nodded toward the snow-blanketed east face of the Sangre de Cristo Mountains.

"That should bring them down," he said. "Elk or deer?"

"Elk," I said.

"Where you hunting?" he asked.

"Costilla Peak, if I can get near it with the mountain roads the way they are."

"You'd do a lot better with four-wheel and snow tires," he said.

"That's for sure." He ran a few more clicks on the meter and replaced the cap. Counting out the change, he handed me the money

and turned toward the warmth of the office at the service station.
"Good luck," he said.

I got in and closed the car door. Good luck. It had been a long
time since a stranger said that to me before a hunting trip. Last
year, driving through Connecticut after hunting white-tailed deer
in New Hampshire, a friend and I had pulled up at a stoplight in
a small town. We had one nice buck under canvas in the back of
a big suburban van and were wearing hunter-orange hats. The car
beside us held a couple of college-age young men and two girls.
Before the light turned green, the man on our side rolled down his
window.

"Any luck?" he asked. My friend nodded.

"Dynamite!" the young man said. "That makes you a hero, right?
Proved your manhood."

The light changed and the car tires squealed as the other man
floored the gas pedal.

My friend gradually picked up speed.

"Now there," he said, giving me a quick wink, "is a kid not only
with an open mind, but one who knows a great deal about hunting."

"Probably a vegetarian, too," I said. "Five will get you ten the
four of them are eating plastic hamburgers at the next drive-in."

It was 4 P.M. by the time I reached Raton, the small ranching and
lumber town in the extreme northeastern corner of the state. I
called the ranch and was told a plow had broken through from the
lodge to the main highway just after noon. That still meant a drive
of almost an hour. The drive to the ranch—the pines laden with
heavy clouds of snow and the last light of day fading slowly to a
wine color on the peaks—made up for the long day. The early
Spanish explorers, upon reaching Santa Fe, must have seen this
light when they named the mountain range to the east Sangre de
Cristo (Blood of Christ).

Dinner that night with my host, Bob Haslanger, ranch manager,
saw us talking hunting shop over mule deer steaks cooked on an
open charcoal fire. My guide had joined us for coffee just before
I headed for bed—early.

"Bob Dougherty," Haslanger said to me as the young man and
I shook hands. "A first-class guide. Knows the ranch and knows elk."
Bob smiled and sat down. "Jack here spent a lot of years climbing
around New Mexico looking for elk and deer," Haslanger said, "so
don't try to snow him with a lot of guide talk. He used to be with
the Game Department in Santa Fe and learned about the Vermejo
back in the days when W. J. Gourley imported the first elk from
Yellowstone to start the herds here in the late 1940s."

Dougherty nodded quietly and stirred his coffee. I looked at the dozen or so mounted elk heads on the wall of the dining room. Half of them probably were in the record books. Massive six- and seven-point heads towered over the room. Along with them was a handful of mule deer racks that could only be topped or equaled by bucks from the Four-Corners area of New Mexico—the land of the Jicarilla Apaches.

Each time I come to the Vermejo it is like moving back into history. The big ranch is not only an institution, but a state of mind. Vermejo today is the core of what was once the famous Maxwell Land Grant of 1841, deeded by Governor Manuel Armijo of the provincial government of Mexico at Santa Fe about the same time Kit Carson was leading Fremont's expeditions west to free California from Mexico.

But this was another time, and the following day, Bob Dougherty and I climbed mountains in the deep, soft snow until my legs were rubbery with fatigue. The ghosts of Carson and the other mountain men may have smiled tolerantly at our tiny figures toiling like heavily clothed ants south of the gleaming peaks just across the border in Colorado. But still the elk eluded us.

That night sleep came as it does to tired children, and no taxi horns or police sirens grated against the silence, which was broken only by the sound of the chill winds moaning against the logs of the small cabin.

I had been up again far before first light today—and still no elk. A lunch of a sandwich, a handful of raisins, and a cup of scalding tea brought strength back, and we crossed through a crevice in the Wall in early afternoon. The Wall is an igneous extrusion formed by the writhings of a volcanic upheaval millions of years ago. It extends in a southwesterly direction across the entire ranch from the Colorado boundary in the direction of Eagle Nest Lake, cupped in the crater of an extinct volcano high above to the west of Cimarron.

We cut elk sign about 3 o'clock in the afternoon, with the sun already dropping close to Costilla Peak, towering 12,931 feet above the horizon to the west of us. There were two separate signs—the prints close together. The animals were in no hurry.

"Fresh," Bob said, dropping to one knee and poking a finger into the tracks.

They were heading up a steep slope that ended in a high ridge to the west of us.

"About the same size," I said. Bob nodded.

"Could be two bulls," he said, standing up. "With the rut over, the bulls stay together feeding and gaining weight after all the carrying on of the past month or so. Let's go."

The climb was tough—even for Bob. We stopped every dozen yards or so, grasping a spruce limb or a mountain mahogany bush to keep from sliding back down the slope. When we had almost reached the top Bob moved ahead, motioning me to keep my head down as he peered over the ridge top. Suddenly he dropped flat in the snow and waved me forward, still holding his hand flat, palm down, for me to stay low.

"Two bulls," he whispered hoarsely, "going up the far slope. It's a long way off, but they're in range. They're not spooked, but climbing and feeding slowly as they go."

I nodded and we inched our way to the top. The pounding in the temples and chest was as much from the age-old excitement as from altitude and exertion. Bob looked across the valley at the slope of Little Vermejo Peak, up which the elk were climbing. He handed me the glasses.

"Both good bulls," he said. "Almost the same size. What you think?"

I raised the binoculars. They were both mature bulls—each with five points. They would not be tough old bulls yet. I handed him the glasses and began to work into the sling. The cropped top of a stunted clump of buckbrush, almost buried in the snow, would make a good rest. The worn military sling cinched up tight against the left arm bicep and I worked a 175-grain Core-lokt-tipped shell into the chamber of the 7mm magnum. I checked the 2x7 variable scope to see that it was on 4X—the best for me on a long shot. The two bulls were moving slowly through a sparse growth of aspen, stopping to paw through the snow for grass. About the size of grasshoppers to the naked eye, they jumped to something approximating the size of chipmunks as I settled a cheek tightly against the stock and looked through the scope.

The rear elk was more exposed in the slanting rays of late afternoon sun. The bull was at least 400 yards away. The rifle had been zeroed-in to shoot 3 inches high at 100 yards. Theoretically it should have been dead-on at 300 yards. It was impossible for me to estimate the exact range. I thought perhaps it was more than 400 yards, and the best I could do was to assume the slug would drop anywhere from 6 inches to a foot at that range. Wind, fortunately at that time of the day, was no longer a problem. The crosshairs settled on the top of the back, just a bit behind the hump of the shoulder, as the bull continued feeding. As usual, in hunting big game, everything began to go into slow motion. The squeeze had to be smooth and gradual. The rifle must move with the animal as it placed one foot slowly in front of the other. The recoil came as a surprise—as it should—and I do not remember hearing the blast of the shot. I never do. I raised my head and as I did the sound of the bullet striking carried clearly across the canyon on the cold still air.

"He's hit," Bob said excitedly, still using the binoculars.

Another shell slid into the chamber and the grove of aspens hid the animals as the cheek came back down on the stock. There was movement behind the aspens.

"Better hit him again," Bob began, then: "Wait, wait, he's down and kicking! Good!" My cheek came off the stock as Bob stood up, still using the glasses. "He's stopped, almost," he said. "The other bull only moved off a few yards. No, he's figured out something is up and he's trotting up the slope. Nice shot," he said, grinning. "Let's get there."

It took us nearly half an hour to climb down into the canyon and back up the other slope. The elk, a nice, young, five-point bull, was motionless in the deep snow. There was that combined feeling of sadness at the death of the magnificent animal and the elation of the shot—the completion of the total experience. The 175-grain slug had gone in behind the leg and exploded in the heart.

It was 4 P.M., and the sun was almost down behind the mountains to the west by the time we had, with the use of a belt ax, bone saw, and two knives, gutted the bull and turned it belly-down in the snow to drain. The great expanse of foothills, canyon mouths, and distant mesas below us was bathed in the last glow of golden light from the setting sun.

"It's going to be well after dark by the time we get pack animals up here," Bob said, sheathing his skinning knife.

I nodded. A feeling of peace pervaded my world.

"I'll stay while you go to get them," I said. "I'll keep a fire going. It'll be easier to find with a light."

Bob nodded and turned away for the long walk down to the base camp.

"You got enough to keep warm?" he asked.

"Matches, tea, some sandwich meat," I said. "I'll be fine."

"OK," he said and shrugged. "Long as you don't get lonesome."

"I won't be lonesome," I said. "I've got a lot of old friends up here."

He looked at me for a moment, smiled, and then began to make his way down the slope in the powdered snow. Young Bob Dougherty is a hunter. He didn't have to ask me who my old friends were.

BASKETBALL

THE BEST OF AL McGUIRE

By Dave Anderson

From The New York Times
Copyright, ©, 1977, The New York Times Company
Reprinted by permission

"Sports," said Al McGuire once upon a time, "is a coffee break."
His coffee break is about over. He will retire as Marquette's basketball coach after the National College Athletic Association championship game Monday night. He is 48 years old, which means he is
retiring on his schedule. "Can you imagine being in your fifties," he
once said, "and still worrying if some cheerleader is pregnant." Or
even worrying about winning a basketball game. "Winning is only
important," he has said, "in war and surgery." Long after Al Mc-
Guire's success as a coach is forgotten, his philosophy and his phrases
will be remembered and repeated. Some of his words deserve to be
chiseled on stone tablets or at least carved into the boardwalk at
Rockaway Beach, where he grew up.

On aggressiveness: "If you haven't broken your nose in basketball,
you haven't really played. You've just tokened it."

On his coaching habits: "I've never blown a whistle, looked at a
film, worked at a blackboard, or organized a practice in my life."

On his coaching style: "Every coach coaches the way he played.
I couldn't shoot, so I coach defense."

On handling players: "My era is over. Dictator coaches are finished. I was good for the 'Burn, Baby, Burn' atmosphere. It's time
now for coaches who sit in dens."

On his team's style: "The team should be an extension of a
coach's personality. My team is arrogant and obnoxious."

On fundamentals: "I'm not sure I have the basketball knowledge
of a good high school coach. I don't know if I coach. I think I'm
like the master of ceremonies. I create a party on the court and keep

it going. I have people with me who do a lot of coaching, but I never know what leg to tell a kid to put out first to make a lay-up."

On his team's philosophy: "We run a black defense and a white offense. Nobody could be a star under our system."

On strategy: "It's a Simple Simon game. Most of the time it's like a kindergarten. When you have the ball, you are king. But when I have it, I am king. When you dribble, you are king. But when you stop, I am king."

When his black players once threatened to stop playing during a nationally televised game to honor the memory of Dr. Martin Luther King: "You don't have to stop playing, I'll call a time-out."

On the value of pregame meals: "Give me kids who'll win on a pizza and a Coke."

When some Marquette rooters questioned his players screaming at him: "It's healthy. I also notice that the screaming always comes when we're 15, 20 points ahead. When it's tied, they're all listening very carefully to what I have to say."

On his type of player: "I can't recruit a kid who has a front lawn. Give me a tenement and a sidewalk."

When he was trying to recruit Ernie Grunfeld, now an all-America at Tennessee: "Look, Ernie, if you want to wear a blazer, go to Tennessee: if you want to play basketball, come to Marquette."

When leaving on a vacation: "I'm going to Tibet, maybe I can recruit the Abominable Snowman."

On recruiting: "I got to get the best because that's the only way I can be good. If I want shrimp cocktail, I got to get shrimp, I can't get octopus."

On his New York accent: "Back in New York, I sound like just another bartender, but in Milwaukee, it's music, like a southern accent."

On how to determine if a player has hung on to the rim after a dunk, a technical foul: "Electrify the rim. If a guy's hand touched it, you leave the juice on until he turns blue."

On coaching's social value: "Help one kid at a time. He'll maybe go back and help a few more. In a generation, you'll have something."

On teaching history at Belmont Abbey when he coached there: "All you do is stay six pages ahead of the class. When somebody asked me a question I couldn't answer, I said, 'It'll take too much time to explain, see me after class.' We had two doors in each classroom. When the period ended, I ran out whichever door the kid wasn't near."

On barroom brawlers: "If a guy takes off his wristwatch before he fights, he means business."

On racial philosophy: "The only two things blacks have dominated are basketball and poverty."

On education: "I think everyone should go to college and get a degree, then spend six months as a bartender and six months as a cab driver. Then they'd really be educated."

On priorities: "You have to know what's important. Don't come to me with a haircut problem. Come to me with a hit-and-run problem. Go after a parrot with a slingshot, not a cannon."

When a busboy dropped a tray of dishes: "The most expensive thing in the world is cheap help."

On his critics: "They call me eccentric. They used to call me nuts. I haven't changed. The only difference between being eccentric and being nuts is the number of security boxes you own."

As the vice-chairman of Medalist Inc., a sports equipment firm, Al McGuire owns several security boxes. He's retiring as a coach in order to devote his time to that business. Without him, college basketball won't be quite the same.

"But you got to remember it's a game," Al McGuire once said. "If we lose, a new star will appear in the East."

But a new coach like Al McGuire will not appear anywhere. His legacy is that there will not be another like him.

HORSE RACING

A NEW HISTORY OF RACING, OR,
"BET TWO, BRUTUS"

By Lenny Anderson

From The Seattle Post-Intelligencer
Copyright, ©, 1977, The Seattle Post-Intelligencer

Seattle Slew's appearances here are attracting to Longacres a number
of fairly casual racing fans who think a filly is a National League
ball player, a furlong is a GI vacation, and a $15 combo an orchestra
that works cheap.

Seeking to fill the void with a vacuum, this department offers its
new, expanded, half-baked history of horse racing, Semi-Turf. This
digest of racing ignorance supplants tired old myths and legends
with tired new myths and legends, as follows:

To begin with, horse racing is one of the oldest pursuits known
to man, or horse. Long before human beings appeared, horses
roamed the earth, looking for a jockey. While they waited, they
invented blinkers, stickers, the tote board, and the $2 window.

So when the first Cro-Magnon arrived, everything was set. The
first major event of which there is a record was a match race at
Piltdown Downs.

"How can you have a match race when we haven't even invented
matches, yet?" one caveman demanded.

"Matches can wait," replied his friend, Stone Broke Stan, the
dawn of history's first plunger. "Let's get some money down on the
two horse."

(The one horse won it. His name was Trigger.)

Wily Greek warriors gave history the first phony thoroughbred,
the Trojan horse. They put the bogus filly together with wood and
Elmer's glue, dragged it to the entrance of the walls of Troy and
pretended to abandon it. This was the first time a horse was left at
the gate. Hector the Selector, the dead-broke handicapper for the

Athens *Chronicle,* learning the steed was made of lumber, bet it to win.

At the height of the Glory that was Rome, Caesar not only conquered Gaul and got Cleopatra a starring role in an epic by De-Mille, but made book on the chariot races at the hippodrome. Historians bobbled the quote, so no one knew till now that Big Julie, who liked the No. 2 horse in the Ides of March Handicap, tried with his dying breath to give his best friend a horse. What he really said was, "Bet two, Brutus."

More than 15 centuries later, it was Hello Columbus, who, it now can be revealed, discovered more than a new world.

"All right, Chris," Isabella had said in that historic scenario, "what do you want this time?"

"The *Nina,* the *Pinta,* and the *Santa Maria,*" the peerless navigator replied.

"Eureka, Columbo," the queen exclaimed, "you just invented the trifecta. For this, you win a trip to America."

"Thanks a lot, Iz," Chris grumbled. "I'll probably get a mile and sixteenth out and fall off the edge. The world is flat, you know."

"Wanna bet?" she said archly.

He made it to the new world, all right, but arrived on a Sunday, when all the tracks were closed except Longacres and, alas, Hollywood Park.

As is generally known, George Washington liked the ponies. The picture of Washington standing up in a rowboat which the troops are rowing across the Delaware is a graphic portrait but fails to provide the text. What George is saying is, "A little faster, boys. We want to get there for the exacta."

Less than 100 years later, the ponies surfaced again in U.S. history.

Riding up to Little Big Horn, General Custer bumped into Chief Sitting Bull, and, dismounting, said, "We just want to water the horses, Chief. Then we'll be on our way."

"Wanna bet?" the chief said archly.

If all this won't help the newcomer to a better understanding of racing, nothing will.

GENERAL

WHEN A GIRL PICKS BASEBALL OVER BALLET

By Murray Chass

From The New York Times
Copyright, ©, 1977, The New York Times Company
Reprinted by permisison

My daughter is a second baseman. That is, she's a second basewoman. Second baseperson? Whatever she is she plays second base and she plays it darn well.

Debbie Chass (known only to her father as Deborah) is 12 years old, a girl and a full-fledged, uniform-wearing, glove-carrying member of the Paramus (N.J.) Junior Baseball League, Triple A Division.

She plays for a team called Corey's Maintenance and her 12 teammates are all boys—10-year-old, 11-year-old, and 12-year-old boys. Debbie is not the only girl in the Paramus baseball program; there are seven others. However, she was the first girl ever to play on the Triple A level, which is one step below the major league, or top, level.

Having played in the Continental League (the lowest of the three divisions) the first two years girls were allowed to play with the boys in Paramus, Debbie nearly made it all the way to the majors this season. But the boy she would have replaced started showing up for practice so she had to be content with Triple A.

"There are some guys who wouldn't consider taking a girl into the major leagues," said Dick Schwartz, the manager, who not only considered but also took Debbie into Triple A.

"There had been no response to anyone else, but when I picked her, the other managers said, 'You picked a girl. Oh, the first girl. There's a girl in Triple A.' Like it was a whole undertaking. Everyone else, including her manager last year, chose not to take her. But I'm thrilled to death with her. Debbie's been a great asset to the team."

Until 1974, no one knew whether girls could be assets to boys' baseball teams because they weren't allowed to play on the teams. Then girls and their parents started suing for equal rights on the diamond, and the Little League and similar programs reluctantly conceded those rights. Today there are about three million youngsters, ages nine to 18, playing Little League baseball and softball, which doesn't include the independent programs such as the one in Paramus.

A Little League spokesman in Williamsport, Pennsylvania, estimated that 120,000 girls were included in that total, but that most played softball. The number playing baseball, he said, is "very, very minimal."

Debbie, however, chooses to play baseball rather than softball. "I think it's good competition," she explained, removing her necklace and bracelet before a recent game. "When there are all girls, there's no competition because most girls are not very athletic."

Debbie, despite her diminutive size (4-feet-5¼, 65 pounds), is athletic. She also is interested in such things as gymnastics, ballet, and baby-sitting, and these have conflicted at times with her baseball games, forcing her to make decisions she rather would not have to make.

When she chooses gymnastics, ballet, or baby-sitting, it's the team's loss.

"She's better than some of the boys! She's our best second baseman," said Carlos Gandiaga, a 12-year-old member of the team. "She covers her position well, she has a rifle arm, and she's a good, good, good, good hitter. I used to be opposed to girls playing, but when I saw how Debbie was, I changed my mind. Now it makes no difference to me if a girl plays. She just has to compete, show that she wants to do it. If she doesn't, the boys would mock her out."

When Debbie started playing in the league at the age of 10 (she actually started playing baseball at the age of 3 or 4, joining her older brother in backyard games), she was afraid that the boys would drive her away with mockery. Before her very first game, she discovered that one of the boys on the opposing team was her classmate in fourth grade. She was certain he was set to pounce on her if she played badly, but in her first time at bat she lined a single to left field, thus silencing the would-be critic.

She also has helped shatter the myth fostered by antigirl Little Leaguers that girls were too fragile to play a boy's game. On her first stolen base this season, Debbie was hit in the head by the catcher's throw, but she survived as well as any boy could have.

Another time she was hit on the arm with a pitch but shrugged it off and ran to first. Still, some boy chauvinist piglets aren't convinced that girls belong on the same field and in the same uniform with them.

"One time," sixth-grader Debbie related, "there was a throw to second and I missed the ball, and a kid said that'll teach you for having a girl. That kind of thing bothers me for a little while and then I forget about it."

She showed how good she is earlier this season when she snared a line drive and pulled off an unassisted double play, not a routine play in that level of baseball. In a more recent game, she ended an inning by grabbing a wicked one-hopper and throwing the runner out, she alertly fielded a smash off the pitcher's glove and threw the runner out, and she effectively blocked the base against an advancing runner, took the throw from the catcher and tagged him out.

When the spectators, mostly parents of other players, see Debbie making those plays, they aren't always aware it is a girl making them.

"Is that a girl?" one woman asked, seeing Debbie's short blond hair peeking out from her green cap.

"I don't know," her friend replied. "A lot of boys look like girls today."

"It's a girl," I said, walking by the stands.

"A girl," the first woman exclaimed. "Golly gee whiz! And look— she plays the infield."

Most of the managers are so boy-oriented that they have difficulty adjusting to Debbie's presence. "OK John," an opposing manager shouted to his pitcher when Debbie was on third base, "keep your eye on him."

"That's a girl," Debbie's third-base coach pointed out.

Each season brings a new manager and it takes the new man several games to grow accustomed to referring to Debbie as a girl. "Steven," her manager said at one point well into last season, "you have to throw the ball to your cutoff person, Debbie."

And then there was Dick Schwartz's lament one time this season after Debbie got a timely hit. "I can't even pat you on the backside," the manager complained. Debbie has registered many timely hits in her career. She remembers three of them best: the first double she ever got, a line drive to left field two years ago; a home run that was a birthday present to herself April 28 of this season ("A girl"); and a double that helped win a game this season.

In that game, Debbie bobbled two consecutive ground balls, a rare occurrence, that would have been the second and third outs of the inning. The opposing team went on to score six runs and take an 11–10 lead into the last inning.

"I was mad at myself," Debbie said. So mad that she doubled in the tying run and, when the next batter singled, raced home with the winning run.

SQUASH RACQUETS

SQUASH RACQUETS, ANYONE?
DEFINITELY YES!

By John S. Radosta

From The New York Times
Copyright, ©, 1977, The New York Times Company
Reprinted by permission

Squash racquets, as the song would say, is bustin' out all over. Its growth resembles the booms in tennis, golf, and bowling in the last two decades. Squash even has its own Arnold Palmer to help project it into public consciousness. He is Sharif Khan, a charismatic professional and one of the stars in the Boodles Gin open, a three-day tournament in New York.

Squash has been around for at least two centuries, but for the most part it has been a hidden sport, played in private clubs patronized by the wealthy and in some colleges.

But something has been happening. Squash has acquired corporate financing, a lively pro circuit that stimulates interest, a growing amateur program, and possibly up to a million players in the United States.

People looking for recreation, exercise, and fun have discovered that squash is moderate in cost and that it can be played without regard to weather or season.

Squash is more a participant sport than a spectator show. It is related to tennis in the sense that two players hit a rubber ball with a racquet. But in play it is closer to handball and jai alai. Opponents do not face each other; they play side by side in a court, hitting shots off a front wall, two sidewalls, and a back wall.

The game is compressed into a tight cubicle 32 feet long, 18½ feet wide, and between 16 and 18 feet high. Because of that compression, action is extraordinarily fast. Its followers say a half hour of squash, the usual unit of play, is equal to an hour and a half of tennis. Squash demands great stamina and speed.

What has helped squash grow is its new accessibility and modest expenses. Anyone can play without having to be a member of some exclusive club. In Manhattan a court rents from $5 to $9 a half hour, the charge depending on the time of day. Clubs also offer a membership deal, ranging from $25 to $50 a year; its main advantage is the privilege of reserving court times.

One of the movers and shakers in the squash industry is a 36-year-old entrepreneur named Harry Saint, who worked in computers and real estate before he got into this business. As a player Saint is just an average amateur, but as an organizer he is the industry's current model.

Saint's company owns three clubs in Manhattan, including the Uptown Racquet, with 3,000 members at $35 a share. In just three and a half years he has become so successful that club owners in other cities are willing to pay for his advice, expertise, and experience.

Another builder, Phil Monahan, has been comparably successful in the Philadelphia area. Rodney Brent and Tony Spencer have brought public squash to Westchester.

"I have a stack of letters I haven't had time to open," Saint was saying as Sharif Khan and Stu Goldstein, Uptown Racquet's home pro, were warming up for the Boodles tournament. "Squash offers a better return for your investment than the usual tennis facility."

Saint also is planning to open squash complexes in other American cities.

"This is one sport ideally suited to cities," Saint says in explaining the new popularity of squash. "A player can stop in during lunchtime, before work or after, play as little or as much as he wants to.

"It is just as interesting as tennis and is much, much easier to learn. If anything has hurt tennis, it is that players who are not at least fairly good cannot carry on rallies—hitting the ball back and forth with your opponent—and therefore cannot enjoy themselves. That's not true in squash."

Most players in Saint's clubs are in their twenties and thirties, he says, "but we have plenty of men and women in their forties, fifties and even older."

Players do not need regular partners. The bulletin boards carry notices from individuals looking for partners to play with, and several leagues have been organized to formalize competition.

The United States Squash Racquets Association estimates at least a million adults play regularly in more than 3,000 clubs around the country. In the New York metropolitan area there are more than

25,000 players, 40 percent of them women—office workers, professional people, students, housewives, and others.

Squash is catching on elsewhere, too. In Canada it is believed to be second only to hockey as the national sport. There are claims it has displaced tennis as the leading sport in Australia. In the United Kingdom, surveys suggest one of every four "mature males" plays squash at least twice a week.

As a legacy from Britain's colonial era, squash is played extensively in India, Pakistan, and Egypt. Latin-American countries are turning out skilled players.

So far most of the growth has been in the participation side of the sport. As a spectator sport, squash has had problems because of the physical limitations of the arena. For all practical purposes the play can be seen only from above, which means crowds of no more than 150 to 200.

Television has been wary about covering squash because the ball moves so fast the cameras cannot follow it.

But the World Professional Squash Association and the United States Squash Racquets Association are working on those problems. Physicists and other specialists are working to develop a ball whose optical quality will make it easier to see.

TENNIS

THE NEW LOOK IN TENNIS

By Bud Collins

From The Boston Globe
Copyright, ©, 1977, The Boston Globe
Courtesy of The Boston Globe

Yu Li Chao was very "jin jang." Nervous. She had made the two-and-a-half-day boat trip on the Yangtze River from her home in Wu Chang a week before to play in the Chinese National tennis championships at Shanghai's Hsu Wei courts. And Yu, a 19-year-old worker in an electromagnet factory, had startled her country's small tennis faction by winning the women's title. But now she was the first player of the People's Republic in its nearly three decades of existence to oppose an American and Yu Li Chao had the wobbles against Annie Smith, a trim kid from Dallas who almost beat Billie Jean King at Wimbledon and Forest Hills. Yu lost the opening point by klutzing a backhand which bounced twice on her side of the net. She lost the first two games as the Chinese crowd of 500 watched in silence. The only emotion ventured by the full-house gathering at Hsu Wei courts came when Yu butchered an easy overhead, knocking the ball well wide of the court. That amused the customers, who paid 10 cents apiece to witness the first tennis contract between the United States and the People's Republic since Mao Tse-tung won his revolution in 1948. In fact, the last clash of these two countries on a tennis court had been a U.S. victory in the first round of the 1935 Davis Cup tournament.

This occurrence last Friday amid pines, willows, and ivy-trimmed mansions—Hsu Wei had been a European club in imperialist days—was not, however, a full-blooded match. It was just the starter on a three-city exhibition tour by a team of American professionals and amateurs which will include Peking and Canton. Nevertheless, this is another sporting breakthrough in Sino-American relations and, "The longest road trip I can imagine just to eat original chow mein," said Tom Gorman, player-coach of Seattle in World Team Tennis.

After a couple of games Yu Li Chao had her nerves back in line. A sturdy, extremely fit youngster in pigtails, shorts, and tennis shirt, she lost the first set, 6–4, but won the second by the same score. The 12 encounters were all two sets and Yu left the court quietly pleased. Annie Smith, an 18-year-old who won the French junior title in June and attends Trinity (Texas) on a tennis scholarship, is among the top 30 players in the world. "She is the best I have ever seen," Yu said. Annie said, "Yu was a lot better than I thought they'd be— although I never really thought about it. She surprised me the way she served and volleyed all the time on a clay court."

But the coach of the Chinese National team, Chu Cheng Hua, reminded his listeners that Chairman Mao had said attack is the best defense and Chu's players were going with the Chairman.

Like Annie Smith, few Americans have given Chinese tennis a thought. No Chinese has made an impact on the game although Kho Sin Khie did win the British hard court title in 1938. The Chinese have been out of sight internationally for ages and the sport is not very popular within this country where basketball, Ping-Pong, swimming, and volleyball are mass diversions. Beginning with the renowned Ping-Pong diplomats who paddled their way into Chinese hearts in 1971 and cleared the way for Nixon's serve the following year, several American sporting delegations have played China.

The tennis troupe is the sixth, following swimming, basketball, track, and volleyball invaders. Jan Berris, the tour leader for the National Committee on U.S.-China Relations, says, "We offered basketball or volleyball teams for this visit, but the Chinese surprised us by asking for tennis. We were happy to comply."

They rounded up pros Stan Smith, Tom Gorman, Valarie Ziegenfuss, Mona Guerrant, and amateurs Larry Gottfried, John Benson, and Annie Smith—all students at Trinity—and Sherry Acker, a student at Florida, as well as advisers Dick Gould and Ann Gould, a husband-wife duo who coach the men's and women's varsities, respectively at Stanford.

Why tennis? It is not certain, but the All-China Sports Federation, the controlling body of games-playing in this country, seems aware of the planetary Tennis Epidemic and may be planning a great forward leap over the net. One official says, "Tennis has been pretty much out of reach economically and in practicality. In the space occupied by one tennis court you could have a basketball court in use by 10 people needing only one ball which can be played with indefinitely."

A tennis racquet costs at least eight dollars and balls are $3.50 for a can of three. Ping-Pong paddles come as low as 35 cents, and balls a nickel apiece.

GENERAL

ROOTS AND SPORTS

By Edwin Pope

From the Miami Herald
Copyright, ©, 1977, Miami Herald Publishing Co.

Beyond its impact on general America, television's *Roots* has to hit sports like a jackhammer against a forehead.

One of our most persistent national myths is that sports is the most democratic area of society.

It may be on the playing level where the antediluvian postures of management finally were overcome by skills of black athletes.

The lie is on executive levels—coaching and managing—where qualified blacks are still victims of atrocities as brutal in their subtlety as *Roots* depicted in the most unsubtle terms.

Predictably, in dramatic license taken in mass merchandising, *Roots* suffers from oversimplification. Some segments are over-drawn. But just as surely some are underdrawn.

If nothing else, in its application to sports today, *Roots* should remind us that the so-called militancy of some black athletes runs centuries deeper than chronic bellyaching: boxing's Muhammad Ali and baseball's Curt Flood for openers, then the gentler "militants" such as Minnesota Viking Alan Page and New York Yankee Dock Ellis and Los Angeles Ram James Harris.

Roots brings to sharpest focus yet the innermost and largely unspoken feeling of many blacks that coaches and managers, stunningly white in terms of numbers, are merely extensions of overseers and/or slavemasters of ages past.

No matter that some of these coaches and managers may be the most color-blind of men. The point is, a black athlete cannot obliterate epochs of persecution simply by telling himself, "Well, I'm making $100,000 a year now, so everything must be OK."

In more than 100 years of organized baseball, the only black to manage a major-league team is Cleveland's Frank Robinson. This is an incredible three decades after Jackie Robinson busted up the no-black-player policy.

In some 50 years, the National Football League has never had a black head coach. Black assistants are in pathetic ratio to whites, considering the black-white player ratio.

In more than 100 years of college football, no major school (except for black-oriented institutions) has hired a black head coach.

The 22-team National Basketball Association, with a majority of black players, includes just three black head coaches, Bill Russell of Seattle, Elgin Baylor of New Orleans, and Al Attles of Golden State. NBA Deputy Commissioner Simon Gourdine is No. 2 to Commissioner Larry O'Brien, but Gourdine's is the only black face among the top 12 executives in the league's front office.

Major college basketball, also dominated by black stars, has a bare handful of black head coaches. Washington State's George Raveling, Arizona's Fred Snowden, Wisconsin's Bill Cofield, and Georgetown's John Thompson are among the few.

Sports journalism shares in the travesty.

I received a calmly thought-out letter from a black. Essentially the letter asked if I agreed that white athletes get more favorable newspaper comments than blacks, simply because they are white.

The answer was yes. An overwhelming majority of sports writers are white. We are more comfortable talking with white athletes; this obtains regardless of geographical origin of either writers or players. The fault is ours. If we are made to feel uncomfortable by black athletes, *Roots* helps show precisely why, and the solution is not to shrug and walk away in search of a more willing subject.

One of the most poignant conversations in my memory was with the late Milton Gross of the *New York Post*. "I was the first white sports columnist to stand up for equality for black athletes," Gross told me on our way to a late-1960s World Series game. "Even so, when I try to talk in personal terms with them, I can get just so far. Then, whap! They pull the curtain on me."

Gross said he thought black athletes did not appreciate what he had tried to do for them.

After a moment, he added quietly, "But after everything else that's happened to the black race for so long, why should they?"

Sports' cruelest statistic, beyond the intolerable racism in management selection, is that only in boxing (and, in far rarer instances, track and horse racing) have blacks had a long opportunity to compete on parity.

Even in boxing they were victims of the rankest bias, not to mention outright thievery. After white (and black) associates helped reduce Sugar Ray Robinson's fortune to zero, he was asked what he would do if he woke up and found $1,000 in a pocket. "I'd think," Sugar Ray said, "that I had on somebody else's pants." All he has left is his sense of humor.

What would pass for minor aberrations in white fighters has been considered arrogance in blacks such as Jack Johnson, Sonny Liston, and most notably Ali. They could do a *Roots* on boxing alone.

Closer to home, in football, the University of Miami did not award a scholarship to a black until Ray Bellamy in 1966. That was a year before Florida State invited its first black, Calvin Patterson (he committed suicide in 1972), and three years before Florida recruited Willie Jackson and Leonard George.

Now few count athletes by color. History is none the less horrifying for that. The danger in *Roots*, God help us all, black and white, is that it will arouse or re-arouse racial hatreds. The hopeful positive is that it will bring perspective and fairness to issues previously dismissed out of hand. Or whip.

HORSE RACING

A RELIGIOUS RITE WITH THE RICH AND FAMOUS

By Billy Reed

From The Louisville Courier-Journal
Copyright, ©, 1977, The Courier-Journal
Reprinted with permission

As another steamy Bluegrass day turns slowly into a night full of mystery and promise, the big cars begin arriving at Keeneland's sales pavilion. Cadillacs, Continentals, Rolls-Royces. Out of each climbs somebody fabulously beautiful or wealthy or famous, the sort of person who can spend, oh, $250,000 with the nod of the head.

Inside, the money-green seats in the semicircular, air-conditioned pavilion slowly fill with oil barons, playboys, tycoons, sheiks, magnates, and horsemen. The men wear cool summer suits, their ladies chic gowns designed in New York and Paris. Everyone has a smashing tan.

At precisely 8 P.M. auctioneer Tom Caldwell pounds his gavel to begin the final session of Keeneland's blue-ribbon summer yearling sale. Caldwell wears a tuxedo. So do the bid-takers who roam the aisles, heads bobbing crazily as they frisk the audience for bids.

Caldwell sits high above the crowd, behind what can only be described as a pulpit. Indeed, the scene is invested with a certain kind of religious mysticism. As Caldwell, the high priest, chants his mysterious incantations ("WHO'LL GIMME FIFTYNOW, WILL YA . . .") the congregation sits mesmerized, clutching their hymnals —the thick sales catalogs.

The audience looks like a *People* magazine convention. Elizabeth Taylor asked for seats, but was a no-show. But over here sits Leslie Combs II, the smiling old Kentucky breeder who likes to call himself "Poor l'il ol' Leslie." Poor, indeed. Combs's Spendthrift Farm is a slice of heaven that produces million-dollar babies for the Keeneland sale.

And over there is Nelson Bunker Hunt, the Texas oilman worth $700 million or something silly like that. And here is a Madden and there is a Whitney and so on. In the hallway outside the pavilion, working people stand on tiptoe and press their faces near the glass, hoping to catch a glimpse of somebody rich or famous.

In the bars at the back of the pavilion, the children of high society play their own games. Handsome young men in polo shirts and khakis hold drinks just so as they chatter away with sweet young things with long tawny hair, flashing eyes, and perfect teeth. (Rich kids ALWAYS have perfect teeth.)

Through the hum of conversation and the layer of blue cigarette smoke comes the tinkle of ice cubes and the champagne bubbling of laughter. Romance is in the air. Those with harder hearts can look up and watch the sales on closed-circuit TV.

Outside, under the stars, grooms lead the yearlings from the barns to their appointments with destiny. The yearlings are the equine equivalents of the buyers in the pavilion, all sons and daughters of such uptown, high-class sires as Sir Ivor, Nijinsky, Northern Dancer and, of course, Secretariat.

Identified only by a number pasted on the hip, each yearling is led into the pavilion by a groom in green coveralls. Sometimes the glare of the bright lights or the dull roar of conversation can frighten a yearling, causing it to whinny or pace nervously on the tanbark floor of the sales ring.

The buyers speak many languages, coming as they do from 12 countries. But the universal language, of course, is money. Over the last two days, the Americans, English, Irish, Japanese, French, and Arabs have been spending their dollars, pounds, francs, pesos, yen, marks, and lira with a vigor that is remarkable, even by Keeneland standards.

Oh, nobody broke the world record of $1.5 million for a yearling set here last year. But six-figure bids were as common as the flies buzzing around the barns. On Monday night, a British syndicate bought a son of Secretariat for $725,000. The average for the two days was about $20,000 higher than ever before.

The actual bidding is a special kind of game, sort of a cross between Monopoly and high-stakes poker. The competition is so fierce that buyers often hire agents to do their bidding, to keep their moves and plans secret. If word got out, for example, that Bunker Hunt was interested in a particular horse, the price might be driven up several thousand.

Trying to figure out who is bidding takes a sharp eye. A bid of $50,000 can be as subtle as a slight nod of the head. In the next section, a man can scratch his nose and up the ante to $100,000. Auctioneer Caldwell and the bid-takers must be careful not to mistake a yawn for a $25,000 bid.

While the buyers are trying to outsmart each other, the breeders are trying their best to look impassive. For many, the Keeneland summer sale will determine the success or failure of an entire year's work. Sometimes telltale signs betray their inner turmoil. On his aisle seat, Seth Hancock's left leg jiggles in time to the auctioneer's cadence. E. V. Benjamin chain-smokes.

Soon as a horse is sold, a Keeneland functionary hustles to the buyer's seat so he can put his name on a sales slip. If a yearling brings a record, or if the bidding has been particularly spirited, the audience might applaud until the breeder and buyer stand to take a bow.

So it goes at Keeneland. By the time that last yearling is sold, the sales pavilion is near empty. The beautiful people already are on their way to the next party or the next continent or wherever it is that they go for kicks when they aren't buying horses.

196   Edwin Pope

mention outright thievery. After white (and black) associates helped reduce Sugar Ray Robinson's fortune to zero, he was asked what he would do if he woke up and found $1,000 in a pocket. "I'd think," Sugar Ray said, "that I had on somebody else's pants." All he has left is his sense of humor.

What would pass for minor aberrations in white fighters has been considered arrogance in blacks such as Jack Johnson, Sonny Liston, and most notably Ali. They could do a *Roots* on boxing alone.

Closer to home, in football, the University of Miami did not award a scholarship to a black until Ray Bellamy in 1966. That was a year before Florida State invited its first black, Calvin Patterson (he committed suicide in 1972), and three years before Florida recruited Willie Jackson and Leonard George.

Now few count athletes by color. History is none the less horrifying for that. The danger in *Roots*, God help us all, black and white, is that it will arouse or re-arouse racial hatreds. The hopeful positive is that it will bring perspective and fairness to issues previously dismissed out of hand. Or whip.

GENERAL

IT'S NOSTALGIA TIME AGAIN

By Jeff Caponigro

From the Midland (Mich.) Daily News
Copyright, ©, 1977, Jeffrey R. Caponigro
Reprinted with permission

Nostalgia, trips back to yesteryear, the Good Ole Days . . . blah, blah, blah.

I'm sick of it.

The 1970s have been filled with various monotonous hoopla concerning past eras—the twenties, thirties and, the most popular, the fifties.

I keep waiting for it all to end. But some people still insist on getting dressed up like Fonzie even though the wet head has been dead for 10 years.

When will nostalgia-mania stop? It may never.

The dreadful disease struck helpless victims again last weekend. Although the Troy (Mich.) Hilton Inn was not quarantined, it had those nasty nostalgia amoebas in four huge ballrooms.

The occasion—the Midwest Sports Collectors Convention.

This, thankfully, was a nostalgia presentation of a different type. There were no baseball players modeling black leather warm-up jackets or former football linemen sporting flattened heads from playing too long without helmets.

No, this was a bit more interesting.

Most of the United States' top sports collectors were in Troy to show off their extravagant assortments of old uniforms, books, and various sports charms from the past.

The gamut of the weekend collections varied from an autograph picture of Jersey Joe Walcott to Greg Luzinski's (Philadelphia Phillies) 40-ounce Adirondack "Big Stick" bat.

There were Gordie Howe ashtrays, glasses and Hank Aaron trash bags.

Sports celebrities were on marbles, mirrors, clocks, cartoons, posters, puzzles, beer bottles and, of course, baseball cards.

Ah yes, baseball cards. They were the main attraction at the convention. There were cards from the day they began in existence.

The cards were smaller then. I looked and looked but I didn't know a Joe Schmedler from a Bill Carmichael. They all looked like Ty Cobb to me.

There were tables and tables of baseball card exhibits at the hotel. People were buying and selling their cards and spitting off names with the precise knowledge and wizardry of a sports columnist.

"I need a Frankie Frisch."

"Boog Powell—1967, please."

"Where can I find a 1960 card of Mickey Mantle?"

These were common requests that you could hear barked above the noisy rustling of the crowd.

The collectors were old and young, and, even more surprisingly, a good percentage were female. But all were very serious about their hobby.

Each representative had rented a small card table, or series of tables, to boost his product. Every collector was very friendly, gladly answered questions and, most of all, did not push his product in your face and pressure you to buy.

There is nothing more upsetting than to walk into a shoestore and be pressured into buying sandals when you came in for dress shoes.

I appreciated this relaxed atmosphere.

I also appreciated the reasonable prices that the sellers were asking.

The only items that were truly high-priced were the uniforms. Clete Boyer, formerly of the Milwaukee Braves, had his uniform up for a modest $60. Old San Diego Padre uniforms were selling for $65 apiece. The pants, hats, socks, and sliding pads were not included.

What did I buy? Well, since spending a lot of money to me is buying a new ribbon for my typewriter, I wasn't about to splurge to great extremes.

I did, however, go all out and spend one dollar. Laugh if you will but I thought it was one of my best spent dollars.

I bought a circular pin with a black and white photo of the great Jackie Robinson. A red, white, and blue ribbon dangles from the pin with a plastic ball and glove attached.

The photo has a coffeelike stain on its right side but I think it is easily worth the hard-earned money I gave up for it.

If I save it for years, many, many years, the Baseball Hall of Fame will be begging me to sell it to them for thousands of dollars. Remember, I bought it for four quarters.

What a buy!

I have a feeling that many people left the collectors convention with the same satisfied, enjoyable sensation that I had.

As I was going up and down the aisles, I had a continuous flow of memories.

Willie Mays, Hank Aaron, and Sandy Koufax were just a few players that I could envision seeing on the field again.

Memories. . . . I guess it could be called (yech) nostalgia.

Nostalgia, I guess, is the umbilical cord that ties us to the past and to our pleasant memories.

Sports collecting and a show such as in Troy the past weekend can bring back those memories that fans like me love.

One of these days I will have to go to Cooperstown.

FOR THE RECORD

CHAMPIONS OF 1977

ARCHERY

World Champions

Men—Richard McKinney, Muncie, Ind., team: United States.
Women—Luann Ryon, Riverside, Calif.; team: United States.

National Archery Assn. Champions

Amateur—Richard McKinney, Muncie, Ind.
Women's Amateur—Luann Ryon, Riverside, Calif.
Collegiate—Richard Bednar, Akron.
Women's Collegiate—Pat O'Callaghan, Washington.
Collegiate—Washington.

National Freestyle Assn.

FREESTYLE

Open—George Gorman, San Antonio, Tex.
Women's Open—Janet Boatman, Alden, N.Y.
Amateur—Jack Cramer, Gettysburg, Pa.
Women's Amateur—Sherilyn Doyle, Taft, Calif.

AUTO RACING

World—Niki Lauda, Austria.
USAC—Tom Sneva, Spokane, Wash.
USAC Stock—Paul Feldner, Richfield, Wis.
NASCAR—Cale Yarborough, Timmonsville, S.C.
IMSA Camel—Al Holbert, Warrington, Pa.
Can-Am—Patrick Cambay, France.
Trans-Am—Group I: Bob Tullius, Herndon, Va.; II: Peter Gregg, Jacksonville, Fla.
Bosch Gold Cup—Bob Lazier, Vail, Colo.
Indy 500—A. J. Foyt, Houston.
U.S. Grand Prix—James Hunt, Britain.
U.S. Grand Prix, West—Mario Andretti, Nazareth, Pa.
Daytona 500—Cale Yarborough.
24 Hours of LeMans—Jacky Ickx, Belgium; Jurgen Barth, West Germany; and Hurley Haywood, Jacksonville, Fla.

BADMINTON

World Champions

Singles—Flemming Delfs, Denmark.
Women's Singles—Lene Koppen, Denmark.
Doubles—Tjun Tjun-Johan Wahjudi, Indonesia.
Women's Doubles—Etsuko Toganoo–Emiko Ueno, Japan.
Mixed Doubles—Steen Skovgaârd–Lene Koppen, Denmark.

United States Champions

Singles—Chris Kinard, Pasadena, Calif.

Women's Singles—Pam Bristol, Flint, Mich.

Doubles—Jim Poole, Westminster, Calif.–Mike Walker, Manhattan Beach, Calif.

Women's Doubles—Dianna Oesterhues, Torrance, Calif.–Janet Wilts, Claremont, Calif.

Mixed Doubles—Pam Bristol–Bruce Pontow, Lombard, Ill.

Senior Singles—Jim Poole.

Masters Singles—Ed Phillips, Warwick, R.I.

BASEBALL

World Series—New York Yankees.

American League—East: New York; West: Kansas City; playoffs: New York.

National League—East: Philadelphia; West: Los Angeles; playoffs: Los Angeles.

All-Star Game—National League, 7–5.

Most Valuable Player (AL)—Rod Carew, Minnesota.

Most Valuable Player (NL)—George Foster, Cincinnati.

Leading Batter (AL)—Rod Carew.

Leading Batter (NL)—Dave Parker, Pittsburgh.

Cy Young Pitching Award (AL)— Sparky Lyle, New York.

Cy Young Pitching Award (NL)— Steve Carlton, Philadelphia.

AL Rookie—Eddie Murray, Baltimore.

NL Rookie—Andre Dawson, Montreal.

BASKETBALL

National Association—Portland Trail Blazers.

National Collegiate—Marquette.

NCAA Div. II—Tennessee-Chattanooga.

NCAA Div. III—Wittenberg.

NAIA—Texas Southern.

Women's College (AIAW)—Delta State.

Women's Small College—Southeastern Louisiana.

National Invitation—St. Bonaventure.

BIATHLON

World Champions

10 Kms.—Aleksandr Tikhonov, Sov. Union.

20 Kms.—Keikki Ikola, Finland.

BILLIARDS

World 3-cushion—Raymond Ceulemans, Belgium.

World Pocket—Allen Hopkins, Cranford, N.J.

World Women's Pocket—Jean Balukas, Brooklyn.

U.S. Women—Jean Balukas.

BOBSLEDDING

World Champions

2-Man—Hans Hiltebrand–Heinz Meier, Switzerland.

4-Man—East Germany.

AAU Champions

2-Man—Brent Rushlaw–Dennis Duprey, Saranac Lake, N.Y.

4-Man—Plattsburgh B.C.

BOWLING

American Bowling Congress Champions

Singles (Regular)—Frank Gadaleto, Lansing, Mich.

Singles (Classic)—Mickey Higham, Kansas City, Mo.

Doubles (Regular)—Bob and Walt Roy, Glenwood Springs, Colo.

Doubles (Classic)—Tie between Frank Werman–Randy Neal, Los Angeles, and Kevin Garron, Long Beach, Calif.–Don Bell, Santa Maria, Calif.

All-Events (Regular)—Bud Debenham, Los Angeles.

All-Events (Classic)—Dick Ritger, River Falls, Wis.

Team (Regular)—Randel's GMC, Joliet, Ill.

Team (Classic)—Columbia 300 Bowling Balls, San Antonio, Tex.
Team (Booster)—Greater Richmond B.A. Capitals, Richmond, Va.

Women's International Bowling Congress

Singles—Akiko Yamaga, Japan.
Doubles—Ozella Houston–Dorothy Jackson, Detroit.
All-Events—Yamaga.
Team—Allgauer's Fireside Restaurant, Chicago.

National Duckpin Bowling Congress

Singles—Dick Najarian, Cheshire, Conn.
Women's Singles—Linda Rosen, Salisbury, Md.
Doubles—John Garrison–Al Hauser, Hamden, Conn.
Women's Doubles—Denise Przbyz–JoAnn Russell, Baltimore.
Team—Lambis 5, Silver Spring, Md.
Women's Team—Craan TV, Baltimore.

BOXING

World Professional Champions

Heavyweight—Muhummad Ali, Chicago.
Light Heavyweight—Victor Galindez, recognized by World Boxing Association; Miguel Cuello, Argentina, recognized by World Boxing Council.
Middleweight—Rodrigo Valdez, Colombia.
Junior Middleweight—Eddie Gazo, Nicaragua, WBA; Rocco Mattioli, Italy, WBC.
Welterweight—Jose Cuevas, Mexico, WBA; Carlos Palomino, Westminster, Calif, WBC.
Junior Welterweight—Antonio Cervantes, Colombia, WBA; Saensak Muangsurin, Thailand, WBC.
Lightweight—Roberto Duran, Panama, WBA; Esteban de Jesus, Puerto Rico, WBC.
Junior Lightweight—Sammy Serrano, Puerto Rico, WBA; Alfredo Escalero, Puerto Rico, WBC.

Featherweight—Cecilio Lastra, Spain, WBA; Danny Lopez, Los Angeles, WBC.
Junior Featherweight—Son Hwang Hong, Korea, WBA; Wilfredo Gomez, WBC.
Bantamweight—Jorge Lujan, Panama, WBA; Carlos Zarate, Puerto Rico, WBC.
Flyweight—Guty Espadas, Mexico, WBA; Miguel Canto, Mexico, WBC.
Junior Flyweight—Yoko Gushiken, Japan, WBA; Luis Estaba, Venezuela, WBC.

CANOEING

KAYAK

500 Meters—Steve Kelly, New York.
Women's 500—Ann Turner, St. Charles, Ill.
1,000—Steve Kelly.
Women's 5,000—Ann Turner.
10,000—Brent Turner, St. Charles, Ill.
500 Tandem—Kelly–Turner.
Women's 500 Tandem—Ann Turner–Julie Leach, Laguna Beach, Calif.
1,000 Tandem—Turner–Kelly.
Women's 5,000 Tandem—Sue Turner, St. Charles, Ill.–Jean Campbell, Webster Grove, Mo.

CANOE

500 Meters—Roland Muhlen, Cincinnati.
1,000—Muhlen.
10,000—Muhlen.
500 Tandem—Kurt Doberstein, Lombard, Ill.–Dan Lyons, Odell, Ill.
1,000 Tandem—Doberstein–Lyons.
10,000 Tandem—Doberstein–Lyons.

CASTING

World Overall—Steve Rajeff, San Francisco.
U.S. Inland Overall—Rajeff.
U.S. Anglers All-round—Rajeff.
U.S. All-Distance—Rajeff.
U.S. Inland All-Accuracy—Rajeff.

U.S. Women's Inland All-Accuracy—Mollie Light, New Albany, Ind.

COURT TENNIS

U.S. Open—Gene Scott, New York.
U.S. Amateur Doubles—Northrup Knox, Buffalo–Dennis M. Phipps, New York.

CROSS-COUNTRY

AAU—Nick Rose, England.
AAU—Colorado TC, Boulder.
Women's AAU—Jan Merrill, New London, Conn.
Women's AAU Team—Iowa State.
NCAA Division I—Henry Rono, Wash. State.
NCAA Division I Team—Oregon.
NCAA Division II—Mike Bollman, North Dakota.
NCAA Division II Team—Eastern Illinois.
NCAA Division III—Dale Cramer, Carleton.
NCAA Division III Team—Occidental.
NAIA—Garry Henry, Pembroke State.
NAIA Team—Adams (Colo.) State.
Women's Collegiate (AIAW)—Kathy Mills, Penn State.
Women's Collegiate Team—Iowa State.
IC4A—John Flora, Northeastern.
IC4A Team—Massachusetts.
IC4A University—Paul Steeds, Fairleigh Dickinson.
IC4A University Team—Fairleigh Dickinson.
IC4A College—Dom Finelli, Brandeis.
IC4A College Team—Brandeis.
World—Leon Scholts, Belgium.
World Women—Carmen Valero Omedes, Spain.
World Junior—Thom Hunt, San Diego.

CURLING

World—Sweden.
U.S.—Hibbing, Minn.

U.S. Women—Westchester (N.Y.) Wicks.
U.S. Women's CA—Indian Hill, Ill.
U.S. Mixed—Seattle.
Canada—St. Laurent, CC, Montreal.

CYCLING

Road—Claudio Corti, Italy.
Sprint—Hans-Gergen Gesche, E. Germany.
Time Trial—Lothar Thoms, E. Germany.
Pursuit—Norbert Purpisch, E. Germany.
Motor-Paced—Gaby Minnebo, Netherlands.
Pro Road Race—Francesco Moser, Italy.
Pro Sprint—Koichi Nakano, Japan.
Pro Pursuit—Gregor Braun, W. Germany.
Women's Road—Josiane Bost, France.
Women's Sprint—Galina Tsareva, Soviet Union.
Women's Pursuit—Vera Kuznetsova, Soviet Union.
Tour de France—Bernard Thevenet, France.

United States Champions

ROAD RACING

Senior—Wayne Stetina, Indianapolis.
Women—Connie Carpenter, Madison, Wis.
Veteran—Jack Hartman, Nevada.
Junior—Greg LeMond, Nevada.
Junior Women—Beth Heiden, W. Allis, Wis.

TRACK RACING

Sprint—Leigh Barczewski, W. Allis, Wis.
Women's Sprint—Sue Novarra, Flint, Mich.
Kilometer—Jerry Ash, California-South.
Pursuit—Paul Deem, San Pedro, Calif.
Women's Pursuit—Connie Carpenter.

DOGS

Major Best in Show Winners

Westminster (New York)—Ch. Dersade Bobby's Girl, Sealyham terrier, owned by Dorothy Wimer, Churchtown, Pa. 3,029 dogs entered.

International (Chicago)—Ch. Rimskittle Bartered Bride, white standard poodle; Margaret Durney, Moraga, Calif.; 3,811 dogs.

Santa Barbara (Calif.)—Ch. Liz-Bar Magic of Music, cocker spaniel; Mary W. Barnes, Ellenwood, Ga.; 4,254 dogs.

Westchester (Tarrytown, N.Y.)—Ch. Funfair's Pinto-O Joe Dandy, Pomeranian; Loraine Patterson Munter, Rye, N.Y.; 3,247 dogs.

Boardwalk (Atlantic City)—Ch. Green Starr's Colonel Joe, Dalmatian; Mrs. Alan Robson, Glenmoore, Pa.; 3,340 dogs.

FENCING

World Champions

Foil—Aleksandr Romanvok, Soviet Union.
Epée—Johan Harmemberg, Sweden.
Saber—Paul Gerevich, Hungary.
Women's Foil—Valentina Siderova, Soviet Union.

United States Champions

Foil—Mike Marx, Portland, Ore.
Epée—Leonid Dervbinskiy, New York U.
Saber—Tom Losonczy, New York AC.
Women's Foil—Sheila Armstrong, Jersey City, N.J.
Foil Team—New York AC.
Epée Team—New York AC.
Saber Team—N.Y. Fencers Club.

UNDER 19

Foil—Mike Marx.
Epée—Peter Schrifrin, Los Angeles.
Saber—Steven Renshaw, Wayne, N.J.
Women's Foil—Jana Angelakis, Peabody, Mass.

National Collegiate Champions

Foil—Pat Gerard, Notre Dame.
Epée—Hans Wiselgren, New York U.
Saber—Mike Sullivan, Notre Dame.
Team—Notre Dame.

Women—Vincent Hurley, San Jose State.
Women's Team—San Jose State.

FOOTBALL

Intercollegiate Champions

Eastern (Lambert Trophy)—Penn State.
Eastern (Lambert Cup)—Lehigh.
Eastern (Lambert Bowl)—Westminster (Pa.).
Ivy League—Yale.
NCAA Division II—Lehigh.
NCAA Division III—Widener.
NAIA Division I—Abilene Christian.
NAIA Division II—Westminster (Pa.).
Heisman Trophy—Earl Campbell, Texas.

National League

American Conference—Denver Broncos.
National Conference—Dallas Cowboys.
Super Bowl—Dallas Cowboys.

Canadian League

Grey Cup—Montreal Alouettes.

GOLF

MEN

U.S. Open—Hubert Green, Bay Point, Fla.
U.S. Amateur—John Fought, Tuslatin, Ore.
Masters—Tom Watson, Kansas City.
PGA—Lanny Wadkins, Advance, N.C.
British Open—Tom Watson.
British Amateur—Peter McEvoy, England.
Canadian Open—Lee Trevino, El Paso.
U.S. Public Links—Jerry Vidovic, Blue Island, Ill.
USGA Senior—Dale Morey, High Point, N.C.
USGA Junior—Willie Wood Jr., Lake Charles, La.
NCAA Division I—Scott Simpson, Southern California.
NCAA Division II—David Thornally, Arkansas-Little Rock.

NCAA Division III—David Downing, Southeast Missouri.
NAIA—Jim Bromley, Campbell Coll.
Walker Cup (Amateur)—United States.
Ryder Cup (Pro)—United States.
World Series of Golf—Lanny Wadkins.
Tournament of Champions—Jack Nicklaus, North Palm Beach, Fla.

WOMEN

U.S. Open—Hollis Stacy, Hilton Head, S.C.
U.S. Amateur—Beth Daniel, Charleston, S.C.
LPGA—Chako Higuchi, Japan.
USGA Senior—Mrs. Mark Porter, Cinnaminson, N.J.
USGA Girls—Althea Tome, Honolulu.
LPGA Player of Year—Judy Rankin, Midland, Tex.
College (AIAW)—Cathy Morse, Miami.
U.S. Public Links—Kelly Fulks, Phoenix, Ariz.

GYMNASTICS

AAU Champions

MEN

All-Round—Koji Saito, Toledo, Ohio.
Floor Exercise—Saito.
Pommel Horse—Robert McHattie, U. of Minnesota.
Horizontal Bar—Gene Whelan, NYAC.
Parallel Bars—Whelan.
Still Rings—Victor Randazzo, NYAC.
Vault—Guy Spann, Arizona State.
Team—New York AC.

WOMEN

All-Round—Stephanie Willim, Silver Spring, Md.
All Other Events—Stephanie Willim.
Team—Philadelphia Freedoms.

NCAA Champions

DIVISION I

All-Round—Kurt Thomas, Indiana State.
Floor Exercise—Ron Galimore, Louisiana State.

Pommel Horse—Chuck Walter, New Mexico.
Still Rings—Doug Wood, Iowa State.
Vault—Steve Wejmar, Univ. of Wash.
Parallel Bars—Kurt Thomas.
Horizontal Bar—John Hart, UCLA.
Team—Tie between Indiana State and Oklahoma.

DIVISION II

All-Round—Casey Edwards, Wisconsin-Oshkosh.
Team—Springfield.

AIAW Champions

All-Round—Ann Carr, Penn State.
Floor Exercise—Connie Jo Israel, Clarion State.
Balance Beam—Jeanie Beagle, Louisiana State.
Uneven Bars—Cheryl Diamond, Southwest Missouri.
Vault—Karilyn Burdick, Cal State-Fullerton.
Team—Clarion State.

NAIA

All-Round—Casey Edwards, Wisconsin-Oshkosh.
Team—Wisconsin-Lacrosse.

HANDBALL

United States Handball Assn.

FOUR WALL

Singles—Naty Alvarado, Pomona, Calif.
Doubles—Skip McDowell-Matt Kelly, Long Beach, Calif.
Masters Singles—Jim Faulk, Dallas.
Masters Doubles—Burt Durkin-Jack Stebbin, Milwaukee.

ONE WALL

Singles—Al Torres, New York.
Doubles—Torres-Artie Reyer.
Open Masters—Dr. Claude Benham, Chesapeake, Ohio.
Collegiate Singles—Mike Lloyd, Memphis State.

HARNESS RACING

Leading Race Winners

TROTTING

Hambletonian—Green Speed.
Dexter Cup—Cold Comfort.
Kentucky Futurity—Texas.
Yonkers Trot—Green Speed.
Roosevelt International—Delfo (Italy).
Prix d'Amerique—Bellino II.

PACING

Little Brown Jug—Governor Skipper.
Cane—Jade Prince.
Messenger—Governor Skipper.
Adios—Governor Skipper.
Monticello-OTB—Big Towner.
Meadowlands Pace—Escort.

HOCKEY

Stanley Cup—Montreal Canadiens.
National League—Patrick Division: Philadelphia; Smythe Division: St. Louis; Norris Division: Montreal; Adams Division: Boston.
NHL Most Valuable Player—Guy Lafleur, Montreal.
NHL Leading Scorer—Guy Lafleur.
World Association (Avco Cup)—Quebec Nordiques.
World Association—East Division: Quebec; West: Houston.
WHA Most Valuable Player—Robbie Ftorek, Phoenix.
WHA Leading Scorer—Andre Lacroix, San Diego.
World Amateur—Czechoslovakia; Class B: East Germany.
NCAA—Wisconsin.
ECAC—Division I: Boston U.; Division II: Merrimack; Div. III: Worcester State.
WCHA—Wisconsin.
NAIA—St. Scholastica (Minn.).
Allan Cup—Brantford Alexanders.
Memorial Cup—New Westminster Bruins.

HORSESHOE PITCHING

World Champions

Men—Elmer Hohl, Wellesley, Ontario.
Women—Debby Michaud, Raynham, Mass.
Senior—Marvin Richmond, Pequot Lakes, Minn.

HORSE RACING

Horse of the Year—Seattle Slew.
Triple Crown (Kentucky Derby, Preakness, Belmont Stakes)—Seattle Slew.
Metropolitan Handicap—Forego.
Suburban Handicap—Quiet Little Table.
Brooklyn Handicap—Great Contractor.
Woodward Handicap—Forego.
Washington, D.C. International—Johnny D.
Epsom Derby—The Minstrel.
Jockey Earnings—Steve Cauthen.

HORSE SHOWS

American Horse Shows Assn.

Hunter Seat—Elizabeth Sheehan, Plymouth, Mass.
Saddle Seat—Carol Reams, Ashland, Ky.
Stock—Doug Evertz, Santa Ana, Calif.

Dressage Awards

Champion, 1st Level—Chrysos, owned by Susan Rotson, Oakland, Calif.
Champion 2d Level—Whozit, Holly Essex, Midland, Tex.
Champion, 3d Level—Pinchbeck Lord Peter, Linda Oliver, Great Falls, Va.
Champion, 4th Level—Adagio, Deann Cramer, Webberville, Mich.
Junior—New Horizons, Judy Bird, Farmington, Mich.

National Horse Show Equitation

ASPCA Trophy (Maclay)—Francie Steinwedell, Flint Ridge, Calif.
Saddle Seat (Good Hands)—Carol Reams.

ICE SKATING

FIGURE

World Champions

Men—Vladimir Kovelov, Soviet Union.
Women—Linda Fratianne, Northridge, Calif.
Pairs—Irina Rodnina–Aleksandr Zaitsev, Soviet Union.
Dance—Irina Moiseyeva–Andrei Minenkov, Soviet Union.

United States Champions

Men—Charles Tickner, Littleton, Colo.
Women—Linda Fratianne.
Pairs—Tai Babilonia, Mission Hills, Calif.–Randy Gardner, Los Angeles.
Dance—Judi Genovese, Vernon, Conn.–Kent Weigle, West Hartford, Conn.

SPEED

World Champions

Men—Eric Heiden, Madison, Wis.
Women—Vera Bryndzey, Soviet Union.
Sprint—Eric Heiden.
Women's Sprint—Sylva Burka, Winnipeg.

United States Champions

Outdoor—Jim Chapin, St. Louis.
Women's Outdoor—Liz Crowe, St. Louis.
Indoor—Jack Mortell, Wilmette, Ill.
Women's Indoor—Celeste Chiapaty, Skokie, Ill.

JUDO

National AAU Champions

MEN

139 Lbs.—Keith Nakasone, San Jose, Calif.
143 Lbs.—James Martin, San Francisco.
152 Lbs.—Michael Vincenti, Boston.
172 Lbs.—Steve Cohen, Chicago.
189 Lbs.—Irwin Cohen, Chicago.
109 Lbs.—Leo White, Monterey, Calif.

Over 209—Shawn Gibbons, San Jose, Calif.
Open—Shimitchi Otaka, North Glen, Colo.

WOMEN

110 Lbs.—Lynn Lewis, Peabody, Mass.
120 Lbs.—Linda Richardson, Milwaukee.
130 Lbs.—Diane Pierce, Minneapolis.
142 Lbs.—Dolores Brodie, Los Angeles.
154 lbs.—Christine Penick, Los Angeles.
166 Lbs.—Amy Kublin, Peabody, Mass.
Over 166—Margaret Castro, New York.
Open—Maureen Braziel, Brooklyn.
Grand Champion—Maureen Braziel.

KARATE

World Form—Masahiko Tanaka, Japan.
World Fighting—Yoshiharu Osaka, Japan.
Women's Form—Hiromi Kawashima, Japan.

LACROSSE

NCAA Division I—Cornell.
NCAA Division II—Hobart.
U.S. Club—Mount Washington LC, Baltimore.

LAWN BOWLING

Women's Singles—Mrs. Pat Boehm, Tacoma, Wash.
Women's Doubles—Mrs. Edith McWilliams–Dora Stewart, Euclid, Ohio.

LUGE

World Champions

Men—Hans Rinn, East Germany.
Women—Margit Schumann, East Germany.
Doubles—Rinn–Norbert Hahn, E. Germany.

United States Champions

Men—Jim Moriarty, Chicago.
Women—Lisa Clune, Schenectady, N.Y.

MOTORBOATING

World Offshore—Betty Cook, Newport Beach, Calif.
U.S. Offshore—Joel Halpern, Bronxville, N.Y .
Unlimited Hydroplane—Atlas Van Lines, driven by Bill Muncey, La Mesa, Calif.
Bacardi Cup—Preston Henn, Pompano Beach, Fla.
President's Cup—Atlas Van Lines.
Gar Wood Trophy—Atlas Van Lines.
Gold Cup—Atlas Van Lines.

MOTORCYCLING

National Champion—Jay Springsteen, Lapeer, Mich.
125 Motocross—Tie between Broc Glover, El Cajon, Calif., and Danny LaPorte, Yucca Valley, Calif.
250 Motocross—Tony DiStefano, Morrisville, Pa.
500 Motocross—Marty Smith, San Diego.
Class A Hill Climb—Earl Bowlby, Logan, Ohio.
Class B Hill Climb—John Williams, Markham, Ont.

PADDLEBALL

U.S.—Steve Keeley, San Diego.

PADDLE TENNIS

U.S. Doubles—Brian Lee–Greg Lawrence, Santa Monica, Calif.
U.S. Women's Doubles—Annabel Rogan, Pacific Palisades, Calif.–Nena Perez, Venice, Calif.

U.S. Mixed Doubles—Annabel Rogan–Rick Beckendorf, Los Angeles.

PARACHUTING

United States Champions

MEN

Overall—Jim Hayhurst, U.S. Army.
Style—Tie between Royal Hatch, Raeford, N.C. and Hayhurst.
Accuracy—Jack Brake, Salt Lake City.

WOMEN

Overall—Perry Hicks, Raeford, N.C.
Style and Accuracy—Perry Hicks.

PLATFORM TENNIS

United States Champions

Men's Doubles—Herb FitzGibbon, New York–Hank Irvine, Milburn, N.J.
Women's Doubles—Louise Gengler, Locust Valley, L.I.–Hilary Hilton, Pacific Palisades, Calif.
Mixed Doubles—Hilary Hilton–Doug Russell, New York.

POLO

United States Champions

Open—Retama, Wichita Falls, Tex.
Gold Cup (18-22 goals)—Lone Oak, Texas.
America Cup (16)—Boca Raton, Fla.
Continental Cup (14)—Milwaukee.
Copper Cup (10)—Mallet Hill, Cochranville, Pa.
Collegiate (indoor)—Xavier (Ohio).

RACQUETBALL

Amateur—Jerry Zuckerman, St. Louis.
Women's Amateur—Karen Walton, San Clemente, Calif.
Pro—Davey Bledsoe, Kingsport, Tenn.

Doubles—Dave Charlson–Roger Sanders, San Diego.
Women's Doubles—Jan Pasternak, Houston–Linda Siau, Riverside, Calif.

RODEO

Professional Rodeo Cowboys Assn. Champions

All-Round—Tom Ferguson, Miami, Okla.
Saddle Bronc Riding—Bobby Berger, Norman, Okla.
Bareback Bronc Riding—Joe Alexander, Cora, Wyo.
Bull Riding—Don Gay, Mesquite, Tex.
Steer Wrestling—Larry Ferguson, Miami, Okla.
Calf Roping—Roy Cooper, Durant, Okla.
Team Roping—Jerald Camarillo, Oakdale, Calif.
Women's Barrel Racing—Jimmy Gibbs, Valley Mills, Tex.

ROLLER SKATING

World Artistic Champions

Men—Thomas Neider, West Germany.
Women—Natalie Dunn, Bakersfield, Calif.
Pairs—Karen Mejia–Ray Chappatta, Melrose Park, Ill.
Dance—Fleurette Arsenault–Dan Littel, East Meadow, L.I.

United States Champions

Singles—Dean Mayard, San Diego, Calif.
Women's Singles—Robbie Coleman, Memphis, Tenn.
Int. Figures—Alexander Kane 4th, Toledo, Ohio.
Women's Int. Figures—JoAnne Young, Virginia Beach.
Figures—Tony St. Jacques, Virginia Beach.
Women's Figures—Jean O'Laughlin, Waltham, Mass.
Int. Dance—Dan Littel–Fleurette Arseneault, East Meadow, L.I.

Pairs—Karen Mejia–Ray Chappatta, Melrose Park, Ill.
Speed—Chris Snyder, Irving, Tex.
Women's Speed—Marcia Yager, Loveland, Ohio.

ROWING

World Champions

Men's Singles—Joachim Dreiske, East Germany.
Women's Singles—Christine Shieblich, East Germany.
Doubles—Chris Baillieu–Mike Hart, Britain.
Eights—East Germany.
Women's Eights—East Germany.

United States Champions

Singles ¼-Mile—Jim Dietz, New York AC.
Singles—Sean Drea, Ireland.
Doubles—Dietz–Larry Klecatsky, New York AC.
Pairs—Bud Ibbotson–Tom Wafenpaugh, Philadelphia.
Pairs with Coxswain—U. of Pennsylvania.
Eights—Penn AC.

WOMEN

Singles, ¼-mile—Joan Lind, Long Beach, Calif.
Singles—Joan Lind.
Doubles—Liz Hill–Lisa Hampton, Long Beach, Calif.
Eights—Vesper B.C., Philadelphia.

Intercollegiate Champions

IRA—Cornell; second varsity: Penn; Freshmen: Syracuse.
IRA Team Trophy—Penn.
Eastern Sprints—Heavyweight: Varsity, Harvard; Team Trophy (Rowe Cup): Penn; Lightweight: Varsity: Harvard; Team Trophy (Jope Cup): Harvard.
Western Sprints—Varsity: British Columbia; Junior varsity: Orange Coast; Freshmen: Orange Coast.
Women's Eastern Sprints—Heavyweight: Yale; lightweight: Radcliffe.

SHOOTING

Grand American Trapshooting Champions

Men—James Edwards, Fairfield, Ohio.
Women—Mildred Paxton, Charleston, W. Va.
Veterans—Verne R. Harkins, Desoto, Iowa.
Senior—George Tony, Indianapolis.

National Skeet Shooting Assn. Champions

Men—John Shima, San Antonio, Tex.
Women—Conni Place, Pompano Beach, Fla.
Veterans—Tom San Filipo, Fairfield, Calif.
Senior—K. E. Pletcher, Bellevue, Neb.

Pistol Champions

Men—Hershel L. Anderson, Tracy City, Tenn.
Women—SPS Kimberly Dyer, U.S. Army.

Rifle Champions

Smallbore Position—Maj. Lones Wigger, U.S. Army.
Smallbore Women Position—SP4 Karen Monez, U.S. Army.
Smallbore Prone—Mary Stidworthy, Prescott, Ariz.
Highpower—Carl R. Bemosky, Giordon, Pa.

SKIING

World Cup Winners

Men—Ingemar Stenmark, Sweden.
Women—Lise-Marie Morerod, Switzerland.

U.S. Alpine Champions

MEN

Slalom—Cary Adgate, Boyne City, Mich.
Giant Slalom—Phil Mahre, White Pass, Wash.

WOMEN

Slalom—Christin Cooper, Sun Valley, Idaho.

Giant Slalom—Becky Dorsey, Wenham, Mass.

U.S. Nordic Champions

MEN'S CROSS-COUNTRY

15 Kms.—Stan Dunklee, Brattleboro, Vt.
30 Kms.—Tim Caldwell, Putney, Vt.
50 Kms.—Dunklee.

WOMEN'S CROSS-COUNTRY

7.5 Kms.—Shirley Firth, Banff, Alberta.
10 Kms.—Sharon Firth, Banff, Alberta.
20 Kms.—Shirley Firth.

JUMPING

Class A—Jim Denney, Duluth, Minn.
Combined—Jim Galanes, Brattleboro, Vt.

National Collegiate Champions

NCAA

Slalom—Stephan Hienzsch, Colorado.
Giant Slalom—Hienzsch.
Cross-Country—Heigelge Aamodt, Colorado.
Jumping—Ron Steele, Utah.
Team—Colorado.

AIAW

Slalom—Toril Forland, Utah.
Giant Slalom—Toril Forland.
Cross-Country—Liz Carey, Middlebury.
Team—Dartmouth.

SOCCER

United States Champions

North American Soccer League—Cosmos.
Challenge Cup—Maccabi, Los Angeles.
Amateur—Denver Kickers.
Junior Cup—Santa Clara, Calif.

Collegiate Champions

NCAA Division I—Hartwick.
NCAA Division II—Alabama A&M.
NCAA Division III—Lock Haven State.
NAIA—Quincy.

Other Champions

English Assn. Cup—Manchester United.
Scottish Assn. Cup—Glasgow Celtic.
English First Division—Liverpool.
Scottish Premier Division—Celtic.
European Cup—Liverpool.
European—Czechoslovakia.
European Cup Winners Cup—Hamburg, W. Germany.
Uefa (European Union)—Juventus, Italy.

SOFTBALL

MEN

Fast Pitch—Billard Barbell, Reading, Pa.
Slow Pitch—Nelson Painting, Okla. City.
16-inch Slow Pitch—Republic Bank Bobcats, Chicago.
Industrial Slow Pitch—Armco Triangles, Middletown, Ohio.

WOMEN

Fast Pitch—Raybestos Brakettes, Stratford, Conn.
Slow Pitch—Fox Valley Lassies, St. Charles, Ill.
College—Northern Iowa.

SQUASH RACQUETS

U.S. Squash Racquets Assn. Champions

Singles—Thomas E. Page, Philadelphia.
Doubles—Victor Harding, Toronto—Peter Hall, Hamilton, Ontario.
Veterans Singles—Lee Harding, Toronto.
Senior Singles—Henri Salaun, Boston.
Veterans Doubles—Thomas Jones, New York—John Swann, Toronto.
Collegiate Singles—Michael Desaulniers, Harvard.

U.S. Women's Squash Racquets Assn.

Singles—Gretchen Spruance, Wilmington, Del.
Doubles—Gretchen Spruance—Mrs. F. A. C. Vosters, Wilmington, Del.

Senior Singles—Marigold Edwards, Pittsburgh.
College—Gail Ramsay, Penn State.

SQUASH TENNIS

U.S. Open—Pedro Bacallao, New York.

SWIMMING

Men's U.S. Long-Course Champions

100-M. Freestyle—Jonty Skinner, South Africa.
200-M. Freestyle—Jim Montgomery, Madison, Wis.
400-M. Freestyle—Brian Goodell, Mission Viejo, Calif.
1,500-M. Freestyle—Brian Goodell.
100-M. Backstroke—Mark Tonelli, Australia.
200-M. Backstroke—Peter Rocca, Orinda, Calif.
100-M. Breast-stroke—Rick Hofstetter, McKeesport, Pa.
200-M. Breast-stroke—Rob Lang, Wayne, Pa.
100-M. Butterfly—Greg Jagenburg, Drexel Hill, Pa.
200-M. Butterfly—Mike Bruner, Los Altos, Calif.
200-M. Ind. Medley—Scott Spann, Greenville, S.C.
400-M. Ind. Medley—Jesse Vassallo, Mission Viejo, Calif.
400-M. Freestyle Relay—Beach SC, Long Beach, Calif.
400-M. Medley Relay—Cummins Engine SC, Bloomington, Ind.
800-M. Freestyle Relay—Beach SC.
Team—Beach SC.

Women's U.S. Long-Course Champions

100-M. Freestyle—Wendy Boglioli, Ocean, N.J.
200-M. Freestyle—Gail Amundrud, Ottawa.
400-M. Freestyle—Rebecca Perrott, New Zealand.
1,500-M. Freestyle—Alice Browne, Corona Del Mar, Calif.

100-M. Backstroke—Linda Jezek, Los Altos, Calif.

200-M. Backstroke—Linda Jezek.

100-M. Breast-stroke—Robin Corsiglia, Beaconsfield, Quebec.

200-M. Breast-stroke—Kathy Treible, Brookfield, Wis.

100-M. Butterfly—Wendy Boglioli.

200-M. Butterfly—Nancy Hogshead, Nashville, Tenn.

200-M. Ind. Medley—Tracy Caulkins, Nashville, Tenn.

400-M. Ind. Medley—Tracy Caulkins.

400-M. Freestyle Relay—Central Jersey.

400-M. Medley Relay—Nashville, AC.

800-M. Freestyle Relay—Mission Viejo Nadadores.

Team—Mission Viejo Nadadores.

National Collegiate Champions

50 Yds. Freestyle—Joe Bottom, So. Calif.

100-Yd. Freestyle—David Fairbank, Stanford.

200-Yd. Freestyle—Bruce Furniss, So. Calif.

500-Yd. Freestyle—Tim Shaw, Long Beach State.

1,650-Yd. Freestyle—Casey Converse, Alabama.

100-Yd. Backstroke—John Naber, So. Calif.

200-Yd. Backstroke—John Naber.

100-Yd. Breast-Stroke—Graham Smith, Calif.

200-Yd. Breast-stroke—Graham Smith.

100-Yd. Butterfly—Joe Bottom.

200-Yd. Butterfly—Mike Bruner, Stanford.

200-Yd. Ind. Medley—Spann Scott, Auburn.

400-Yd. Ind. Medley—Rod Strachan, So. California.

400-Yd. Freestyle Relay—So. California.

400-Yd. Medley Relay—Indiana.

800-Yd. Freestyle Relay—So. California.

1-M. Dive—Matt Chelich, Michigan.

3-M. Dive—Brian Bungum, Indiana.

Women's National College Champions

50-Yd. Freestyle—Sandy Neilson, Cal-Santa Barbara.

100-Yd. Freestyle—Sandy Neilson.

400-Yd. Freestyle—Kim Peyton, Stanford.

500-Yd. Freestyle—Valerie Lee, Stanford.

1,650-Yd. Freestyle—Valerie Lee.

50-Yd. Back-stroke—Bonnie Broyles, Florida.

100-Yd. Back-stroke—Miriam Smith, So. Calif.

200-Yd. Back-stroke—Melissa Belote, Arizona State.

50-Yd. Breast-Stroke—Chris Jarvis, Alabama.

100-Yd. Breast-Stroke—Chris Jarvis.

200-Yd. Breast-Stroke—Chris Jarvis.

50-Yd. Butterfly—Shawn Houghton, UCLA.

100-Yd. Butterfly—Susan Sloan, Arizona State.

200-Yd. Butterfly—Valerie Lee.

100-Yd. Ind. Medley—Bonnie Brown, North Carolina.

200-Yd. Ind. Medley—Melissa Belote.

400-Yd. Ind. Medley—Melissa Belote.

200-Yd. Medley Relay—Miami (Fla.)

400-Yd. Medley Relay—Arizona State

200-Yd. Freestyle Relay—So. Calif.

400-Yd. Freestyle Relay—Stanford.

800-Yd. Freestyle Relay—Stanford.

1-M. Dive—Chris Seufert, Michigan.

3-M. Dive—Chris Seufert.

Team—Arizona State.

Small College Team—Clarion State.

U.S. Outdoor Diving Champions

MEN

1-Meter—Scott Reich, Dallas.

3-Meter—Phil Boggs, Ann Arbor, Mich.

Platform—Phil Boggs.

WOMEN

1-Meter—Jenny Chandler, Columbus, O.

3-Meter—Christine Loock, Fort Worth.

Platform—Christine Loock.

TABLE TENNIS

World Champions

Singles—Mitsuru Kohno, Japan.

Women's Singles—Pak Yung Sun, North Korea.

Doubles—Li Chen-shia–Liang Ke-liang, China.
Women's Doubles—Pak Yong Ok, North Korea–Liang Ke-liang, China.
Mixed Doubles—Jacques Secretin–Claude Bergeret, France.
Team (Swaythling Cup)—China.
Women's Team (Corillon Cup)—China.
World Cup—Soviet Union.

United States Champions

Singles—Jochen Leiss, West Germany.
Women's Singles—In Sock Bhushan, Columbus, Ohio.
Doubles—Jochen Leiss-Peter Stellwag, W. Germany.

TENNIS

International Team Champions

Davis Cup (Men)—Australia.
Wightman Cup (Women)—United States.
Federation Cup (Women)—United States.

U.S. Open Champions

Singles—Guillermo Vilas, Argentina.
Women's Singles—Chris Evert, Fort Lauderdale, Fla.
Doubles—Bob Hewitt–Frew McMillan, South Africa.
Women's Doubles—Martina Navratilova, Palm Springs, Calif.–Betty Stove, Netherlands.
Mixed Doubles—Betty Stove–Frew McMillan.
Boys—Van Winitsky, Miami.
Girls—Claudia Casablanca, Argentina.

Other United States Champions

Team—New York Apples.
Indoor—Bjorn Borg, Sweden.
Indoor Amateur—Matt Mitchell, Palo Alto, Calif.
Clay Court—Manuel Orantes, Spain.
Women's Clay Court—Laura DuPont, Matthews, N.C.
Junior—Van Winitsky, Miami.
Junior Women—Tracy Austin, Rolling Hills, Calif.

NCAA—Division I: Matt Mitchell, Stanford; Division II: Juan Farrow, Southern Illinois-Edwardsville; Division III: A. J. Shaka, Harvey Mudd.
NAIA—Gordon Jones, Flagler.
Women's Collegiate (USTA)—Barbara Hallquist, So. California.
Women's Collegiate (AIAW)—Lindsay Morse, California-Irvine.

Wimbledon Champions

Singles—Bjorn Borg, Sweden.
Women's Singles—Virginia Wade, Britain.
Doubles—Ross Case–Geoff Masters, Australia.
Women's Doubles—Helen Gourlay, Australia–Joanne Russell, Miami Beach.
Mixed Doubles—Bob Hewitt–Greer Stevens, South Africa.

Other Foreign Opens

Australian Men—Roscoe Tanner, Lookout Mountain, Tenn.
Australian Women—Kerry Reid, Australia.
French Men—Guillermo Vilas, Argentina.
French Women—Mima Jausovec, Yugoslavia.

TRACK AND FIELD

World Cup

MEN

100 M.—Steve Williams, San Diego.
200 M.—Clancy Edwards, Los Angeles.
400 M.—Alberto Juantorena, Cuba.
1,500 M.—Steve Ovett, Britain.
5,000 M.—Miruts Yifter, Ethiopia.
10,000 M.—Miruts Yifter.
3,000 M. Steeplechase—Michael Karst, West Germany.
110-M. Hurdles—Thomas Munkelt, East Germany.
400-M. Hurdles—Edwin Moses, Dayton, Ohio.
400-M. Relay—United States.
1,600-M. Relay—West Germany.

Long Jump—Arnie Robinson, San Diego.
High Jump—Rolf Beilschmidt, E. Germany.
Triple Jump—Joäo Carlos Oliveira, Brazil.
Pole Vault—Mike Tully, Long Beach, Calif.
Hammer—Karl-Hans Riehm, West Germany.
Shot-Put—Udo Beyer, East Germany.
Discus—Wolfgang Schmidt, East Germany.
Javelin—Michael Wessing, West Germany.
Team—East Germany.

WOMEN

100 M.—Marlies Oelsner, East Germany.
200 M.—Irena Szewenska, Poland.
400 M.—Irena Szewinska.
800 M.—Tonka Petrova, Bulgaria.
1,500 M.—Tatyana Kazankina, Sov. Union.
3,000 M.—Grete Waitz, Norway.
400-M. Relay—Europe.
1,600-M. Relay—East Germany.
High Jump—Rosemarie Ackerman, East Germany.
Long Jump—Lynette Jacenko, Australia.
Shot-Put—Ilona Slupianek, East Germany.
Discus—Faine Melnik Veleva, Soviet Union.
Javelin—Ruth Fuchs, East Germany.
Team—Europe.

Men's U.S. Outdoor Champions

100 M.—Don Quarrie, Los Angeles.
200 M.—Derald Harris, Los Medanos JC.
400 M.—Robert Taylor, Phila. Pioneers.
800 M.—Mark Belger, Phila. Pioneers.
1,500 M.—Steve Scott, Irvine, Calif.
5,000 M.—Marty Liquori, Florida AA.
10,000 M.—Frank Shorter, Boulder, Colo.
3,000 M. Steeplechase—James Munyala, Phila. Pioneers.
110-M. Hurdles—Tie between James Owens, Los Angeles, and Charles Foster, Phila. Pioneers.

5,000-M. Walk—Todd Scully, Shore AC.
High Jump—Dwight Stones, Desert Oasis TC.
Long Jump—Arnie Robinson, Maccabi, TC, Los Angeles.
Triple Jump—Milan Tiff, Los Angeles.
Pole Vault—Mike Tully, Pac. Coast Club.
Shot-Put—Terry Albritton, Pacific Coast Club.
Javelin—Bruce Kennedy, San Jose Stars.
Hammer—Emmitt Berry, Maccabi.
Discus—Mac Wilkins, Pacific Coast Club.

Women's U.S. Outdoor Champions

100 M.—Evelyn Ashford, Maccabi TC, Los Angeles.
200 M.—Evelyn Ashford.
400 M.—Sharon Dabney, Clippers TC.
800 M.—Sue Latter, Michigan State.
1,500 M.—Francie Larrieu Lutz, Pacific Coast Club.
3,000 M.—Jan Merrill, Waterford, Conn.
10,000 M.—Peg Neppel, Iowa State.
100 M. Hurdles—Patty Van Wolvelaere, Los Angeles.
400 M. Hurdles—Mary Ayres, Prairie View (Tex.) TC.
5,000 M. Walk—Sue Brodock, Rialto (Calif.) Roadrunners.
440 Yd. Relay—Tennessee State.
880 Yd. Relay—Tennessee State.
Mile Relay—Atoms TC, Brooklyn.
High Jump—Joni Huntley, Sheridan, Ore.
Long Jump—Jodi Anderson, Los Angeles.
Shot-Put—Maren Seidler, Chicago.
Discus—Jane Haist, Canada.
Javelin—Kathy Schmidt, Pacific Palisades, Calif.
Team—Los Angeles Naturite TC.

National Collegiate Outdoor Champions

100 M.—Harvey Glance, Auburn.
200 M.—William Snoddy, Oklahoma.
400 M.—Herman Frazier, Arizona State.
800 M.—Mark Enyeart, Utah State.
1,500 M.—Wilson Waigwa, Texas-El Paso.

5,000 M.—Josh Kimeto, Wash. State.
10,000 M.—Samson Kimombwa, Wash. State.
3,000 M. Steeplechase—James Munyala, Texas-El Paso.
110 M. Hurdles—James Owens, UCLA.
400 M. Hurdles—Thomas Andrews, So. California.
400 M. Relay—So. California.
1,600 M. Relay—So. California.
High Jump—Kyle Arney, Arizona State.
Triple Jump—Ron Livers, San Jose State.
Discus—Svein Wavik, Texas-El Paso.
Javelin—Scott Dykehouse, Florida.
Pole Vault—Earl Bell, Arkansas State.
Long Jump—Larry Doubley, So. California.
Shot-Put—Terry Albritton, Stanford.
Hammer—Scott Neilson, Washington.
Team—Arizona State.

Other Champions

AAU Decathlon—Fred Dixon, Beverly Hills, Calif.
AAU Pentathlon—Linda Cornelius, Texas A&M.
Boston Marathon—Jerome Drayton, Toronto; first woman finisher: Miki Gorman, Los Angeles.
USTFF Marathon—David Jones, Owatoon, Minn.
USTFF Decathlon—Steve Alexander, Houston.
NAIA Marathon—Tim Terrill, Saginaw Valley.
NAIA Decathlon—Bill Waters, Point Loma, Calif.

TRAMPOLINE

AAU Champions

Men—Ron Merriott, Rockford, Ill.
Men, Double-Mini—Ken Kovach, Cleveland.
Women—Shelly Grant, Springfield, Ill.
Women, Double-Mini—Diane Goldsworthy, Rockford, Ill.

VOLLEYBALL

USVA Open—Chuck's Steak House, Santa Barbara, Calif.
USVA Women's Open—South Bay Spoilers, Hermosa Beach, Calif.
AAU—Maccabi Union, Los Angeles.
AAU Women—Nick's Fish Market, Santa Monica, Calif.
YMCA—Countryside, Westchester, Ohio.
YMCA Women—Stonestown, San Francisco.
NCAA—Southern California.
NAIA—George Williams College.
Pro—Orange County Stars.

WATER POLO

AAU Men—Concord, Calif.
AAU Women—Merced, Calif.

WATER SKIING

World Champions

MEN

Overall—Mike Hazelwood, Britain.
Slalom—Bob LaPoint, Castro Valley, Cal.
Tricks—Carlos Suarez, Venezuela.
Jumping—Mike Suyderhoud, Petaluma, Cal.

WOMEN

Overall—Cindy Todd, Pearson, Fla.
Slalom—Cindy Todd.
Tricks—Maria Carrasco, Venezuela.
Jumping—Linda Giddens, Eastman, Ga.

United States Champions

MEN

Overall—Ricky McCormick, Winter Haven, Fla.
Slalom—Kris LaPoint, Los Banos, Calif.
Tricks—Ricky McCormick.

WOMEN

Overall—Camille Duvall, Irving, Tex.
Slalom—Cathy Marlow, Pinole, Calif.
Tricks—Pam Folsom, Boynton Beach, Fla.
Jumping—Linda Giddens, Eastman, Ga.

WEIGHT LIFTING

AAU National Champions

114½ Lbs.—Curt White, Charleston, Ill.
123½ Lbs.—Patrick Omori, Honolulu
132¼ Lbs.—Phil Sanderson, Billings, Mont.
148¾ Lbs.—James Benjamin, Columbus, O.
165¼ Lbs.—David Reigles, York, Pa.
181¾ Lbs.—Robert Napier, Richardson, Tex.
198¼ Lbs.—Phil Grippaldi, York, Pa.
220¼ Lbs.—Mark Cameron, York, Pa.
242½ Lbs.—Ray Blaha, Garfield Heights, Ohio.
Superheavyweight—Sam Walker, Dallas.

WRESTLING

AAU Freestyle Champions

105.5 Lbs.—Bill Rosado, Bakersfield (Calif.)
114.5 Lbs.—Kayoto Shimizu, Japan.
125.5 Lbs.—Aikiro Yamati, Japan.
136.5 Lbs.—Jim Humphrey, Bakersfield.
149.5 Lbs.—Chuck Yagla, Ames, Iowa.
163.1 Lbs.—Stan Dziedzic, New York AC.
180.5 Lbs.—Mark Lieberman, NYAC.
198 Lbs.—Ben Peterson, Comstock, Wis.
220 Lbs.—Harold Smith, Toledo, Ohio.
Unlimited—Greg Wojciechowski, Toledo.
Team—New York AC.

National Collegiate AA Champions

118 Lbs.—Jim Haines, Wisconsin.

126 Lbs.—Nick Gallo, Hofstra.
134 Lbs.—Pat Neu, Minnesota.
142 Lbs.—Steve Barrett, Oklahoma State.
150 Lbs.—Mark Churella, Michigan.
158 Lbs.—Lee Kemp, Wisconsin.
167 Lbs.—Rod Kilgore, Oklahoma.
177 Lbs.—Chris Campbell, Iowa.
190 Lbs.—Frank Santana, Iowa State.
Heavyweight—Jimmy Jackson, Okla. State.
Team—Iowa State.

World Champions

105.5 Lbs.—Anatoli Beloglazov, Sov. Union.
114.5 Lbs.—Yuji Takada, Japan.
125.5 Lbs.—Tadashi Sasaki, Japan.
136.5 Lbs—Vladimir Uymin, Soviet Union.
163 Lbs.—Stanley Dziedzic, Lansing, Mich.
149.5 Lbs.—Pavel Pinigin, Sov. Union
180.5 Lbs.—Adolph Seger, W. Germany.
198 Lbs.—Anatoli Propopchuk, Sov. Union.
220 Lbs.—Aslanbek Bisultanov, Sov. Union.
Unlimited—Soslan Andiev, Soviet Union.

YACHTING

U.S. Yacht Racing Union Champions

Men (Mallory Cup)—Marvin Beckmann, Houston, Tex.
Women (Adams Cup)—Cindy Stieffel, Bay Waveland, Mo.
O'Day—(single-handed)—Dave Chapin, Springfield, Ill.
Mertz (Women's single-handed)—Poppy Truman, Berkeley, Calif.
Adams Memorial (Women's double-handed)—Jan C. and Pat O'Malley, Mantoloking, N.J.
Sears (junior)—Will Petersilge, Buckeye Lake, Ohio.
Smythe (junior singlehanded)—Paul Yost, Stockton, Calif.

Prince of Wales Bowl (Club)—Coronado YC, San Diego.

Distance and Ocean Racing

Annapolis-Newport—Overall: Jack Knife, Jack Greenberg, Miami.

Trans-Pacific—Merlin, Bill Lee, Santa Cruz, Calif.

America's Cup

Courageous, United States, defeated Australia.

WHO'S WHO IN BEST SPORT STORIES–1978

WRITERS IN BEST SPORTS STORIES—1978

THE PRIZE WINNERS

THOMAS BOSWELL (The Right-Field Sign Says "Reg-gie, Reg-gie, Reg-gie"), winner of the 1978 news-coverage award, has been a sports reporter with the *Washington Post* since 1971. His major beats are major-league baseball (World Series and playoffs), tennis (Forest Hills), and general assignment coverage of the Washington Redskins, Washington Bullets, college football and basketball. He is a graduate of Amherst College, class of 1969. He won a Baltimore-Washington Newspaper Guild Front Page Award honorable mention in 1974. This is his third appearance in *Best Sports Stories*.

DAVID KLEIN (Wells Twombly, 41; The Laughter Still Echoes), who captured the news-feature award, is a second-time winner in the *Best Sports Stories* anthologies. As a columnist for the *Newark Star-Ledger* and associated Newhouse Newspapers, he won the news-coverage prize with his story on the Billie Jean King-Bobby Riggs tennis match in *Best Sports Stories—1974*. In addition, he is the author of 14 books, including *The New York Giants: Yesterday, Today and Tomorrow*. He has also contributed to most of the national periodicals. He attended the University of Oklahoma and Fairleigh Dickinson University in New Jersey. Klein has appeared in *Best Sports Stories* on many occasions.

A. BARTLETT GIAMATTI (Tom Seaver's Farewell), winner of the best magazine story award, is the president of Yale University, elected in 1977. He has written two books on literary subjects, edited several others, and written many essays for literary anthologies and magazines, but this is his first important sports story. He received a doctor of philosophy degree from Yale in 1964 and before being named president of that university he was the Frederick Clifford Ford professor of English and comparative literature as well as the director of the division of the humanities. This, of course, is his first appearance in *Best Sports Stories*. He was born in Boston, Massachusetts, in 1938, making him one of the youngest presidents ever to serve at Yale. He is also interested in community affairs at New Haven as a member of the Board of the Arts Council of Greater New Haven and a member of the Board of the Connecticut Ballet.

OTHER WRITERS (*In Alphabetical Order*)

DAVE ANDERSON (The Best of Al McGuire) is a sports columnist for *The New York Times* and was the winner of the news-feature award of *Best Sports Stories—1972*. He also won the 1965 magazine story award for a profile of Sugar Ray Robinson. He was born in Brooklyn, New York, and began his newspaper career with the now defunct *New York Sun*. After graduation from Holy Cross in 1951, he went to work for the *Brooklyn Eagle*, also defunct, and then for the *New York Journal*, likewise out of business. As a columnist and reporter for *The New York Times*, he covers the entire range of sports and has appeared in *Best Sports Stories* many times.

LENNY ANDERSON (A New History of Racing, or, "Bet Two, Brutus"), after attending the University of Washington, worked as reporter and columnist for the *Tacoma News-Tribune, Seattle Times* and, for the past 13 years, *Seattle Post-Intelligencer,* where this story appeared—23 years all told in sports. This is his first appearance in *Best Sports Stories*.

PETE AXTHELM (Racing's Boy Wonder), a 1965 graduate of Yale, has been a general editor of *Newsweek* since 1970. He had previously been a writer for *Sports Illustrated* and a reporter and horse racing columnist for the *New York Herald Tribune*. Axthelm has written more than twenty *Newsweek* cover stories since becoming a member of the staff. While a majority of them dealt with sports subjects, he has also written covers for the Music and News Media sections and reported on scenes from the Munich Olympics for the International section. His honors include a Schick Award from the Professional Football Writers for his cover story on "The Running Backs"; writing honors for his cover story "Superhorse" on Secretariat; and the Newspaper Guild's Page One Award for "Olympics '76: A Star Is Born." He has contributed to many other major magazines and authored four books, of which *The City Game* received the finest accolades. His work has merited a number of appearances in *Best Sports Stories*.

PETER BODO (Paging Joe DiMaggio!) lives in Manhattan. He writes frequently about tennis and soccer and is a contributing editor of *Tennis Magazine* and co-author of the book *Pele's New World*. His work has appeared in numerous magazines, including *New York, Sport,* the *Star,* the *Australian,* and the magazine section of the *New York Daily News*. This is his second appearance in *Best Sports Stories.*

PETER BONVENTRE (Coming Back Blazing) has been a general editor in *Newsweek*'s Sports section since 1976. He has covered the Olympic tragedy in Munich, Bobby Fischer's chess playoff in Iceland, the Ali-Foreman title bout in Zaire, and the Ali-Frazier fight in Manila. He joined *Newsweek* in 1969 as an assistant editor and two years later was promoted to associate editor. He has shared two Newspaper Guild of New York Page One Awards with General Editor Pete Axthelm for his reporting from Manila on the Ali-

Frazier fight and from Montreal on the 1976 Summer Olympic Games. Before joining *Newsweek,* Bonventre was a news assistant to the sports editor at *The New York Times* for two years. He is a 1967 graduate of the University of Pennsylvania where he received a bachelor of arts degree in journalism. He has appeared in *Best Sports Stories* on numerous occasions.

JEFF CAPONIGRO (It's Nostalgia Time Again) is a free-lance writer who specializes in sports. He has done work for the *Observer & Eccentric* newspaper chain in lower Michigan, the *Mt. Pleasant Daily Times-News,* and is currently working for the *Midland* (Mich.) *Daily News* where he is a reporter and columnist. Currently he is also a senior at Central Michigan University and has a double major in journalism and English. This is his first appearance in *Best Sports Stories.*

MURRAY CHASS (When a Girl Picks Baseball Over Ballet) began working for *The New York Times,* where this story was printed, in 1969 after serving with the Associated Press in Pittsburgh and New York for nearly 10 years. With the *Times,* he has concentrated on baseball in recent years and has gained a reputation for his coverage in legal and labor areas of sports. This is his fifth effort in *Best Sports Stories.* He is married and has five children, one of whom he has written about in the current volume.

BUD COLLINS (The New Look in Tennis) is one of America's best-known tennis writers and television broadcasters and one of the most respected reporters of all sports. As a columnist for *The Boston Globe,* he has received warm critical acclaim for his books on Rod Laver and Evonne Goolagong and has been a regular contributor to *World Tennis* magazine for five years. He has made many appearances in *Best Sports Stories.*

BILL CONLIN (The Ten-Minute Collapse) is currently in his thirteenth season as *Philadelphia Daily News* baseball writer and also covers Penn State football, college basketball, and off-season baseball between November and the end of February. He shared the best news-feature story award in *Best Sports Stories—1965* with Robert Lipsyte. He lives in Washington Township, New Jersey, and enjoys all types of surfing, sailing, tennis, and photography.

BILL DIXON (The Cosmos Dance to the Title) is a first-timer in the *Best Sports Stories* series. At 29 he is sports editor of the *Coos Bay World.* A native of North Carolina, he has covered sports for 12 years in Oregon and the two Carolinas. He holds a master's degree in education and has worked as a teacher and coach.

TRACY DODDS (A Mile of Style), at 25, has been working as a sports writer for the *Milwaukee Journal* for four years since her graduation from Indiana University in January 1974. She covers Big Ten football and boxing as her primary beats, but she also does extensive coverage of auto racing. This story marks her debut in the *Best Sports Stories* series.

MAYNARD EILERS (The Enjoyable Chess Game), 33, is executive sports editor of *The Florida Times-Union,* where this story appeared. He is a graduate of Tulane University and attended law school at the University of Oklahoma before deciding on a journalism career. He is married and the father of two daughters. This marks his first appearance in *Best Sports Stories.*

WILLIAM BARRY FURLONG (When a Fight Breaks Out It Doesn't Always Play Well on TV) reflects the broadening perspective of the modern sports writer. He has a degree in engineering and was a ghost writer for the astronauts; he is a consultant in communications for many of the largest corporations in the nation; and has covered—as a reporter—everything from the White House to plane crashes to international economic conferences. During the last 16 years he has spent most of his time as a free-lance writer covering finances space, medicine, science, politics—and sports. His books also suggest the vast range of up-to-date sports writers: He has published one book on sports—*Go for Broke* with Arnold Palmer; one book on medicine; and one book on classical music. He writes for *The Washington Post* and has merited other appearances in *Best Sports Stories.*

JOE GERGEN (Three Sheets to the Wind, and More) is celebrating his third year as sports columnist for *Newsday* after seven years on the baseball and pro football beats. In the course of that role, he has interviewed everyone from Miz Lillian to The Big Dodger in the Sky, both of whom, he says, attended the 1977 World Series, although not as a couple. He is a 1963 graduate of Boston College and spent five years on the UPI sports desk in New York attempting to compute box scores before moving on to *Newsday.* He won the National Headliner Award for sports writing in 1971. He has appeared in *Best Sports Stories* many times.

PAUL HEMPHILL (The Second Coming of Jerry West) is the sports world's answer to William Faulkner. His roots are deep in the South. He went to college at Auburn University. He began his newspaper career with the *Birmingham News* and did further stints as sports editor of the *Augusta Chronicle* and the *Tampa Times.* His last newspaper job in this area was with the *Atlanta Journal* before getting a prized Neiman Fellowship at Harvard. After that he free-lanced for a short time, wrote a fine book, *The Nashville Sound,* went West and back into newspaper work with the *San Francisco Examiner;* got married and went to *The Washington Post* at its sports desk, where he now works a bit nearer to Faulkner territory. He has merited inclusion in *Best Sports Stories* on many occasions.

JENNY KELLNER (Derby Week: Parades, Parties, Pressure), after graduating from Hofstra in 1975, continued working at *Newsday* as a sports assistant, covering scholastic sports and equestrian events. In July 1976, she began working for *The Record* (Hackensack, N.J.) as horse racing writer and harness racing handicapper. She left *The Record* in July 1977 to become the racing writer at United Press International in New York, where she is now. This is her first appearance in *Best Sports Stories.*

TONY KORNHEISER ("Love! Love! Love!" Cries Pele) has worked at *The New York Times,* where this story appeared, for the last three years. Before that he was at *Newsday* as a sports reporter, a rock music critic, and the life-style specialist for the daily magazine section. His stories have appeared in *Rolling Stone, New York,* and *Sport Magazine.* He has also been a regular contributor to the *Street & Smith Basketball Annual* and a story of his from this publication was reprinted in *Best Sports Stories—1976.* This is his sixth appearance in *Best Sports Stories.*

ROBERT LIPSYTE (A Legend of the City Game), a former sports columnist for *The New York Times* and general columnist for the *New York Post,* where this story appeared, is the author of nine books including *Sportsworld: An American Dreamland,* and the novels *The Contender* and *One Fat Summer.* He has appeared in this collection 11 times and won the top award four times, in each of the three categories.

BARRY LORGE (British Glow: Wade Wins Wimbledon), a native of Worcester, Massachusetts, is a 1970 graduate of Harvard University, where he majored in government. He started writing sports for the *Worcester Telegram & Gazette* while he was in college, happened on the tennis beat and since 1971 has been a free-lancer, specializing in tennis. He has covered the sport in more than a dozen countries for a number of publications. In 1975 he achieved the grand slam, covering the Australian, French, Wimbledon, and U.S. opens. He is a contributing editor of *Tennis Magazine* and his stories appear frequently in the *Washington Post.* Lorge has been represented many times in this anthology.

GENE LYONS (If They Don't Win It's a Shame), a former teacher turned free-lance writer, has written for *Harper's, The New York Times* magazine, *The New York Times Book Review,* and several smaller magazines. After stints at the University of Massachusetts, the University of Texas, and the University of Arkansas, he abandoned the teaching profession in 1976 and since then has been a free-lancer with *Texas Monthly,* where this story appeared. He also presently writes a book review column in the *Nation.* This is his first appearance in *Best Sports Stories.*

JEFF MEYERS (Foul Play for Foul Balls) has been sports columnist of the *St. Louis Post-Dispatch* since 1972, but this is his first appearance in *Best Sports Stories.* He covered the St. Louis football Cardinals from 1970 through 1974 and won the Sigma Delta Chi Award in 1977 for outstanding reporting. He attended Miami of Ohio and was graduated with a B.A. in 1964.

NEIL MILBERT (Seattle Slew Wanted to Run) covers racing, professional and college football and boxing for the *Chicago Tribune*. A graduate of Marquette University, he served in the Marine Corps and worked for WEMP Radio (Milwaukee), the *Ottumwa* (Iowa) *Courier,* and the *Jersey City* (N.J.) *Journal* before joining the *Chicago Tribune*. He has made four appearances in *Best Sports Stories*.

HUBERT MIZELL (The Tampa Bay Bucks Win One at Last) is 38 and sports editor of *The St. Petersburg* (Fla.) *Times*. He was formerly feature sports writer for the Associated Press in Miami and New York. He has covered almost all of the world's great sports events, including the Olympic Games, and has been included in *Best Sports Stories* many times. Mizell, who is also a contributing editor of *Golf Digest,* began his career on the *Florida Times-Union* in Jacksonville at age 17.

MONTY MONTGOMERY (Far Afield, Far from Home) is 39 years old and has been what he calls a "professional student," with a B.A. from Stanford, an M.A. from the University of Oregon, and "two utterly useless degrees from the Harvard Graduate School of Education." He wanted to spend the rest of his life writing about trout but he is occasionally required to cover snow sports, including skiing and ice skating, for *The Boston Globe*. He has been employed there for six years and "works there frequently," he says. He was once home and gardens editor of the *El Cajon* (Calif.) *Valley News,* a biweekly.

SHEILA MORAN (A Wimbledon Story Waiting to Begin) began her sportswriting career in 1969 with the Associated Press in New York City. She continued covering golf, tennis, and other sports while working full time on the news side rewrite bank at the *New York Post*. She joined the *Los Angeles Times* sports staff in October 1976 and is currently covering hockey. This is her first appearance in this anthology.

EDWIN POPE (*Roots* and Sports) was born in Athens, Georgia, and maintains he fumbled his way through the University of Georgia. Nevertheless, he has established a warm readership as a columnist and reporter for his paper, the *Miami Herald,* of which he became sports editor in 1957 and in which this column appeared. He was formerly with the *Atlanta Journal Constitution* and United Press International. He is the author of four books: *Football's Greatest Coaches, Baseball's Greatest Managers, Encyclopedia of Greyhound Racing,* and *Ted Williams: The Golden Years*. He is a veteran contributor to this anthology.

JOHN S. RADOSTA (Squash Racquets, Anyone? Definitely Yes!), once a reporter for the late *New York Herald Tribune,* has been with *The New York Times* for 32 years, during which he has performed all kinds of writing and editing assignments. He was a picture editor for 13 years and a sports writer for 11, during which he covered motor sports, golf, and ice hockey, as well as many other assorted sports. He is the author of *The New York Times Guide to Auto Racing,* published in 1971, and won the magazine award this sports anthology offers in 1975. This is his third appearance in *Best Sports Stories.*

BILLY REED (A Religious Rite with the Rich and Famous) is sports editor of *The Louisville Courier-Journal,* in which this story appeared. He is a graduate of Transylvania College and began his journalism career in 1959 with the *Lexington* (Ky.) *Herald,* later serving as assistant sports editor for both the *Herald* and the *Leader.* He joined the sports staff of the Louisville *Courier-Journal* and the *Louisville Times* in 1966 and later spent four years as a writer for *Sports Illustrated* before returning to those newspapers in 1972. In 1973 Billy Reed and reporter Jim Bolus won national journalism awards from Sigma Delta Chi and the Headliner Club for a series of investigative stories on thoroughbred horse racing. This is his first appearance in this anthology.

BOB RUBIN (What Some People Will Do for Money!) is a sports reporter and columnist for the *Miami Herald.* For four years he covered sports for *Newsday.* He has also had considerable magazine experience, as assistant managing editor of *Sport Magazine,* editor of Pyramid Publications, *Basketball News, Gridiron News, Kyle Rote's Jets/Giants Newsletter,* and *Week End Sports.* He is the author of 12 books, including biographies of Satchel Paige, Pete Rose, Tony Conigliaro, and Ty Cobb. He is currently researching a bio of Lou Gehrig. This is his first appearance in *Best Sports Stories.*

JACK SAMSON (The Day of the Elk) is the editor of *Field & Stream.* His outdoor writing career has spanned 27 years and almost as many countries. He wrote an outdoor column for the Associated Press for nine years and his stories have appeared in all the major outdoor magazines. He is the author of numerous books, ranging from trap and skeet shooting to big game fishing. This is his second appearance in *Best Sports Stories.*

LOEL SCHRADER (Who Are Those Guys Anyway?) has been a sports writer and columnist for 36 years, all in the Ridder (now Knight-Ridder) chain. At the *Long Beach* (Cal.) *Independent Press-Telegram,* where this story appeared, he has covered college football, professional baseball, college basketball, and college hockey. He is a bachelor of philosophy, with a major in journalism, and also a J.D. from Western State University and its College of Law. This is his first appearance in *Best Sports Stories.*

JOHN SCHULIAN (No Garden Party for Ali) worked on the defunct *Chicago Daily News,* where this story appeared, and specialized in prose portraits of athletes. But he has also been known to write about touchdowns, home runs, stuff shots, and left hooks. Before coming to the *News,* Schulian, who has a B.A. from the University of Utah and an M.S. from Northwestern, worked on *The Washington Post* and spent five years as a cityside reporter and rock-and-roll columnist at the *Baltimore Evening Sun*. His free-lance work has appeared in a variety of magazines ranging from *Sports Illustrated* to *American Film*. He has appeared in this anthology on numerous occasions.

NICK SEITZ (Nicklaus!) is one of the few writers who has hit the over 10-time mark in this sports anthology. He is now the editor of *Golf Digest*. His alma mater was the University of Oklahoma, where he majored in philosophy. Then, at the age of 22, he became editor of the *Norman* (Okla.) *Transcript*. His majoring in philosophy was excellent background for his golf articles, which not only concern themselves with the techniques of the game but also with the frustrations and tribulations of ordinary mortals who are constrained to watch the epic golf events on the tube and then attempt to emulate them. He has won numerous prizes in golf and basketball writing contests.

BLACKIE SHERROD (Randle's Big Explosion), the executive sports editor of the *Dallas Times Herald*, has garnered just about every important sports-writing prize in the country. To name a few: The National Headliners Award; seven citations as the outstanding sports writer by newspapers, radio, and TV colleagues; and over a dozen inclusions in *Best Sports Stories*. As a master of ceremonies and banquet speaker he has made a reputation almost equal to his reputation for writing. He also has his own radio and TV programs.

D. L. STEWART (The Bullring) spent 10 years as a sports writer, including seven covering the Cincinnati Bengals of the NFL for *The Dayton* (Ohio) *Journal Herald*, in which this column appeared. In 1975 he switched to a general humor column and 80 of these columns have been combined into a book entitled *The Man in the Blue Flannel Pajamas*. This is his second appearance in this anthology.

PHIL TAYLOR (Watson Is the Master) has been a sports writer for 41 years, but his writing style is strictly today. His stints include work with the *Tacoma News-Tribune, Seattle Star, Seattle Times,* and *The Seattle Post-Intelligencer*. He has covered every major sports beat, and for the past 26 years has been a golf editor. He also covers University of Washington football and basketball. Some of his writing honors include two first places in the National Golf Writers Competition, several regional citations, and numerous inclusions in *Best Sports Stories*. His alma mater is the University of Washington.

SAM TOPEROFF (Death of the Don King Tournament) began his writing career in the mid sixties as a poet and fiction writer. More recently, after publishing five novels and numerous short stories, he began to explore sports journalism. He has found the struggles of athletes against themselves and others a theme that interests him deeply. His current story, which appeared in *Sport Magazine,* is his first in *Best Sports Stories*.

JAMES TUITE (Women's Golf Tour: Stained by Tears and Drudgery), who stepped down as sports editor of *The New York Times* this year to devote full time to writing, has authored several books on sports and moonlighted as a journalism professor at Long Island University, Brooklyn, New York, for eight years. This is his first appearance in *Best Sports Stories.*

WELLS TWOMBLY (The Flesh Lottery) died at 41 midway in 1977. This, therefore, is one of his last columns. For a more inclusive biography of a great writer and fine gentleman may we refer you to David Klein's fine prize-winning feature story in the front part of this book. But may we quote from his short biography that appeared in *Best Sports Stories—1977:* "His family and the sports world have been bereft of a man who had a beautiful way with words. They flowed from his pen and accounted for his meteoric rise. Since coming to the *San Francisco Examiner,* he had published more than six books, contributed to many magazines, and written a daily column in his paper. His work was usually involved with the sports world but he had no hesitation in going beyond his particular arena to write about a slice of life that delighted or disturbed him. But whereas a bright meteor quickly disappears without a trace, Twombly left behind him a legacy of marvelous and exciting talent that will be remembered. The only thing is that he left us much, much too soon."

MAURY WHITE (Three Seconds to Go) has been with the *Des Moines Register* since 1946 and has been writing sports columns for a good share of that time. A graduate of Drake, and a three-time letterman in both football and baseball, he has been fortunate enough to sit in on some of the high points in national sports during that time. He is a past president of the Football Writers Association, a 1966 Sports Illustrated Silver Anniversary honors winner, the 1977 recipient of the Jake Wade Award for distinguished sports writing from the College Sports Information Directors of America. He has merited many appearances in *Best Sports Stories.*

DAVID WOLF (In This Corner: The Fighting O'Gradys!), now an editorial consultant at *Sport,* where this article appeared, did his undergraduate work at the University of Wisconsin and received his M.A. from the Columbia School of Journalism, where he was awarded the Grantland Rice Fellowship. As a sports reporter and editor with *Life,* he wrote a 1969 investigative article that cleared basketball player Connie Hawkins of involvement in the 1961 gambling scandals. His book about Hawkins, *Foul!,* was a best seller. A former contributing editor at *True* and writer of the documentary basketball film, *The American Game,* he has made two previous appearances in *Best Sports Stories.*

PHOTOGRAPHERS IN BEST
SPORTS STORIES—1978

THE PHOTO WINNERS

GEORGE D. WALDMAN (The Day the Seismographs Broke Down) has now won the action-photo award in *Best Sports Stories* for the second time. His first win came with a shot titled, "Head in Groin, Shoe in Belly, Cleats in Face and Other Items," showing a bruising, rough and violent encounter among a group of soccer players struggling for the ball. After that shot, which he took for the *Colorado Springs Sun* in 1976, he went East and joined the *Detroit News* photo staff. As a young man he held many odd jobs; delivering milk, digging ditches, and even working as a weather observer in Greece. Soon he found he liked taking pictures, got himself a camera, and now has two winners for his portfolio.

CHARLES R. PUGH, JR. (A Child Shall Come Forth; But He Wanted to Be First), feature-photo winner, has been a three-time victor since the inception of the *Best Sports Stories* series in 1944—once in 1969, again in 1977, and now in 1978. Two of his earlier prizes were in the action category. He began his distinguished photographic career with the *Johnson City* (Tenn.) *Press-Chronicle* and is now with the *Atlanta Journal-Constitution*, where this photo was published. He has garnered many state and national prizes and has merited a number of appearances in this sports anthology.

OTHER PHOTOGRAPHERS (*In Alphabetical Order*)

MICHAEL A. ANDERSEN (Yankee Eruption at Fenway Park) has made eight previous appearances in *Best Sports Stories*, winning the feature-photo award in 1977. He has been a general assignment photographer for *The Boston Herald American* for nine years, after working for papers in Kansas, Iowa, Arizona, and Texas. He has been named Photographer of the Year on two occasions by the Boston Press Photographers Association.

TONY BERNATO (If Looks Could Kill) is one of the fine veterans among eastern lensmen. He has often appeared in *Best Sports Stories* and has won many eastern and regional honors. He makes this statement in his bio: "Have been a photographer for 40 years and have enjoyed every bit of it. New cameras make our task easier; no more chasing and running. Competition is not what it was in the old days. I like it better this way. More sports are covered today than in the old, and more people are involved." Tony has been with the *Philadelphia Bulletin* since 1963.

PAT BERRY (Cowboys of Another Stripe) received a B.A. in Journalism in 1974 and became a photographer in Vietnam. While in school he worked for the *San Marcos Record.* He is now a free-lance photographer. His photos have appeared in *New Times, New York,* and *Texas Monthly.* He has also been a stringer for the Associated Press in Houston and has done documentary work for NBC. Awards: Internal Exhibit of Media Arts, Communication Arts Award 1976 and 1977; bronze and silver medals and awards of excellence in the 1977 Houston Art Director's Show.

JOSEPH CANNATA, JR. (Grabbing Hold of the Situation) has been a staff photographer for *The Hartford Courant* for four years. He is editor of the National Press Photographers Association's Region 1 Newsletter and a member of the Connecticut News Photographers Association. Aged 24, he is married and lives in New Britain, Connecticut. This is his first appearance in this sports anthology.

RAY COVEY (Player Flips) is assistant chief photographer at *The Houston Post.* Both he and his wife, Shirley, are from the Connecticut area and moved to Houston in 1956. Previously he had worked for the Connecticut State Police in the Hartford Headquarters Division. He has been with *The Houston Post* for 21 years.

RICHARD DARCEY (Slew Who? Seattle, That's Who!) has the reputation of being one of the nation's most talented photographers. He is the director of photography at the *Washington Post,* where he has worked since 1948. His past honors include *Look's* Sports Pictures of the Year award and many prizes in press association competitions, both national and regional. He has won two prizes for his action shots in this anthology.

ROBERT EMERSON (Time in Their Hands) attended the University of Rhode Island and then started taking photographs for the *Narragansett Times* and the *Standard-Times* in South County, Rhode Island. While at those papers he was named New England Photographer of the Year by the New England Press Association in 1971. He moved in 1974 to *The Providence Journal* and in 1976 was named Photographer of the Year for New England by the National Press Photographers Association (Region 1).

JOHN P. FOSTER (Rodeo Clown Gets the Point) is a most talented rodeo photographer, and every one of his shots shows a remarkable eye for a dramatic situation. He is a stringer for the *Seattle Times* and has taught photojournalism for 10 years at Central State University, Ellensburg, Washington. He was promoted to an associate professor this year.

BERT L. FOX (Guess Whose Wife Uses Tide) is the photo-editor-photographer for *The Coos Bay* (Ore.) *World,* a position he has held since early June 1977. At college he was the photo editor of the school paper, supervising a student staff of 20 part-time photographers. They put out a newspaper five days a week, a weekly feature supplement, and a monthly magazine. Fox is a member of NPPA and has consistently placed high in their monthly clip competition. He has also received photo awards from Sigma Delta Chi, from the Utah-Idaho Associated Press Association and in the Utah State press photo competition. This is his first appearance in *Best Sports Stories.*

STORMI L. GREENER (A Six-Year-Old Hangup) has been a newspaper photographer for the past two and a half years. She came to the *Minneapolis Star* from the *Idaho Statesman* in January 1977. Stormi has an art background and attended Boise State University in Boise, Idaho. She too is a freshman in *Best Sports Stories.*

CLETUS M. "PETE" HOHN (See No Evil, Hear No Evil, Speak No Evil) has been a newspaper man for 25 years, ever since his graduation from the University of Minnesota in 1953. He has been with the *Minneapolis Tribune* for the past 23 years. His pictures have appeared in *Best Sports Stories* for the past three years and in 1976 he won the feature-picture award with a hilarious shot of Patty Berg teaching how to avoid a slice.

LIL JUNAS ("Call Me Offside, and I'll Ram This Right Up . . .") is the chief photographer for the *Log Cabin Democrat* in Faulkner County, Arkansas. Her previous stints were with the *Hazelton* (Pa.) *Standard Speaker* and the *Harrisburg* (Pa.) *Sunday Patriot-News.* She is a native Pennsylvanian and was also on the staff of Juniata College in that state, serving mostly in the public relations area. Later she free-lanced for 12 years for assorted media, mostly magazines, and for several years taught photojournalism on the university level. She is making her first appearance in *Best Sports Stories.*

LARRY KASPERAK (They Forgot to Look Back) makes his first appearance in this anthology. He was graduated from the University of Missouri in 1974, majoring in photojournalism. After graduation he was employed as a summer intern at the *Des Moines Register and Tribune* and later at the *Sentinel* in East Brunswick, New Jersey. He is currently associated with the *Jackson* (Miss.) *Clarion.* His hometown is Salamanca, New York.

EDWARD L. LALLO (A Head for Winning) is on the staff of the *Dallas Morning News.* He had been employed by several photo-oriented newspapers before going to work for the *News* in June of 1977. Now 26, he was graduated from the University of Kansas School of Journalism and worked for the

Colorado Springs Sun, New Iberia (La.) *Daily Iberian, Kingsport* (Tenn.) *Times-News,* and the Scottsbluff (Neb.) *Star-Herald.* He is a newcomer to *Best Sports Stories.*

JOHN LONG (Bleep, Bleep and Jeepers!) has been a photojournalist for six years, working for *The Hartford* (Conn.) *Courant.* He presently holds the office of president of the Connecticut News Photographers Association. This is his third appearance in *Best Sports Stories.* He lives in Manchester, Connecticut, with his wife and three daughters.

JIMI LOTT (Even Pele Doesn't Want to Mix in This One) started his career directly after college at *The Coos Bay* (Ore.) *World* as a darkroom helper. After two and a half years as part-time employee, he became a staff photographer, even though he lacked previous experience in photojournalism. His interest had always lain in creative design and art photography until he discovered the excitement of journalistic lensing. This is his first appearance in *Best Sports Stories.*

FRED MATTHES (Football Can Get Hairy) is 47 years of age and has been a staff photographer with the *San Jose Mercury-News* for 16 years. He has been in *Best Sports Stories* consecutively from 1973 to 1978. He is a member and officer of every important news photographers association. His awards have been manifold, including first places with the California Newspapers Association and the Pro Football Hall of Fame, and commendations and awards of merit from many others.

WILLIAM MEYER (One of Him Should Get a Hit) is a 28-year-old staff photographer for *The Milwaukee Journal* and the *Milwaukee Sentinel.* He is a graduate of the University of Wisconsin and has merited five inclusions of his pictures in *Best Sports Stories,* thanks to his innovative style and perceptive camera.

JAMES A. (JIM) RACKWITZ ("Get Lost!") has been a photographer for the *St. Louis Post-Dispatch* since April 1959. He is married and has two children. He lives in suburban Manchester, Missouri. Prior to his employment by the *Post-Dispatch* he was with the St. Louis bureau of United Press International.

KENNETH R. RANDOLPH (A Little Goose Is No Stymie) has been with the Register Publishing Co. for 10 years. He is at present chief photographer of the *New Haven* (Conn.) *Journal-Courier,* one of the two newspapers owned by the Register. In addition to working on his bachelor of fine arts in photography degree at the University of Bridgeport, he is minoring in graphic design, art history and social work. He presently is in his senior year.

KEN REGAN ("I *Was* the Greatest!") has photographed numerous major news and sports events during the past 12 years, including three Olympics and two national conventions. His work has appeared in magazines such as *Newsweek, Time,* and *Life* and he has won a number of awards on these and other assignments. This is his first appearance in *Best Sports Stories.*

VINCENT T. RIEHL (A Net Loss) started his career in photography in the United States Air Force. He served from 1951 to 1955 as an Air Force photographer, spending three and a half years in Japan during the Korean War. He began work with the *New York Daily News* photo lab in 1956, becoming a photograper on the *News* in 1964. This is his first appearance in this series.

JAMES ROARK (A New Play?) is a Chicagoan who completed the Famous Photographers School course and then joined the *Los Angeles Herald-Examiner* as a copyboy. Later he became a staff photographer there. For the past three years he has been staff sports lensman. His shots have made this sports anthology for the last four years. Last year he won first prizes for his work from the Los Angeles Press Photographers Association, and the Los Angeles Press Club, the California Press Photographers Asosciation, and the California State Fair.

JOHN ROUSMANIERE (It's a "Keeling" Job) is a senior editor at *Natural History Magazine* and was formerly an associate editor of *Yachting Magazine,* with writing, photographing, and editing responsibilities that covered the entire sport of boating. He has B.S. and M.A. degrees from Columbia, with some Ph.D. work in history. He taught American history for three years at the United States Military Academy before coming to work for *Yachting* in 1972. For two years he was the magazine's West Coast editor, living in Newport Beach, California. He now lives in Stamford, Connecticut, and is the author of a glossary of modern sailing terms and co-author of *No Excuse To Lose,* a book on sailboat racing.

LESTER SLOAN (A Legal Squatter) has been a staff photographer at *Newsweek's* Los Angeles bureau since 1970. Before coming to the magazine he free-lanced in Detroit for three years. Sloan graduated from Wayne State University in 1969. While attending school he worked full time as a television news cameraman and made free-lance contributions to magazines. He is a member of the society of professional journalists, Sigma Delta Chi. In 1972 Sloan's work was featured at the Los Angeles County Museum in a five-man show entitled "L.A. Flash." In 1976 Sloan completed a nine-month Neiman Fellowship at Harvard. This is his first appearance in *Best Sports Stories.*

BILL STAHL, JR. ("Yer Outta the Game") was raised with a camera by his award-winning photographer dad, Bill Stahl. After college, young Bill became a free-lance photographer. His work appeared in outstanding magazines throughout the world. He joined the staff of the *New York Journal-American* in 1960 and then, in 1966, went to the *New York Daily News.* He has won numerous awards for photography, including the Page One Award for Best Sports Photography presented by the New York Newspaper Guild. He has also been named the leading photographer .in the New York City area by the National Press Photographers Association in its yearly competition. This is his first appearance in *Best Sports Stories*.

JOHN H. WHITE (They're Having a Big Ball) won the feature award that this anthology offers in 1972 with his shot of a child's footrace, "Happiness Is Winning a Race." He is a staff member of the photo division of the *Chicago Daily News* and has been honored by being named Chicago Press Photographer of the Year three times, a record. He was also chosen as Illinois Photographer of the Year in 1971 and has won numerous other awards. He was born in North Carolina and received his higher education at Central Piedmont Community College.

THE YEAR'S BEST SPORTS PHOTOS

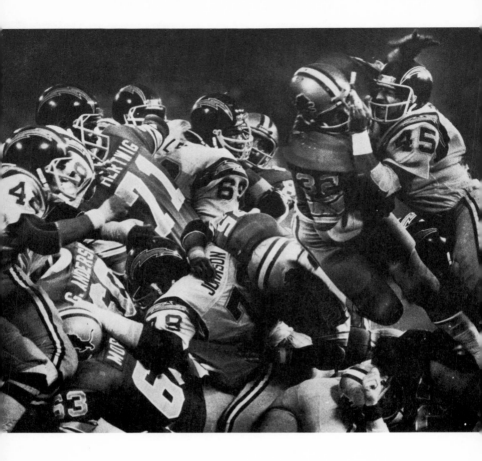

THE DAY THE SEISMOGRAPHS BROKE DOWN

by George D. Waldman, *The Detroit News.* The violent tremor of the earth that resulted from this play when the Detroit Lions charged the San Diego team, only to be held at the one-yard line, is alleged to have alarmed many seismologists throughout the country. The judges, in looking for a good action picture, felt this shot met every requisite for the prize in that category. Copyright, ©, 1977, *The Detroit News.*

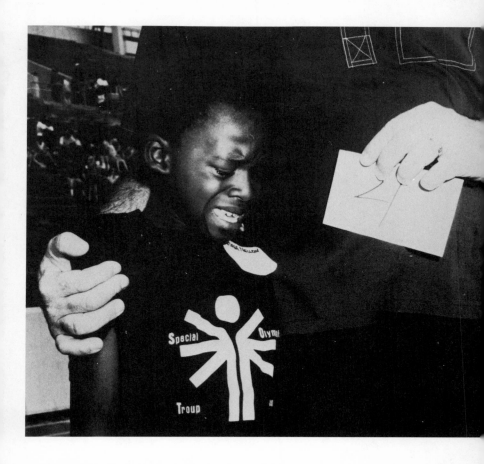

A CHILD SHALL COME FORTH; ONLY HE
WANTED TO BE FIRST

by Charles R. Pugh, Jr., *Atlanta Journal-Constitution*. This lovely bitter-sweet shot speaks for itself and the judges, too. It captured first prize in the feature category. Copyright, ©, 1977, Charles Pugh, Atlanta newspapers.

YANKEE ERUPTION AT FENWAY PARK

by Mike Andersen, *The Boston Herald American-Advertiser*. The abrasive
feelings that permeated the Yankee team throughout 1977 are best exemplified in this shot. Manager Billy Martin is rebuking Reggie Jackson for loafing
in the outfield. Reggie tried to explain but as the argument heated up,
Yankee players intervened and Jackson was spirited from the dugout. Martin, seething, went for him but was bodily restrained. That this fragmented
team cohered to win the World Series is a miracle. Copyright, ©, 1977, *The
Boston Herald American*.

IF LOOKS COULD KILL

by Tony Bernato, *Philadelphia Evening and Sunday Bulletin*. This picture
snaps Phil Boone, a Phillie player with mischief in his eyes, trying to steal
a base while Mike Tyson of the Cards stares him down with a steady,
malevolent glare. Copyright, ©, 1977, *The Evening and Sunday Bulletin*,
Philadelphia.

SLEW WHO? SEATTLE, THAT'S WHO!

by Richard Darcey, *The Washington Post.* As Seattle Slew (Triple Crown winner and 1977 horse of the year) crosses the Preakness finish line, jockey Jean Cruget takes a glance over his shoulder to see runner-up Iron Constitution finish second. Copyright, ©, 1977, the *Washington Post.*

COWBOYS OF ANOTHER STRIPE

by Pat Berry, *Texas Monthly*. These four inmate cowboys are the aristocracy of the Prison Rodeo. For these men the rodeo means a chance to wear boots, spurs, and leather belts and to walk around for a few hours without having to stand in line. Copyright, ©, 1977, *Texas Monthly*. Reprinted by permission.

GRABBING HOLD OF THE SITUATION

by Joseph Cannata, Jr., *The Hartford Courant.* Phil Larsen (54) grabs hold of Fred Hill's jersey to stop the Woodrow Wilson runner during the third period of a Northwest Conference football game in Middletown. Berlin won, 26–6, for its sixth consecutive victory of the season. Copyright, ©, 1977, *The Hartford Courant Company.*

ONE OF HIM SHOULD GET A HIT

by William Meyer, *The Milwaukee Journal*. Cecil Cooper of the Milwaukee Brewers is pictured during his swing in these multiple exposures taken at Milwaukee County Stadium. Copyright, ©, 1977, *The Milwaukee Journal*.

"CALL ME OFFSIDE AND I'LL RAM THIS RIGHT UP . . ."

by Lil Junas, *Log Cabin* (Ark.) *Democrat*. A Southeast Missouri runner is making this threatening gesture on his way to a touchdown in the second quarter against the University of Central Arkansas. Southeast beat Central, 17–6. Whether or not the ref was intimidated is not known. He did, however, signal a touchdown immediately. Copyright, ©, 1977, *Log Cabin Democrat*.

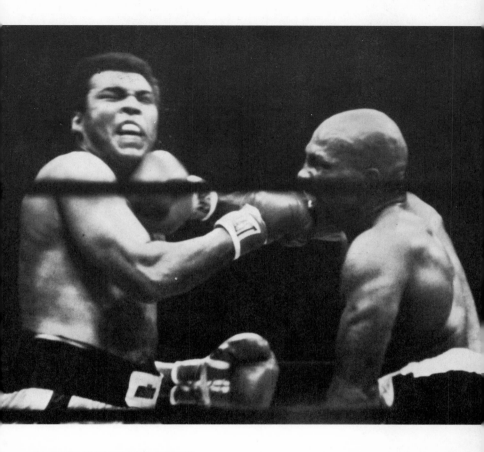

"I *WAS* THE GREATEST!"

by Ken Regan, *Newsweek*. Ali attempted to make a stumblebum out of Earnie Shavers long before the fight. He psyched, scolded, and belittled him. He didn't succeed. Many in the fight crowd, and many sports writers, believed that Shavers had won. However, weary and almost punched out, Ali staggered out for the fifteenth round and put on a magnificent comeback that was just enough to tip the scales in his favor. He was voted the winner in a split decision. Copyright, ©, 1977, Ken Regan, Camera 5.

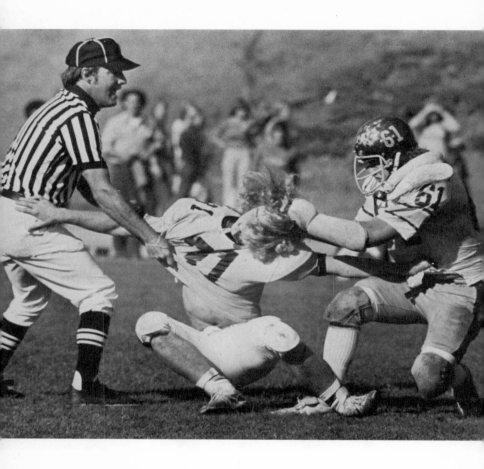

FOOTBALL CAN GET HAIRY

by Fred Matthes, *San Jose Mercury-News*. Del Mar's Pete Narlesky is caught in the middle as an official tries mightily to comb out matters between the hapless Pete and Steve Johnson of Camden High, who appears to have a good grip on matters. It is alleged the ref did separate them with a can of "Head and Shoulders," after which the groundkeepers cleared the field of dandruff. Copyright, ©, 1977, *San Jose Mercury-News*.

A LITTLE GOOSE IS NO STYMIE

by Kenneth R. Randloph, the *New Haven (Conn.)* Journal-Courier. Clay-ton Larsen is doing his best to ignore a new batch of fledgling geese wandering around the fairway and they are returning the compliment. The golfer was taking part in the local U.S. Open qualifying event at the New Haven Country Club. Copyright, ©, 1977, the *New Haven Journal-Courier.*

A HEAD FOR WINNING

by Ed L. Lallo, *Dallas Morning News*. Chuck O'Neal of Flagler High School pushes his head just far enough into the tape to garner a victory over Mullen's Dick Barry in the 440 semi-finals of the meet for high schools at the U.S. Air Force Academy in Colorado Springs. Copyright, ©, 1977, *Dallas Morning News*.

A NEW PLAY?

by James Roark, *Los Angeles Herald-Examiner.* The kicker belongs to the Los Angeles Rams and his flying opponent is a Viking, Nate Allen, who is on his way over the goalpost. At least that's the way it looks. We could be wrong, and it's merely a Ram linesman earning his wages by blocking out Nate. Copyright, ©, 1977, *Los Angeles Herald-Examiner.*

A NET LOSS

by Vincent T. Riehl, *New York Daily News.* As Buffalo goalie Dan Edwards turns around to watch, the puck rolls across the goal line into where the net should have been standing. However, at just that moment Islander Denis Potvin is being checked into the top of the net by Jocelyn Guevrement, leaving a gaping nothing to receive the puck. Copyright, ©, 1977, *New York News,* Inc. Reprinted by permission.

GET LOST!

by Jim Rackwitz, *St. Louis Post-Dispatch*. A half-dozen St. Louis Cardinals vigorously and unceremoniously shoving Calvin Hill, fullback for the Washington team, back into his own territory after he tried to penetrate their line. Copyright, ©, 1977, *St. Louis Post-Dispatch*.

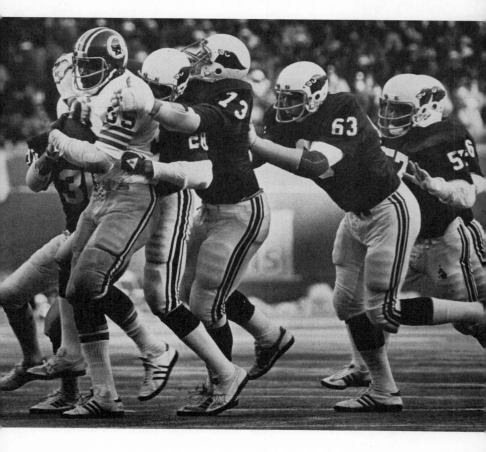

BLEEP, BLEEP AND JEEPERS!

by John Long, *The Hartford Courant.* Jimmy Connors, always a man of taste and good manners, is caught by this cameraman in a most exasperated moment while playing in the Aetna World Cup Tournament at the Hartford (Conn.) Civic Center. It is obvious he did not agree with a call by the line judge but treated the incident with tolerance, courtesy, and tact. However, he could not understand the mood of the spectators, who razzed him a lot. Copyright, ©, 1977, *The Hartford Courant* Company.

RODEO CLOWN GETS THE POINT

by John P. Foster, *Seattle Times*. This dramatic situation was created when Jordie Thompson took on a big bull at the Ellensberg (Wash.) Rodeo and was momentarily hung up as his left hand was trapped in the harness. Bob Romer, a rodeo clown, rushed in to help and the bull decided that the clown made a much more interesting target. Fortunately nobody was hurt. Copyright, ©, 1977, John P. Foster.

A SIX-YEAR-OLD HANGUP

by Stormi L. Greener, *Minneapolis Star*. Casey Ratcliffe was a beginning student in a gymnastic class for boys 6 to 10 years old. He had just been shown how to bring his legs up to his chin and straight into the air. He lost control, his feet flopped downward, he panicked. One of his instructors sensed the situation, made the proper response, and the episode was forgotten. The boy is from Mendota, Minnesota. Copyright, ©, 1977, The *Minneapolis Star & Tribune* Company.

SEE NO EVIL, HEAR NO EVIL, SPEAK NO EVIL

by Cletus M. "Pete" Hohn, *Minneapolis Tribune.* New Prague, Minnesota, High School cheerleaders Sandy Miller, Dawn Vaunhtka, and Becky Bisek strike this classic pose to show their misery as they watch Rick Tietz lose a 145-pound match in the Minnesota high school wrestling tournament. Copyright, ©, 1977, *Minneapolis Tribune.*

THEY FORGOT TO LOOK BACK

by Larry Kasperak, *Jackson* (Miss.) *Clarion-Ledger*. In agony and holding
his injured knee, an Ole Miss wingback lies ignored and untreated as his
own teammates walk away unheedingly. He later was rushed to the hospital,
where he underwent knee surgery. Copyright, ©, 1977, *The Clarion-Ledger*.

EVEN PELE DOESN'T WANT TO MIX IN THIS ONE

by Jimi Lott, *The Coos Bay* (Ore.) *World.* Bone-crushing collision by Sounder goalie Tony Chursky (1) and Cosmo defensive man Werner Roth (4) is viewed with open mouth by superstar Pele (10), also of the victorious Cosmos. Other members of the pile-up are Sounder Tommy Ord (8) and Dave Gillett. Chursky was credited with eight saves in the game but the Sounders couldn't match the two Cosmo goals. Copyright, ©, 1977, Southwestern Oregon Publishing Co., *The World.*

A LEGAL SQUATTER

by Lester Sloan, *Newsweek*. Strain and bulging eyes show to some extent the tremendous effort involved in this "squatting" phase of powerlifting. The athlete is Larry Pacifico during the National Powerlifting Championships in Santa Monica, California, last August. Copyright, ©, 1977, by *Newsweek*, Inc. All rights reserved. Reprinted by permission.

PLAYER FLIPS

by Ray Covey, *The Houston Post.* In this Texas high school game Port Neches Grove player Hebert inadvertently flipped over when his opponent from Forest Brook gained yardage against Hebert's team. The photographer also caught a conglomeration of linear lateral movement that gives the shot an almost abstract artistic composition. Copyright, ©, 1977, *The Houston Post* Co.

TIME IN THEIR HANDS

by Robert Emerson, *The Providence Journal*. Has shot a strange group of people to be in a sporting event of any kind. A young man at the bottom of the picture holds a tape. There is an intense staring look on all the other characters. Each holds a watch but all stare straight ahead in different directions. What has this to do with sports? Well, these people are all members of the Rhode Island Track Timing Guild who are waiting patiently at the finish line of a race. They are practicing. Copyright, © 1977, *The Providence Journal* Company.

"YER OUTTA THE GAME!"

by Bill Stahl, Jr., *New York Daily News*. Umpire Joe West makes a valiant effort to exercise his authority and order cat off the field during Mets' game with Expos. The albino feline was having none of that, however, and stayed around to toy with some of the box seat fans before going back into the stands to resume its main occupation, patrolling the grounds. Copyright,

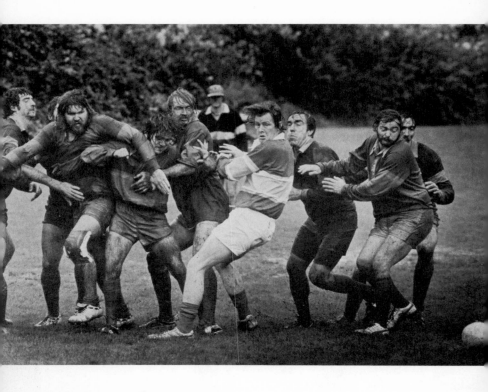

GUESS WHOSE WIFE USES TIDE

by Bert L. Fox, *The Coos Bay* (Ore.) *World.* The Coos Bay rugby club wrestles in the mud and pouring rain with the Portland (Ore.) club. This throw-in play caught both teams going the wrong way, as their faces grimace in an effort to get headed in the right direction. Copyright, ©, 1977, Southwestern Oregon Publishing Co., *The World.*

THEY'RE HAVING A BIG BALL

John H. White, *Chicago Daily News,* caught this delightful and playful shot at a primary school while waiting for an interview to do some official shooting. It is this extemporaneous shooting with a ready camera that exemplifies the real craftsman. Copyright, ©, 1977. Field Enterprises, Inc.

IT'S A "KEELING" JOB

by John Rousmaniere, *Yachting Magazine*. Keeping this little job on an even keel is a rigorous and delicate job that entails a certain sense of balance and teamwork. These two young sailors on their surfboardlike tandem at *Yachting Magazine*'s One-of-a-Kind Regatta on Lake Carlyle, Illinois, seem to be doing a most adequate job. Copyright, ©, 1977, John Rousmaniere, *Yachting Magazine*.